The Rebel Seer

Other Books by Lexi Blake

ROMANTIC SUSPENSE

Masters and Mercenaries
The Dom Who Loved Me
The Men With The Golden Cuffs
A Dom is Forever
On Her Master's Secret Service
Sanctum: A Masters and Mercenaries Novella
Love and Let Die
Unconditional: A Masters and Mercenaries Novella
Dungeon Royale
Dungeon Games: A Masters and Mercenaries Novella
A View to a Thrill
Cherished: A Masters and Mercenaries Novella
You Only Love Twice
Luscious: Masters and Mercenaries~Topped
Adored: A Masters and Mercenaries Novella
Master No
Just One Taste: Masters and Mercenaries~Topped 2
From Sanctum with Love
Devoted: A Masters and Mercenaries Novella
Dominance Never Dies
Submission is Not Enough
Master Bits and Mercenary Bites~The Secret Recipes of Topped
Perfectly Paired: Masters and Mercenaries~Topped 3
For His Eyes Only
Arranged: A Masters and Mercenaries Novella
Love Another Day
At Your Service: Masters and Mercenaries~Topped 4
Master Bits and Mercenary Bites~Girls Night
Nobody Does It Better
Close Cover
Protected: A Masters and Mercenaries Novella
Enchanted: A Masters and Mercenaries Novella
Charmed: A Masters and Mercenaries Novella
Taggart Family Values
Treasured: A Masters and Mercenaries Novella
Delighted: A Masters and Mercenaries Novella
Tempted: A Masters and Mercenaries Novella

Masters and Mercenaries: The Forgotten
Lost Hearts (Memento Mori)
Lost and Found
Lost in You
Long Lost
No Love Lost

Masters and Mercenaries: Reloaded
Submission Impossible
The Dom Identity
The Man from Sanctum
No Time to Lie
The Dom Who Came in from the Cold

Masters and Mercenaries: New Recruits
Love the Way You Spy
Live, Love, Spy
Sweet Little Spies
The Bodyguard and the Bombshell: A Masters and Mercenaries New
Recruits Novella
No More Spies
Spy With Me, Coming September 16, 2025

Butterfly Bayou
Butterfly Bayou
Bayou Baby
Bayou Dreaming
Bayou Beauty
Bayou Sweetheart
Bayou Beloved

Park Avenue Promise
Start Us Up
My Royal Showmance
Built to Last, Coming May 27, 2025

Lawless
Ruthless
Satisfaction
Revenge

The Rebel Seer

Outlaw: A Thieves Series, Book 4

Lexi Blake

The Rebel Seer
Outlaw: A Thieves Series, Book 4
Lexi Blake

Published by DLZ Entertainment LLC
Copyright 2025 DLZ Entertainment LLC
Edited by Chloe Vale
ISBN: 978-1-963890-14-3

Acknowledgments

I'm going to be honest. This is one of the toughest books I've written. My daily writing partners will tell you I was kind of lost while working on this one. I knew where I wanted to go, but getting there proved difficult, to say the least. I questioned myself about a million times writing this book. Not simply the usual "is it good enough" stuff. That's a daily thing for me. I think for the most part authors tend to rank pretty high on the insecure scale. It's one of the reasons we flee into our own worlds and never want to come out.

Thieves has been my world since before I started publishing. It was the world I lived in when I was healing from a near-death experience. It was a fantasy world, and I think it might touch too close to reality now. But I got through it and once again figured out something about myself.

I always associate myself with Zoey. I think every long-time writer has a core character or characters who they closely relate to. Mine would definitely be Zoey. She carries my worries about the world, her children's futures, and my own soul, but I found something of myself in this remarkable young woman, too. Shy is young and just finding out that sometimes what we see isn't always what is there.

I'm going to leave that enigmatic piece of information there. It'll make sense at the end of this book, but it was a long journey for me. I didn't know how long. I tend to sink into research when I write a book like this, and part of that for me this time around was getting into all things witchy. I wrote this book in one of the most active astrological times we've seen in the last hundred years. Depending on who you listened to, it was the end of a seven- or twelve-year cycle for a Virgo—which I am. As it was explained, the planets aligning would bring an end to an era that began years before, bring peace and wisdom and the ability to start a new cycle.

I didn't think much of it until I sat in my backyard watching the parade of planets and realized that I was writing a book about a woman who needs to look at death differently. Who needs to figure out the difference between grief and mourning. Who needs to see her worth and talent even when much of the world vilifies what that talent is.

As I sat there, I felt a peace come over me when I realized it has been seven years since my mother died. I realized she is both gone and still with me. I can move on because that's life, and moving forward doesn't mean leaving anything behind. It means holding memories close while I make more.

So I learned much from this mess of a book I wrote. The pain—as is usually the case with creative projects—was worth the wisdom.

The wheel turns and so do we.

It's time to begin again. To confront a new cycle and all it has to offer.

Spring is here.

Prologue

Shy

Dallas, TX

My hands shake as they shut the door and I'm locked in with my nightmare.

Water flows not three feet away from me, like a waterfall, but in a never-ending churn that comes from nowhere and goes nowhere. There is nothing peaceful about this waterfall. This waterfall is death and despair.

"Shahidi Davis," a deep voice says from behind the locked door. "She's fifteen. An orphan. Her family died in a house fire a few years back, and she went into the system. Eighteen months ago, her foster mother found her screaming about something she called a water demon."

I know it's not a demon now, but in the moment I saw those hollow bones behind the water and it was the only word I could think of. No one believed me, of course. No one. I'm cut off from the supernatural world since my parents died, and I can't get anyone to call me back.

I tried our family friends when I had a phone. No one answered. I called Sarah Day, a witch who worked with my mom and aunt from time to time, but the number was disconnected.

Like I'm disconnected.

"She was in quite the state when she was brought in. We believe she's got early onset schizophrenia," the doctor explains. "Tell me. What course of treatment would you begin?"

Drugs. Lots of drugs.

They keep me… Not calm. I'm never calm when that thing is close to me. The drugs simply keep me from being able to defend myself.

I sit on the bed, not able to really get up because the drugs make me dizzy. I can't defend myself from anything in here. They make sure of it.

I wish my mother was here.

I feel a tear slip down my cheek because this is what every day looks like. I try to tell the doctors what's happening, what I'm seeing, what I am now. Some nod sympathetically and up my dosage. Others sneer and tell me I'm lying because I'm lazy and don't want to go to school.

I wish I was in school. I used to love school. I was told once my power manifested, I could join the school where all the werewolf and Fae and witch kids went.

I haven't seen a supernatural creature in years. My family died and they sent me straight into the human foster care system. I remember waiting and hoping someone would come looking for me. We had friends in that world, friends at the Council.

No one ever did. I never got to that school.

Instead, they bring in a tutor a couple of hours a day for us and they treat us like we can't read or understand mathematics.

I glance over and wonder what would really happen if I walked into that water. Would I be free? Would darkness take me and it could all be over? Or would I be somewhere worse. Some hellscape the spirit owns.

"Hello, Shy."

Even through the fog of my brain I hear the man talking to me. From inside my room.

"Don't panic," he says and drops to one knee in front of me. "I'm not a spirit, though you shouldn't fear those either. You're so damn young and have had no one to guide you. These ghosts you see are not the enemy. You were born for a specific purpose, though I'm sure you don't care about that right now. I'm so sorry this happened to you."

"Who are you? How did you..." Sometimes it's hard to find words. Especially right after they give me the medicine. "The doors are always locked."

"I suppose it doesn't matter since there's almost no way you'll remember." He's a handsome man with dark hair and his eyes... I never saw eyes that color before. Violet. And they nearly glow in the low light. Even on one knee he looms above me. "I'm what you would call a prophet. I witness the important events of our world. Needless to say, I've been busy lately."

So I'm asleep and dreaming. At least he seems nice. This dream guy. "Why would you be here?"

"For the same reason I convinced your friend to have a sleepover the night your parents were murdered."

The words send a shock through me. "What?"

He stands and then moves to sit next to me. "Shy, I see the possibilities of how the world will go. They are laid out like infinite roads. Technically I'm simply here to observe, but what I've learned is that sometimes I can choose the path. Or at least who I can put on the path. You are important. More important than you can imagine. More important than anyone can know."

I shake my head. "I should have been home."

"If you had been home, you would no longer be on this plane of existence. You would not be able to do what you were born to do. Myrddin doesn't know it, but you are the one he was trying to take out. He only wants the psychics he can control. For him it was a power play. He never realized he could have won the war with one fire."

"I'm not a soldier." His words don't make sense except that this prophet person kept me from being with my family. From holding my mother's hand as we went to the next life together.

"No, and that is why you are so important. I prophesize, but I cannot explain, so sometimes things get interpreted improperly," he explains. "Especially when you're dealing with a very literal wolf. And sometimes a prophecy can go more than one way. No matter what is written down, there is almost never only one way. Life doesn't work like that. We all think fate is a through line, but there are almost always many roads that come to the same place. By saving you and hiding your value, I am giving us options. Options Myrddin will overlook in favor of the ones he understands."

This is a damn weird dream. "I don't understand you. I'm not important. I'm never leaving this place. They won't ever let me leave."

"Because you don't know how to say and do what you need to in order to get out and take your place with the rebels," he explains. "That's what I'm going to do today. Or rather I've simply come to watch an important event. If anyone from Heaven or Hell asks, that's what I am doing. I didn't lure him here or anything. I'm sorry it took so long. He was trapped for a while, but he's ready now."

"Who is he?" I ask.

Suddenly there's another man standing in front of me looking like he's ready to go play a round of golf. He's much shorter than the prophet guy and older. He's like my grandpa's age. If my grandpa was alive.

"Hello, Shy. My name is Harry Wharton, and according to Gray here, we can help each other out." He has the most lyrical Irish accent, and something about him is infinitely warm. "I have a granddaughter who's only a bit younger than you. Her name is Evangeline."

"Uh, I thought we talked about not using my name," the prophet says.

Harry waves him off. "We both know neither of us will remember this encounter. The way you explained it, bonding to her soul will make this brief time foggy and dreamlike, if anything at all. I won't even remember you were the one who guided me here, so I can't tell Heaven and Hell on you."

"It's Hell I'm worried about. Heaven would stop me if they wanted to. Lucifer might get upset if he thought I was playing favorites," Gray says.

"Lucifer Morningstar?" I ask. My mother was careful around demons. I had heard many a lecture on staying away from them. "He watches you?"

"As you can see some of her delusions are biblical in nature," the doctor outside says.

"Does she always talk to people who aren't there?" another asks.

"Oh, yes. Though she usually begs them to leave her alone. This might be a further decline," the doctor explains. "She also claims this very institution is filled with ghosts."

I ignore their laughter because I'm starting to think this isn't a dream.

Also, this place is unbelievably haunted, and I hope one of those ghosts binds to the doc and gives him hell.

"Lucifer watches me carefully," Gray says with a sigh. "Which is precisely why I will never mention this day to anyone. I will keep my distance so they never suspect. The next time I see you will hopefully be the day you join the rebellion and meet... Well, I'll leave that to fate."

"Leave it to me," Harry offers. "Shy, I died fighting Myrddin Emrys. My daughter is Queen Zoey of Vampire and the High Priestess of Faery. My grandchildren are on the run. I need to help them, and you need to get out of this place. It's killing you."

"They won't ever let me out." I look to the door, but the doctor and his students have moved on. They'll be back, of course, but not for hours.

Harry kneels down, and we're eye level. He has kind eyes. "I promise, I'll teach you what to do and say and how to act so we can get out of here. It will take a while, but I promise I'll get you out. Once we're out, we'll make our way to Iceland, where the rebels are. There are vampires and wolves and witches and Fae who are resisting Myrddin's new world order. They're growing stronger by the day."

"I didn't tell you that either." Gray seems concerned with plausible deniability.

"Of course you didn't." Harry's eyes never leave mine. "Shy, I will do everything I can to help you. I know I'm not a psychic, but I actually collaborated with your dad from time to time. He was the best telekinetic I ever worked with."

"You knew my dad?" Tears start to roll. It's been so long since I even talked to someone who understands the world I grew up in. I started to wonder if maybe I'm wrong and they're right. Maybe I made up all of this in my head to disassociate myself from trauma. But Harry knows who my dad was. Knows what his powers were.

If this is a dream, maybe I don't want to wake up. It's the first time I believe someone wants to help me.

"I did, and I respected the hell out of him," Harry says. "We'll take down Myrddin for him, too, me darlin'."

The idea of taking down the wizard… Maybe there is something I want more than peace. But it won't work. "Even if you can teach me how to get out of here, we can't get to Iceland. I would go back into the foster care system. I don't have money or ID or anything like that."

His smile widens, and there's an impish quality to the expression. "Oh, don't worry about dat none, girl. I'll teach you one more thing. I'll teach you how to steal. We'll be right and fine. I'll teach you how to talk to those ghosties, too. You and me will be all right, Shy. I promise. I'll take care of you."

I sniffle and look back at the prophet. There is only one way to go. "What do I have to do?"

Gray's eyes soften. "All you have to do is welcome him in. Your soul is unique in all the world. Your soul has a space Harry can reside in. But he needs an invitation, and you'll both be a little out of it afterward. Hold on to who he is and why he's here. You do the same, Harry."

I'm desperate. This might be a trap. I'm not foolish. I know there are creatures willing to prey upon the weak, and I am so weak now.

If there's no hope, then I don't care what happens. I can take this chance or stay here all of my days. Waste away until I don't even remember who I used to be, where I came from. "You are welcome, Harry Wharton."

There's the slightest feel of tension in my chest and then the world goes hazy and I'm not sure what's happening. Darkness fills my eyes and I fall back. The last sight I see is the water ghost moving in, looming above me like she's trying to find a way in, too.

When I wake, I'm lying on my bed with the vaguest recollection of a visitation. But I can't quite remember from who.

"Shy? Are you there? It's Harry."

I force myself to sit up and put a hand on my chest. It's warm but not in an unpleasant way. I feel…stronger. Like some place that was empty is now filled.

Harry. Harry Wharton. He's going to help me. I can hear Harry in my head. His lyrical accent is warm and friendly, and suddenly I'm not so alone. "You made it."

I can feel the man smile. "I did, darlin'. And now we're going to get you out of here. I'll do everything I can."

I feel far more centered than before, like whatever we did dispelled the effects of the drugs. I can think again. And be sarcastic. "I wish you could get rid of the Drowning Woman."

"I don't think she's here," Harry says. "I saw something odd before, but it's gone now."

I turn and he's right. For the first time in over a year, she's not here.

I breathe a sigh of relief and start to listen to my new mentor.

Chapter One

Shy

Frelsi, the rebel encampment, Iceland
Six years later

I remember when I saw my first ghost. I call her the Drowning Woman. It was one year after my entire family was murdered by Myrddin's witches. I'm fairly certain he didn't do the deed himself. He was busy killing vampires at the time. A group of psychics would be easy to kill as long as he found a way to dampen their powers of prophecy. It was my auntie who saw into the future. It's funny the things you remember years later. She'd been sick for weeks. It's how I know the whole idea that Myrddin simply took advantage of the mistakes the queen and king made is false. He might have not planned for the king to fall into his trapped painting, but he intended to take over. Why else would he have cursed the only woman in the world who might have been able to see his plans?

Up until that moment, I had not a hint of power. My cousins manifested early. So did my sister. I worried I was going to be the only Davis without power.

And then I was simply the only Davis.

I should have died with them. We lived in this rambling old

house in the woods. We were close enough that we could get to Dallas within an hour, but far enough out that it felt like the country. I miss the house with its sounds and smells and rich laughter coming from every room. When I close my eyes, I'm there, surrounded by obnoxious siblings and cousins. By wise aunts and uncles, and my parents who loved me. I can still smell my mother's cooking. She used to say her caramel cake recipe came from a famous and very dead pastry chef she met in her travels.

The Davis family was known throughout the supernatural world for our mental and spiritual gifts. My father could move heavy objects with nothing more than a thought. I had uncles who could astral project across the planet. They worked for some scary men from time to time. One aunt could hear sounds from other planes of existence. She described it as a radio playing in her head. I always thought that would be weird, but she enjoyed it since apparently the people who lived in our house on the other plane were extremely dramatic.

My mother was a medium. She could see and speak to the dead. It's not like what you see on television. At least not some programs. She didn't need a séance or to hold something the dearly departed once owned. That's called psychometry, and you do not want it. My cousin thought she was picking up a hunting knife once and spent two hours screaming because it belonged to a serial killer.

"You'll find your power, Shy," my mother would always say.

She didn't tell me my power would lead me to a mental institution.

She certainly didn't tell me the first ghost I would ever see would be the most terrifying vision, nor that she would still be hanging around so many years later.

"She's back." Josie Albertson stands to my left, her hands on her hips as she watches the Drowning Woman from a distance. "I wonder what she wants. You ever talk to her? Anytime I try to get close, she disappears."

I can see her out of the corner of my eye even as I stand in the garden of the home I share with Lily Tucker and Hannah Jenkins. I love a good garden, and no one takes a garden quite as seriously as a witch. I stand among the herbs and flowers and vegetables they've spent half a year growing, and in the background, I see ghosts.

I turn to Josie, who is a fairly recent addition to the dead of

Frelsi. Not that there are many. We're a community of supernatural creatures and located in an isolated part of the world. Josie showed up a few months before, having fallen into a crevice while attempting to climb the mountain we live in. She presents as most ghosts do, with some form of how she died printed on her body. In her case, her left side is always stained with blood, and her left arm bends at an odd angle. She's got a really nasty knot on her head. Other than that, she could be any sarcastic tourist who happened to die, find herself in a supernatural world, and freak out.

When I first saw her, I calmed her down, asked her the salient questions. There are a few when dealing with the dead. Do you see a light being the most important. Josie was adamant. Yes, it was there, but she wasn't going through. I explained about how every soul has a limited amount of time to complete the whole death journey before things go sideways. She was cool with it, and we've been hanging ever since.

"No," I admit and kneel down to start harvesting the mugwort Lily told me is needed for the spell of protection she intends to work before we leave this place. "She's the oddest spirit I've ever seen, and when she gets close, it's hard to look at her. I can't see her face through the water. I know she's not the scariest-looking being I've ever come up against, but I fear her more than all the rest of you combined."

Josie huffs. "I don't know. That dead thing freaks me out." Her head tilts as she watches the Drowning Woman, whose limbs move in and out, every finger dripping with blood.

I wonder if she can follow me to Faery. I've never been off plane before. Until I came here to Frelsi, the only thing I knew about other planes of existence was that someone named Jill was cheating on her husband, Lewis, and it was only a matter of time until he found out, and my aunt was pretty sure they had a prenup.

Like I said before, my childhood was weird and wonderful at first, and then a horror movie.

And now...now I wonder if I am walking into a romance. I wonder if I am finally ready for it.

"See, that kind of freaks me out, too," Josie says.

I nearly start when I feel something on my cheek. And then the smell hits me. Roses.

"But he sure doesn't." Josie smiles and smooths back her hair like she's trying to make a good impression on a man who cannot see her.

I close my eyes and let the silky petals caress my skin, let them give me the strokes and kisses I haven't been able to take from the man who controls them.

Rhys Donovan-Quinn. My love. My problem. Probably my downfall.

"I thought I would find you out here," his deep voice says.

I open my eyes and the rose is staring at me. It grows from its home bush and vibrates like a happy puppy. I can't hold back a smile. Rhys is a Green Man. He's always been, but when we were younger he couldn't control plants the way he can since his ascension. We call him a Green Man, but since a day he spent with his mother a few weeks back, he's become a god.

"Lily needs some herbs for her spell," I tell him as I stand back up. The rose is still playing around me.

"See, he couldn't do that a couple of weeks ago." Josie moves in, getting close to Rhys. "All us dead folk are talking about how the energy feels off when this hottie is around. What did you say he is? He was a Green Man and now he's what?"

"First off, respect his space," I tell her.

Rhys's eyes go wide, and he gets that slight smile that takes over whenever he realizes I'm using my power. "Not alone?"

I shake my head. "It's Josie, and she thinks you're hot. She also has questions." I turn back to her. "He's an elemental, if you want to get technical. There are beings that take on aspects of the seasons or elements. It happens almost exclusively with Fae, but some demons have been known to have the power as well. I heard Kelsey once tangled with a winter elemental."

Rhys looks to where I turned, always the polite man even when it comes to the dead. "Yes, Trent says it was a close thing, and naturally my brother, Lee, was the reason Kelsey had to risk her life. I love my brother, but he's an asshole sometimes. And if Josie would like the religious term for what I have become, it's Walking Spring."

Yes, I heard the term before. He is life, and I feel so mired in death.

I turn to look at him, and the proof of the differences in our circumstances stands roughly fifty feet away, a watery figure near the spruce. The wave shifts and mirrors the world around it before showing ghastly limbs. I look at that water and know I can drown in it. One drop and I would be caught.

Rhys stops, and his handsome face goes serious. "She's here?"

I must have winced. I try not to do it, but it's impossible. Rhys knows about the Drowning Woman. Once when we were much younger, she screamed in my face, her illusion of cold water turning my skin clammy. We were planning on going into Reykjavík for supplies, but I ruined the trip because I couldn't stop crying. I had to tell them what only Harry and I knew.

Harry. I miss Harry. I'm still mourning him.

I wish it was Harry standing next to that tree, but he's moved on. He's happy now. For so many years he shared a space in my soul, and now he's gone and I feel a bit empty.

And a whole lot…excited. Tempted. Aroused. Because now that Harry's gone, there's zero reason for me not to take Rhys up on everything he's willing to offer me.

Everything except forever.

"She's keeping her distance," I tell him and lean my cheek slightly against the rose he controls. I frown at Josie, who is way too close to Rhys. "As we all should."

Josie frowns my way but moves back. "I'm sorry. He's really pretty, and his brother isn't here so I don't have porn to watch."

My jaw drops. "You can't do that. Josie, that is private. You can't watch Lee when he's…"

Rhys laughs and looks genuinely amused. "Does Lee have a ghost peeping Tom? Don't worry about it. It's not private for my brother. He would say the more the merrier."

Josie points his way and smiles so I can see she broke three of her teeth in the fall that ended her life. "See, sensible man. I wish I met faeries before I died. And the vamps. Who would ever want to leave this place? Not me."

This is her attitude. She says it with a hint of arrogance, but I know there's fear underlying her refusal to leave. "You'll end up stuck here for all of time if you aren't careful. Like that one. She might not be bothering me right now, but she's rarely not around. Does she look like she's having fun?"

"Ah, the should I stay or should I go now discussion. You should listen to her, Josie. She knows what she's talking about. If you were Fae, I would be worried you'll turn sluagh, and that is not pretty." Rhys Donovan-Quinn is six and a half feet tall, with dark as midnight hair and the greenest eyes I've ever seen. Those eyes draw me in every time. They shift with the light or his mood. Sometimes they're emeralds. Other times I see the evergreen of the forest there. Sometimes they're almost hazel, warm with gold tones. He's got a foot on me, and when he stares down at me, my stupid heart flutters. My heart doesn't care that I'm not in his league.

Josie sighs. "Tell me again why you haven't hopped into bed with him? He's so hot, and unlike his brother, he seems ready to settle down."

I do not need to have this conversation right now. "Are you sure you don't want to walk into the light?"

There are so many reasons I haven't jumped all over that man. He's a prince of two realms. He's the son of the King of All Vampire—though right now his father doesn't wear the crown. And he's the son of the High Priest of Faery. Both the Seelie and the Unseelie recognize his father and Rhys as fertility gods.

I'm an orphan who's one skill in the world is to see and talk to the dead. I don't think that will help us much in the war that is coming. Although sometimes the dead are bitter and willing to give up some secrets. I tried to convince Sasha to let me hang around the Council building and see who talks to me, but Rhys lost his shit.

Josie's head shakes. "I don't know what's in that light. You don't know. Sure they say it's all warmth and sunshine, but I'm more of a shadows girl. I want to hang around until I figure out if that vampire is going to get his fangs in Lily. He's trying hard."

I look to Rhys. "She's literally risking her eternal soul because she likes gossip."

"We do pretty good gossip here," he says, his hand coming up to cup my other cheek. "Did you hear that Benedict has been leaving Lily flowers? Night blooms, of course, since he's dead during the day. I've also heard there's a small war going on with the gnomes. Colin hid Fergus's hat, and now they are pranking each other like mad. No one pranks like a gnome."

"See, all good reasons to not risk that light." Josie takes a seat on the bench in the pretty gazebo Rhys and Lee built for us a few years back.

"She's hopeless," I tell Rhys and my eyes stray back to that horrifying slash of water that disturbs the peace of my space.

Rhys's hand tilts my head up, gently bringing my focus back on him. "Do you think you'll get a break in Faery? Can souls follow you off plane? What if we get to Faery and it's all quiet. Wouldn't that be nice?"

"Somehow I doubt it." I wish I didn't feel so warm when I'm with him, so deeply connected to a man I cannot have. "You know I see dead of all kinds, and I bet there are many on the Faery plane."

A brow rises. "Yes, I suppose so. Was it easier when it was all humans? At least you might have understood humans."

I have to laugh at the thought. Everyone thinks they know what it would be like to see the dead. It's scary until you get used to it. Except you never get used to it. "It was never all human. I was in a foster home and there was a dead dog who haunted the backyard. He was still tied up in the heat. His body was gone but his soul never stopped being tortured. That dog terrified me. Then I went to the hospital, and let me tell you, you don't get more haunted than a psych ward. I was in the hospital until Harry taught me how to manipulate the system. You know adulting is a lot easier with an old Irish guy in your head."

Rhys groans and then pulls me close, his arms going around me as the rose shrinks back to its place. "You're missing my grandfather. I do, too. Even though he spoke through you the last couple of years, it was like we had him around. So are supernatural dead creatures worse?"

I breathe him in. I love the way this man smells, how warm I am with his arms around me. "I wouldn't say worse. Though there aren't many. A lot of them are immortal or hard to kill, or they simply walk into the light with more ease than some humans. There's a small troll who strolls the streets here from time to time. No idea why. He's never approached me. I saw a witch in the bookstore in Reykjavík a few months ago. She's waiting for her sister so they can go through together. Her sister's ninety-two but still going strong, so she hangs in the bookstore and judges people's purchases. She is very judgey about crystals. Told me the amethyst I was about to buy was a piece of crap."

He smiles, an expression that can light up the darkest night. "Why didn't you tell me?"

Because I don't like to talk about the things I see with him. I talk to his sister, Evan. She's become my closest friend. I talk to Lily and some of the witches. I've talked about it with Sasha and Trent, but only when I've learned something that could possibly help in the war effort.

I don't like to remind my sunshine god of an almost lover that I live in the shadows.

"You were off plane when I met the witch. I think you were meeting with someone on one of the alternative planes. You got back and then you saw that little pig and started planning your own mission to retrieve your parents. You know the one you didn't tell me about. You avoided me for weeks, so I didn't mention my new dead friend."

"I wasn't avoiding you. I was avoiding my grandfather. I couldn't be sure he wouldn't decide it was too dangerous and get Trent and Sasha involved. We didn't tell anyone," he says softly. "Not even Uncle Neil."

"Well, Uncle Neil can't keep a secret to save his life, but we both know I can." I keep so many of them. I understand why they didn't let me in on the plan to rescue their parents. They fell through a trapped painting and ended up on another plane. Even when they found their way back, they were stuck in stasis for twelve years. What seemed like a few days for the royals and Kelsey Owens was in reality years. From the moment I was allowed inside this rebel encampment, the witches of the group were trying to find a way to contact their lost leaders. After a lot of chanting and manifesting and taking some really good-looking drugs/religious herbs, they came to the conclusion that the royals would return to the place from whence they left on one of four dates. While Sasha and Trent decided to focus all their energy on one date, Rhys had an encounter with Arkan Sonney and decided to change plans.

There are still omens and prophecies and wee creatures that bring both. You simply have to have your eyes focused in the right way to see them.

Rhys's fingertips brush along my jaw. "Are you still angry about it? You should know I won't ever keep anything from you again. Now that you're…"

"Alone." I step back because I feel it again. Harry chose to leave after seeing his daughter safely returned. He said it's time for me to be on my own, that I'm strong enough now. That's what I told everyone.

What he actually said to me in the quiet of our shared soul was something more.

You were always strong enough, Shy. You never really needed me, but oh how I needed you. You are more than you think you are, but I can't tell you. You have to discover it for yourself. Remember this. Death is a doorway not an end. It's one more step on the path we all take, and you help them along. One day you'll understand the gift you are to this world and the next.

The words are imprinted on me, though I think he was being optimistic.

I only know I miss him. I mourn him.

Rhys goes still. "I'm sorry. You know I miss my grandfather, too. But there is a part of me that is relieved to finally have you to myself." He takes a long breath and steps back as well, the space between us plain. "However, maybe we should rethink the trip to Faery. My parents can handle the situation."

"Oh, he's getting antsy," Josie says, crossing one leg over the other as though settling in for the show. "His magic pours off him when he's anxious. It's green and blue and yellow. So pretty."

I know I should think about her words, but I'm caught on his. It's my turn to stare at him. "I'm not going to Faery? You want to go without me?"

We've been preparing for the trip for days. Ever since the queen realized it might be her only chance to find her friend Sarah Day, and Sarah's husband and daughter. Sarah is a powerful witch, so powerful she managed to evade Myrddin's slaughter and take her family off plane. She also apparently left a way for the queen to find her. Except the queen blew up the Council House and that doorway with it. So Faery it is.

I'm supposed to go, but it seems Rhys changed his mind. Likely because I didn't sleep with him yet and he knows the pleasures that await him in Faery.

The idea makes me ache despite the nagging voice in my head

that says he's right and I should think about taking a break from him. Time moves differently on the Faery planes, and he'll be gone far longer in Earth plane time than he'll experience. If it takes them three weeks to complete the mission, at least three months will have passed here. By the time he returns we'll have moved from Frelsi to our summertime home in New Zealand. We call it chasing the night. During the winter we're here in Iceland, and then when the days grow longer, we move so the vampires among us have more time awake.

He frowns my way, and I swear the grass is growing beneath my feet. I can feel it tickling my ankles. "No. I meant I won't go. Shahidi, I've told you before. You are my goddess. I knew it the moment I saw you, and I'm willing to wait until you're ready. Unless you're ready to tell me once and for all you don't want me."

"Oh, this is down bad stuff. What are you doing to this man, Shy?" Josie asks.

I ignore her. Don't want him? I dream about Rhys at night. He's in my good dreams. He's in my bad dreams. He's in all of them because somehow Rhys has become the touchstone of my life, and I can't imagine it without him. I thought we might have a shot, but then he ascended in a way no one could have expected. He must marry someone of royal blood. Or someone Fae, who can unite the rebels with the Seelie and the Unseelie and help win this war.

I knew the moment the King of All Vampire returned my time with Rhys would be limited.

"Is that what you're saying, Shy?" Rhys asks the question in a quiet tone but the grass is halfway up my calves, and I see his hand tremble. "Are you saying you don't want me?"

"Uh, Shy," Josie begins, "those pretty colors are taking on a dark edge."

Control. Since his ascension he's always on the edge of losing control. His magic is starting to go wild, and that can be dangerous for all of us.

"Son, what's happening?"

"Papa's here so we know it must be bad," Josie announces. "Damn, that man is fine."

I turn slightly and see Devinshea Quinn standing at the edge of the garden. He looks so much like his son they could be brothers, but then His Grace is locked in his youth by the blood he shares with his partner, Daniel. He looks worried, and he frowns as he stares out over the garden. Which is blooming like mad weeks before it should. Rhys planned to come through and do this in a controlled way so we would have a harvest before changing camps. Those planned "grows," as we call them, are focused. This unintentional one goes wild, and I can see clearly the grass and weeds aren't limited to this one place. They are everywhere.

Rhys takes a long breath, and his fists clench and unclench. "Nothing. We're fine. We've just changed our minds about going to Faery."

"Rhys, you have to go," his father says in an even tone. He stands there perfectly paternal, like Rhys is still a child in his mind. Which he likely is since it was only days ago for His Grace that Rhys was eleven. "I know they haven't treated you with the respect they should have. We'll deal with it."

Rhys's jawline tightens. "I don't care about the Fae. I'm not going because Shy wants to stay here. Unless she tells me she doesn't want me, I will stay with my goddess. I will not leave her unprotected and alone."

The blueberry bush to my left kind of explodes, and I hear His Grace curse under his breath. I can't see Rhys's magic the way Josie claims she can, but I can feel it, and it's got a desperate edge to it.

"Rhys, I need you to be reasonable." His father takes a cautious step forward. "You're emotional right now, and we both know why. But you're spilling magic out like a waterfall."

"And here's Dad. This family, I cannot tell you how much I enjoy them. They are the best TV show ever," Josie says as the vampire flies in. "But you need to handle this, Shy, because while I enjoy watching those two, I don't want to see them die because that wizard person tracks you down through faery magic. I can see it spreading all over. I hope the goats are hungry because…that's a lot of grass."

There's a slight shake to the ground and the King of All Vampire lands beside his partner. Daniel and Dev might share their wife, but they share each other, too. Donovan is a strongly built man with sandy blond hair, blue eyes, and dimples when he smiles. Those dimples look sweet, but he is the ultimate predator in our world. "Rhys, the witches are worried. Myrddin has spies in the country, and they're looking for Fae magic."

I can see Rhys trying. He's trying so hard to control himself, but he can't control his magic the way he should. The way a Green Man would.

And I'm the reason.

He's a Green Man. A twenty-three-year-old Green Man. As a class of beings go, they tend to rank high on the promiscuous scale. He's an actual sex god.

A virgin sex god. Because he thinks I'm his goddess and has refused to take a lover despite them all being paraded in front of him whenever his uncle Declan manages to get some time with him.

His father was shocked at the state of his sexual purity and horrified at what it might mean now that he has all the power of a season at his fingertips.

I move into his space since that distance between us is absolutely contributing to his control issues. I put both hands on his cheeks and look into those glorious green eyes of his. Right now there's a light in them that's almost wild. I can't stand the thought of him losing the control he's fought so hard to gain. Like me, he was left to fend for himself when it came to his powers. Oh, he had parental figures, but the one who could truly understand his power was taken from him. "I would never say that, Rhys. I'm nervous about going. I'm nervous I'll cause trouble for you, but if you want me to go, I'll go."

"Trouble? You won't cause trouble." A root breaks through the surface of the earth, popping up like a sea creature rising. "If they do, I swear…"

"Shy, he might need more than words. He's on edge and has been for days." Dev starts to move toward us, but the king stops him.

More than words. Well, it isn't like I don't enjoy what he needs. I go on my toes and brush my lips against his. "I'll go with you," I whisper.

Then his hands are on my waist and the nape of my neck, holding me in place while he kisses me like I'm the last woman on earth. I can feel a wave of heat roll across my skin. It comes from him. That wave is seduction and affection and need. The need of a god for his goddess.

Unfortunately, I am no goddess.

Still, I let him kiss me, let the intimacy of his mouth against mine cocoon us in a place that feels warm and infinitely safe. Our space. If only we never had to leave it.

"Shy, uhm, I hate to tell you this but the whole kissing thing is revving the Green Man up," Josie says. "Not that I mind. You know one of the fun parts about being dead is the wide and never-ending opportunities for voyeurism, but I'm hearing some panic among the lesser beings. Something's coming."

And that's when I hear it. The clanging of an alarm.

The alarm that tells us Myrddin is coming.

Chapter Two

Zoey

"**I** have intelligence that places Myrddin's witches around both doors to the Faery plane," Sasha Federov says as he sits at the conference table. The big Russian vampire is awake and seems to enjoy being a daywalker since I gave him Alexander Sharpe's ring. I took it from his ashes when I killed the fucker. Sasha's eyes go down to the ring he wears on his left hand. On his ring finger. "Your Highness, I think we should consider postponing the trip."

My Fae husband frowns. "I think it's important to get Rhys to Faery. I'm worried about the state he's in since his deeply unexpected ascension."

I have to wonder if he blames me for that. I was there with Rhys when it happened. Naturally, like most of my life right now, we were in terrible danger, and not wanting to watch his recently returned mother be murdered by a troll had caused him to accept his power. The trouble was his power had turned out to be way stronger than any of us dreamed.

My son is Walking Spring. Sounds innocent, right? Like how can being able to grow flowers be a destructive power? You wouldn't think it if you saw what Dev can do. On many occasions he's used the trees around us to stab our enemies or the roots to drag and hold them underground. We're still not certain what all Rhys can do, but it's been raining a lot lately. Raining in a pocket world that shouldn't have much weather. I think we can safely say it's not Lee or Evan.

Who chose Kelsey.

I try to shake off that invasive thought. When the *Nex Apparatus* and I decided to split our group for these missions we're on, I knew she would need her son Fenrir with her, and where goeth that wolf king so goeth Evangeline Donovan-Quinn. Kelsey is trying to save our friend we found on another plane. His name is Dean Malone, and according to prophecy, he is going to help my son, Lee, destroy Myrddin Emrys. So beyond the fact that I like the kid and don't want him to die, we kind of need him. It's one of those dire, this-is-the-only-way prophecies that prophets like to give us.

I often think the universe would be way more fun if instead of prophecy leading us, we could do one of those Mad Lib things and figure out how to save the universe that way.

So Kelsey is on the Hell plane trying to steal a feather from Lucifer Morningstar with the help of two of my kids, and I'm sure Rhys would have tried to go if his papa hadn't told him absolutely no. Not that his papa's views would mean a thing. It was only when my vampire husband, Daniel, pointed out the Hell plane might be disturbing to someone with Shy's powers that Rhys agreed to come to Faery with us.

My son's love can speak to the dead, and I know sometimes they can frighten her. I would like to keep her away from a place where the dead are tortured and will likely overwhelm her. I hope in Faery we can spend time together and become closer.

"I think Rhys's powers will also help loosen some tongues," the King of All Vampire says. Danny was once my childhood sweetheart. Then he died and our lives truly began. We spent years bringing the supernatural world together and building a Council that worked for everyone. We also built a family. A family I love.

Myrddin took it all away from us. He stole twelve years from me and Dev and Danny. Twelve years where our kids and the people we love struggled and fought to stay alive while waiting for us to return.

"You really think the faeries know how to get to the celestial planes?" my bestie asks.

Neil Roberts, the most fab werewolf in all of the planes. We've been through a lot together, and having him here with me brings me so much comfort. In the years since we disappeared, Neil and his vampire husband, Chad, adopted two wolves and made a home for themselves within the rebel force.

"I think my mother has access to information." Dev sits back, his gaze going to the window that looks out over the yard. "The Faery plane connected directly to the Earth plane is rather unique. It's been posited that faery planes are close to celestial planes. There has to be a way. My brother gave Zoey a relic to use to speak with our ancestors. Unfortunately, my lovely wife chose to use it as C4 to explode my beautiful club."

Yeah. We're still processing that. "Babe, Myrddin turned Ether into something terrible. I had to do it. We can start again after we off him."

Danny stands and frowns Dev's way. "According to what your brother told us, it's back in Faery. It was the process of dematerializing to go back to the amulet's base that caused the explosion. So the amulet is safe and sound in your mother's palace. We simply need to access it."

It's more complex than that. I have to prime it first, so it's not like we're going to walk in, find it, and use it. According to my brother-in-law, I have to wear the amulet close to the chain Devinshea gave me when we wed. The Goddess Chain is one of the Fae treasures, and its proximity can allow the wearer to use the amulet.

Dev nods. "Yes, and we can use it to talk to the ancients, who might have some wisdom when it comes to finding Sarah, Felix, and Mia."

We have come to believe Mia plays a huge role in the prophecy we risked our lives for on the outer planes. The prophecy speaks of a weapon. I believe Mia is that weapon.

My other bestie is a powerful witch, and her husband is a fallen angel. Mia's powers were off the charts as a kid. She was so powerful Myrddin came for her on the day of his coup. According to the intelligence Kelsey received, Sarah was forced to take her family off plane because Myrddin tried to claim her not-even teen daughter at the time as his bride.

Yeah, I hate that man.

"Beyond finding Sarah, we need to get to Faery to help Rhys

control his powers," Dev says. "I don't think you understand how bad it could get. His powers seem soft…"

"There's nothing soft about Rhys." Sasha waves him off. "Rhys is a hell of a fighter, and his powers can help us win this war. What is it about being in Faery that will help him? I would think having his father back in his life would be what he needs to learn to control these new powers of his. His fathers. Has Bris spoken to him?"

My faery husband's eyes shift in a heartbeat, the change so quick, going from his normal green to an emerald color that takes over the entire eye, leaving no white behind. Unlike my son, who ascended to godhood all on his own, my husband did it the old-fashioned way. He opened his soul to a non-corporeal ancient god. Bris, an Irish fertility god. They bonded at our wedding. Which I mostly didn't know was a wedding. Let me tell you it's a shock when you realize the public proof of sexual compatibility ritual you're performing with your honey has been taken over by a sex god.

Though now I simply love Bris. He looks my way and sends me a warm smile. "My Goddess."

"My Lord," I reply with a smile of my own.

Once he's greeted me, he turns to Sasha. "General, being in Faery will amplify Rhys's powers. My host believes being in Faery will push our son to have sex. Rhys is a sex god. He requires sex to exist. It is not natural for him to be a virgin, and that state is causing him to struggle to contain his magic. If he were having sex as he should, his partners would absorb some of his magic."

"He's apparently really good at masturbating," Neil offers helpfully. "I mean I mostly stay in the forests with the wolves, but we've all heard stories about gardens exploding around Rhys's house after a late-night session." He sighs. "I never thought of it. He can't even jerk off without the world knowing. If the grass around his place grows a couple of inches, everyone assumes he's been one-fisting it. The only way I knew Brendan had figured it out was those socks. Socks aren't supposed to be sticky. That was when I realized the boy needs to do his own laundry."

"Thank you for the clarification, Neil," Danny says with a long sigh. "Bris is right, of course. We have to find a way to get Rhys to… I can't believe I'm having this conversation. When I thought about having kids, never once did I imagine I would be sitting around a table with my wife and partner and the living god inside him discussing how the hell to get our sex god firstborn laid."

"There are many temptations in Faery," Bris says slowly as though he knows it will be controversial. "My host thinks being there will put Rhys on a proper footing."

They are forgetting one important fact.

"You tell your host that our son is in love with Shy." Of the three of us, it's Dev who is having the most trouble adjusting, and it's affecting his relationships with our kids. He tried to meddle in Evan's relationship with Fenrir already, and that went south. I'm not about to allow him to ruin Rhys's relationship with that smart, brave and gorgeous girl. "He isn't going to be tempted by anything. She is his goddess."

Bris shakes his head. "I know he is in love, but she hasn't proven to be his goddess yet. Not only does she have to bring forth his magic, she has to be able to contain it, to calm him. As far as I can tell, being close to Shahidi merely heightens Rhys's issues since they won't do what they need to do. There is also the fact that my host believes Rhys is too young to take a goddess."

I feel my brows raise at the hypocrisy. "His brother said the same thing to me. It was his justification for withholding the Goddess Chain."

"He's four years younger than Dev was," Danny points out. "I'm with Z on this one, but we need to all be on the same page."

Dev's back, his eyes normal again, but I'm getting used to that frown of his. "And that page is the one the king chooses to be on, I assume."

Danny sighs and sits back. "Devinshea, you are pushing our children away. You have to accept that they are adults and understand their hearts. Evan loves Fenrir."

"And Fenrir is destined to be the king of the wolf packs," Dev points out. "They will never accept a companion as a queen. There have already been attempts on her life."

"Which we have successfully stopped," Sasha interjects. "Your Grace, the situation with the wolves is complex, but I need you to understand Fenrir has called for her. There is no other mate for Fen. He will never give her up. So his father and I have a plan, one which we will implement when Fenrir is ready."

Danny grins, but it's a predatory expression. "Kill every fucking wolf who refuses to accept their marriage?"

"That seems extreme," Neil begins.

Sasha shrugs. "I figure we only need to have Fenrir challenge ten or so of the strongest alphas to let the packs know we won't stop. They can accept Fen's mate or they can lose a generation of alphas and unite under Fenrir only. He can be a modern king or a ruthless dictator. It's up to them."

"Evan is seventeen." Dev's hand slaps at the table. "She should be finishing high school, not be in the middle of a fucking political campaign."

"I assure you, Your Grace, that neither Fenrir nor Evan sees their relationship in those terms." The Russian sits back and seems to consider my faery prince. "I know you have anger because you lost those years with your children, but that is the reality of the situation. I watched those children grow. Those children have been the center of my life for the last twelve years, even while my own child grew up with a different family. Fenrir loves Evan and Evan loves him. It is the same with Rhys and Shy. Did you know the dark prophet visited Frelsi when Shahidi first came here?"

Dev studies Sasha for a moment. "No, I did not. Do we know why Gray thought Shy was important? Or was it Harry? Shy brought Harry with her. I know he had a profound impact on the rebellion."

Sasha's head shakes. "No, it was Shy. I know this because he came in full prophet mode. He did not speak to the rest of us. Merely watched for the moment he was supposed to witness. Would you like to know what that moment was?"

I can guess. "When Rhys first met Shy."

Sasha nods.

Dev takes a long breath and seems to calm. "I am not trying to alienate our children. I will accept whatever Evan and Fenrir decide, but we have a problem with Rhys. He and Shy have known each other for a long time. I don't think she wants him. Lee's been having sex for years. The only reason Fenrir and Evan aren't sleeping together is he promised her brothers to wait until she's eighteen."

Which is coming up on us like a freight train, but I'm not about to point that out to my husband. "And until a few weeks ago Shy had my father in her head. Do you honestly believe she was going to go to bed with Rhys with his grandfather talking in her head? I love my father, but he could be bossy at times and very opinionated."

"Look, let's give them some time," Danny says, obviously trying to placate Dev.

"I don't know how much time we have." Dev looks out the window and then stands. "What the... Well, this is exactly what I'm talking about. I've got to find him."

I stand and see what he means. The grass around the house was perfectly cut this morning. It's a mess of weeds now, and it's at least four inches taller than it was. I seriously doubt Rhys meant to do that. One of the goats is standing in the yard, looking around and trying to figure out how she's suddenly knee high, lost in a field that had been easy to walk in mere moments before. To the goat's credit, she simply puts her head down as though she's ready to eat her way out.

Danny starts to follow Dev. "I'll fly up and see how bad it is." He turns his attention Sasha's way. "But you need to get us into Faery. Any way you can. We have to find the Days, and there's that other project the ancients might know something about."

Danny walks out the door, and I see his feet dangling above the window. Because he can fly.

"What other project?" Neil asks. "I think finding our way to the Heaven plane is project enough. Especially if we're going to have to fight our way through Myrddin to get there."

Sasha's head shakes. "I'll find a way to distract them. I'll think about it, but I'll get us in. As to the other project, that is for Her Highness to say."

It's not like it's a big old secret. Not in my inner circle. "Harriet."

The child I'm carrying. The one Danny and I made when he was briefly human on the outer planes. Dev facilitated the pregnancy.

When Myrddin realized I was pregnant with Danny's baby, he flipped out. Like lost his cool, and not in a congrats way.

In a "you're carrying a creature who might destroy the world" way. It is precisely why he locked me up with Lee rather than taking me prisoner. He thought my dying son would kill me in his turn. He was wrong, but his reaction got me thinking.

So I need to figure out why the baddest of all magicians is scared of a fetus.

It was pointed out to me that if I used the amulet in the way it was intended to be used, I could have asked the ancients. So now I get to go to Faery, face my mother-in-law, who thought her son was dead for twelve years, and ask for the super-exclusive way to call really old dudes.

Of course, I'll also be talking to Miria about the fact that she refused Lee and Fenrir entry to Faery. She was willing to allow Rhys and Evan in, but she closed the doors to my seemingly human son and Kelsey's werewolf boy. Sasha and Trent decided to not break the kids up, a decision I approved of.

I thank the universe that Sasha and Trent stepped up.

And I'll explain to my mother-in-law that she won't ever get Rhys to live in Faery and be a proper priest.

After I get the other stuff. I'm pretty sure my guys will be pissed if I throw down with Miria before we get what we need.

I have a job to do. I get that amulet via persuasion…or I can steal it. Either way, I'm going to get what we need. I'm going to find Sarah. I once pulled my friend out of a torture chamber on the Hell plane. Surely I can find her in Heaven.

I hope she's still alive and wants to come home.

"There's nothing wrong with Harriet," Neil insists. "Daniel was human when you conceived. So Harriet might end up being a companion, but she's probably human. We can handle a human. She won't even be a latent vampire like Lee, so we won't have to deal with the recklessness."

"I'm not so sure about that," Sasha says. "Daniel might have seemed human, but from what I can tell he was under the influence of some truly unique magic. Summer Donovan is a magical creature of immense power. She managed to make her father seem human, and Dev's fertility magic did its work. So in essence the queen's child was created with several kinds of magic, and we can't know what she is."

"She's mine." It's all I need to know. The girl Bris promises me is growing normally is my baby. I don't care what kind of supernatural creature she turns out to be. But I need to know so I can protect her.

"And she's perfect." Neil is one hundred percent Team Harriet. Or rather he's always on my team. Even after all these years. "Sasha's right. We'll figure a way to get in without Myrddin's hunters knowing. I think this might be a job for my husband. It's been a while since Chad did a really fabulous illusion. He'll be thrilled since he's not actually coming on this trip."

"Someone has to stay and represent the vampires as Lily and the others move to New Zealand. The wolves trust Chad and so does Zack." It was decided we would keep our group tight. I would feel so much better if Zack was with us, but he has a young son and just regained his health. He's the alpha of our wolf pack. He and Chad and Lily can oversee the safe shift to New Zealand while we're gone, and Neil and their kids will serve as our wolves.

I'm excited to spend time with Brendan and Cassie.

I'm nervous about what will happen with my son when he's in Faery. I know there is trouble with both the Seelie and Unseelie. Both tried to claim Rhys. With my husband off plane, they had no priest, and at the time Rhys was the next best thing.

Now he's beyond any Green Man they've seen in centuries. Beyond his ascended god of a father.

I wonder if I'll be giving up the Goddess Chain soon. I'm attached to it, but I can pass the torch on after one more job. I'm not sending sweet Shy in to deal with the Fae royals.

I walk to the window to see if I can tell where Rhys is when the alarms start to go off.

Neil is at my side immediately. "Z, let's get you somewhere safe."

But I'm not a safe girl, and he should remember that. "The safest place is with my family."

I hear both Neil and Sasha curse as I race out the door, desperate to find my son.

Chapter Three

Shy

Rhys's arms tighten around me as the alarm clangs and our people start to come out of their homes, worried looks on their faces and weapons in hands.

"Well, that was expected," Josie says. "You need to get that boy laid and properly or that wizard dude is going to murder everyone."

I ignore her, trying to figure out what to do. This has only happened once before. Right after the royals returned. "We need to bring the wolves inside."

Our pack tends to stay outside the mountain. While the pocket world Frelsi exists in seems to be a wide-open valley, we're actually inside the mountain, and the magic can't completely fool wolf senses. They're happy outside, but they're also vulnerable.

If Myrddin's found us, we need to bring them in. They will be his first strike.

"We need to get Shy somewhere safe," Rhys tells his fathers.

If Myrddin's found us, I'm not sure anywhere is safe. Beyond that I'm not about to hide if we're going into a fight.

"You need to calm down and stop the magic that's pouring off you, son." Devinshea Quinn wades through the grass. "Shy, it might be best if you put some space between the two of you. It has to be

40

your decision. He can't think straight long enough to let you go."

"He won't like that." Rhys has gotten so much more protective, and he was pretty much a nightmare before his ascension. He's always treated me like something precious he needs to preserve. In a fight, he'll insist I stay hidden or he can't do what he needs to do. I want to be more like Evan and Fen, who fight like a team.

"Rhys, you're putting Shy in danger," the king says calmly. "Right now, we still have some shot at not giving away a precise location. The magic around Frelsi will ping it through the countryside, but Myrddin will figure it out if you give him enough data. And that will hurt Shy and your mother. You should know he likely won't kill them. He'll take them and hurt them."

The king knows how to talk to his son.

Rhys takes a deep breath and steps back, his hand still holding mine.

"That dude is wound tight," Josie says, looking around and shaking her head. "Poor goats are going to get tummy aches."

I turn her way. She might be my best lead on what's really happening. "Do you sense anything outside?"

The dead can be sensitive to certain magics. Like Josie can see Rhys's magic. She might be able to sense Myrddin's.

"Is someone here?" His Highness asks, and there's a certain tension to his stance.

Rhys lets my hand go and allows his Fae father to approach him. He shifts his hands out, giving Dev access to his chest. "It's Josie. She was a tourist who died on the mountain and got stuck here. She's human."

Josie frowns. "He says that like it's a bad thing. Prejudice, much? Oh, hey, what's that?"

I look over and Bris is in the house. He places a hand flat against Rhys's chest and Rhys almost immediately relaxes.

"Whoa. He's pulling the excess magic out of him. Holy shit, Shy. Is that like a god or something?" Josie asks.

I need her to stay on task. The lecture about the Fae pantheon is going to be a short one. "Yes, Rhys's father is what we call an ascended god. It's what happens when Fae bond with non-corporeal ancient beings. This is an Irish deity named Bris."

Josie cocks her head. "Like the thing where they cut a baby's penis off?"

"No," I say with a sigh as I watch Rhys. Am I hurting him by being close? If I were to leave, would he settle down and find a proper goddess? I love this man. It's an emotion that's sat in my chest pretty much since the moment I met him. I don't want to hurt him. "It's just his name."

"Did she ask if he's named after the Jewish ritual?" the king asks, his lips quirking up.

"Yes, she's not up to date on Irish gods," I admit. "But she is pretty good with seeing magic. Josie, do you sense anything? If Myrddin sent an eye, it'll feel like something is pressing in on you."

I'm pretty sensitive to certain types of magic, too. I remember how the last eye Myrddin sent made me nauseated and anxious. I don't feel it this time.

Josie seems to think for a moment and the alarm stops, bringing blessed quiet with its cessation. She finally turns and points to the north. "I sense something from there, but it's not like what happened a while ago. I did feel that. This is different. I would bet it's coming through the portal."

Which means whatever set off the alarm is in Reykjavík. Where I happen to know some people. Oh, they're all dead, but they can tell me things.

"Is everyone okay?"

I look over and the queen is running into the yard followed by Neil Roberts and our general. I would bet they didn't want to be running after her, but she is the queen. They likely told her to stay put, but she does what she wants.

"I'm fine, Mom." Rhys steps back and straightens his shirt. "I lost control for a moment."

"And now we have an eye outside," His Grace declares, his eyes back to normal. "We need to get the wolves inside somehow."

"I don't think it's an eye," I explain. "We don't have to panic."

One of our witches walks in and whispers something to Sasha. He stands tall and faces the royals. "The witches agree with Shy. They do not believe it's Myrddin. The energy is wrong, they say. They are going to investigate but believe the wolves are safe for now."

The queen moves in and looks her baby boy over. "Rhys, are you sure you're okay? What set you off?"

Despite the fact that everyone seems to relax slightly, I feel anxious again. There's only one answer, and I give it before Rhys can come up with some bullshit no one will buy. "It was me. It's always me. But the witches are right about the eye. Josie says it's something else. Something she hasn't felt before, and it's coming through the portal."

The queen turns my way, and her gaze softens. "Shy, he's in an emotional state. That is not your fault."

I like the queen, but she doesn't fully grasp what's going on between me and her son. "I told him I shouldn't come to Faery."

The king curses under his breath and the queen winces.

"If she doesn't want to come, we shouldn't make her," His Grace says.

And the grass starts to grow again.

The queen turns to her Fae husband, her eyes narrowing. "Stop it."

I hold up my hands. "I'm going. I was worried I would be a distraction. It was a brief thought. I'm sorry I brought it up. Of course I want to go."

I reach for Rhys's hand, and he seems to calm at the contact.

"Shy comes with me or I stay with her. I will not leave her," Rhys states quietly, bringing my hand to the same place where his father recently pulled magic from. He cradles it there. "Papa, if you have a problem…"

His Grace's hands come up in obvious concession. "No problem."

"Oh, we have a problem," Sasha argues. "Apparently we need to go to the portal and figure out what's out there. It's big enough to set off our alarms. Even if it isn't Myrddin right now, that kind of magic will attract attention. I will gather some people to go into town with me and figure out what's happening."

"I'll go," Donovan says, and his eyes narrow when Sasha starts to argue. "I have a magic dampener on. I'm not foolish, General, and I won't put the community at risk, but I can't have Rhys go, and he'll feel better if I'm protecting Shy."

What? I was prepared to fight to go. I can talk to some of the dead. I hope the living haven't seen anything or we have a real problem. That means our witnesses will be the supes of the city or the dead. I'm the only one who can talk to both.

"Why the hell would Shy go?" Rhys asks, his hand tightening around mine. "I'm not putting her in danger. Dad, you can handle it. If you need backup, I'll go, but I'm not risking Shy."

"Shy is the reason we're not panicking and locking down the mountain," the king points out. "She's the only one with any idea what is happening, and I believe she'll be invaluable figuring out what's going on. Shahidi, I'm making a request as your king. Will you aid Frelsi?"

I don't hesitate. A spark of…I don't know what to call it…pride, eagerness…hits me hard. "Of course, Your Highness. I was going to suggest I take… Well, normally I would ask for Fen and Evan or Lee if I couldn't go with Rhys. I was going to offer to talk to some people I know. Dead people. Like I said, they can be sensitive to certain magics."

"It's strong," Josie says, and I notice her eyes close as she seems to sigh. "It feels…good. Not like I think whoever is working the magic is good. I mean, it's nice. It's kind of vibrating along my system. But then I felt some of that from King Hot Stuff before he started wearing the amulet thing Lily gave him."

The King of All Vampire gives off a lot of death magic. I can sense it when I open myself to it. Which means others can as well. So Lily found a way to dampen it.

"They don't need you," Rhys insists. "You can't fight whatever's out there. I won't let you get hurt."

I turn to the man I love. The man who sometimes smothers me. "Babe, I need my hand."

His grip tightens. "You are not leaving the town. I forbid it."

Yeah, he's started using that word, and I don't like it one bit.

"Rhys, she is not a possession," the queen says in a firm, slightly pissed-off tone. "She is an adult woman who has been through things you cannot imagine, and you will lose her if you continue to treat her like a doll you own. This is not love. This is obsession, and if that's all it is, then I assure you, son, I will make it my life's work to get her somewhere safe, somewhere she can be herself."

Whoa. I did not expect that. I kind of expected everyone to tell me how I need to be gentle with Rhys and understanding. Like Harry had. Harry always told me Rhys loves me and he doesn't mean some of the toxic shit he can fall into. So I expected the same from the queen.

I didn't expect her to understand me.

"Zoey, I just got him calm," His Grace complains.

The queen's head shakes. "I will not force another woman to put up with this possessive shit. I do believe Rhys loves her, but he'll drive her away or break her if he refuses to see her as a whole human being who can make her own damn decisions. Who has a whole life beyond being his goddess. If she's your goddess, son, then you should trust her to know what she can and can't do."

I kind of love the queen. All this time I was intimidated at the idea of Rhys's mom. Not that I haven't heard the stories about her, but I expected she would side with her son no matter what.

"Rhys, your mother is right," the king says in a calm voice. "Do you think I don't know what you're feeling? My instincts are to protect your mother at all costs. Even her own autonomy. I have to check myself all the time because that kind of obsession can break a soul, and you don't want that for Shy. I will watch over her. I won't let anything happen to her, but you need to let her use her gifts to help her family."

"Unless she's not family and she's merely a possession." The queen is staring at her son.

"Zoey," His Grace says again, her name an admonition.

But Rhys slowly lets go of my hand. "She is everything to me. I do not mean to make her less than she is."

The look he sends me threatens to bring me to my knees. He looks at me like I'm the sun in the sky and I'm going to leave him in darkness.

But what he doesn't understand yet is that I *am* darkness.

"She is a warrior, Rhys," Sasha says quietly. "I made sure of it. She is perfectly capable of defending herself. Like your sister is. She is part of our army and she has a job to do, one you cannot help with because your magic might give away our position and put everyone in Frelsi in danger. Do you understand?"

Rhys's eyes close and when they open, he looks grim. "Of course, General. I forgot myself."

I feel for him. He's trying, but Sasha is right. I do have a job to do, and if Josie feels the magic, maybe I can, too.

Suddenly the Drowning Woman is close. She stands right next to Zoey Donovan-Quinn, so close I worry for her, but I hold back the warning. I have to be stronger than this. She cannot harm the living. Is she trying to scare me? Well, I'm done being scared. If she's working with whoever is out there, then she'll find out how badass a warrior that big Russian made me.

I close my eyes and try to access my power the way Harry taught me. It's a space inside me, he explained. When I breathe deep and listen to my body, I can feel it.

And I can feel what Josie is feeling.

The magic is weak here, but then it's coming across hundreds of miles and all our wards. I can still feel its pull.

I thought it would feel like some of the magic I've had worked around me. Some of it soft, like the slightest caress. Some of it scratches and claws at me.

This one calls to me. This one tells me I could master it if I tried.

This magic feels familiar. Like some song that plays in the back of my head all the time. It feels like it's mine, but I don't have magic beyond my abilities.

I open my eyes and look to Sasha first. It's a habit. Since I came to Frelsi, Sasha has been the authority figure in my life. Well, the one who didn't live inside me. Sasha trained me in combat and strategic thinking. Sasha taught me to trust my instincts in the field. When I've been allowed in the field. Rhys tends to find a way to get me to stay out of the line of fire. "It's death magic. I can feel it. It's powerful, but I don't think it's here to hurt us. I know that sounds weird, but it's almost like an invitation. It's definitely not an eye. I know how that feels."

"All right," Sasha says. "Then you will go into the city with the king and perhaps Neil while I talk to our witches about how this affects our plans to leave. Please talk to your friends and try to get a better feel for whatever is out there and what they might be inviting us to."

"And me." The queen steps beside me.

"Zoey," His Grace begins.

"Don't," the king says with a sigh. "Devinshea, do not push her. Settle our son down and then perhaps the two of you could have one of the witches teleport you to Nimue to see if she's got legs yet. We need to leave soon, and the last time I saw her she was barely a head and some shoulders."

"I would rather..." Rhys began and then stopped as though thinking better of it. "Yes, sir." He looks my way, the saddest expression on his face. "Shy, I'm sorry."

I'm sorry I put him in the position. The queen is wrong. It is my fault, but I'm starting to change my mind about the whys. While Harry was with me, I knew there could be nothing physical between me and Rhys. In the weeks since he's been gone, grief consumed me at first, but something about the queen's words sink in and give me strength. Sasha did teach me how to fight.

The queen might teach me how to fight for myself.

But that's no reason to be angry at Rhys. He's scared. I move in close. I crave this man. It is something like obsession, but it's also love. "I'll be fine."

The truth is I'm scared to have sex with him. I'm scared I won't be enough. Everything I know about sex is creepy assholes at the psychiatric hospital who tried to touch me. I swear even though Harry had no body, he would work some kind of magic. When anyone would try something on me, the walls would seem to shake and a cold would skim over my skin and the men would back away, utterly terrified. So I avoided what happens to lots of women in places like that, but I still know nothing. He's a sex god.

He's a virgin who somehow connected with me on a level that I don't understand.

We've kissed, but only a few times because it hasn't been long since Harry passed over. Still, it feels normal and natural to go on my toes and brush my lips to his. His hands go to my waist but he lets me control the kiss, lets it be the tender promise I mean for it to be.

"Be careful, Shy," he whispers when I break it off. His forehead rolls against mine. "I'll listen to my mother. I'll work on it. I promise."

I step back and can't even find the will to be mad at this gorgeous, amazing man. "Say hi to Nim for me."

He nods and I notice I'm surrounded by pansies, beautiful colorful flowers. His gift to me.

I also notice the Drowning Woman is at a distance again.

"I wish I could go," Josie says. "The portal never lets me through."

Because she's tied to roughly the place where she died. I don't know why it's different with the Drowning Woman.

"Let's go," the king orders.

The queen moves in close to me and threads her arm through mine. "Maybe we can do some shopping if it turns out to be harmless. I saw the prettiest sweater that would look beautiful on you, and I think you're due for some new boots."

I am actually not much of a fashion girl. I wore hospital gowns for years, and then Sasha and Trent had us in practical clothes in case of a life-threatening fight breaking out. So I hope she's talking about combat boots. Or all-weather boots. I could use a pair of Birkenstocks.

"When we get back from Faery I'm going to talk Devinshea into letting us have a girls weekend in London," the queen announces as we start making our way toward the portal at the north end of the pocket world. "You and me and Evan. We can see if Neil wants to come and bring Cassie."

"Do you have any idea how long it's been since I went shopping at anything that isn't Iceland's version of an Army Navy store?" Neil is suddenly on my other side. "I swear Z I missed you, but I missed Dev's black card more than anything. And Chad's dressing like a Nordic dad these days. I swear I saw him looking at a pair of Birkenstocks."

I am going to be so out of place. Still, I like the queen's affection and how the king asked me to share my gifts. With my family.

How I long for that word. How that word scares me.

We reach the portal and I take a deep breath, ready to face whatever is on the other side.

Chapter Four

Zoey

We emerge from the portal that connects Frelsi to Reykjavík. Frelsi is located in the northwestern most point of Iceland, while the city is on the opposite side of the country, but magic makes the trip roughly a two minute-walk.

We're connected to a bookstore called Sun and Moon Books in a quiet part of town. Daniel walks through first, and then me and Shy, with Neil bringing up the rear. We find ourselves in the storage room. It's surprisingly roomy, and I appreciate the smell of old books, though Neil's nose twitches. I was told this is where they keep the really old stuff and the magical books. So I'm not touching anything because you never know when a magical book is going to bite.

Danny turns at the door leading to the sales floor. "Let me talk to Tinna and Magnus before we head out. Neil?"

My bestie takes a long breath and shrugs. "I don't sense any desperate threat. There's a pack of dogs somewhere. They smell weird, but I can handle some puppers if they decide to misbehave."

"You are not hurting puppies," I declare.

Danny sighs. "Shy, do you sense anything?"

Her big brown eyes seem to darken as she obviously opens some space inside herself to access her power. "It's here. Much closer. But again, I don't feel threatened by it. It wants me to find it. And by me I mean it wants to be found. I don't think it's particularly looking for me, but it definitely wants attention."

"Well, that can be an excellent reason to stay away," Danny points out. "I'll be right back. Neil?"

"I remember what to do, Daniel," Neil assures him as he starts to look at the stacks around us.

"Hey," Shy says.

I turn and give my son's girlfriend a grin. "Hey, yourself."

She gives me an apologetic nod. "Sorry, Your Highness. I was talking to Anna. She haunts the bookstore. She says there's something going on. She can sense the energy, but she can't leave the store to go look for it." She turns to a space to my right. "What does it feel like to you?"

Neil stands back, watching Shy now.

What must it be like to experience a whole world the people around you can't see? How isolating must that be? I know she was in an institution for a while because her foster parents were scared of her.

How weird is it to know there's a ghost standing so close to me? Like how many are around at any given time and how much do they see?

"She describes it as a beckoning warmth," Shy tells me. "She's not afraid of it. I'm going to be honest. It's somewhat similar to the magic I feel coming off the king at times, but I didn't want to mention that to Rhys because the minute I start talking about death magic he's sure I'm going to die. Like he's not surrounded by it. We live with vampires. Sasha is nearly his second dad. Sorry, third dad."

Neil shakes his head. "Fourth dad. Trust me, Bris counts. I often think about what would have happened if we didn't lose twelve years. I would love to have sat in on Bris's version of the birds and the bees."

My life is complex, but I know the type of magic Shy is talking about. "Any number of beings have some form of death magic. It doesn't mean they kill everything in sight. So we're fairly certain it's not demonic in nature. Their magic isn't the same."

Demons aren't dead. Technically Daniel is. My hand goes to my belly. I'm carrying proof that no matter the technicalities, Danny's alive in all the ways that count.

"I don't even get a hint of brimstone," Neil replies.

Shy shudders slightly. "No. It's definitely not demons. Demonic energy is like ants crawling on my skin. At least the kind I've been around. Even Kelsey's husband gives off the slightest bit of it. Not enough to make me really uncomfortable, but I feel it."

"He's a halfling, though he takes after his human side." We're talking about Grayson Sloane, the dark prophet who witnessed Shy meeting my son. I don't hear anyone coming so I lean against the bookcase and hope I'm not bisecting Anna. "Does this Anna person have anything else to say?"

Shy sighs. "Not anything important. She thinks my leggings are going to attract the wrong attention. Also, she wants me to tell Tinna to stop selling sage. It disturbs her. She doesn't understand the whole the-bookstore-needs-to-make money thing."

Neil's eyes sparkle in the low light. "Does she say anything else? She sounds like a fun ghost."

Shy's head shakes. "She's not. She's really salty. She thinks the queen should cover up more and you should find a nice girl to settle down with and then you'll be a better man. Sorry. She's super old, and the dead can be cranky."

Neil smiles. "See, I've been in Frelsi for way too long. I haven't been judged in forever. I forgot how good it feels to be all morally superior. And Z, don't listen. The girls look magnificent. Anna, do you know how old this woman is? She is in her damn forties and looks this good. She should show those puppies off as often as she can."

Shy's lips turn up. "I am not saying that."

I'm curious. "Is she from here?"

"Yes," Shy replies. "She was a housewife, and then her husband died and she lived out the last of her years in an apartment above the bookstore. Her sister still lives there. I've met her. She's pretty salty, too."

"So she's Icelandic." I want to know more about Shy's power. "Did she speak English in life?"

Shy seems to understand where I'm going. "Oh, I'm sure she thinks she's speaking Icelandic, but I hear English. Harry told me it was something unique to my power. I understand all of them. One time I came across a ghost chicken and even then I got some images. Hence me entering my vegetarian era. It was not pretty."

"But that's not how most mediums work." I knew a couple in the day, and the hardest part when they weren't in their native countries was dealing with translations. One of them learned how to say "go into the light" in twelve different languages. "Ghosts speak the language they did when they were alive. Mediums aren't like vampires. Vamps learn languages quickly."

"I don't know Icelandic. If a living person spoke Icelandic to me, I would be lost," Shy admits. "I don't know. My mom was a medium, but we didn't travel a lot. She told me she wanted me to take either French or Spanish in high school. We lived in Texas but had a lot of relatives in Southern Louisiana, and some of them still speak some form of French. I don't think she had this ability. I don't know why I'm different. Harry told me I was born that way. It's been really helpful. That's what Sasha says. I can absolutely understand Fae languages, too. Rhys thinks I'll be helpful in Faery. At least with the dead."

I've made her uncomfortable. If we have some time to talk, I'll take it. "Are you okay?"

Shy seems surprised at the question. "Of course. I've felt magic many times before."

"She's asking if you're okay with all the questions. And if you're okay with Rhys. That was a heavy scene back home." Neil gestures my way. "She knows what it means to have some dude think he owns her, and she's real expensive, if you know what I mean. The funny thing is that dude was Danny and not Devinshea. Dev actually figured out pretty quickly she wasn't going in a cage and behaved accordingly. If only he put that knowledge to use when it comes to his daughter."

Didn't I know it, but there are some differences. "Dev didn't meet his goddess before he attained maturity."

"By maturity she means before he got his freak on with half of Faery and a whole lot of the Earth plane," Neil adds helpfully.

Shy frowns at a space to my left. "You do not have to be so judgmental. He's a Green Man. Do you know what that means?" She pauses. "I don't think faeries can carry syphilis." Her head is shaking as she looks back at me. "Sorry. She was really old and set in her ways when she died. You know some ghosts revert to the form they were happiest in. Some stay frozen the way they died. Anna apparently likes being a mean old biddy."

The lights flicker slightly.

Shy waves it off. "She'll be back. I'm the only one she can talk to. As for Rhys, I didn't mean to…I don't know…stunt his growth. I know he should have way more experience than he has, and it's my fault."

"You need to stop using that word, sweetie. Fault is loaded and not applicable here," I explain. "If anyone is at fault, it's his fathers and me for being dumb enough to fall into that painting and cause the world to explode."

"It would have done that anyway," Shy says firmly. "Myrddin would have found a way. He was always going to bring this darkness to our plane."

I wonder about that. I know Myrddin thinks I'm little more than the king's bang buddy, but I have some power of my own. I'm a nexus point. It means I have no fate. I don't show up on that endless tapestry, and the things I do and choices I make can change that sucker for good or bad. I have to wonder what could have happened if I were here when Myrddin made his move. But I've been told thinking that way will get me nowhere, so I let it go. I have inroads to make with this someday daughter-in-law of mine. Including cleaning up some of my son's mess so he has a chance at making her exactly that. "The point being if Devinshea had been here when Rhys reached puberty, he likely would have taken him to Faery to begin his training as a priest, and let me tell you it does not involve denial of pleasure the way it does here on the Earth plane."

Shy's head cocks slightly, a curious expression coming over her. "A priest? Like a high priest?"

I nod. She knows the terminology, but there's more to it. I wonder if anyone explained this to her. Likely not. The kids were too young to really grasp their father's role in the Fae world beyond he was called His Grace and given deference. It wouldn't occur to Trent or Sasha to talk about it beyond telling the kids their dad was important. I'm pretty sure Trent, at least, hadn't explained that their parents got it on in public and a whole lot of voyeurs got pregnant. "Yes. Simply by his nature he's already a priest of Faery. Dev is the high priest, though I suppose in his absence they declared Rhys for the position. It's why they tried to kidnap him. The issue is a priest usually spends years in training that begins when the Green Man hits puberty. When he should have been in Faery making Lee look like a prude, he was on the run."

"From the stories I've heard, it didn't stop Lee," Shy says quietly. "I was sixteen when I met him. Harry managed to teach me how to act normal. How to be normal, and I finally got out of the institution. Naturally they sent me to a group home, but Harry taught me how to get out."

I smile. "He taught you how to steal, didn't he? My father was a menace. He was also the best thief in all of the supernatural world. I wondered how you managed to get across the globe and find your way here."

"It wasn't exactly stealing," Shy admits. "Harry kept a bunch of cash in his old house. By then it had been sold by Myrddin, and he pocketed the money. You do not want to know how your father felt about that."

I can guess. "I suppose Myrddin used magic to falsify the records."

"Almost certainly," Shy allows. "Harry walked me through breaking into his old house and getting the fifty thousand in cash he hid under the baseboards of his old office. From there he taught me where to get a fake ID, and it was pretty easy. I got here. They were freaked out some unknown American was living in a tent outside the mountain. I met my first actual Fae creature and after a while, they let me in and I met my second. And realized how different they can be."

I heard a bit of this story. It doesn't surprise me my dad hid money in his office. He always had a plan. "You never saw a faery before?"

She shook her head. "My parents never went to the Council building. Every now and then a vampire or a witch would show up for consultation, but they look human, of course. The wolves I met were always in human form. So meeting that brownie was a lot. And then I met Rhys."

It's easy to forget how young she was when Myrddin killed her family, and only coincidence saved her. "How old was Rhys?"

"He was seventeen," Shy answers. "Lee already had quite the

reputation. He managed it even though Fen and Rhys wouldn't join him in the partying. Oh, they would drink and start fights and stuff. But they wouldn't pick up women the way Lee did. Or men. Lee doesn't discriminate. From what I understand it's not like Rhys has no experience. He had encounters but he never finished the act."

"Because something deep inside told him not to." Neil gets serious, his arms crossing over his chest. "I know I wasn't on the outer planes with the kids, but I was still their Uncle Neil. When they would come home, they would always spend time with me. Rhys and I sat up many a night talking about his future and how weird he felt not doing what his body so clearly told him to do."

The idea of my best friend being there for my kids brings tears to my eyes. I know Sarah would have done the same if she had the chance.

"But why wouldn't he follow his instincts?" Shy asks. "Trust me. I've heard a whole lot about Rhys's instincts."

I'm curious about that as well. It's not like Rhys wants to talk about his sex life or lack of one with his mother. Lee is so much more open. So is Evan. Rhys is the one I'm having a hard time getting close to.

"He told me he dreamed at night of his goddess. He said he knew she was out there, and he didn't want anyone but her," Neil explains. "No amount of teasing or pointing out the obvious problems of a virginal Green Man could persuade him. I think one of his deep fears about being taken to Faery was being forced to perform rituals."

Oh, he's being generous. The Fae treated my children poorly while we were away. "He was afraid they would facilitate his rape. I don't care that he would have likely gotten some pleasure out of it. It's rape, and they should be happy they didn't pull it off. I assure you they will feel my wrath."

"Zoey, you should know both King Angus of the Unseelie and Queen Miria disavowed having anything to do with those attempts," Neil says. "From what we can tell, they were rogue elements of the Fae world."

Sure. Like they didn't know. Like they wouldn't have found a way to use my son and his fertility powers. "What's important is the fact that Rhys knew he would have a goddess at a young age. Devinshea thought he was a simple priest. So he had no reason to hold back. However, the situation can't stay this way. It's not sustainable. Are you afraid of him?"

Shy's eyes come up and she smiles slightly. "You remind me so much of Harry."

I can only imagine why. "Because I have no filter right now? I actually am pretty good at politics, but not when it comes to my family. I'm blunt and plain and not afraid to ask the hard questions."

"Honestly, she's not that great at politics, which is why I'm worried about her getting to Faery and starting another war," Neil admits.

Shy seems to ignore him. "To answer your question, Your Highness, yes I am afraid, but not for the reasons you might think."

"Because he's so possessive? His dad was much the same. The vampire/companion relationship is an intense one, to say the least."

"Yes, the vampire is addicted to companion blood," Shy says in an academic fashion, and I'm sure she's been through some lectures on the nature of supernatural creatures. "A companion's blood makes the vampire faster, stronger, far more powerful than a vampire without a companion. Rhys isn't addicted to me."

"He is in a way," I explain. "If you truly are his goddess, then you will enhance his powers. Part of my wedding vows to Devinshea included the fact that his magic flows from me and only me. It's why he calls me goddess, though I don't actually have any real power. I'm his connection to the divine. The way Rhys believes you are for him. But Shy, this is your choice. Always. I love my son, but I won't allow anyone to push you into a relationship you're not ready for."

Shy looks down at the floor for a moment and then her head tilts back up. "I know how sex works, but I don't know the other stuff. I...my mother died before we got around to that particular hard conversation. I talked about it with Evan, but it kind of grossed Harry out and the truth is she doesn't know any more than I do."

This I can handle. "I will answer every question, Shy. I'm a mom who missed so much with my kids that I want to take you all in and hold your hands and steal some of that time back. I know I'm not your mom, but if you let me, I can be your friend and your mentor. I can teach you how to handle these men."

"She can," Neil affirms.

I finally get a real smile out of her. "I really do love him."

"I know you do, sweet girl, and I will do anything to help you feel comfortable," I vow but I have some rules. "You have to stop calling me Your Highness. Zoey will do."

I can't replace her mother, but I can be something close. As I settle in to this reality, I realize my kids' partners are going to be my kids, too. If things were normal and they got regular jobs and moved and traveled for fun and had their own lives, it would be understandable to be a bit more distant. But we're at war and we need to be as close-knit as possible. My father loved Shy. Shy gave my whole family the gift of a lifetime. I will honor and love this young woman the best I can.

There's the slightest sheen of tears in her eyes as she nods. "All right, Zoey. Then I do have some questions for you." She straightens up and seems to find some courage. "I would like to know how the Fae will welcome me if I agree to be Rhys's goddess."

See, I'm all for Sasha's "take out all the wolves who would get rid of my daughter so the love of her life can find a proper wolf mate" plan. I don't like the word *proper*. Not the way they use it. "My darling girl, it doesn't matter what they think. I assure you if they don't welcome you in a manner that pleases this family, they can do without a high priest. Rhys won't touch them and neither will Devinshea. They can rot for all I care."

She stares at me for a moment as though trying to figure me out. "That's not practical, Your...Zoey. We're in the middle of a war. Having the Fae on our side would do a lot to help us."

I shrug because I'm not known for being practical about the people I love, and she'll come to know that I mean what I say. "We'll figure it out. I won't sacrifice my children's lives and happiness. I'll find a way, and one of those ways is using every ounce of power we have. This is nothing you need to worry about, Shy. Dev and Danny will handle the politics. I'll handle Dev and Danny. Neil will handle danger, and also all the weird food. Seriously, don't eat any meat he doesn't give you a name for."

"Hey, the last time I was in Faery, the frost giant burgers were delicious," Neil adds.

It's good to know nothing has changed for my bestie. Though I remember that he got a terrible tummy ache and Sarah had to whip up a tonic.

I miss Sarah so damn much.

"I'm a vegetarian, so no worry about meat." Shy's nose wrinkles. "I ate a chicken once and its ghost chased me around for three days before I tricked it into going into the light. You know what doesn't leave behind a psychic signature? Celery."

Neil shudders. "Z, I'm so glad I'm a werewolf and not a medium. That would be terrible."

Neil would definitely have troubles with all the creatures he eats.

The door opens and Danny stands there. "They haven't seen anything, but they got a call from one of the women in their circle. She's not a natural witch but she has some knowledge. She says there are the markings of a god-like being in town. We should go question her."

I nod, happy that I got this time with Shy. I feel like I know her better. And hopefully she knows I'll protect her while we're dealing with my in-laws. Who will likely absolutely think Rhys should be with a proper *sidhe* girl who won't mind him performing crazy fertility rituals with numerous partners and spreading his seed all through the *sithein*. "Of course. And then we can do some shopping."

I want Shy to feel confident in everything she wears while she's in Faery.

Danny sighs but doesn't argue as he lets us walk past into the bookstore that smells like coffee and baked goods and old books. I kind of love it.

We're almost to the front door when Neil stops. "Huh, those dogs are closer now. Be careful. We don't know if they're feral. I'll handle them."

"I feel something, You... I feel something, Zoey," Shy says. "The magic is closer. It's calling to me."

I look to Danny—who is legit made of death magic. He shrugs. "I feel nothing except an instinct that tells me you're going to spend a shit ton of money."

He knows me well. Neil steps out of the store and I follow.

"Can you tell us which way it's coming from?" I ask Shy.

But both she and Neil answer. They point to a place around the side of the shop.

"Is there something supernatural walking around in the open?" That could be bad for us.

"Don't worry," Danny reassures me. "The place is warded. If you have supernatural blood, you can see everything. If you don't, well, there's a reason people think this place is haunted."

"Oh, it's super haunted." Shy moves down the stairs. "But then pretty much everywhere is."

And that's when I hear it. A low growl, and then Danny is cursing, trying to get me behind his back as a big animal moves around the side of the bookstore and into the parking lot.

It's a dog, though it's as big as a horse, it's fur a stark white and eyes blood red.

Cŵn Annwn.

We're in serious trouble because I left my treat bag at home.

Chapter Five

Shy

I was serious when I told the queen I never saw a real live Fae creature until I came to Frelsi. I definitely have never seen an adult hellhound, but that's what this feels like. Except the magic pouring from the massive creature doesn't feel demonic.

The eyes, though… They look a little like a portal to Hell.

If Rhys hears about this, he's going to lose his shit and try to find a way to never let me leave Frelsi again. Even as this deadly creature growls my way, I'm thinking about how Rhys is going to explode. The plant thing does seem harmless, but you've never seen what a root can do to a home's foundation. Even magical ones.

"Shy, I need you to get behind me," the king says. He stands in front of the creature, his arms out like he's trying to show he isn't a threat.

Except he is, and it's not like the big predator is buying it. The hound growls, and the hair on the back of his neck stands up. That is not a happy puppy. And yet I'm not entirely afraid. Which kind of makes me afraid.

I find myself with the queen, letting the king stand between us and the dog who does not look like he did well at obedience school.

"Neil, shouldn't you change?" Danny asks. "Let's see the

werewolf that loves to take a bite out of strange creatures."

I hear Neil's long sigh. "My wolf is not going to scare that buddy there. We're all safer if there's not another canine to try to dominate. That is a Ci Annwn. It's a Welsh hellhound. He's not going to be impressed with a werewolf, so I'll keep my favorite pair of jeans intact, thank you, very much. I no longer have access to Dev's endless cash, so my wardrobe is important to me now."

I manage to get a look at the creature Neil calls a Ci Annwn. It's like an oversized dog with stark white fur, except there are streaks of red around its long ears and on its tail. And yet the magic coming off it still feels…right to me.

"Danny, we've got another one." The queen moves from my side, pressing herself to my back so I'm surrounded by Rhys's parents. Rhys isn't the only one with a protective instinct.

I manage to turn just enough to see our friend is not alone. There's another Ci Annwn coming around the opposite side. And yet another follows him. "Uhm, shouldn't they be in Wales?"

Out of the corner of my eye, I see the Drowning Woman has joined us. She's closer than before, and I wonder if she wants to attack like the dogs seem to.

"Not if Myrddin sent them," the king says, his voice tight.

"They don't belong to Myrddin." The queen sounds worried, too, but then I would be worried if she wasn't. "They belong to Arawn. There are some bonds not even Myrddin can break. They're not of this plane, nor of the Hell plane, so Myrddin shouldn't be able to influence them."

"The dude who used to be involved with Nim?" Neil joins our circle. "Good puppy. You don't want to eat me. I'm gamey. Go for the vamp."

"Thanks a lot," the king says. "And yes, they belong to Arawn, the asshole Welsh King of the Dead. I say that because the fucker drained me once. He fed off my magic because it got him high. Only Bris was able to save me. Why would he send his hounds?"

"Maybe he's looking for Nim," the queen offers. "They were involved, and it wasn't his idea to break up."

"But that was over ten years ago," Neil argues.

"He's a god." The king keeps shifting us around, shuffling in a circle like he's waiting for one to pounce. "I assure you a couple of decades are like giving his girlfriend some time to cool off. But why not come himself if he's worried?"

"We can take you to Nimue," Neil offers, and then his voice goes low. "How do we get a bunch of crazy-looking hellhounds all the way across the country? I don't think we should take them through the portal. Is there an Uber?"

"Also, how upset will they be since best-case scenario she's starting to grow her legs back," the queen points out. "I don't know how much they understand. We didn't do it. Could we sic them on Myrddin?"

"I don't think they want an escort," the king growls. "If he wants to find Nimue, he should simply send a representative who won't try to kill us."

"They are not looking for Nimue, Your Highness," a deep, feminine voice says. She sounds like a pack-a-day smoker for maybe three hundred years. "Though I assure you my king feels her absence."

Then I get a look at her and raise that estimate up. Like three thousand maybe.

"Then what are they looking for? Perhaps you could call them off and introduce yourself." The king sounds irritated. "Is this the way Arawn treats his hosts?"

"Are you our hosts? I should also ask if you can truly be considered a king at this point," the really, really old chick asks. She's dressed in all black, the color making her hair look stark against it. She wears her white hair in thick braids. She points the king's way, long nails forming what looks like talons. "From what I can tell, you don't have a crown anymore, Daniel Donovan. And you have no real ties to my people."

"Oh, but I do," the queen says, moving so she can face the woman.

No. That's not what she should be called. I might not have met all the supernatural creatures of the world, but I did take classes. This is a crone. Maybe a hag. I'm hoping for a crone.

She stills for a moment, and then her head drops. "Your Grace."

It must be good to have all those titles. Makes it easier to pivot when one doesn't do the trick.

I wonder if the crone can sense the Drowning Woman, who

stands right beside her, menace pouring from her form.

"Yes," the queen says. "I am the high priest's goddess, and I would like to know why Arawn would send his hounds to hunt us. I would also like to know your name and why he didn't come himself."

"The hounds will calm down when you allow *yr un sanctaidd* to greet them," the woman says, standing behind the largest of the hounds. "My name is Mallt-y-nos. You can call me Matilda. I serve the King of Annwn."

See, here is where my dead translator would be helpful, but apparently Matilda is considered alive because I got nothing.

"The Sacred One?" the king asks. "Who are you talking about? Is this being in the bookstore? We have no one from Annwn among our people."

"*Yr un sanctaidd* is of the world. Is more than ours. She belongs to the world. *Mae hi y llwybr i dragwyddoldeb*," Matilda says, her voice even deeper than before. Like it's coming from someplace inside her. "My invitation is for her, though you are welcome."

"Danny, I think she's talking about Shahidi," the queen says, turning my way.

The dogs growl and move in closer when the queen takes my hand.

"I don't understand Welsh." I'm confused, and I don't have a handy ghost translator. Although the ones I would likely find here wouldn't help me. I doubt there are a bunch of dead Welsh tourists hanging around.

The queen lets my hand go and steps slightly back. The dogs stop growling. "I don't either, but she's an emissary from a dead land, sweetie. You can talk to the dead."

Matilda frowns, deepening the wrinkles and crevasses of her face. "You make light of her. Or you don't understand her."

"She says you're the path to eternity," the king explains. "Mallt-y-nos, you need to understand I consider this young woman a daughter, and if you harm her, I will find a way to make your slice of hell even worse."

The crone's brow rises. "How little you know, Your Highness. But your ignorance is none of my concern. If you will allow my hounds to assure themselves *yr un sanctaidd* is safe, I think you will find they will calm and we can have a talk."

"What do you want, Shy?" the king asks. "We can back off and let you handle this or we can fight here and now. I'm perfectly happy to do that. I think I can handle some hellhounds."

"No, it's fine." For some reason I don't think they're here to hurt me. And I would love to know why she thinks I'm some sort of gateway to eternity. I'm just the chick who tries to get dead folk to walk into the light.

"We'll be right here," Neil promises as he moves to the steps again. "And I assure you I will change if I need to. Jeans be damned."

The queen is the last to join them, and then I am surrounded by three hellhounds.

It's not my first time around dogs. My family kept several along with cats. It is the stupidest thing, but I'm kind of following my instincts here. I put a hand out to the largest, palm down, to allow him to catch my scent. Or take my hand off with those insanely sharp choppers of his.

I hear the queen's deep intake of breath as I offer my hand.

The hound takes a sniff and then makes a huffing sound, and I find myself surrounded by bouncy, happy hellhounds. They change utterly from snarling death machines to puppies who want attention. I find myself on my ass, laughing and trying to not let them lick my mouth.

"Hey, guys, you are very sweet," I say as they start to settle down.

"I told you they would be fine once they knew she was all right," Matilda says, walking toward me.

The Drowning Woman stays where she is.

Matilda moves in front of me and bows formally. "*Un sanctaidd,* my king wishes to meet with you. If you will allow me and my hounds to escort you to the Faery plane, we can be on our way."

"Whoa," the king says. "She's not going anywhere."

"You should listen to him," Neil adds. "Your sacred one is kind of spoken for, and you will have one pissed-off elemental following you. He's getting good with weather, so think about it."

"I fear not the Green God," Matilda replies. "Of course he is welcome to join his goddess. The fact that Rhys Donovan-Quinn has selected one of ours as his goddess gives all the kings hope. We are entering a new age. The stars have aligned, and we will either be destroyed utterly or we shall make this age one of peace and prosperity."

"I wouldn't think a death crone would care about peace and prosperity," the king notes.

"Because for all of that death magic clinging to you, Your Highness, you do not understand death at all. You may deal it. May feel yourself mired in it. But you do not know death at all if you think it only darkness."

"I've been to the Hell plane," the queen admits. "It was a fearsome thing."

"That is the Hell plane, a place created by and for very specific people. Annwn is our underworld. You only call it Hell because you have no imagination, Your Grace. And I also happen to know Shahidi is planning a trip to Faery along with the rest of you. Tell me, how are you planning to get through the wizard's guards?" Matilda asks, summing up one of our problems.

I manage to get to the steps, sitting down. The hellhounds come with me. One on the step above me. One at my feet below. One beside me, his big head resting on my lap.

The queen sits with me and gives me a grin. "This is the fun part. I made friends with some black dogs once. Such sweeties. They get a bad rep. I mean, sure, throughout human history they've been death omens, but if you get past that they make excellent pets." She looks at Matilda. "Will they let me pet them or try to bite my hand off?"

The mysterious crone—isn't there always one—smiles slightly. "As you explained, you are the high priest's goddess. They are Fae creatures. They had one mission, and it is done. I think you'll find them to be happy for some affection. They are canines, after all. Despite the magic they carry, they also harbor the deep instincts. For love. Companionship. Like all dogs, they are as open as they've been taught to be. You'll find my master takes care of his own."

The one behind me moves to the queen's side and his tongue lolls out, giving him a smiling expression. The queen practically melts as she starts to pet the creature.

I stroke the head on my lap and feel the oddest connection to the hound. "Are you saying you can get us into Faery without having to get past Myrddin's guard?"

"I want to understand how she knew we were going to Faery at all." The king stands close as though watching over the situation, but I see that Neil is behind us now. So we have a vampire king at our front and a werewolf on our six. As Rhys would call it. Rhys is a good soldier. Rhys is the one who follows commands and gets things done. At least he had before his power went insane. How hard is it for him?

Can I make it easier?

"While my master does not believe it to be safe for him to come to the Earth plane right now, he does keep up with what is happening here. After all, what happens here affects all of the planes. The inner planes are the working heart of the universe, though there is an outer plane that forms the…how would you say it…the engine of the universe. I believe you were recently there, Your Highness."

The king nods. "Yes. My daughter, Summer, and her husband, Marcus, have taken their rightful places on that Fae plane."

Matilda chuckles. "It's closer to a celestial plane, but I doubt you've been on one of those."

"Are you talking about Heaven?" Neil asks.

"Heaven is a human construct," Matilda corrects. "Like what you would call Hell, Heaven is made of many different planes. The celestial planes."

"This doesn't answer my question." The king is determined, but then I bet Sasha would be, too, if he was here.

"My master is a lord of the dead. Do you think he doesn't have a network?" Matilda asks. "He keeps watch on what is happening here. On what is happening on all planes where he has a presence. He also has allies who exchange information with him. The underworlds are worried, Your Highness. They are worried about Myrddin."

"I assure you Hell is not," Neil says with a bitterness that can't be denied. "They're working with him."

"Some of the Hell planes are," Matilda allows. "Some are not. Some are ready to resist should Myrddin fulfill his plan to close off the planes. My master will not allow it. Cutting off the celestial planes will harm those in transition. It will cause millions to be stuck. So he will aid you in doing what you need to do, Your Highness."

"I'm supposed to trust the man who nearly killed me so he could get high?" The king's voice goes dangerously low.

"He would rather like to speak to you on that subject himself." Matilda's head lowers deferentially. "Your Highness, I cannot tell you how important the girl is. He would never place her in danger."

"I'm not important." I think I'm the only girl here. Not many people would call Zoey Donovan-Quinn a girl. She's a badass woman queen. I'm just… Well, I've been trained and can take care of myself in a fight, mostly. But I feel like a girl.

Matilda gets to one shaky knee in front of me before I can stop her. "You are *yr un sanctaidd,* lost from our kingdom for millennia. The fact that you are resurrected in this time means something. You are here to save us, to be what you were created to be. You are walking death."

The words bring tears to my eyes. I don't know why. She's not saying anything I don't know.

Rhys is life, abundant and rich. I simply cling to shadows.

"You think I insult you," Matilda says softly. "Because you do not know death, either. Come to the Faery plane and learn who you are, what you can do. Death is not the end. Death is change. There can be no rebirth without death. No end to suffering and hope of something new without death. You can see yourself as a cold, pointless thing, or as necessary and warm and loving as birth itself. Like all things, you decide how to see the world around you and by choosing your vision, you form reality. Come to meet my master and let him show you all the lies this world has told you. You are nothing to fear, Shahidi Davis. You are a miracle."

"You mistake me for someone else." She has to because I'm just a girl from Texas. Seeing and talking to the dead is the only thing special about me. I don't have any power beyond a good gossip session with the recently deceased.

She straightens up. "The Cŵn Annwn do not make mistakes. They know you." She turns to the king. "So what should I tell my master?"

"I need to think about it." The king looks my way, considering me. "I don't know that I like how interested the King of the Dead is in my son's goddess."

"She isn't his goddess yet," Matilda whispers. And looks straight at me, her lips not moving. "And you never have to be. You could take your place in Annwn. You do not need the spring. You are so much more." That's when I realize the whole time she was speaking in my head, her other face was turned to the king. "I will leave you with the key. There is a secret door to the Fae plane that my master and Nimue have used many times over the years. No one else knows of its existence. It is in the Welsh countryside. Go to Snowdonia. The hounds will guide you from there. If you carry these stones with you, the door will open."

"Neil," the king says.

Neil moves in and takes the stones. They look like crystals to me. He sniffs them. "I think they're safe, but I'm not a witch."

"Take them to your witches," Matilda offers. "But do not wait too long, Your Highness. There are plans the wizard makes that you do not understand."

"You could tell us," the queen asks, but she says it offhandedly like she knows the crone isn't going to take her up on it.

"I will tell you only this, be careful in Faery. Give nothing away. Your lives depend upon it." And then she's gone. She is simply there one moment and gone the next, and we're left with three massive hellhounds and a bunch of blue crystals.

And about a million questions.

"We should get back to Frelsi." The king frowns his wife's way. "You are not keeping those dogs, Z."

The queen has her arms around one. "Not forever, but they're our guides." She goes nose to nose with a ferocious beast. "I'm going to get you some treats. Yes I am. Yes I am, you good boy."

The ferocious beast's tale wags enough it's creating its own wind system.

The one on my lap flips over and wriggles, asking for a belly rub. Which I give as I think about everything the crone said and know I have to go. I have to meet this god of the dead and see what he might want of me.

I also know exactly who I have to fight to get there.

Rhys Donovan-Quinn.

Chapter Six

Zoey

I oftentimes wish my life was calm enough that I could keep a pet. The pixies who cling to my hair don't count. They have their own whole society, and I can't run a hand along their fur because one, they don't have any, and two, they would probably consider petting to be some form of crime against their dainty personhood, and I don't fuck with pixies. They know about revenge.

But the puppy with his head in my lap simply wants some treats. My daughter has a hellhound. The kind from the actual Hell plane, so he's got darker fur and eyes, but he's the sweetest puppy. Naturally when she decided to take a trip to Gray's kingdom, she took Puff with her. I miss him.

"Did you tell her we are not keeping hellhounds?" Devinshea says as he paces the floor to the designated conference room/dining room. "Zoey, are you feeding that dog under the table? You have no idea what that is going to do to his belly."

"Mother might not be, but I assure you Shy is." Rhys seems calmer now, but he might not be in a few minutes. "Baby, I need you to understand that I adore you, but I'm not cleaning that up."

"They're hellhounds," a familiar voice says. "They don't poop the way other dogs do. It comes out as fire. You need to be careful, though, because it can catch you off guard. Now, I need to know everything that happened because Arawn wouldn't send the hounds on an everyday errand. I don't know these hounds personally, but Arawn is serious about all his creatures. It's been a long time since I was in Annwn but I still know a bit. They are telling me their names are Caddoc, Bledig, and Emyr, though the truth is you can call them whatever you like. They are not smart creatures."

I look down the table where Dev and Rhys set up a…well, a system to keep Nimue upright in a chair because she is not all there. And I do not mean her mind. Myrddin chopped her head off when he realized the thrall stone he'd placed there had made its way out and she was no longer under the influence of his magical roofie. He placed her head in a magical box that became her prison for years until I sent some huldrefólk to do a little recon in the Council building and they brought back Nim. She's been hanging out in a cold-ass lake for a couple of weeks, but apparently regrowing a body takes time.

"You should know that Arawn is one of the Unseelie who fought the idea of forcing me to play priest for the *sitheins*." Rhys sits beside Shy. When we returned, he was still on the errand with his papa to bring Nimue back. He breathed a sigh of relief when he saw Shy. He hasn't let her out of his sight again. "When a group dragged me and Lee to the Unseelie *sithein*, it was Arawn who stopped them. And maybe one of these guys. They're sweet now, but you should know I've watched them take apart an ogre."

My heart clenches because I think he's talking about the incident that led to his twin brother losing an eye. Oh, it grew back after he died and rose as a vampire king, but I'm sure it was incredibly traumatic at the time. I know Rhys still dreams about that day and carries guilt with him like a millstone around his neck. I have to wonder if there's a part of that trauma in his deep desire to avoid Faery. "I'm glad to hear Arawn helped you."

Nimue sighs. Her hair is far longer than her body at this point. Apparently it kept growing when the rest of her did not. "In the last couple of hundred years, I'm afraid Arawn has grown apathetic. Once he was a true believer in justice. It seems a few centuries without his original body have taken a toll. He took on some of his hosts' more hedonistic tendencies, but then I did as well. Until I had a cause again."

"My father," Rhys prompts.

"Your parents," Nim corrects. "I know Daniel Donovan is the King of the Sword, but it was obvious from the first meeting that he was a member of a royal trio. When I found your family I remembered my purpose. If only I remembered how duplicitous the wizard can be. There's a reason I lock the fucker up when he's done."

"It wasn't your fault, Nim," Danny sits at the head of the table, Sasha on the opposite end. A king and his general.

"Technically, it was." The Russian watches Nim with dark eyes. "She took you to the wizard. She allowed the plan that ended in the king and His Grace receiving thrall stones that kept them in Myrddin's pocket for years, that led you all to lose twelve years of time."

"I had one, too," Nim argues and then sighs. "I can't tell you how sorry I am. What a fool I have been, and I do not have the excuse of youth."

I'm not sure what Sasha is trying to do, but I can't let Nim think I blame her. "You were doing your job, and Myrddin certainly didn't treat Arthur or the other kings of the sword in such a fashion."

"I wonder about that now," Nim admits. "But there's nothing I can do but move forward. I know what Myrddin's planning. He must be stopped. I assume Arawn has figured it out. Closing off the celestial planes would be devastating for the dead, so of course Arawn is concerned. If he requested a meeting with you, perhaps you could do it on some neutral site."

"I got the feeling the meeting he's requesting isn't with me," Danny says, and I fear his next words but know they're coming. Danny isn't one to play politics with his family. He does too much of that in his job. He'll rip this bandage right off. "He wants to meet Shy."

Shy winces. "I think they have me mixed up with someone else."

Rhys has gone quiet and still. Like really still. Like "trying to keep his cool so we don't find ourselves in a prison of grass and leaves" cool.

"Rhys, we would never let Arawn hurt Shy," I say, trying to calm my son down.

"He wants to meet Shy? He sent the Cŵn Annwn to find Rhys's girlfriend?" Nim asks.

"His goddess," Dev corrects.

At least he's on board supporting Rhys's choice now. In public. The problem is I'm not absolutely certain Shy wants to be his goddess. Or thinks she can be. One I can work with. The other will break my son's heart.

"And that Matilda person," Shy adds even as I see her sneak one of the hounds a piece of cheese. Gotta pay the cheese tax.

Nim goes still. Or rather stiller. There's not a lot she can do with those stubby things growing out of her shoulders. "He sent Mallt-y-nos?"

Danny nods. "I believe that is what the crone called herself, though she allowed us to call her Matilda."

"It's her informal name though she hasn't been around in centuries. I thought she was on another plane. She's a crone who often traveled with the Cŵn Annwn. She acted as Arawn's eyes from time to time. If he sent her, then he believes Shahidi is important," Nimue explains. "You're a psychic, correct? From a family of psychics?"

Shy nods, more somber now. "Yes. My family was famous in the supernatural world for their abilities. I took after my mother. I'm a medium."

"Matilda called her the sacred one," Danny says.

"Like I said. She's confused." Shy puts a hand on Rhys's, obviously offering him comfort.

Rhys threads their fingers together and brings their hands to his chest, holding them over his heart. "I doubt that. Shy is afraid of her power. I believe she is far more powerful than anyone knows. Even her. If the King of the Dead sent his hounds to find her, then he understands things we do not. Nimue, Lady of the Lake, do you know what Arawn wants with my goddess?"

"Rhys, technically she isn't your goddess," Nim says with quiet sympathy. "You are not married. You're not sleeping together."

"How would you…" Rhys growls a bit. "My brother, of course. He doesn't know when to shut up."

"Rhys, you have to know that in the Fae world there is no marriage without a properly witnessed ceremony. Like your parents," Nim reminds us. "You can call her your goddess, but you have no technical claim on Shy. Not one any Fae will recognize."

"My parents' marriage had to be witnessed because my father was taking on a god. I didn't need to take on an old one to ascend. I did that all on my own. My goddess is powerful, but she was traumatized at a tender age. Myrddin wiped out her family and forced her to take on her power with no support. My grandfather found her and took care of her, but he shared what she calls a soul space with him up until recently. I will not push her and traumatize her further because the Fae have rules I care nothing about." In this moment my son reminds me so much of his papa I can barely stand it.

In the beginning Dev couldn't care less what Fae society thought. He wanted to be with me and damn the consequences. But then we found ourselves in a place where we had to deal with them. I fear Rhys will learn this lesson far too soon.

"Rhys, you are Fae," Dev begins carefully. "You are considered divine. No one in the *sitheins* has seen an elemental in millennia. From a religious standpoint, you're important."

"I don't care," Rhys replies with a shrug. "I need you to understand this, Papa. I know you think I'm going to get to Faery and become like this super *sidhe*, but you're wrong. You can be the high priest for all of time on the Fae planes. I will remain here with my goddess. I will serve the Fae on this plane. For me, this is nothing more than a trip to facilitate Mom's mission. Finding the Days. However, if Arawn has some sense of my goddess's power and thinks he can claim her, he's in for a surprise."

Shy's head comes up. "I'm sorry, what? Claim me?"

"I don't think Arawn is trying to claim her as his bride," Nim replies.

"Whoa." Shy moves closer to Rhys. "I am not Persephone. I am also not playing out *Twilight* fantasies because I'm assuming the god of the dead is super old."

"As old as time." Nim manages an amused smile. "I think you're safe. Young women were never Arawn's thing. I was his woman for a couple of hundred years. I would be surprised if he's trying to move on. No. I assume he's intrigued with Shy's power."

"Does the god of the dead need a medium to speak to his subjects?" Rhys asks.

I know the answer to that one. I watched him not merely speak to the dead, but reanimate them and have their corpses fight for him.

"He doesn't need her medium powers. Which makes me wonder what power he thinks Shy has. The crone called her the sacred one. That sounds pretty specific."

If Nim had arms, she would have waved that one off. I can tell from her expression. "You would be surprised. The old ones use the term sacred a lot. Like when Arawn was forced to give up his corporeal body, he had to divest himself of his sacred objects. Every Fae deity had objects of magical power and when they began to pass through into immortal life, leaving behind those objects was considered dangerous, though some of course remain. Then he would call his hounds sacred. His torc. You would call it a crown. They can't be destroyed, so they were changed into things humans or Fae wouldn't recognize as magical to hide them. He's been obsessed for the last hundred years with finding them. It might be that he thinks Shy can help him."

"But Shy is a human," Devinshea points out. "She has no real connection with Fae planes. She's lived her whole life here."

"A human who can speak to the dead, a power considered sacred to Arawn," Nim returns. "I'm trying to not put too much into his crone calling her the sacred one. There are a lot of sacred ones in Fae lore."

"So this king is like Devinshea," Sasha begins. "He holds the soul of a non-corporeal god within? Is there any possibility he would see Shahidi as a better vessel given her unique abilities?"

The general always asks the pertinent questions.

"No, he has never taken a woman as a host. Arawn's particular power is masculine in nature. It's why I was such a good mate for him. The power I hold is of the feminine divine." She frowns. "However, the feminine divine can get fucked over by a wizard just like the rest of you. I left Arawn behind because I had a job to do. I always intended to go back. Over the hundreds of years we've been together, we've taken these breaks often. I didn't mean to be gone for so long." She looks my way. "Zoey, I'm not ready to see him. I'm not ready to see Rourke. Not yet. I need to be whole again before I admit what happened. What I got myself into."

"Nim, you were raped." I know what it means to be forced into some asshole's bed to save the people around me. It doesn't matter that he didn't have to beat me. Threat is coercion, and drugs and spells certainly are, too.

"And yet I remember how eager I was." She looks behind me as though she can't quite meet my eyes. "It's there. Those memories are there. I can see them. Feel them deep inside my mind. I was happy with him. I did things, things that hurt people, but at the time it felt right. Like what I allowed to happen to the pixie queen."

"You mean when Olivia spelled her to find Devinshea and she died?" Danny asks, his voice cold.

"And her priest brought her back to life." Dev's tone is softer, more forgiving. "Daniel, you know how the thrall stones work. You know we betrayed our wife's trust time and time again because it seemed like the right thing to do. I know how good I felt when Myrddin would praise me. Like I was worthy. What I wasn't is a fool. Nor were you, Nimue. You were caught in a trap. We were lucky enough to find a way out, and so were you. There is nothing to be ashamed of."

Tears well in Nim's violet eyes. "I remember when the coup began. I didn't kill anyone myself, but I remember crying even while I knew...I knew...it was necessary. And then one day the veil lifted and I realized it was all blood and murder and pain, and it only benefits one man. The rest of us don't matter. We all live to serve Myrddin. Our wants, needs, desires, who we are as individuals mean nothing to him. He truly believes he can control the demons and force the humans to worship him. To make him their god. And then they will matter to him no more."

"Can Arawn aid us?" Sasha asks.

"We shouldn't trust him," Danny adds quickly.

"Yes, he can and he will," Nimue says with obvious confidence. "Arawn is serious about Annwn. It's his home, his place of power, and it is not like Hell. It is connected to the celestial planes. If Myrddin cuts off Heaven, he cuts off Annwn, too. And I don't know what happens to Arawn if he can't spend time there. He is dual natured. Of Annwn and of the Earth plane. Rourke, his host, is Fae and must have access to those energies. Myrddin's plan could kill him. So yes, you can trust that he will aid you in taking down the wizard."

"What do you mean Annwn is connected to the celestial planes?" I ask and the crone's words come back to me. "Matilda said Annwn wasn't like Hell. What does that mean?"

"It means the underworld isn't the same for all cultures. Annwn is closer to Valhalla than Hell," Nim says, and then gasps a little. "I wonder if Odin's still around. He'll be pissed, too, and that old guy does not hold back. His son is an asshole, though. I'm not joking. Marvel makes Loki look good. He's a little shit."

"So all of the old gods are hanging around?" I've only really dealt with the Fae, which I should be forgiven for since they're my in-laws. Luckily Danny didn't come with a whole religious background. Vampires are pretty pragmatic.

"Some of them," Nim explains. "Some left for the outer planes. Some became like Arawn when people stopped worshipping at levels that could keep their godhood up. Some cling to their places of power and never leave. Some are whispers, still trying to influence the humans. You can trust Arawn in this, Your Highness. It serves his interests to do anything he can to stop Myrddin. Your mission will be his mission."

And if I'm right, it might serve my personal mission. "I believe Sarah took her family to one of the lesser celestial planes. Felix and Mia would be able to move on them. Sarah would need magic, but she would do anything to save them."

"Arawn might be able to help. He knows doorways no one else dreams exist. If he doesn't, he knows someone who does," Nim affirms.

I know what I'm going to vote for. "So if we take Arawn's invite, we don't have to worry about getting around Myrddin's guards and we might have a handy way to find my friends that means I don't have to grovel to my mother-in-law. And we get to hang with the puppies."

"I'm afraid Z's right." Danny sighs but looks resigned. "I don't want a fight with Myrddin while the *Nex Apparatus* is on the Hell Plane."

"I'll handle my mother," Dev assures me. "And I'll get Nim back to her lake if it's really her will to stay."

"I can't face him, and I will be a burden without my hands and heart. There is magic I can do with my mind, but Myrddin knew what he was doing. He cut me off from heart and body magic," Nim explains.

Sasha stands. "Then we will be going to Wales. I will alert our allies and get the plane ready. We can be there tonight. I, for one, would like to get this mission started so we can rejoin our group in New Zealand. I'm leaving Chad and Lily in charge since the rest of my team is either coming with me or in Hell." He chuckles. "It's fun to say that."

Kelsey and Trent aren't exactly in Hell as we think of it. They're in Gray Sloane's territory on the Hell plane. I was told it's called a midnight plane, and Fenrir will be powerful in that night kingdom. I hope so because my children Lee and Evan intend to either negotiate with or steal from Lucifer Morningstar.

All in all, it feels like I'm getting the easy end of this particular stick.

And I'm worried sick about my babies.

Danny stands, too. "We're ready to go. Dev, did you pack enough Scotch?"

My Fae hubby sends my vampire hubby a smile. "Oh, Your Highness. We are packing light, but I assure you we can find something in the palace to get in trouble with."

See, that makes me perk up. I love it when my guys go at it.

"I'm not letting Shy get anywhere close to this male," Rhys announces. "Mother, I understand that you need to go. You need to find the Days. You need good relations with the Fae. But Shy and I are staying here. I will ensure our safe transfer to New Zealand."

"Rhys..." Dev begins.

But Shy is standing up, pulling her hand from Rhys's. "You are not my master, Rhys Donovan-Quinn."

Rhys's eyes narrow. "No. I am your commanding officer, however."

"And I am yours," Sasha says, his voice deep. "Or do you forget your place?"

"I think things have changed, General." Rhys stands, his shoulders back like the good soldier he is. "I think our little army unit has shifted since my parents returned, and I know my powers have grown. I know Faery better than you."

"You know it from your childhood and you fear it from your adolescence," I say, trying to reason with him. "Rhys, we all need to go. Shy most of all because if Arawn knows something about her power that we don't, we have to explore it."

The hounds take up positions around Shy, and I feel the minute this could go poorly.

Rhys doesn't seem to feel the shift. His hand slaps on the table. "She is my goddess, and I will not have her in danger."

Not the way he should have gone.

I hear thunder in the distance.

"And this is how I know she is not your true goddess," Dev says with a frown. "Not yet. If she was you wouldn't be about to bring a storm down on our heads in the middle of a pocket world. Do we even have drainage? Are we about to flood?"

Shy looks my way, a frown on her face. "If I have sex with your son, will he be easier to control?"

There's only one answer to that. Though it's not a question I thought I would ever be asked. I should have known better. "Infinitely. And you'll be the only woman he's ever had so you won't even have to compete with faulty memory."

"Excellent," she declares as she stands. "Then we'll be ready to go when it's time. Let us know, but you should probably knock, Your Highness."

She takes Rhys's hand and my stunned son follows her out. Along with two of the hounds. The third finds his way back to me and sits, obviously asking for a treat. I give the good boy some of Albert's bacon.

I know how to deal with a hellhound.

And it feels like Shy is about to figure out how to deal with my son.

"It really should be..." Dev begins.

Danny picks up an orange and fast balls it at Dev's head.

"Oww." Dev's hand goes to his head as he frowns Danny's way. "Fine. I'll stay out of it."

Words we should all follow.

Chapter Seven

Shy

There's a light rain falling as I hold Rhys's hand and lead him out of the big house his parents call home in Frelsi. Earlier in the day, the sun was shining, but now there's a distinct gloom. So Rhys's magic can override the magic of the pocket world. Even in a world made of magic, Rhys's can hold sway.

"Shy," Rhys begins.

I'm not in the mood. Honestly, it's been a day, and I'm sick of feeling like I'm not doing what I should be doing. Even when the what I should be doing is offering my virginity up to a Green Man. I knew when Harry left I would have a choice to make. I've been putting it off because there's a part of me that knows giving myself to Rhys will make it so much harder to leave him.

But he's been kind of an asshole today, so I'm willing to risk it. Maybe I won't miss his annoyed ass at all. I do a quick pros and cons list. The man is a sex god. I have zero intention of staying virginal all my life, so why not do it with the sex god I'm irritated with?

I pull him out into the rain he's creating. The two Cŵn Annwn who follow us don't seem to mind the rain. One of them starts doing zoomies and the other wags his massive tail.

"Shy," Rhys insists, planting his feet in the grass that is still too high from his earlier issues. "I am not going to make love to you because you want to control me. My father is right about one thing. We should do this properly. We waited this long. We should have a proper ceremony."

"A proper ceremony would be in Faery." I know that much. My best friend in all the planes is Evangeline Donovan-Quinn. We've been talking about our weddings since I was roughly seventeen. She wants hers in a sacred forest and I knew mine—if I married this stubborn asshole—would be in the high priest's temple on the Faery plane. I don't know about the wedding right now, but I do intend to get to the Faery plane. "The good news is I'm already packed."

"My parents married right here," Rhys counters. "We don't have to risk putting you in danger. I'll start preparing for our ceremony. We can perform it in Herekoretanga."

"Hey, Green Man, what the hell," a voice calls out, his Irish accent thick. "You know we get our water from the ground here. There's no need for this bullshite."

I look over and the gnomes have joined us. Three small men with red pointy hats and long white beards who are responsible for the big gardens here in Frelsi. Seamus, Tiddle, and Enoch. The one in the middle is obviously their leader. Seamus looks to Rhys with a fierce frown on his face.

"First you grow so much grass we're going to be digging the crops out for days," Seamus complains. "You know it will take us a while to establish crops in Herekoretanga. These are supposed to sustain us."

Rhys turns as the rain starts coming down harder. He faces the gnomes, hands in fists on his hips. "I'll grow more."

Enoch steps up, his pointy hat drooping a bit under the rain. "Will you now, Green Man? Because you seem to be struggling. Did you mean to grow the grass so high? Did you know the strawberries were caught in your whatever this is. They grew and rotted in the course of moments. And I was planning a strawberry pie."

One of the goats joins the gnomes, bleating like she has something to say, too.

"And now poor Maeve has a belly ache," Tiddle proclaims. "How is she supposed to keep up? You're treating her like one of those human mowing machines."

I wanted that strawberry pie, too. I face Rhys. "Now you've pissed off the gnomes. Do you know what it takes to piss off the gnomes? Come on. Everyone says if I spread my legs, you'll calm down and the world will be a better place."

Enoch sighs loudly and puts a hand to his heart. "Thank the goddess. Someone is thinking straight. Carry on."

"Yes, turn off the waterworks or we'll all drown," Tiddle says as he waves and walks away.

The goat bleats and runs when the hellhound tries to sniff her backside.

"Hey, no eating the goats," I call out. If the hounds start eating our livestock, everyone will revolt.

"What are you doing, Shy?" Rhys stands in the rain, his dark, longish hair slicked back after he runs a hand through it.

It does not make him any less sexy. The rain simply drenches the tunic he's wearing, plastering it to his perfectly cut chest.

Yeah, I watch this man a lot. I watch him when he's training. I watch him when he chops firewood. I watch him when he swims in the pond, but always find a way to avert my eyes when he starts to walk out. I don't have that right. But I want it.

It's kind of nice to not have his grandfather inside my head trying desperately not to vomit because he can somehow feel what I feel.

Don't you think for a second you aren't worthy of him. He's my grandson and I love him, but I know your soul. You make sure he's worthy of you.

Sometimes I still hear Harry like he's here. Like he's still the strong ground I stand on.

But he's not and I'm alone, and the only way I'll ever figure out if there's more to me is to meet with this Arawn person.

"I'm doing what everyone in the supernatural world needs me to do." It's good. I can get it over with and then we'll know. Then he'll know if I'm his goddess or not. He'll see that I can't ever keep up with him sexually because I don't know how good I'll be at it. I don't know if I'll like it. I think about it, but how will I know?

When he kissed me earlier... I liked that. Maybe I can get through the rest of it if he'll kiss me. I love it when he wraps his arms around me and holds me until I fall asleep. When he stands in front of me even though he can't see the ghost or spirit that frightens me.

When his hand holds mine and the world seems warm…

But since he ascended there's an intensity to him I don't understand. A need to control me.

All I know is I love this man and he needs me, and after this I'm putting my foot down and he better be reasonable enough to understand that I am going to Faery.

Rhys stares at me for a moment and thunder cracks right before he reaches out and hauls me close. The hound growls, but I hold out a hand as Rhys leans over and hauls me high against his chest. He strides through the muddying yard toward the road that leads through the center of town.

"My place is closer," I say as he keeps walking. He moved to a cabin on the edge of town when his parents returned. He stays there with his brother and Fen, who claim they can't handle all the fertility magic that flows whenever the royals get it on. Which they do a lot. Only Evan is still staying at the big house.

"Your house is full of witches," he says, not looking down at me, though I note there's only a light drizzle now. "Everyone who might be at mine is currently in Hell. I really should have gone with them."

"What is that supposed to mean?" I glance around, and there are a whole bunch of townsfolk out trying to figure out why it's raining.

The minute they see Rhys, the pointing begins. Then it looks like they have some questions about the hounds trotting behind us.

Rhys really is getting a bad reputation, and while it wouldn't bother Lee at all, it will upset him. Rhys has played the peacemaker over and over again. Rhys loves these people and enjoys when they come to him with their problems. The benevolent god.

"It means if I'd gone to the Hell plane with Fen and my siblings, I wouldn't be in this position," he mutters. "I wouldn't be fighting with you. I hate fighting with you."

We never fight, but now I wonder if that's healthy. Rhys and I formed a friendship at a tender age that quickly became a romantic attachment. But the years have rolled by, the war keeping us apart at times, my own unique circumstances at others. We've never been a normal couple. We've leaned on each other, supported each other, been awkward around each other. We've never simply been.

"Well, get used to it if you intend to be this overly possessive asshole you seem determined on becoming." Despite my harsh words,

I don't move my arm from its position around his broad shoulders. I don't struggle to be released.

"I am trying to protect you as I always have," he insists as his long legs take us to the edge of town and his small cabin.

He takes the steps quickly and closes and locks the door behind us.

"No, you are trying to control me." My feet find the floor as he sets me down and stares at me, his eyes bleeding out to full emeralds.

In his father, this would symbolize Bris taking over the body. But Rhys is his god and his god is him. Those eyes are spring and fertility and rebirth.

How can he want a woman so mired in death?

Death is not the end. Death is change. There can be no rebirth without death.

The words have taken root inside me. I wasn't told lies, as the crone said. But what if I misunderstood what I was told? What if I am not using this power I have in the best way possible? What if my power fits with Rhys's in a way I never imagined?

Still, I don't think giving him my arguments will sway him when the thunder cracks all around us. "Could I control you?"

His eyes flash. "Do not push me, goddess. I want to do this with gentleness. With the love I feel for you. You're angry with me. It matters not. In a few days, you'll see I was right."

"I am going to Faery." I won't allow him to cage me. I spent much of my childhood in a version of hell, and I won't go back into the cage. Not even when its gilded and comfortable.

"You are not. I will not allow Arawn to get his hands on you," he says, his arms crossed over his chest. "Tell the hounds to sit or something. I don't want to have to hold them myself, but they should understand if they come between me and my goddess, I will show them what I can do."

That's the moment I realize the hounds are scratching at the door he locked. One of them howls. I'm glad one had the sense to stay out of the rain with the queen. At least I know where Fenrir keeps the treats. I cross to the pantry and pull out the jerky Evan makes. I do not ever ask what it is made of.

"They're hellhounds," I say as I move to the door. "I think they're tougher than you make them out to be."

He waves me off. "They're Welsh. I bet I can handle them with a nice spot of tea and an afternoon game show on the telly."

I seriously doubt that, but I also don't want to start a war. "Could you at least stop the rain? Otherwise start a fire and I'll bring them in to get warm."

The rain stops immediately. It's good to know he's got some control when he really wants it. I give each hound a handful of jerky. "I'm fine. Stay here. He's touchy, but he would never hurt me."

Both hounds settle on the porch, curling their bodies around each other as they dig into their treats.

If only all males were so easy to deal with.

Rhys is staring at me when I close the door again. "My parents will not take you. I know my mother sounds like she's pissed at me, and she likely is, but she will not go against me if I put my foot down."

I'm not so sure about that. I think Rhys has an idealized vision of his mom, but he's missing the point. "I was sixteen when I left everything I knew and made it here. I might have had Harry as a guide, but I assure you I handled most of it myself. I had to lie and fake my way across several countries to get here. I had to pitch a damn tent in the middle of Iceland and wait for your people to decide I wasn't a threat. Do not think for one second that I can't do it again. I will meet with the death god. I can do it with you or I can take those hellhounds and find my own way. Or I can simply explain to your parents that I am the cost of a ticket past Myrddin's guards. They need to find Sarah Day. It sounds like Arawn might be able to help them. But they go nowhere without the Cŵn Annwn, and for now they are mine."

His eyes narrow, and I can practically feel his anger vibrating off him. "You would not dare."

I know I'm supposed to be all intimidated since I can see a tree popping up in the front yard. A big one. It shakes the ground. Oak, naturally. The masculine in its essence. But I can't live in fear. Not of him. I would rather live utterly alone than fear him. "I dare. If you think I will make some kind of submissive, quiet and meek goddess, you have underestimated me, Rhys Donovan-Quinn. I will not be ruled by you."

He moves toward me. Moves is the wrong word. Stalks is better.

"But you would rule me with sex."

I sigh. "I would put this tension between us to rest, Rhys."

"And you will not listen to reason?" he asks as he gets close.

I hold my ground. "I am listening to reason. Reason states I should learn as much about my own power as I can." I'm starting to shiver because my clothes are soaking wet. "I should get dry before we have this conversation."

He holds up a hand and a warm wind embraces me. Heat skims across my skin and I'm suddenly warm and dry. "As you command, goddess. Now, if there is no other way to convince you then I might as well take what you offer me."

Suddenly his hands are on me, dragging me close. He dried his own clothes as well, so I'm warm as he pulls me in. His mouth is on mine in an instant.

"You think you can rule me with sex," he whispers against my lips.

"I think you need it, and you won't take it from anyone but me," I reply as my heart rate ticks up and I feel… My body feels both languid and on edge.

"At least you admit that truth. I will have no one but my own goddess," he says, those emeralds of his staring into my own. "You believe I have been faithful, Shahidi?"

"Yes." It's a simple truth.

"And I know you have been." His hands skim down to my hips. "I wonder how far you've gone. Tell me, Shy, when was the last time you had an orgasm?"

"What do you mean?" I ask, confused.

Two big hands cup my backside and draw me against his body. I try to drown the gasp at the feel of his hardness against my belly. I've felt it briefly before, but he's never been so blatant. Never rubbed it against me like some big predator. "I mean when was the last time you slipped your hand down your panties and stroked your little clit until you came, Shy? How long? I'll tell you how long it's been for me. A couple of hours. I woke up thinking about you. I dreamed about you working over me, your breasts bouncing as you took the whole of my cock. And I wrapped my hand around my dick and stroked until I called out your name and ruined a perfectly clean set of sheets. It's okay. We have many sets. Lee alone can go through five in a week. So how long?"

Every word seems to work some magic on me. I can feel my…vagina seems clinical…core too undefined…pussy. I can feel my pussy pulse as he rubs against me, his words forming a cloud blanketing my senses in him. In the smell of him—woodsy and masculine. In the feel of him. In the rough sound of his voice. But I realize how out of my depths I am. I don't want to admit this but I also don't want to lie. "Rhys…I was young when I went into the asylum. I was older when Harry found me."

His eyes flare as though I've confirmed some long-held belief. "You were too young to be interested in it, and then you had my grandfather and he could feel what you feel, know what you're doing. Shy, you've never had an orgasm."

It's the truth. And he's right about the timing. Sex was something I feared for the longest time, and then when I was curious, I wasn't alone. It's been such a short time since Harry passed that I didn't think about it. I'm thinking about it now. I'm thinking about how woefully inexperienced I am. Rhys might not have had actual penetrative sex with a woman before, but he certainly knows what to do. He's watched before. He's had encounters on the outer planes. "I don't know how." I step back, embarrassed. "You're right. This is ridiculous. I don't know what I was thinking. Of course I can't control you with sex."

He pulls me toward him with a grunt, though this time he's shifted me so my back is to his front, his arm winding around my waist in a possessive grip. "I never said that. I assure you I will do a lot to get inside those panties of yours. Stop thinking. We both think too fucking much. This is the way you want to go, then we'll start it right."

His mouth is against my ear, warm breath sending a shiver through me as his free hand finds the waistband of my pants and eases under.

My head falls back against his strong chest. I should protest. This isn't the way I wanted this to go. It was supposed to be quick and fast, an easy way to get it over with, but that plan kind of flees as my breath hitches and I feel my nipples get hard. "Rhys…"

"Yes, it's Rhys who's about to give you what you need. You think I'm the only uptight one, the only one who is slightly out of control? You are not made of stone, my love. You need this every bit as much as I do. You just don't know it yet."

My body tenses as I feel his erection against my backside. For a second, it makes me freeze, but then I know this is Rhys and no matter how much he can hurt my heart, he won't ever harm me physically. I'm safe with him in this.

I want this. I want this in a way I didn't when I started it. I began because I was sick of waiting, sick of the anticipation. Now I simply want to know where this feeling is going to lead me. I want to know why Lee has women walking out of his bedroom with smiles on their faces and sighs of satisfaction. And men. I want to know why their cheeks flush and they seem happy in a way I don't understand.

Rhys's arm moves from around my waist to right under my breasts, which seem way more important than they did before. My body is a tool to use, except now it feels like an instrument to be played, a way to make something beautiful.

"Do you have any idea how many times I've done this in my mind?" Rhys rasps the question against my ear as his fingers move between my legs, easing under the band of my underwear. My breath seems to catch as he continues. "A thousand times since that first day. I know the humans don't have fated mates, but I knew you were mine and I thanked the goddess that night. I sat under the full moon and offered her blessings for sending you to me."

Tears pierce my eyes at the sweetness of his words. They resonate. "I...I knew you were special, too."

I remember the moment. I remember I was scared and he grew a flower for me. When I dream about him, I still smell that flower, still feel it caress my cheek.

"You were always able to tell the difference between me and my twin. You didn't have to get close enough to see our eye color. Even before..."

I can finish his sentence, though not aloud. Before he lost his eye. Before he sacrificed to save Rhys. Their eye color was the only difference between them before then. Lee's were a dark brown. But I could always tell them apart from how they held themselves. "You are very different. It's easy to tell. Ohhh."

The pad of his finger slips over my clitoris, and I feel a jolt of arousal rushing through me.

He nips at my ear, sending another pulse. "Poor goddess. How long you have suffered without the pleasure due you. A goddess is to be worshipped. When I'm done you'll simply look at me and I'll know what part of my body you wish me to use. My fingers." He slides them over my clit again, making a circle that has my vision blurring. "My tongue." He licks my earlobe, which I would say shouldn't be sexy, but that warm stroke shoots through me like lightning. "My cock." He rolls his hips, and I can feel how much he wants me. "I will call on all of spring to please my goddess."

I feel a warm breeze surround me, and the scent of roses is delicate in the air as his fingers work. He rubs my clit gently and I feel another finger running lower, starting to breach me in the sweetest way. I'm wet and hot and my hips move against his hand as I catch the rhythm. My body starts to shake with anticipation because this is something new and vibrant and real. This is connection in a way I haven't felt before. I've felt love from a father figure, but this is something else. This is something for us. Something only the two of us can experience. Pleasure and connection like an invisible thread binds us together.

He groans behind me as his hand cups my breast and he presses me tighter against his body. "Come for me. I'm going to be the only man in the world you ever come for, so come for me now."

Heat flashes through my body, and I am so connected to him. I can feel his will and intentions in my veins. To love me. To worship me. To make me safe and warm and happy.

I let go, allowing his magic to flow over my body, heightening the pleasure that threatens to scorch me. My whole body is humming and he hasn't even gotten my clothes off yet.

I'm starting to get my breath back when his hand pulls away and he retreats slightly. When I turn I watch him put his fingers in his mouth. His eyes close as he tastes the arousal he brought forth from me. I should think it's weird but damn he's hot. "Take me to the bedroom."

He shifts uncomfortably and frowns. "No. I can't stop you from rushing into danger, but I can take this part of our relationship seriously, Shy. I haven't waited years to shove you on a bed where my brother has had a hundred lovers. You want to go to Faery, then we'll go. I'll have you in my father's temple with all proper rites."

There's a reason the queen doesn't like that word. Proper. I don't either. My body is perfectly primed for more and he's turning me down? I can see his erection, so I know it's not that he doesn't want me. This is a power play. "And if I'm not ready to be married?"

His fists tighten. "Then we wait." He growls. "Shy, I'm not going to force you into marriage, but I'm also not going to allow the relationship between us to be less than it is. I love you. You are the best part of me, and I cannot honor you by throwing down. I need you to hear what I am going to say to you. You are not responsible for my loss of control. You are everything that is good about my life. You are the reason I meet each day with any kind of joy. You should feel no guilt about what happened today because I am responsible for my loss of control. Not you. I will talk to my parents and every single person in this town to let them know I will not accept anyone putting this on you."

My body still pulses with the pleasure he gave me, but the feeling wars with the emotion I feel at his words. I feel his guilt and anxiety, and yet he will not take what I'm offering him because it's more important to honor his love for me. How the hell am I supposed to be upset with him? I move to him, placing my hands on either side of his face and kissing him soundly. "I love you, too." I have to be honest with him. "But I don't know that I am the right goddess for you."

He frowns, his eyes going a softer shade of green. "Why would you think that?"

"You are life," I whisper. "Walking Spring. My only power is to see the dead of the world. I don't know how you expect your magic to flow from me. I know you say I'm not responsible, but your goddess will be. Your mother soothes your papa. His power grew when he married her. I know Bris is there, but from the stories I've heard Bris came for your mother, not only because he wanted a host."

His head drops forward, nestling against mine. "Then I'll show you. I'll prove it to you. If you don't want to be married to me, then we'll figure something out. Until you tell me you cannot love me, I won't give up on us. But Shahidi, you need to understand I won't go to bed with you because you're afraid. I won't sleep with you because you want to experiment. I won't fuck you because you feel some sense of responsibility to me. I will sleep with you because you want me. Because you crave me the way I crave you. I'll fuck you when you beg me for it because you can't stand another second without knowing what it feels like to have my cock inside you. I will take you to Faery and when you want me, really want me, I'll show you how perfect you are, Goddess."

He kisses my forehead and steps back, longing plain on his face. I want him touching me, feel bereft without his hands on my skin.

"Rhys," I begin because the truth is I really want him now.

"You should get your things ready. I'm sure my parents will want to leave soon." Rhys takes a long breath. "Tell me if I should pack condoms. I want to be prepared, but if you want to avoid temptation, it would be a good way to do it. I'm afraid birth control isn't a thing in Faery."

My head shakes as I realize what he's saying.

Sleeping with Rhys means taking a risk every woman takes. Except times a thousand. He's a damn fertility god. He's offering me a way out, and I believe him. I believe he would never touch me without protection unless I wanted a child with him.

"Pack the condoms, Rhys." I take a deep breath and head for the door. "We will figure this out. I promise."

It's a promise I pray I can keep.

Chapter Eight

Zoey

I pull my cloak around me, grateful we've changed into Fae clothes for once. It's almost the spring equinox, but it's cold here in Wales. Eyri—or as it's known to the rest of the world, Snowdonia—is the site of a national park and the tallest mountain in the UK south of the Scots border. We followed Matilda's instructions, allowing the hounds to guide us.

And making sure to not be too close because everyone was right and bacon is apparently screwing with my hound's belly.

As Dev dodges a small fireball, he frowns my way. It's his "I told you" look.

I'm starting to worry my faery prince is having even more trouble than I am settling into this new life forced upon us. He's treating the kids like they're still young and haven't been forced to grow up. Like they're incapable of making decisions, and it's alienating them. Evan barely talks to him. Rhys is reserved around him. Lee is…well, Lee is Lee. My vampire son seems like the perfect "roll with the punches, nothing bothers him" young man, but I know his emotions run deep.

Rhys walks ahead of us, a grim expression on his face. He turns every now and then to ensure Shy is following. Shy looks lovely dressed in a flowy yellow gown that cinches in her waist and shows off her curves. Her naturally curly hair flows around her face, brushing the tops of her shoulders. The dress is concealed by her heavy cloak, though I can see the sturdy slippers Rhys insisted on. Dev tried to get her to wear heels.

The Fae are all about appearances. Oh, a brownie gets to wear whatever she wants, but I get my ass shoved into a ballgown. Though I am happy for the cloak since it's chilly up in here.

Danny stops and looks back our way. "Take a break, guys. The dogs are splitting up. Sasha, Neil, and I will follow them. We'll be back as soon as we can. Rhys?"

My son nods his dad's way. "I'll take care of them."

Brendan Thomas gives the King of All Vampire a big grin. "I will, too, Your Highness. My wolf hasn't had a good fight in weeks."

Neil turns on his son, pointing a finger his way. "Brendan, we are traveling light. Do not explode those clothes if you don't have to. No showing off."

"He's not showing off," Cassie Thomas says, nudging her brother with her elbow. "He's smarter in wolf form. Dad, you know he's not really a wolf, right? Let's see. He's a complete weirdo with abandonment issues and weird prey instincts who makes the most ridiculous sounds. He's obviously a Husky shifter."

Neil snorts but opens his arms. The two supernatural kids he and Chad adopted move easily in, accepting his affection. He bows his head and kisses the top of Cassie's. "Be nice to your weirdo brother. And be safe. Listen to Z. I'll be back."

He takes off after his hellhound escort.

Rhys sits on a rock roughly fifty feet from his papa, Shy next to him. Brendan and Cassie join them.

So the old folks are on their own.

"I don't think they did it." Dev stares at our son. "I would have felt it. There was no release of magic. I was ready to contain it, but it didn't come."

"No, but I'm pretty sure Shy did." I find a big log and settle in, thanking the universe it's not raining.

Dev's brow rises. "Yes, I rather had that energy coming off her. I suspect Rhys is making a power play. Withholding himself is not the right call here. It's going to get him in trouble."

It's a good time to remind my husband he's not in control of this situation. "You have to let him make his own mistakes, Devinshea."

He shakes his head and paces the length of the log in front of me. "That might be fine if his mistakes were something like staying out too late and getting in trouble at work. His mistakes can call Myrddin to us. We're not ready. I worry we're not ever going to be ready."

"Why would you say that?" I need him positive. Danny and I are the ones who get mired in the what ifs, in the dark questions. Dev is the one with faith. "I think once we find Sarah, and more importantly, Mia, we'll at least have the tools we need."

Dev's jaw tightens. "You truly think one girl can defeat Myrddin? We had an army when we took out Marini and he was just a vampire. And back then, the witches were on our side. They killed…so many of us. Even if we win, have we thought about what we do with the witches who fought on his side?"

I don't like to think about it. In my head, they've all got thrall stones. I know it isn't true and we will have to ask the hard questions. "We should cross that bridge when we come to it. Winning the war is all that matters now."

He stills, his hands on his hips as he stares down at me. "And if we cannot win?"

I don't think about that either, but I can see the thought has my faery prince in a bind. I stand and put my arms around him, offering the affection he needs. "There is no option and you know it. With Marini if we stayed in Faery he might have left us alone. We will not get the same courtesy from Myrddin. He cannot allow us to live. Daniel walking the plane—any plane—subverts his authority and gives the supernatural world a figure to rally around. And you should consider that until a few weeks ago, Rhys had taken that mantle. He was the figurehead of this rebellion, and that's heavy. You are being too hard on him."

He huffs but holds me close. "Yes, I've heard that a lot. I question if we would be in this situation if I had been harder when they were children. Damn it, my goddess, I can see the mistakes they're making, how reckless they're being. How can you not try to stop them? You and Daniel are far too calm, if you ask me."

I have to wonder if he's actively rewriting history or just forgetting. "Says the man who cut his hair and vowed to never return to Faery. You left with nothing more than a pack on your back."

He chuckles. "Well, I did steal a bunch of gold, and my favorite brownie packed some sandwiches, but I get your point. However, I had to leave Faery. My mother forced my hand. I had no great desire to leave the only place I'd ever… Shit. You think Rhys is afraid to go to Faery because he was kidnapped by Fae. He's using Shy as an excuse."

I never said he wasn't smart. My faery prince really left the *sithein* to make his way in the world. Having a human father who was a ridiculously successful businessman helped, certainly, but he was brave to leave what he knew behind. No one wanted Rhys to do that. "I'm worried they both think Rhys might have to sacrifice in order for us to obtain the army we need."

Dev steps back, frowning. "He thinks I would ask him to… What?"

I hold a hand out. "Please don't take this personally, babe. I'm not saying he thinks you are going to ask him. He thinks he's going to have to make the decision and weigh the greater good with his own wants and needs. The Fae won't simply fall in line. They will ask for concessions, and one of them might be Rhys. If you recall, your brother thought it would be best if I remained your mistress and allowed you to find a proper Fae wife."

"And I punched him for even suggesting it. My goddess, I know we've had trouble with my family in the past and I will talk to my mother about how she handled our children, but the truth of the matter is…"

"We need them." I wish we didn't. "I intend to behave until I have what I need, but you have to understand where Rhys is coming from. Shy is everything to him. The way Fenrir is to Evan. And before you tell me they need time to see the world or find themselves, I'm going to ask you when you expect them to do that. They don't get to go off to college. They didn't get to graduate from high school and backpack through Europe. They got blood and sweat and fear. They had to spend their childhood on the run, and in the midst of all of it, they found family."

"We are their family," Dev says stubbornly.

"Of course we are, but not the way Fenrir and Shy are right now. Not the way Sasha and Trent are. You have to respect what they went through. We were not there. It wasn't our fault but we weren't there."

"And that is why I will kill Myrddin."

I need to get him to the place I am, the place where he's honest, but first he has to be honest with himself. "Tell me what you're feeling."

"Rage." He steps away, pacing again. "I don't understand this fucking world. It's like we came home to utter chaos."

"Not true. We came home to a well-run rebellion. Sasha and Trent did a magnificent job."

"They turned our children into soldiers." Dev runs a hand through his hair, a frustrated gesture.

"They had to be soldiers. They tried to hide the kids and when they couldn't, they raised them to be a marvelous unit who love and care about each other."

His eyes darken. "Yes, and that is my mother and brother's fault."

This is well-worn ground. "And you are angry with them."

"I have considered killing them both."

I sigh and move into his space again, placing a hand on his chest. It's good to acknowledge the impulse even if I know he won't follow through with it. "What else do you feel?"

"It's wrong. It's all wrong, Zoey. It's not supposed to be this way." He grinds the words out, his discomfort plain.

I can't care about his discomfort now. "I need you to think about this, my love. Don't tell me now. I want you to sit with the question for a few days. Have you felt this before? This feeling, this all-encompassing, drowning feeling. If you have, what name did you give it?" It took me a while to name this feeling. This emotion that threatened to take my heart. But I had to come to this conclusion myself. Knowing what was truly ruling me, saying the name plainly, made it easier to deal with. I need my husband to come to the revelation on his own. "Now tell me what you sense from Shy. Does Bris have any thoughts? What could we be missing? What power would tempt Arawn into being willing to help us?"

I've been asking the question since we met with the crone. Shy is good at what she does. I know her powers are impressive, but I fail to see how Arawn would need her. He can already talk to the dead. I'm asking the question now because I think my husband could use a few moments to calm down.

His eyes change and Bris reaches for my hand, bringing it up to his lips. "You are handling him so well, Zoey."

Tears pierce my eyes and I move into his arms, feeling safer than I did before. "Only because I'm already on the other side. Sort of."

I feel him sigh and kiss my hair. "I think it will be a long time before we're truly on the other side, but you are being strong for them all, and you will get Rhys through this trip to Faery. I believe you are correct and he is scared. His fear comes out as anger, and it's easier to protect Shy than to protect himself. Though you should understand he will do anything to protect Shy. Devinshea doesn't want to believe that Rhys is old enough and mature enough to take a goddess."

"Because it's proof of our loss," I whisper, holding him.

"He needs more time," Bris replies, his Irish accent soothing. "I hope being in Faery, seeing the damage his mother did, will make him rethink his stance. He loves them. He loves them so much."

"I know."

"And he loves Shy because we can feel Rhys's love for her," Bris explains quietly. "It's written in his magic. Devinshea is being stubborn. He feels it and it hurts that he didn't get to see them meet, to send them off on dates and worry about them breaking the rules. He didn't get to have talks about sex and how sacred it is. He didn't get to tease them and have Shahidi come to dinners. He didn't get to watch you get close to her. He will come to the proper conclusion. He will call this ache by its name and then he can begin to heal."

Grief. That is this feeling's true name. My husband mourns those twelve years, but it's coming out as denial and anger. This feeling, this pit that opened inside him, is loss. I realize what we're doing and step back. "We shouldn't talk about this. He has to figure it out himself."

Bris's eyes glow in the dim light. "He is resting. It's something we've started to do over the years. When we agree, we can suppress the other so private conversations can be had. He knows this is something I worry about. It is a sign of our respect that he allows this."

"It is a sign of his love," I correct. "We love you. You are a part of us."

A beatific smile lights his face. It's so odd how different his smile is from Devinshea's. How I've come to know all the differences and similarities between them. "And you and Dev and Daniel and our children are everything to me. Which is why I need you to understand there is no other woman for Rhys, but I worry unless she finds her true power, she will not be able to choose him."

"Do you sense this power?"

"In a way. Our powers are different, so I can't explain it fully. In some ways our powers seem oppositional. But there is a connection I cannot name," Bris explains. "I think Arawn might be able to shed some light on what is simmering beneath her surface. She was young when she lost her parents, who could have guided her into her power. Harry did what he could, and I know Lily and the witches of Frelsi tried to help, but by then she was locked into what she believes are her limits. Perhaps a bit afraid of what other power she owns."

"I think so, too." I've studied her a bit and had some dealings with other mediums. "I don't think I've ever met someone with Shy's ability to talk to the dead. The mediums my father and I have dealt with need rituals and the trappings of a séance to get a bit of information from a spirit. Shy sees them everywhere and has long conversations with them. Could Nim be right? Do you think Arawn is looking for his old shit?"

Bris snorts. "You mean the Golden Torc or the Cauldron of Rebirth? Then yes, I think Shy might be helpful in finding them. The dead might be able to feel the objects even though they're hidden to living eyes."

"Is it dangerous if Arawn gets the stuff back?" I don't want to exchange one tyrant for another.

"He can't use them in his current form, but he could be worried about them being out in the world. He could simply miss them," Bris says in a way that makes me think he knows what Arawn is feeling.

"Did you have...things that were important to you?" I never asked about what it was like for Bris to give up his corporeal body. Never asked what his life was like before.

"I had a magic scythe. I could swing it once and the whole field was harvested. I miss her. She was a gift from Brighid," he says with a hint of a smile. "But Arawn's tools were made of parts of him. So he might be feeling nostalgic. He might be worried they will be found and misused. Or he might think the cauldron could swing the tide of war if he can find it and put the pieces back together. We will not know until we meet with him."

"They're coming back," Rhys calls out over the space between us.

I take a deep breath and move into the group of our young people. "Guys, I know you've heard stories about Faery, but whatever you've heard, I need you to be prepared for something much more dangerous. It is beautiful and deadly. Don't trust anyone in there who is not one of our party. Keep your eyes and ears open and mouth shut if you can."

Cassie's eyes go wide. "You make it sound super scary, Aunt Z. Dad said it was fun."

I point Brendan's way because we need to make some things clear. "No eating weird faery creatures. Your dad thought it was fun because he ate a bunch of stuff he shouldn't have."

Brendan's hands go up like *what me?* "I would never eat a faery creature." He frowns as though lying hurts him. "I mean, unless it deserved it or looks really tasty."

"Be careful," Rhys warns. "Some of the sweetest-looking things in Faery can bite back. We're only going to the Seelie *sithein*. Your senses can fool you in there. The Unseelie are a bit more open about their cruelty."

My heart hurts for my son because there's beauty in Faery, too. It should have been his second home.

"I'll have to change your mind." Dev is back and his hand slides into mine, squeezing it as though letting me know he's going to try. "Do you remember our temple?"

Rhys frowns. "Vaguely. I think the last time I was there I was eight. I remember there was a stream that ran through it. We would play in it, Lee and Evan and I."

Dev gives our son a smile. "It is the most peaceful place I've ever been. I can't wait for you to show Shahidi. And Brendan and Cassie, I promise you will be safe in the palace. Your aunt is being cautious, and she has her reasons for it, but I want you to enjoy yourselves."

The hounds reach us first, all three running to Shy as though greeting her before one joins me.

"We found it," Danny says and reaches into his backpack, pulling out the stones Matilda gave us. He passes them around.

"Nimue told us we must each have one of these on our persons, preferably in hand, to go through this door," Rhys explains. "It's blue dolerite, found only here in the mountains. It will allow us to pass through a piece of Annwn, though Nimue says we won't notice it. It's more like a wormhole."

"It's a passageway he uses," Dev explains. "Many ancients connected to other planes have ways to travel that don't involve using the front door. So let's get this going. I would like to be at the palace before nightfall."

Danny places the stone in my hand and takes the other. "Let's get this over with because I want to get to New Zealand. Sasha, whatever you do, don't take off that ring. The sun in the *sithien* has less ultraviolet rays than the Earth plane sun, but it will still damage you."

"I will be careful," Sasha says, taking up a position at the back of the group. "And no one forget that there is cold iron in your packs should you need it."

I carefully sheathe my cold iron knife before we start the walk to the mountain. I hope I don't have to use it.

Chapter Nine

Shy

Rhys's hand is firmly in mine as we reach the entrance to the cave where we will find the doorway to Faery. At least the hounds seem to think so. The biggest is at my side, as though trying to ensure I don't fall off the mountain. I know he has a name. Something Welsh. But I call him Fluffy. He seems to like it.

"My parents will go first." Rhys helps me up the last of the steps, and I'm so grateful he overrode his father's suggestion of designer heels. The slippers I'm wearing are sturdy and don't slip on the wet rock stairs. "And then the two of us. Sasha will watch our six. Stay close to me. No matter what my papa says, it's dangerous until we're in our temple. We'll stay in the rooms there. I won't let them separate us."

It's so odd to think in a matter of hours I'll be presented to Miria, Queen of the Seelie Fae. My boyfriend's granny, though I doubt he calls her that. I've only ever heard Rhys refer to her as Queen Miria. I wish we went over royal protocols but no, I had to make us lunch. I'm wondering if I'm supposed to curtsey, and then panicking a little because I don't know how to curtsey, when a shiver goes through me and I realize the Drowning Woman is here again. I gasp and shift toward Rhys when I realize how close she is.

His arm goes around me. "Are you okay? What do you see?"

"She's here," I whisper and try not to look at her. I can feel her, though. Cold and dead and longing. Longing for what? To take me with her? Fluffy barks and circles the spirit. It surprises me, though I don't know why since it makes sense. "The hellhounds can see her."

"Emyr seems to sense something," the queen says as the hound joins Fluffy.

We find ourselves in a cave, though it's obviously magical. There are faery lights all around, and it's far warmer and drier than it was outside. It reminds me of the entry into Frelsi.

All three hounds circle the Drowning Woman, but they don't seem to see her as a threat. They bounce around as though asking if she wants to play.

So much for their instincts.

"It's a spirit," I tell the queen. "One that has followed me around since I was a child. She's the first spirit I ever saw, and quite frankly, one of the most frightening. Not that the hounds seem to be afraid."

They are literally running in and out of her, playing in the water surrounding her like puppies.

"I hoped she wouldn't be able to follow," Rhys says with a sigh.

"She might not be able to," I reply. There's something desperate about her. I feel energy coming off some spirits. It's stronger the older I get. Or perhaps I'm simply more at ease with it so I feel it more. The Drowning Woman is desperate. "She hasn't come this close in a long time. She might be trying to imprint on me because she knows she'll lose me once I cross the plane."

She shimmers. I can't tell if it's the faery lights or something she's doing herself. But for a moment she glows and I feel...sadness.

"Is there anything we can do to banish her?" The king stares like he's trying to see what I can see.

I face her for the first time. "Do you see a light?" Now that I'm looking at her, the rushing sound of water is so much louder, and I feel her chill. "If you can see the light, you can leave this plane and begin again. It doesn't matter what you've done. The light is another chance. Can you see it?"

A shiver goes through me as a hand breaks through the water, a long finger pointing at me.

She doesn't want to go into the light. She wants me.

"I'd like to pass through now," I say quietly.

Rhys leans close and whispers in my ear. "We can talk to Arawn about banishing her. If anyone will know how to get rid of an evil spirit, it will be the King of the Dead. I promise, I will find a way."

I believe him. I really do. I love this man so much, but as I turn from the spirit that has haunted me since I was a child, I'm back to being worried about the fact that his grandmother is a Faery queen and he has a temple where he's supposed to conduct fertility rites.

"Are we good to go?" Rhys's papa asks. "Is there anything we can do to protect you, Shy?"

I shake my head. "I'm ready. She wouldn't be the first to try to take my body. Harry taught me well. I can expel a spirit with a single breath. I'll be fine."

Devinshea nods and moves toward the back of the cave. We're all lined up. The royals first. Rhys and I after them with our wolves, and Sasha in the back. The hounds seem to know things have gotten serious because they stop playing and take up their spots. Fluffy and Caddoc on either side of me and Rhys and Emyr behind the queen.

Devinshea places the largest stone on the door and says something I can't hear. Likely an incantation or request for entry. The door opens and I can see another world. It's near dark here, but the sun is vibrant in Faery. Time moves differently, I was taught. It passes more quickly here on the Earth plane.

Rhys's hand is in mine as we approach the door his parents walked through. I look back and the Drowning Woman is still there, her monstrous hand reaching out.

I swear I feel sadness. Loss. An ache I haven't felt before. Like I lost something.

I have the oddest feeling I should stay. But then Rhys squeezes my hand, and I know it's just my fear and anxiety. Since the encounter with Matilda, I find myself walking the knife's edge between excitement and worry. I want to know if there's something more inside me, something else I can help our cause with. But I worry the Welsh King of the Dead will take one look at me and realize a mistake was made.

I force myself to turn to that soft light coming out of the door. When I walk through, I feel a jolt on my palm as though the stone in my hand zapped me lightly. I ignore it since it doesn't really hurt. It's one of those magical things. Rhys leads me out and we find ourselves walking into a field, and I know immediately the door worked and we are in the Faery realm.

I know because the air is sweet and the sun warm on my skin. Softer than before. I know because the grass is perfect and green, and I can see a palace in the distance. I know because Rhys takes a long breath, and a shudder goes through his big body like something inside him relaxes simply by being here.

I look behind me as Cassie moves forward with her dad, and I see Sasha walking out of the door. In the back I see the Drowning Woman is gone. The door closes and she is not here. She cannot follow me. I breathe a sigh of relief. She is attached to me. She proved that when she managed to follow me to Iceland. But she's more attached to the Earth plane.

"Is she here?" Rhys asks.

I look around to make sure. "No."

"Good." He kisses the top of my head and looks out over the green fields toward the gleaming palace in the distance. His shoulders straighten. "Well, I suppose we should get going. Did anyone send word we were coming?"

His papa turns our way. "I spoke with your grandmother via the mirror network. I expect there will be an escort waiting closer to the palace. I didn't tell her we were coming in through Arawn's door. I can't be sure if she even knows this door exists, so I explained we would meet them outside the palace walls. We should get going."

"She readily agreed we could bring Dad and the wolves and Sasha?" Rhys asks the question in a challenging tone.

"Yes. She agreed to it," Devinshea replies with what seems like patience. "She understands the rules. When Mom, Dad, and I went missing, the Fae took it as a bad portent. They are deeply superstitious. In their minds they had only recently gotten their fertility back and then it was gone again. They blame my interactions with non-Fae creatures. Once we start setting the fields right and perform a few rituals, they will calm down."

"Fecking bastard."

The words are spat from somewhere over my head as Devinshea continues to explain why it's going to be all right this time, why it's not like when she turned away Lee and Fenrir.

"I hope they kill him."

I glance up, and there's a small creature sitting on the lowest branch of a tree to the left of the door. Not that you can see the door anymore. It disappeared after Sasha walked through it. I move in closer. "Are you all right?"

I think it's a troll. Oh. A dead troll. I can see a gaping wound on his neck and one eye dangles.

The troll nearly falls from his perch.

"So, I think it's safe to assume she can see dead Fae creatures," the queen says.

Rhys nods his mom's way. "She sees them back in Frelsi. I'm not surprised she can see them here."

The hounds circle the tree and the troll shrinks back. "Leave me alone, fecking bastards. Don't let him look at me. Don't let him send his evil eye."

"They can't hurt you," I explain, moving beneath the big oak tree. I tilt my head up. "They're curious."

His head turns down, one big black eye taking me in. "I assure you they can hurt anything they want to. And so can the king."

"I don't think the king is here to hurt anyone." I'm not sure how this troll knows Daniel Donovan, though I'm sure he came to Faery many times with his family. The king has a profoundly calm energy. Not that I haven't seen him mad, but his base energy is good. The queen has this frenetic but lovely energy around her. A little like chaos, but the kind that works for good. Devinshea is the one with hard, purposeful energy.

The troll stares at me for a moment. "Why are you with him? This is not your world. Are you his captive? Is he taking seers now?"

"I'm no one's captive. He's my boyfriend's father." I've found simple replies are best with new "friends."

I swear that dead troll paled. "Then I curse you, too, and all is lost."

And then he's gone.

He is a very dramatic troll.

I turn to the king. "Did you screw over some trolls the last time you were here, Your Highness?"

King Daniel looks confused. "Why would you ask that?"

"Because that was a dead troll who really doesn't like you. And he curses me because I'm with you. How much magic do dead trolls have?" I ask. In all my time in Frelsi I only met witches with my best interests at heart. Rhys keeps me shielded when we're in the field. When I'm allowed in the field. I don't like the thought of being cursed by a troll. Dead humans don't have a lot of magic, but I don't know about the Fae who live in a *sithien*.

Devinshea grins as he puts a hand on Daniel's shoulder. "None at all, Shy, and I think the last time we were in Faery, Dan here did get into a row with some trolls. Apparently they remember."

"They were cheating at cards," the king says with a sigh. "I did call them out on it. I respect a con, but I'm not going to get taken by one."

I stare up where the troll sat, the hounds rejoining us since their curiosity will obviously not be assuaged.

And then I feel it. I feel an invisible tug to my gut. Like I've been hooked but no one is reeling me in yet. That tug forces me to turn and look to the north. Past the rolling fields and forest. Away from the shining White Palace.

A chill creeps up my spine. Not because I'm afraid of those mountains in the distance. Because I want to be there. Because something waits for me there. Something wants me there, cries for me to come forth.

"Shy?" Rhys is at my side.

"What's in those mountains?" I ask, trying to temper my growing anxiousness.

"Well, not a frost giant. That's for sure." Neil gestures the king's way. "Daniel killed that motherfucker years back. It was sad. We killed a frost giant and all I got was a T-shirt."

The queen's eyes widen. "You could have gotten hexed by leprechauns if you had taken even a T-shirt. We made a deal with them. We got the Blood Stone and nothing else. Except apparently the trolls hate us now. That was so long ago I'm surprised anyone remembers."

"The Fae never forget." Devinshea is more sober now as he takes in the mountains I pointed out. "Those are the Shehy mountains. It's the northernmost part of the *sithein*. They're dangerous, as my goddess and Daniel discovered. I think I know what you're feeling. There is a cave system, and it's where the sluagh of our plane reside.

We have quite a few unshriven dead."

I shake my head. "That's myth, Your Grace. Shriven, unshriven, it does not matter. The universe does not constrain a soul based on rituals. The soul itself decides whether to move on. No ritual can hold it back nor can a ritual force it into the light. The sluagh are simply Fae who choose to stay for whatever reason. I've found it's almost always fear, though some stay in a bid to protect those they love. Yes, I believe that's what I'm feeling."

So many souls without light. Souls who choose to cloak themselves in shadow and feast on death itself.

"Well, we stay far from the north, then." Rhys slides his hand against mine. "I want to bathe you in light and life, my goddess. Not expose you to all the death Faery offers."

I follow him as we begin our walk to the palace. The trouble is I find that death very attractive.

And that scares me most of all.

The sun is beginning its long march to evening as we make it to the forest. I was told from here it's only an hour or so into the village that surrounds the palace.

The queen has a lot of memories of Faery.

"This is where I was almost eaten by an ogre," she says, pointing out a small pond.

Most of them involving some kind of bloody battle.

Neil sighs as he looks it over. "Good times."

"I still owe Herne the Hunter for that one," Devinshea admits with a sigh. "Although he did me a solid when he called down the Wild Hunt and slaughtered my enemies."

"All Dad talks about when he tells that story is how he almost lost his favorite pajamas," Cassie points out.

"Pops bought him those." Brendan defends his parents.

They start to reminisce, and Devinshea declares this is a perfect spot to eat the sandwiches I made earlier. I like to joke about the fact that I only cook for productive people, so I carefully put together the brown bread, butter, and ham sandwiches while the rest of our group packed.

I'm not hungry.

My mind keeps going back to those mountains.

Rhys begins a fire with nothing more than the clapping of his hands and pulling from the earth. The royals all sit around it, the wolves and Sasha joining them. The hounds prove their canine instincts as they are far more interested in the food that's being brought out than in anything else around us.

But I feel myself pulled to the pond.

"Hey, Shy. Don't get too close," the queen calls out. "There are lots of things that want to eat you out here."

"The hounds don't seem to think so," Cassie points out. "And I don't smell anything but some small prey."

Brendan grins and suddenly looks very wolfish. "I haven't hunted in a while."

Neil growls his boy's way. "No changing until we need to." He takes a deep breath. "I don't sense any threats. If anything this place smells...different."

"You can't possibly remember how a place smelled decades ago," the queen argues.

Neil frowns her way, taking two sandwiches. "I assure you I remember everything about the day I had to fight with a damn ogre."

"But it was tasty, right?" Brendan asks.

I hear whispers coming from bushes to my left, but they hush as I move closer. I glance back and no one seems to notice except Rhys, whose eyes are on me even as he downs half a sandwich. I have to assume a Fae elemental would sense if there was some terrible danger.

"Why do you aid him?"

The question startles me, more because of the haunting voice that asks it. I turn and Rhys stands, obviously ready to intervene, but I hold a hand out.

A beautiful woman stands in the pond, her torso exposed, her long dark hair tangled with vines and weeds and sticks.

We're far enough away from the party that we're not interrupting them, though I'm sure they can all hear us. Well, the queen might not be able to but the wolves and vampires certainly can.

"I see your light and yet you walk with him." Her skin is pale, lips a deep blue.

"Are you talking about the king?" I ask, walking to the edge of the pond. One of the hounds has left his search for treats and joins me at the water's edge. I'm certain it's only Fluffy's calm demeanor that has Rhys restraining himself.

Her head cocks slightly. "Yes, though I'm surprised I don't see his guards around him. I thought he was never without his dark guard."

"He travels with wolves," I reply. I'm not sure what the Fae call their guard, but the high priest wouldn't have one assigned by the palace unless there was some sort of threat. The way I was told, Green Men are welcome on all the Fae planes. No one would dare harm a fertility deity.

She snorts. "He does? I thought only *sidhe* were good enough for our king."

"He certainly has a fondness for the *sidhe*," I reply.

"I don't think she understands, Shea," a quiet voice says, and then I'm turning to my right where a young woman sits on a rock. I didn't notice her before, so she's either good at hiding or she's just come into this discussion. Like her friend, she has long hair, but there's a warm tone to it, like the bark of a tree. Her skin is so translucent I can see traces of the veins where her blood once flowed. They have a greenish cast.

I frown her way. "You see each other? You can converse?"

It's not that way on the Earth plane. Each spirit is solitary. They exist in some kind of bubble where they are utterly alone, able to see the living world but not interact with it. There is no dead world to live in on the Earthly plane. Death without the light is to be sentenced to a singular prison. Until you find someone like me.

The nymph goes underwater and quickly reappears close to what I might call a sprite. All I know is she is definitely a woodland Fae.

I hear Rhys telling someone to let me be, that I will find more information out if they pretend not to notice us.

So they are listening, though they can only hear one side of the conversation.

"We're Fae, not human," the sprite tells me. "We are more in touch with our energy than any human."

"Why have you not moved on?" I ask. "Do the Fae not see the light?"

The nymph's lips curl up in the slightest smile, the expression a bit cruel on her pale blue lips. "I have seen only darkness here since the king decided to rule with an iron fist. I thought he left for an outer plane. I saw him with his guards."

Time flows differently for the dead. Harry talked about it quite a bit. He died the day the king and queen went missing, but he didn't find me until years later. He remembered nothing of the time in between. His soul got stuck, or rather as Harry died he made the choice to not leave. When his soul picked up enough energy, he could manifest himself again. For others, they immediately start their lives as ghosts. So it's not surprising that she's talking about the king leaving like it was yesterday. For her, it might be. "He means you no harm. I know the king can seem intimidating."

"That one looks to be his son," Shea says, her gaze on the party sitting around the fire. "Did you know the bastard has a bastard, Clem?"

"He does. At least that's the rumor. He had a child with a woman from one of the villages on the edge of the forest," Clem replies as she shifts on her rock. "I suppose that's him. I don't know what's going on, but this is wrong. Can you not feel it?"

"If you're talking about Rhys, he is most certainly the king's son." While not exactly by biology. I've been told I shouldn't have to explain the dynamics of a threesome here in Faery.

Clem gasps slightly, and I can now see the marks on her neck where someone held her, likely until she could breathe no more. "Do you feel it? Sacred One, are you carrying a blue stone?"

I pull out one of the stones Matilda gave us. "Yes, we came through a doorway we wouldn't usually use."

Now Shea's smile is full, and I can see her fangs. She laughs. "Is the king hiding from his own people? Wouldn't that be well deserved."

"I don't think the king is who you think he is," I reply.

Clem is staring behind me. "He certainly looks like our king."

I am confused. "Your king? You have a queen."

"What kind of nonsense is this?" Any amusement in Shea is gone. "Is he trying to hide? He can't hide from the dead. He can't hide from what he did to me."

She turns and her back is a mass of open wounds. Like someone burned her and then beat the pained flesh. So it hurt more. Blood pours from her mouth, and there's a sword in her belly.

"I do not know what happened to you, but I know King Daniel did nothing of the kind." I know the King of All Vampire has done brutal things in his past, but he would never torture a Fae creature like this.

"I don't know who Daniel is, but I assure you I spent time in Seelie dungeons," she hisses. "Anyone who was protected by his brother was tortured."

"The king doesn't have a brother," I point out.

"Of course he does," Shea spits back. "He had a twin. He murdered him and took his throne."

The hound at my feet goes perfectly still, and I hear growling from behind me.

"I don't think that's our king, Shea," Clem says right before a blast comes through the forest and I feel fire all around.

Chapter Ten

Zoey

I'm sitting in between Sasha and Daniel watching Shy talk to a large rock when I hear Neil growl and then feel the blast of heat that threatens to singe my arm.

Then I'm on the forest floor with a werewolf on top of me.

"Brendan, protect your sister," Neil orders. "Z, stay still."

What the hell is happening? There's the sound of a sizzle and a crack and Neil pushes me further down.

"Daniel?" Dev says. "Can you see it?"

"Shy, put your hands at your side," Rhys yells and I can see his hands rise, fingers splayed in a gesture I've seen his father perform many times.

I hear a squeak and manage to turn my head enough to see Rhys has thrown up a wall of thick vines and roots around Shy.

"It's coming from the east. Some kind of sorcerer or witch," Daniel is saying. "Keep your heads down."

I hear a roaring in the distance, but Neil hasn't let up.

"It's a chimera," Shy shouts from her cage of green and brown. "At least that's what Clem says. Your Highness, it's trying to kill the priest. But apparently it doesn't know he's a priest. He thinks the priest is the king."

What? I'm very confused. But then another fireball hits and I hear a chuffing sound.

"What the fuck?"

I have never heard Sasha sound so human. This is a man who kept my children alive on a plane where dinosaurs still rule, but he's disturbed by whatever is coming out of the woods.

"Let me see," I hiss at Neil.

He frowns down at me. "I'm not letting you see. You don't want to see."

He is so bossy when he's working.

The hounds are freaking out now. Whatever is coming at us must have been cloaked in some crazy magic to fool their senses, but it's on their radar now.

"Is that...is its tail a freaking snake?" Brendan asks. "Sasha, watch out. It's definitely a snake. Dad, to your left."

Neil flips me over, rolling us close to Shy. That's when baby boy takes over and I'm suddenly in a cage with his girlfriend.

I can hear what's going on, but I can't see much.

Neil gets to his feet and looks at me through the vines. "Stay there. You are pregnant, and you are not losing another baby to this place. Am I understood?"

Neil was the one who carried my bleeding body to the palace when I lost our first child.

"Fine." I nod and then wince because a fireball narrowly misses him.

"Rhys, shield my daughter so my son can try to take this thing's throat out." Then Neil's favorite jeans are toast, and I foresee some shopping in that wolf's future. Neil's wolf is arctic white, his eyes a crystal blue. He barks my way, and I still speak wolf. He's telling me to stay put.

"Can you see anything?" Shy asks.

I can barely move. I'm going to have such a talk with my eldest child. Cages should have room. I try to move some of the vines, gaining a slit to see out of. "Danny is in the air. Damn. That was close. He dodged a fireball. I've never seen a chimera. Have you?"

"No, but Clem has," Shy replies. "Cassie's going to be pissed. I can see her little cage thing and she's trying to hack her way through it. They never try this shit with Evan. Not after she shot Rhys with an arrow. Your husband is a bad influence on my boyfriend."

I can't exactly argue with her. Dev and Danny have been known to be overly protective in the best of times. And now I'm pregnant with my tiny abomination, so they'll go overboard. And good for Evan. I can say that because my fully Fae son is pretty indestructible.

I feel heat blast in my direction, but the vines don't catch fire. As long as we're here I have questions. "Who is Clem and does she know how to take out a chimera?"

A loud roar breaks through the forest and the ground kind of shakes.

"Did you know it could fly?" I hear Dev yell.

"I was too busy trying to figure out which head to lop off," Sasha replies in a low growl. "Do I take the lion or the goat head?"

That's easy. I would totally pick lion over goat. Goat doesn't scare me much, though apparently my son did piss off the Icelandic goats. So there's that.

"I think she's a sprite." Shy manages to push back some of the vines separating us. I can see her face now. She glances downward. "Sorry. I didn't know. She says she is a woodland Fae and sprites are whores. But she also says some weird stuff, Your Highness." She sighs. "I was not referring to her as the Queen of the Fae. She's the Queen of All Vampire. Yes. I said vampire, though she's also the high priest's wife."

"Zoey, please." I'm going to have to remind her because the idea of my son's goddess calling me by a royal title doesn't sit well. "And I would think almost every creature in the Seelie *sithein* would know who I am. We've done tours of all the districts over the years. She might not know me by sight, but she should know my name. I'm her high priest's goddess."

I can barely make out Shy's head shaking. Rhys seems to have thrown up another wall, and I can't see anything at all outside now. I never get to have any fun.

"That's the thing, Zoey," Shy says. "I'm not sure this is the Seelie *sithein*."

There's a loud crash and Daniel yells for Dev to get out of the way. Then Dev yells for Rhys to duck and something else seems to explode. Cassie calls one of the men an asshole, and I hear a whole lot of growling and barking. "I promise you it is. I've been here many times. This is the place where Herne the Hunter bound me to a tree that might have exploded because he wanted to use me as bait to kill an ogre, but then he got horny and followed a *baobhan sith* home for some loving. Now she was a skanky bitch."

Sasha rushes by our green cell cursing in Russian.

"Clem says there are no *baobhan sith* in this *sithein* and haven't been for centuries. She's surprised the chimera is here. What?" Shy's face disappears for a moment and then she's back, her hands wrapping around the vines. "She said she thinks the rebels must have brought him over from the Unseelie *sithein*."

Rebels? "Someone is rebelling against Miria?"

"Cassie!" Neil must have taken human form again because he's screaming his daughter's name. "Don't you dare try to ride that... Damn it..."

I turn, trying to get a look at Neil's fierce daughter. And make the mistake of actually catching a glimpse of that thing. Creature. I try not to be too judgey. There are a lot of creatures who seem really scary who turn out to be super cool. This...I would bet this is not one of them. The massive beast has two heads—a roaring lion with a matted mane and a goat with nasty horns it's currently using to try to headbutt my vampire husband.

Of course there's also the tail, which could be considered a third head, maybe, since it's a big old snake. Cassie has a machete in her hand. I would bet anything that sucker's made of cold iron. Rhys and Dev seem to have shackled the chimera with various roots, but the lion/goat/snake is giving it a good go.

"Is Cassie okay?" Shy asks.

"Cassie is...oh shit. Cassie lopped off the tail, and the biting snake parts that went with it." I've got a good view now, and I will faithfully recount everything I see to my future daughter-in-law. "Oh, and now it's super pissed. It's strong. Its claws are able to cut through whatever Dev and Rhys are sending his way."

"How do you know it's not a her?" Shy asks.

I frown her way.

Her eyes widen. "Oh."

Yeah, there's big old dangly bits that tell me this is a masculine chimera, although I personally don't know how he identifies. Chimeras could be very fluid. Probably are since they have to deal with all those various animal spirits.

I wince as Cassie manages to leap onto the chimera's back just as he launches himself into the air. A big brown wolf jumps, trying to catch the chimera, but it's too fast.

And Cassie is reckless as hell. She somehow manages to grab one of the goat horns and wrap her legs around the body before she shoves that machete into the beast's side.

"Cassie's going to get in so much trouble," I say, admiring my bestie's daughter. From what Neil has told me, I know she was left behind because she couldn't change. Or she couldn't completely change. I note her fingers have claws.

"Daniel!" Neil yells as the blood starts to flow.

"I'll get her." Daniel takes off, and then they're out of sight.

"I'm pretty sure Cassie killed the chimera, and Danny's got to catch her because she did it midair." I have faith in my vampire hubby. He's caught me many times.

The chimera's body hits the pond and water splashes everywhere.

But no Cassie. She's in Danny's arms as he floats down.

Girl didn't even drop her machete.

"Clem is upset. She hoped the chimera would take out the king."

"Why would she want Danny dead?" I ask, and the vines start to recede, and I can see again. I frown at my son. "You could ask, Rhys."

He rushes over to Shy, not looking my way. "Why would I bother, Mother? I was going to do it one way or another. And don't assume it was to protect you. It was to keep you from doing what Cassie did. You are extremely chaotic in battle. Shy, are you all right?"

Shy allows him to take her hand but holds her position. "Something is wrong."

My son pales.

"Cassandra Elaine Thomas," Neil begins, and I have to admit he's developed an excellent dad voice.

"Damn. I wanted to see what it tasted like," Brendan says, and then he catches the look in his sister's eyes and holds his hands up. Naturally both he and Neil are totally without clothes, but hey, that's the way the supernatural world goes sometimes. We're not precious about our bodies. "Cassie, you heard what Dad said. He told Rhys to protect you. What was I supposed to do? Tackle him?"

Sasha, Danny, and Dev stand by the pond, looking out over the water.

"Should one of us go in and make sure it's dead?" Danny asks.

"It's dead," Cassie assures them. "I killed it, and I would have carved out its heart except everyone freaks out when I do that."

"I can bring the creature up from the pond if need be," Devinshea offers. "Though I'm not sure how it will help."

"Well, I'd like to know why it attacked," Danny replies.

"I assume it was hungry and we look like excellent snacks." Sasha's accent seems deeper when his adrenaline is up. He rubs a hand over his chest like something pains him there. Which it can't because he's a vamp.

"We don't have chimeras in the *sitheins*." Dev glances back my way. "Are you and Shy all right, my goddess?"

I look at Rhys, who seems to be studying Shy to ensure not a hair on her head has been shifted out of place by the fight we've just gone through. Well, the men and Cassie did. I make note. I'm going to start carrying a machete. I'm glad Danny and Dev are through their "treat me like I'm made of glass" phase. "I'm fine, though I didn't appreciate the unwanted cage. I can take cover on my own."

"So can I," Shy says quietly.

"Rhys, you have to know your mother is very capable," Daniel begins.

"Of causing chaos," Rhys replies, ignoring what Shy said.

"Hey." I should not have to take that from someone I breastfed for a year.

"Mother, the last time we were in a bad situation, you nearly brought a troll down on our heads. And you angered the entire village of Hidden Folk," Rhys accuses even as he gets close to Shy.

"And then you ascended and we got them as allies." My chaos can be helpful at times. It's not all bad.

"You could have been killed." Neil grabs his backpack and pulls out his emergency sweats.

"But I wasn't," Cassie replies, pointing her machete his way. "Dolores and I took care of it."

Neil's head shakes. "I should never have taken you to that musical about Kelsey. It put all kinds of thoughts in your head, and do you know how much it pains me to say anything bad about musical theater?"

"If he wasn't from here, then where was he from?" Daniel asks Dev. "Could the Unseelies have sent him? It wouldn't be the first time."

Dev's head shakes. "No. That's what I'm saying. That wasn't a Fae creature. That was an old-school Earth plane monster that died out…thousands of years ago. Not to say a few couldn't have hung around, but how did it find its way here?"

"You're not even going to admit I did a good job?" Cassie asks in a bratty teenage tone, but I don't think she can help that. I'm pretty sure we all sound that way at her age.

"I think you were stellar, babe," I shout across the distance and give her a thumbs-up.

Cassie nods and seems to get a bit teary. "Well, thank you, Aunt Z."

Neil's got his pants on, pulling a T over his head. "I do not need your parental input. You got to skip the teenage years. You have no idea what it's like to deal with an overly hormonal werewolf."

I know he doesn't mean it that way, but the words make me ache. I didn't get the chance.

Cassie gasps. "Are you telling everyone I'm on my period?"

She starts arguing with her dad, but I notice the hounds have turned their attention to the south.

"Let's get you someplace safe where you can rest," Rhys is saying to Shy.

"Why would I need to rest?" Shy asks, some fire in her tone. "It's not like I did anything but get stuck in an organic prison cell with your mom and a Fae ghost who really hates your dad." She looks down, frowning at a rock. "No, he's not the king's twin. And his dad is not the king."

"My father certainly is the king," Rhys insists. "Shy, you know we have to hold the line against Myrddin. My father never gave up his crown. Myrddin is the pretender."

"I think she's talking to a ghost," I point out.

"Of course she is, but we still need to hold the line," Rhys insists.

Shy is caught in a deep conversation with the… Well, I want to say rock, but I know there's some woodland Fae named Clem there.

"Declan Quinn is very much alive, and I don't know why that would matter since Miria is the queen of the..." She stops and looks to the water and sighs. "Cassie, there's this dead water nymph and she wants to thank you for murdering the chimera. She says now she has someone to play with."

Cassie nods. "See. Even the dead water nymphs are on my side, Dad. You are being extremely patriarchal right now."

I swear Neil's head is going to explode.

Shy leads an odd existence. She's back to arguing about Dev's relatives, and that's when I notice the hounds have moved. They were sniffing around, likely looking for more threats, but they seem to have found one.

"Hey, guys. Does anyone smell something?" I point to the hounds who are growling now and have taken up a circular front around our party.

Danny and Sasha move in behind them.

Neil stops arguing with his daughter and moves in beside me. He points to a place beyond the trees. "There's a party coming. I think all Fae from the smell."

Brendan and Cassie are beside him, Brendan now in sweats and a Yankees T-shirt. We're going to have to have a talk about that. We're obviously a Rangers family.

Damn. They didn't grow up in Dallas. Of course they aren't fans.

I shove the grief aside as Dev joins us.

"Can you tell what kind of Fae are coming our way?" Dev asks.

"Oh, I can smell the arrogance from miles away. It's all *sidhe*," Neil replies.

Daniel releases a long breath. "It's the queen's guard. I can see the flag."

Dev nods and smiles. "Yes, that's Mother's standard." He frowns. "But the color's wrong."

"Zoey, I think something is very, very wrong here." Shy puts a hand on my arm, her eyes beseeching me. "I don't think this is the right Fae world, and if what Clem is telling me is true, we could be in real trouble."

The party of Fae crests the hill, and I can see them clearly now. Unfortunately for me I'm not six five like my faery prince. There are six guards, but I don't recognize them. Has Miria turned her guard over or hired a new squad?

"There he is. The king is here," the *sidhe* at the head of the group says. "They were right."

The horses pick up speed.

"King?" Dev is wearing his "what the fuck's going on" expression. "They're looking for Daniel? Why would they want Daniel?"

"No," Shy says, her tone going breathless. "That's what I'm trying to tell you. I think we took the wrong door. I think we landed in a Faery where you're…"

Before she can get the last words out, the horses have reached us, though they stay back because the hounds are growling.

Still, they all dismount and fall to one knee.

"Your Majesty," the leader says, his head down. "Welcome back to your kingdom, King Devinshea. Long live the king."

Chapter Eleven

Shy

The air suddenly feels tense, and I realize I have mere seconds to convince the queen that we've found ourselves in the wrong damn timeline, and a deeply dangerous one at that.

"He's really not the king." Clem stands beside me. Shea completely disappeared, apparently happy to have a chimera corpse to play with, but Clem left her rock and followed me. She's a calm spirit, if still a bit pissed at how she died. I got a bit of that story when we were locked in Rhys's protective…there's really no other word for it…cage.

"I told you," I say under my breath and get close to the queen. "Your Highness, we're in danger. These men believe the high priest is their king. Their king who slaughtered his mother and brother to take the throne and has apparently been brutal with his subjects. I don't understand everything yet, but I know they will not take it well if they figure out he's not who they think he is."

The queen's jaw tightens, and then she obviously makes her decision. "Ask her if I'm his wife on this plane."

"Eoin, you jokester. It's good to know things haven't change." Rhys's father is smiling like he half expected something like this.

"He has no wife," Clem says. "Though he sleeps with any

woman who catches his eye. He's a professional when it comes to debauchery."

I shake my head the queen's way.

The head of the guard stands, his eyes narrowing. "You sound different, Your Majesty. And you're early. We did not expect you for several months. Where is your guard? Who are these... I don't think some of them are *sidhe*."

And that was a problem for this dude.

"You know well who my partner is," Dev says with a laugh. "Where is my brother? Tell him I'll kick his ass."

While Devinshea is looking at the guard, waiting for them to spring the joke, Zoey moves to his side and proves she can act a part. She places a hand on his arm and looks up at him. "Your Majesty, I think they know your brother is dead and that you bravely took him out so all of Faery could be under your...kind rule. Don't pretend we're in some other timeline. You're the one who is joking with them. Your guard is obviously steadfast and true and would never joke with the king."

He frowns down at her. "Zoey..."

Rhys moves next to me. "What's happening?"

"Your father is either going to catch on or we're all about to die," I whisper.

"Wouldn't it be funny, Your Majesty?" Zoey has the bubbliest look on her face. Like there's not a brain in her head. She blinks her eyes, and I swear at some point when I wasn't looking she undid a couple of buttons of the flowy dress she wears. "If we made a mistake coming back and found ourselves in a kingdom where you weren't the ruler of everything? That would be so weird."

I see the moment Devinshea realizes what has happened and damn, but Rhys's papa is good at acting as well. His face loses its quizzical expression and a decadent darkness takes over. A faintly cruel smile plays on his handsome face. "Yes, my dear, that would be, as you put it, weird. And wrong. Eoin, why exactly are you here? I certainly did not order you here."

"Well, at least now I understand why you came back early. I should have known." Eoin's gaze is still suspicious. "You are supposed to be on the outer planes preparing for your marriage. We were surprised when Ostara's oracle told us you were here. She was a bit surprised. She believed her fiancé would take more time. If you ask me, I think she's attempting to avoid the marriage, Your Majesty. And you are going to give her a reason, it seems. I thought you were done with this."

Rhys leans over, his arm around my waist, and whispers in my ear. "What the hell is going on?"

Devinshea's eyes go hard, and I swear he gains an inch or two as he moves in and stands in front of the head of his guard. Well, the head of the other Dev's guard. This is going to get confusing. "I didn't ask you, Eoin. Did I? Do I typically ask the opinions of guards? Have I been gone so long that you don't remember?"

Eoin's eyes find the forest floor. "No, Your Majesty. I have not forgotten. I was merely surprised. I truly did believe you were going to be gone for much longer."

"Well, he's got the nasty bastard down," Clem says, her hands on her hips. Her skin resembles the bark of a tree, peeling up in places. "You're sure he's not tricking you?"

The forest is quiet, so I simply shake my head. She's a good two feet shorter than me so I can't speak out loud for fear I'll gain the guards' attention. As for Rhys, I can whisper. "According to the spirit I'm talking to, we've landed on a plane where your father killed your grandmother and uncle and took the throne. He's been slaughtering non-*sidhe* creatures, and there's possibly a rebellion against him."

"I'm going to kill that death god," Rhys vows.

"I am confused." Cassie and Brendan join us, watching their elders deal with the guards. Brendan scratches behind his ear and doesn't seem worried he's got two hellhounds near him. "I thought your granny…"

"Is dead, wolf," Rhys says and sends Brendan a look that could freeze fire.

"Who is this?" Eoin asks and then winces. "I'm sorry. I do not mean to question Your Majesty, but this is not the group you left with. If you care to recall, my brother, Caden, led your guard as he always does when you seek the pleasure of the outer planes."

Devinshea frowns, his eyes narrowing. "They await my return. I wanted a bit of freedom. I ran into someone interesting on the planes. That boy is my bastard. Apparently I had too good a time some years ago, and he came of it. His name is Rhys, and he could be helpful.

The boy has some fertility powers and a bit of Green Man in him. Nothing like myself, of course."

It was right there in his words. The warning to Rhys to keep quiet, to not give himself away since his powers were so beyond his father's formidable ones.

"Well, the real king would kill any son who was more powerful than him." Clem neatly summed the situation up.

"So I decided it would be fun to show my new friends around." Devinshea waves a hand, gesturing to the world around him. "Perhaps we should go back to the palace for a bit. Tell Ostara I don't need her and my reappearance won't bump up our wedding day. Tell me what day it is. You know how time flows on the outer planes."

"You have been gone for but a week, Your Majesty," Eoin replies. "It is almost time for the equinox feast."

Devinshea nods like that makes sense to him. "Excellent. Then tell the palace cooks to double what they're making. We have wolves and hounds to feed. Now you have been so helpful to bring us horses to ride so we don't have to walk to the palace. My go…Zoey, love, you should ride with me."

"Your Majesty," Eoin begins as the others step away from their horses, obviously conditioned to immediately do their king's bidding. "We cannot leave you with no proper guard. The rebels are known to work in these forests."

"Yes, I know. I killed a chimera they sent to take me out," Devinshea announces as he moves for the horses. "I think my new friends can handle it."

"Your Majesty, this is not right," Eoin says.

The ground begins to tremble and the trees around us sway.

Clem seems to fold in on herself. Though she's dead and he cannot harm her, the trauma still runs deep.

A branch from a mighty oak swoops in and suddenly Eoin is in the air, a slender tendril wrapped around his throat. The branch lifts him, booted feet kicking as his hands go up to try to pull the branch from around his neck. It isn't more than an instant before I see blood starting to trickle around the branch.

The rest of the guard pointedly don't look his direction.

Rhys tenses beside me. I doubt he's ever seen his father be so brutal. Though from what I can see from how Clem reacts, Devinshea is playing the role perfectly.

Dev easily mounts Eoin's horse and holds his hand out, lifting the queen onto the saddle in front of him. She sits sideways between his legs, one of her husband's arms wrapped protectively around her waist.

Sasha and Daniel take two of the remaining horses, and Sasha helps Cassie find her seat behind him. Neil frowns and starts undressing.

"I do not do horses," the werewolf announces.

"You and Brendan and the hounds will be our forward and rear guard," Dev commands. Zoey says something to him and he sighs. Eoin falls to the ground, gasping for breath. "Rhys, you and Shy will take the last horse. Try to keep up, son."

Rhys takes my hand. Before he leads me away, I lean down like I'm tying my shoe. I get close to Clem. "Can you come with me? There's so much we need to know if we're going to survive this."

Clem's rich brown eyes are pools of sorrow as she looks back to the ponds. "No. I dare go no farther than the tree line. There is some kind of spell, and no spirit who leaves here returns. But there should be dead to help you in the palace. He's killed so many. Be careful. Something is happening in the mountains. Something terrible."

"Do you mean the sluagh?" I ask, but Rhys tugs on my hand and I know we have to leave. There will already be a thousand questions without the Seelie guard wondering why the strange girl talks to no one at all.

"He is coming for them," Clem calls out as I'm led away.

I turn and she is staring at me. "Who?" I mouth the question.

A gnarled hand points to the north. "The wizard, of course."

A chill goes through me, and I have to wonder if Arawn didn't know what he was doing all along.

It's not more than ten minutes before Dev slows his horse and allows the rest of us to catch him, forming a close line. I have to admit that Rhys knows how to handle a horse. Something warm went through me when he lifted me into the saddle like I weigh nothing. When he settled me on his lap like his father had done for his mother, I felt precious and cared for.

I should not be thinking about sex when we're all going to die, but we're talking about a fertility god here. It's damn near impossible to not think about what those big hands can do to me. Especially now that I have actual proof of what they can do to me.

Stroke me like silk and heat and power. Worship me. Make me feel like I've never felt before. Like there's a place I can go where I'm safe and loved and the world doesn't matter.

"What the actual fuck?" The king always seems to know how to start a conversation.

Devinshea slows his stallion, his arm fully around his wife's waist. "Yes, I have questions. So many questions."

Neil barks like he agrees. His white wolf has been running next to Brendan's, while Fluffy took the lead and the other hounds protected our backs.

"I think this is your time, my goddess," Rhys says, his lips against my ear. "You are the one who saved us, after all."

"Shy figured it out," the queen announces. "She was talking to some spirits who haunt the pond, and she managed to put the pieces together. Shy, what exactly did they tell you?"

"Clem kept talking about the king," I explain. "At first I thought she meant King Daniel, but it became clear she was talking about the high priest."

"Except I'm not the high priest in this *sithein*." Dev says the words slow, as though he has to process them.

"No," I agree. "It was all very quick, but according to Clem and the nymph in the pond, in this *sithein*, Devinshea Quinn killed his mother and brother and took the throne. I don't know how long ago that was. I do know that Clem hates you. She said something about you killing many non-*sidhe* Fae. I think you might have killed her. She was terrified of you. Well, she was until she figured out you aren't you."

"Also, bastard child? Really, Papa?" Rhys chuckles like this is funny.

"Well, they will obviously have questions, and I doubt you're my child in this world since I don't think he even knew your mother's name is Zoey." Dev's jaw is tight, his anxiety obvious. "Shy, do you have comprehension of what's happened?"

I am no science pro, but I can take a wild guess. "I think we somehow stumbled on a different timeline."

"So like when Aunt Zoey fell into that painting thing?" Cassie asks.

"No, that was a portal to another plane, but it was still the timeline we were born in." The king suddenly sounds very academic. "Or rather the one we understood. There are some who believe our version of reality is merely a layer that we move through. The planes themselves are physical spaces while what we're dealing with is time and fractures of reality. Think of it like a layered cake. They exist on top of one another, related but not the same. That's why the *sithein* looks the same but something happened to make the Fae here radically different from the court we know."

"Yes, apparently I am a massive asshole who killed my family to take the throne," Dev says with bitterness flowing.

"It's not you, babe," the queen replies, and her hand rubs over his arm.

"The king is right about the layers." I do know a bit about this. I remember my family debating endlessly about the difference of moving through physical portals and the walls thinning between timelines. "My aunt could hear near timelines. Like the ones on top of or below us. Or maybe to the left or right. I'm not sure how it runs, but she could hear them. I think it's safe to say that we were either led to the wrong door or the blue dolerite facilitated a switch in timelines. The dead I've spoken to here were all interested in the crystals we carry. I have to believe they have some kind of power beyond simply opening the door. That's why they made sure we had enough, or we might have lost someone."

"Well, I suggest we turn this around and go back to the caves," Dev says. "We can find another way."

Oh, that was not going to work for me. I know I cannot leave this place until I figure out why I feel the tug of those mountains. "Your Grace, we're here for a reason. I don't know why Arawn sent us, but I do know I'm supposed to be here. So I understand if you need to take your family back, but I'm going to stay and figure out why I'm here."

Rhys goes stiff behind me. "You most certainly are not."

A bit of anger thrums through me. First he locks me in that stupid cage, and now he's telling me what I can and cannot do. All of this and he hasn't even slept with me yet, hasn't made me his true goddess. Hasn't found out if I can actually be his goddess. "I am staying, Rhys. I can find my way back. I'll keep the dolerite, and I'll give you a call when I'm ready to come home."

If I decide to go home. I love this man, but I can't be caged. I might be able to handle his over protection in battle, but despite what he says, he is not my commanding officer.

Rhys pulls on the reins and the horse beneath us neighs and slows. "Shy, if you think for a second that I am leaving you on a Fae plane by yourself, you're wrong."

"You will not leave her by herself." Sasha—who is surprisingly comfortable on a horse—pulls up next to us, matching our gait. "I will stay with Shy. I will ensure her safety."

"I'll stay, too," Cassie offers and gives me a grin. "Girl power and all that."

"I think we need to stop and give this some thought." The king turns his horse around and gazes someplace in the distance. "Let's find a quiet place and talk."

"Yes, I definitely think we need to decide how to proceed in a way everyone agrees," the queen offers.

"I think your mother is trying to tell you to chill the fuck out, Rhys." Dev stares at his son with a concerned look on his face.

I can't see him, but I can feel his will.

"I will not chill out," Rhys announces. "We have no idea where we are or if walking back through that doorway will even get us to the timeline we came from. We don't know if Arawn made this a two-way ticket or if this is another plan from Myrddin and we're losing days right now. You simply took the word of some wizened crone who shows up with a couple of hellhounds, and I should have stopped it right then and there."

The queen's eyes narrow. "Do you honestly believe your papa can't tell if those hounds are from Arawn? Do you think there's a place where they adopt Cŵn Annwn for fun? They are far more specialized and rare than a true hellhound. There might be twenty in existence. I assure you I know a Fae when I see one, and that crone was absolutely from Arawn. Nim believed it, too."

"Nim is a set of shoulders, and she got there because she underestimated Myrddin," Rhys says with a huff. "You do understand we've been fighting this war while you've been gone. I love you, but I will not allow you to make mistakes that cost me and my siblings and the ones we love. I am going to figure out a way to get to the proper timeline and then I'm going to do something I never thought I would. I'm going to negotiate with my grandmother so Shy has a place to ride out this war."

"Excuse me?" I'm shocked at his words, but should I be? Now I wonder if that wasn't his plan all along. Did he mean to get me to the safety of the Seelie palace and leave me there, leave me out of the fight I belong in? The fight his grandfather got me ready for?

"I know you want to stay with me, but it's too dangerous," Rhys replies.

Devinshea winces. The king lets out a hiss, and I swear that white wolf is laughing.

"It's not about staying with you. That might have been part of it at one point, but you are proving to be a massive ass who wants to cage me. I'm not going to be your pet, Rhys. Or your plaything. I'm not going to be your sweet goddess who takes care of your sexual needs and keeps your *brugh* clean." I'm so angry I can barely breathe. I manage to get out of his hold and shift off the horse, my slippered feet sliding slightly on the soft grass.

"Shahidi," Rhys begins, and he manages to sound shocked.

And that's on me. The truth of the matter is I have been quiet around him. I've hidden away parts of myself because I was afraid he wouldn't like me, and I wanted so very much for him to like me.

But right now, I don't particularly like him. "Myrddin killed my family. He wiped them and all of their unique gifts out of existence in a single night. He burned down the house I was born in, the house I was raised in. He left me with nothing. If you think for one second that I will hide away in some palace while my brothers and sisters fight this war, you don't know me at all. You don't get to put your prized pussy in a cage so it's waiting for your return, Prince Rhys."

"Shit," Dev says under his breath.

"I have no notes, baby girl." The queen gives me a chef's kiss gesture. "That was a ten out of ten take down."

While I appreciate the support, I can do without everyone watching us like a soap opera playing out. "I wish you luck, Your Highnesses. I'm going to those mountains, and I'll hopefully see you back home soon."

With that I turn and start walking. All three hounds come with me, though the one who has been at the queen's side looks sad about it. I've only taken a few steps when Cassie rushes in and joins me.

"This sounds like some *Lord of the Rings* shit, Shy," she says with a grin. "I'm in. Consider me your Samwise Gamgee, but with a machete and a bunch of weapons I know how to use. I'm full up on the cold iron bullets, if you know what I mean."

I stop. I hadn't considered anyone would really come with me. "Cassie, it could be dangerous. I have to go all the way to the mountains and hope Arawn is waiting there for me."

"Cassie didn't have to dismount since I will be going as well." Sasha looks to the king. "Daniel, if I might ask a boon. Could you perhaps ride with Rhys so Shy and Cass have a horse? I think it might be easier for you to find another ride than for us, and those mountains look to be at least a day away. Perhaps more. It will be much faster if we are on horseback."

"Sasha, while I understand Shy's anger with my son, I think we need to take a minute and talk about this." The king sounds so reasonable.

"You are not running off to visit some faery mountains, Cassandra Thomas." Neil is not. He changed and is staring at his daughter, completely heedless of the fact that he's not wearing a stitch of clothes.

I note that Brendan does not join his dad. He stays behind and in his wolf form.

Cassie frowns at her dad. "Why? Because I'm weak since I can't shift? Because I'm a girl? I would like to point out it wasn't the King of All Vampire who took out the chimera."

"I was going to, though," Daniel offers.

Cassie ignores him and looks to the queen. "How about it, Your Highness? Want to make this an all girls trip?"

The queen gives us a grin. "That could be fun."

I catch a glance at Rhys staring at me like he can make me do his will.

He cannot.

My heart aches. I didn't think we would ever be at this place. I go on missions with them. I don't hide in the background. Why now?

Does it even matter why he's suddenly decided I'm not competent enough to fight in a war I've been preparing myself years for?

"Z, I know he's screwed this up and he's not handling it well, but remember he's your son," the king says.

"And remember that every minute we stay here, we risk getting caught by that palace guard," Devinshea points out. "They will eventually catch up with us. We need to figure out where we can hide while we decide what to do."

"Or we can have some faith that this is what Arawn meant for us to do," the queen says quietly. "He has no reason to fuck with us. If Myrddin's plan works, he'll be cut off from his place of power. Or shut in. He'll have to decide where to live, and either will cause him and his people harm."

"He could have given us a heads-up," Dev says under his breath.

"I have to believe that whatever we need is in the palace." The queen goes serious, her brow furrowing. "This version of Seelie Fae likely has an amulet, too. What if I'm supposed to use this amulet to find the door to Sarah's plane?"

I'm glad the queen is talking sense. "I know I'm supposed to visit those mountains."

"And I know I'm supposed to protect you," Rhys says with a finality that scares me. "Even from yourself."

The ground beneath me shakes, and before I can take a breath, a thick vine shoots up and wraps itself around me. It tightens but I can breathe, though anger chokes me. It rises inside me in a way it never has before. Rage.

"For fuck's sake," Dev says.

"Rhys Donovan-Quinn, you let that girl go right now," the queen shouts.

Cassie twirls the machete in her hand. "You want me to use this on the vine or his ass?"

"Like you can touch me with that, Cassie." Rhys looks so beautiful and arrogant astride that horse. He looks every bit the young Fae royal, and he will have his will done.

And there's nothing I can do about it. I'm trapped, and if Cassie cuts the vine, he'll simply call another one forth. I've seen him play with his brother this way. When Lee was human and causing trouble, every now and then Rhys would wrap him up in vines and then the obedient vine would lift Lee up and place him wherever Rhys wanted. This time I'm sure I'll be bundled on the back of his horse and forced to go wherever Rhys wants me.

I feel small. So small.

There are no dead to talk to, and it wouldn't help me if there were. What would a dead Fae do to help me? I have no control over the plants of the ground. That is the kingdom of life. The kingdom of spring.

But is it? a voice whispers. A deep voice. One that I recognize. Matilda is talking in my head. *There is no spring without winter. No green fields without the cycle. Birth and life and death and decay. That vine wrapped so tightly around you glows with life because its brethren died the year before and sent its lifeforce forward. Ask it. Touch it with your mind and ask if it will take the journey a little early.*

"She is mine to take care of, and I will decide what is best. She knows nothing of Faery, nothing of how dangerous it can be," Rhys is saying as he argues with his parents.

I can sense the hounds are oddly calm. Like they know something I don't. Fluffy actually takes this moment to roll on his back and do that wiggly thing dogs do. I have to wonder if Matilda is talking to them, too.

Cassie is telling Rhys she can wait. He's got to sleep sometime.

I feel the vine begin to lift me.

Ask it, Pair Dadeni, the voice whispers. *Touch it with your mind. Life and death flows through you. Let it flow. Let your unique magic connect you to all creatures.*

I feel my feet lift but my mind is somewhere else. Someplace deep inside me. I can feel it. I can feel the life in this vine like a heartbeat. It pulses with life. It has no sentience, but there is something deep inside, something all living things have.

History. It grows and dies. Grows and dies. It soaks up the sun and then decays in the earth, but it knows that is the only way it lives again. Like a human. Reborn again and again. If it dies now, it will return in another form, nothing lost.

Do you mind? I ask, putting the question in my hands, my skin, wherever we touch.

I do not get an answer back. Not in words. But suddenly the vine withers and dies, and I drop to the grass.

"What the hell?" Dev asks.

"Whoa." Cassie looks down at the desiccating vine.

The hounds get up like they know I'm done playing and it's time to go.

What did I do? Did I do that? Or the weird voice in my head?

Go to the palace, Shahidi, the voice whispers. *Meet the goddess there and see if you can get Spring under control. When the time is right, you'll go to the mountains and you'll see how much power you have.*

"Matilda?" I ask the question aloud, though I know no one else heard the whispers.

Tell the high priest to play his part to the hilt. And yes, you released that bit of green to begin again. It didn't mind. It was happy to help. Let my hounds take care of you. And perhaps one day, you'll forgive me. There was no other way. When the time comes, call for him.

And then she's gone. I can tell she's gone.

I get the feeling that might have been our last communication.

"How did you do that?" Rhys has dismounted and stands over the thick, now dying vine.

I ignore him for a moment and kneel, touching the vine, sending my grateful energy through it. It's not something I've done before, but then we're in foreign territory. When I stand, I try to be calm. It looks like we have work to do at the palace. "Matilda wants us to go to the palace."

"Should we be worried this crone person can speak to Shy in her head?" Neil is still au natural, but he's calmer now that his daughter isn't playing Sam to my Frodo.

Yet.

"I can talk to the dead," I point out. "She's from a land of the dead."

"Ah." Rhys nods as though he's figured something out. "The crone killed my vines."

I don't think so. She told me how to do it, but I rather think it was me. A power I didn't know I possess. "She wants me to go to the palace. But she also wants me to forgive her since she says this is the only way. She also wants me to meet a goddess and get spring under control. I assume she's talking about Rhys since he's lost his damn mind."

"I certainly have not," Rhys complains. "I do not need to be brought under control, and I have questions. How is this crone speaking to my goddess if she's supposed to be in Annwn?"

"So we're to go to the palace where they'll kill us all if they figure out we're not who they think we are," the queen muses, ignoring her son's outburst.

"Shy, I would like to talk to you," Rhys begins, and he sounds slightly less confident.

"And I would like to forget that you don't give a damn about what I need. I guess neither of us is getting what we want," I shoot back. "I'll walk to the palace."

"Shy, come." Sasha offers me his arm. "You can ride with me."

As he was willing to go with me, I trust him. That's not right. I trust Sasha Federov for a million different reasons. I grip his arm and let him help me up, sliding into place behind him.

Rhys frowns up at me. "We will talk, Shy."

He mounts, and I see Cassie has joined the king. It's probably a good thing since I think she might have used that machete on Rhys. Who sends me one of his patented soulful stares before joining his papa. "We should get our stories straight. I am your bastard son and Shy is my wife."

"I am not your wife," I protest. "I'm a...ooo, I'm the queen's like maid or something."

"She's not the queen," Dev corrects. "She's a piece of heaven I picked up on a party plane. She definitely doesn't have a maid. Cassie's her little sis, and Brendan and Neil are supercool werewolves we picked up at a rave. I wonder how hetero I am here. Do you think I'll be able to tell? I would like to work Dan in."

He starts talking and assigning people their roles.

I can feel Rhys's eyes on me and know he isn't going to make this easy.

Is it wrong I am both angry about that and oddly comforted?

Chapter Twelve

Zoey

The White Palace is stunning, as always, and as I sit on the bed in what should be Miria's bedroom, I'm still in shock. Shock that we're in a weird alternative world. Shock that this Devinshea is apparently some kind of a monster.

Shock that my son is acting like an overly possessive caveman moron.

Shock that Shy is far more powerful than we imagined.

There's a lot of shock running through me right now.

"She killed that vine with a mere thought," Devinshea says as he paces the marbled floors. "No one told me that was a power of hers. All I've heard up until now is that she's a medium. What she showed me today goes far beyond a medium. Do you know the last time I met someone who could counter my power like that?"

When we entered the palace, Devinshea walked in like he owned the place, throwing his cloak at one of the brownies who greeted us. He didn't seem to care that his cloak was far heavier than the servant, simply walked right on. Luckily I saw her fellow brownies heft the cloak off her.

We all followed him, hearing him yell out for rooms to be prepared and food and wine to be brought for his friends.

Every single servant was afraid of him.

The rest of our party is sitting in the outer rooms. Dev brought Danny and I back here for a private talk.

"She is not Myrddin," Daniel replies.

I shake my head because I can't believe this is what Dev is contemplating. I really hope Shy's hearing isn't better than we think. Or Rhys's. "You think that sweet young woman has anything to do with the wizard who murdered her family?"

Dev's jaw goes tight. "Well, I certainly never dreamed Olivia Carey would join him and yet she's tried to murder our children several times."

Olivia is a problem Kelsey Owens is working on. We split our missions, with Kelsey taking my son and daughter with her to her husband's home. On the Hell plane. Grayson Sloane is one of the thirteen princes of Hell, and he's also known as the dark prophet. Olivia was once a dear friend and a teacher at our children's school. They loved her. Then the fall came and Liv was left behind. As a witch, she was taken in by Myrddin, and she became one of his most trusted warriors. Kelsey thinks she can bring her back. I hope she can.

Grayson Sloane. Of course. That's some firepower I bet my husband can't counter.

"Gray witnessed Shy's meeting with Rhys," I point out.

My Fae husband nods like I made his point. "Yes. He witnessed something important. Something dangerous. I happen to remember several times when Gray has shown up and things went to shit."

Oh, how he forgets. "He always finds a way to help us. If he was worried about Shy, he would find a way to warn us."

"He cost us twelve years," Dev practically roars back and then stops as Daniel steps in front of me. "I'm sorry. I...I am unsettled being here."

It's so much worse. He's on the edge, and our circumstances are pushing him. Perhaps too fast. I need to show my husband some grace. I brush past Danny—who should know Dev would never hurt me—and wrap my arms around Devinshea. "Of course you are. I am, too. This whole situation is too close to what we just went through."

"We have no idea how time passes here," Dev whispers. "None. We could be losing years."

"I don't think so," Danny says, moving around to Dev's other side. He wraps Dev up, his hands going around Dev to sit on my waist. "I know this sounds odd, but there's a feeling I get when I'm in Faery. It's like a hum. I get used to it after a day or two. I feel it whenever I leave the Earth plane. Some planes it's barely there. Some feel slow. Some fast. I've talked to the academics and they think vampires can sense the differences in time movement from their home plane. The hum here is identical to your mother's *sithein*. I can't be sure, but I think it's the same. I think everything here is the same except the people. I suspect some of them are even the same, though you are not."

Dev breathes a sigh of relief, and I know Danny's gotten through to him. "Well, as I apparently murdered my way to a throne, I would tend to agree." He rubs his head against mine. "We should be careful."

"No one's here," I promise him. "Sasha checked for spells and bugs. Danny will tell us if he senses anyone sneaking around. We're okay in this room, but we have to make sure we don't tip the court off that Devinshea isn't their Dev. And you have to stop being hard on Shy."

"We don't know her," Dev argues, but there's no fire behind the words.

"But Sasha does. Gray does. Trent does and our children do. She's one of them. Or at least she was until Rhys decided to be a butthead." I'm going to have such a talk with my son. "We need to figure out where this court keeps its amulet while we wait for Arawn to show up. I'm worried about his interest in Shy."

Dev takes a step back. "Yes, I am, too. I am also worried that apparently I have a fiancée roaming the halls."

Danny looks like he wants to haul Dev back to us, but he gives his partner some space. It's odd because Dev looks perfectly at home in these posh rooms. Danny wears the same types of clothes—leather pants, tunic—and he still looks so very out of place. Like his body was simply built for the modern Earth plane. "Ostara. Why do I know that name?"

"Well, the name is from a Germanic goddess of spring. You might know her by one of her other names. *Ēostre*. Early pagans celebrated the spring equinox in her name," Dev explains. "Over the years the celebration evolved into what Christians call Easter. But much like Bris, she was an actual goddess of hearth and home. So this woman I'm supposed to marry is named after her. She'll be a high-ranking Fae. I suspect this is not a love match."

"We need information." Danny moves to the windows, touching the glass. "This is different."

Miria's chambers were open to the air. Oh, there was magic that kept the rain out and wards that kept out everything else, but the Faery queen wouldn't have something like glass in her private rooms.

Danny taps on the pane. "This is thick."

Dev nods, his eyes rolling. "I am probably trying to avoid being assassinated. Eoin mentioned something about rebels. So not only am I worried about being murdered for not being Evil Dev, I have to worry about being murdered because the rebels think I *am* Evil Dev."

"You should grow a goatee. It's how you know you're evil," Danny says with a perfectly straight face. Nerd.

Dev frowns. "Why would facial hair be evil? I think I look quite charming with one."

A groan goes through me because even here in the midst of another crisis, Danny's teasing him. "It's a *Star Trek* thing. The 'Dark Mirror' episode. They go through a worm hole and meet their bad selves. It doesn't matter. We need to figure out how much Danny and I can move around. I need to know more. Would this you allow his lovers free rein? Or does he have an iron fist? Who is this Eoin guy? I don't remember him, but you seem to."

"He's been around court since we were both children. When he reached his majority, he became one of my mother's guards, serving under Padric. Who I assume I killed as well." Dev paces, his eyes looking around and taking in the changes in the room. While the structure of the palace is basically the same, there's some serious masculine energy to the place now. The whole place is decadent and dark and slightly sinister. I fear what we'll find in the temple. I'm also surprised by the lack of plants. Everywhere my Devinshea goes, things bloom and grow. This palace is devoid of vegetation. "He is not someone I suspect has ambitions to lead. The Eoin I know is funny and kind. He's married with a daughter."

"Well, I don't trust him. In this timeline he obviously has ties to you, and he didn't like the way you handled him," Danny points out. "Though he also didn't seem entirely surprised. You should play him like a somewhat trusted advisor when he shows up. I think we should modify why I'm here. I can be a lover, of course, unless we suspect your evil counterpart isn't as open minded as you are."

"I would certainly prefer to keep you close," Dev insists.

"A bodyguard has to stay close. If these windows are an indication, your counterpart has a security problem. Sasha, the wolves, and I can be your solution," Danny offers. "It could give me some access I wouldn't have as your plaything."

I don't like the sound of that. "I can be security, too."

It's Danny's turn to groan. "Baby, I need you to do that thing where you show your boobs and no one thinks you can blow up the world. And then you blow up the world."

I can't exactly argue with him. "And Rhys is your bastard child you found out on the planes?"

Dev shrugs. "I have no other explanation. He is damn near my twin. Unfortunately, the women of the group must be attached to a male. I doubt I'm a feminist on this plane, and I happen to know a lot of Fae think they know where a woman's place is. It's likely why I easily took down my own mother."

Miria faces misogyny even with a crown on her head. "All right, so you picked me up at a rave on another plane and hired some security. Shy is Rhys's wife or girlfriend or whatever, and Cassie is my sister. All of that is fine. But why would you completely ditch your guard and what are we going to do if Evil Dev has some way to communicate with home? We don't have a witch with us."

"I'll have to figure out if there's a mirror network," Dev says with a sigh. "I wish we could trust someone. Anyone."

There's a knock on the door and Sasha opens it. "They've sent the tea and wine you requested, Dev...King Devinshea."

Dev nods. "Of course. Send them in."

I sit on the bed and try to look bored and idle as the three small servants walk in carrying trays that look bigger than their bodies. This Dev seems to have an obsession with "lesser" Fae as servants. I saw the brownies cleaning the palace, and now a duo of small trolls from the kitchens. They wear a version of a uniform complete with their spindly tails poking out of their skirts.

I sigh as they place their trays on the tables in the corner of the room. I lean back, looking to Devinshea. "When are we going to be done with all the security stuff, Your Majesty? You didn't bring me here to sit in on boring talks with your bodyguards."

I notice one of the troll's ears perks up. She's turned away from me so I can't see her face, but her body has gone slightly stiff as she opens the wine.

"Well, lover, I was hoping you didn't get killed." Dev's tone has gone all smooth and silky. "At least not until I'm bored with you."

Such an ass. And he can't ever get bored with me. I sigh. "Well, at least I'll go out happy."

He winks my way. "Serve my mistress, troll. She's from an outer plane and has never tried faery wine before."

The troll who brought in the fruit and cheese is already walking out. Like she can't wait to put some distance between her and the royal apartments.

The one who brought the wine turns, and her eyes are wide. "You do not want wine yourself, Your Majesty?"

Those eyes are super familiar. Bibi. I met her the first time I went to Faery. She was a gardener, and the palace mean girls decided to play a joke on me by making her my social secretary. The joke was on them. I quite like a little troll. I grew up around the huldrefólk. She became my friend. When I visit Faery, Bibi is always there to welcome me and make my trip easier.

Dev frowns, remembering his part. "Did I say I wanted wine, servant? My mistress is waiting."

Bibi bites her bottom lip and holds the wine goblet with trembling hands. "But this is the royal wine. It was made for you."

What is happening?

Bibi is one of the sweetest souls I've ever met. She's also brave when she finds the right leader.

Dev sighs. "I do not want wine right now, but my mistress does. I am attempting to be patient with you."

Bibi nods and starts bringing the wine toward me. And then she trips. Or rather pretends to trip, and the wine goes everywhere. She gasps and curls into a ball. "I am so sorry, Your Majesty. So sorry. I will go and bring more wine."

She starts to crawl back.

Dev's head shakes, and it's clear to me he doesn't know what to do with her. Maybe if she was any other servant he could yell and threaten, but Dev loves Bibi, too. She is part of our Fae family. This whole mission is going to be hard on him. "There's half a bottle, troll. Just clean this up and I'll serve her myself, Bibi."

She stops and with tearful eyes turns his way. "You know my name?"

Dev stiffens and pulls his arrogance around him. "Your name does not matter, but of course I know it."

Big, dark eyes narrow. "You recently made a decree that my kind are below even the lesser Fae and do not need names. We are to be called Troll or Servant because that is our place."

I don't like this version of Dev, but I'm starting to see some serious doors cracking open when it comes to Bibi.

Dev pales and takes a step back. He's saved from having to say something by the door opening and Rhys walking in.

"Pa...Your Majesty, I'm taking Shy to..." He stops when Shy clears her throat and sends him a pointed stare, which makes Rhys sigh. "I would request Your Majesty's leave to take my wife to our rooms, please. It's been a long day traveling, and she needs to rest."

Shy snorts. "Oh, there won't be any resting."

There would be some serious ass kicking in my son's future, and I'm here for it.

That's when I notice Bibi staring at my son. Her jaw drops. She knows him.

I think she might be scared for him.

Oh, we're in trouble.

But Eoin didn't seem to know Rhys. He also didn't seem surprised the king would find a bastard kid and drag him into his seemingly never-ending party.

Danny leans over, staring down at the stain on the floor. Red wine looks too much like blood on the white marble floors.

Dev waves his hand dismissingly. "Feel free to do whatever you like. We'll have dinner late. I expect you to entertain me, son."

Rhys turns and walks out, and I notice Bibi trying to sneak out as well.

"Bibi, I don't think you should leave yet," I say, my tone gentle because it's time to start feeling her out.

My Bibi is an excellent spy. No one pays attention to her. No one knows she's coming.

"Neil," Daniel calls out.

Bibi nods and pulls a rag from her belt. "Of course, mistress. I will clean the mess."

I get to my knees in front of her. "My name is Zoey, Bibi."

Her big eyes glance at Dev, and she shakes her head. "I have no name. I am a troll and a servant. I serve the *sidhe*."

Dev groans and turns away, staring out the window.

"Don't touch anything, Bibi." Daniel stands over us as Neil walks in. He points to the wine. "Smell that."

My bestie frowns. "Polite much?"

"Smell that, please." Danny gives Neil a nod. "Is that what I think it is?"

Neil takes a long smell.

"It's metallic." Cassie is next to her brother, standing by the door. She might not be able to change easily, but she has a wolf's sense of smell.

Brendan nods, his mouth full of whatever the trolls left in the outer rooms. I note he's got an apple in one hand and some cheese in the other. Wolves. I have no idea how Neil managed to feed two teenaged wolves.

Grief strikes. It hits in waves. Sometimes I think I'm fine and then I realize I didn't feed my teenaged kids. I didn't get to complain about them being human garbage dumpsters. I didn't watch Albert cook for my babies and call him a kitchen god because he never complained.

I take a long breath. I can't now. I have to push it aside and cry later when Danny and Dev can hold me. Now I have to keep moving. "Why would the wine smell metallic?"

Dev moves in, looking over Daniel's shoulder. "Cold iron?"

Good for Bibi. A genuine smile lights my face. "Bibi, are you trying to assassinate the king?"

Bibi pales and takes a step back, running straight into Neil, who has the biggest grin on his face as she tilts her head and looks up at him.

"Well, aren't you a little rebel, Bibi," Neil says and holds a hand out. "High five, girlie."

Neil adores my Bibi. And she's got the biggest crush on him because as I have pointed out on many an occasion, trolls have no gaydar.

Bibi gasps and turns to run, but Sasha catches her, drawing her up and looking my way. "You know this troll, Your Highness?"

"I do." I think it's worth the risk.

Daniel moves in. "Bibi, is it cold iron in the wine?"

Tears run down her face. "My master will take you all down, and you will not see it coming. You will not know him. You can kill me but I will never give you his name."

Neil looks at me, grinning. "You need to give Bibi a raise or she might assassinate you."

"How do you all know my name?" Bibi shrinks back from me, and it hurts my heart.

I look to Danny. "Can we be honest with her? We need an ally. She can give us history we don't have."

"And it will allow our Devinshea to feel more confident in his conversations with this court of his." Sasha stares down at the troll. "Your Highness, I recommend this course of action. You should know I use many Earth plane Fae as spies. They are some of my best sources of information. It's precisely why Myrddin banned them from the Council House. Well, he did before the queen blew it up."

I'm never living that down. You cause one building to explode...

Danny nods my way, his decision made.

I hope Bibi doesn't, like, have a cold iron tooth her spy master gave her to chomp down on in case of capture. "Bibi, I know this is going to sound odd, but we know each other. Or rather there's a version of you I know on another plane of existence."

Danny clears his throat. "Timeline. Technically this is absolutely the same plane."

I bite back a growl. First I had to deal with other planes. Now all the planes have different timelines. If I ever meet the maker of this whole existence, we will have such a talk... But for now I'm talking to a troll. "Fine. Timeline. Bibi, my name is Zoey Donovan-Quinn."

The troll gasps and tries to step back, but Neil is right there. "But the king has no wife. He is supposed to marry Ostara and gain all of her power."

Yep, that's something I would like to have a chat about. We need to know if Evil Dev's chosen bride is going to aid us or be a real problem. "And yet I am married to the Devinshea you see here." I pull out the necklace that lay under the bodice of my dress. The Goddess Chain. "I am his goddess."

Bibi bites her bottom lip. "I do not understand. That is supposed to be for Ostara, but my master..."

"It's okay, Bibi. You can talk to us. The real King Devinshea is off plane partying it up somewhere. The Devinshea you see before you is not a king. He is the High Priest of Fae. Seelie and Unseelie alike."

She looks up at him. "Unseelie?"

Yeah, it was a good bet Evil Dev probably did the purity thing. Which my Dev has zero time for. "We spend as much time with the Unseelie as we do his mother, Queen Miria, who in our timeline is probably pissed that we're late."

"And just so we're clear, my brother is perfectly alive and annoying even though there are times when I think seriously about how much easier my life would be without him," Dev says with a sigh.

A look of hope crosses Bibi's small face, but I see the minute she tamps it down. She nods as though she knows she must survive the next few moments. "Of course. Well, if you want to get back to your home, I fear I don't know how."

It's going to take more. "Bibi, is your king an ascended god?"

"Like Ostara?" Bibi asks. "No. King Devinshea would never share his body with a god. He would never give up control."

"Then look into my eyes, Little One, and know the truth." Bris has control of the body, and he bends to one knee in front of Bibi, holding out his hand. "Devinshea and I bonded many years ago, and my host is one of the best men I have met in my long existence. He shares his body and soul with me, and he shares his love. We share a goddess and a partner and several children, including the one who just walked out. Seeing him frightened you. Not Devinshea, but our son, Rhys. Why were you frightened of our boy? I assure you he means no harm."

Bibi stares for a moment and then places her hand in Bris's, tears beginning to fall. "You are truly not our cruel king."

"I am your friend, sweet Bibi," Bris says. "We will help you. But we're going to need some help from you as well. Why were you afraid of Rhys?"

"I wasn't afraid of him, My Lord," Bibi says, her voice tremulous. "I was afraid for him. I was afraid he is here to steal something and will get caught."

Danny huffs. "Well at least we know who's leading the rebellion."

"You know Master Lee?" Bibi asks.

Oh, I know him well. I thought sending him to Hell with Kelsey would save him. Apparently his counterpart here is going to be every bit as troublesome.

Chapter Thirteen

Shy

I follow Rhys out of the magnificent rooms that apparently belong to an evil version of his papa. Cassie gives me a long look as if asking if I need backup.

I do not. I apparently don't need a machete to take out what Rhys can send my way, so I'm pretty comfortable having this throwdown in complete privacy.

Well, as private as anything can be when there are probably always eyes on us.

That makes me worry. "Maybe we should leave the palace if we're going to talk."

Sasha hasn't checked all the rooms yet, and I worry that the butterflies I see all around are actually pixies, and I know how we use them as spies.

Rhys stops in the middle of the hall and turns my way. "I have a charm my sister gave me. When I activate it no one I'm not making eye contact with will be able to hear us. Are you worried about the pixies?"

There are several on him right now—a brilliant blue one on his shoulder and a couple more clinging to his arms. "Sasha uses them as spies. It occurs to me the king might do the same."

Rhys's head shakes. "They hate the king. They followed Papa and I in and they are trying to ensure no one from the king's council sees them. Apparently they have not been welcome in the palace for a long time."

"How are you hearing them? You used to require a wolf or vampire to tell you what they…" It hits me. "You are more attuned to them since your ascension."

He gestures to his shoulder. "This one is called Hallow. He's mated to the queen. She sensed our presence the minute we walked into the *sithein*. They are well aware we aren't who we look like. They are begging us to save Ostara. They think the king is going to kill her. Papa is not well liked here." He stops for a moment, listening, and then his face falls. "Seriously? Ugh. I will never hear the end of it." He looks my way. "Also, they work for the rebellion which is led by the king's actual bastard son who is a famous thief."

Despite our precarious situation, I snort. "Lee's here, then."

Rhys huffs and continues toward the rooms we were given. "Yes, and I'm sure he'll cause an enormous amount of trouble. My brother as a full Fae is likely as annoying as he is as a vampire king. Come along. We have things to talk about."

Yes, we do. "I'm not staying with you in that room, Rhys."

He opens the door and invites me inside. "Where else would you stay, wife?"

He put me in that corner, though the way some of these males look at me, I find a bit of comfort in it. When we entered the palace, the staff was surprised and obviously terrified. But the courtiers seemed delighted their decadent king returned so soon. They looked all the women in our party up and down like they were sizing up how much fun they could have with us. I noted a few high Fae women, but they mostly ignored us.

I also noticed they whispered about Zoey. Almost like they knew her, too, but when Dev introduced her, they seemed like it was the first time meeting her. Something is off, but before I could try to figure it out Rhys put an arm around me and declared me his wife.

I hate it when the only way I can feel safe is to be connected to some powerful man.

"I can stay with Cassie."

His head shakes. "Cassie is with her brother and father. Neil doesn't want to split them up. She has two men watching over her, and Mom has Papa and Dad. Sasha is next to us, and I assure you he'll be listening. Now tell me what I can do to make up for being a massive ass." He reaches for my hand and takes it between both of his. "Shy, I'm not handling this well. I'm on edge, and I'm not even sure why. The minute I walked into this *sithein*…"

His hand feels restless on mine, and my heart rate ticks up because I have a good inkling of why he's on edge.

Whether or not this is his timeline, the land is the same. It pulses with Fae energy in a way the Earth plane does not. Rhys vowed to reside on the Earth plane, the priest to all the Earthly Fae left behind long ago, but that doesn't mean his body fails to receive the energy this plane has for a fertility god.

And it certainly doesn't mean his body doesn't need a place to send the energy pouring through him.

See, it sounds like a good idea to date a fertility god. Especially one who isn't a player. One would suspect an actual sex god would screw his way around the world, but when his papa met his mother and took the ancient god Bris into his body and ascended, he took a vow of monogamy. I suspect it got easier for him because Zoey is his true goddess, and Bris is known for loving one woman at a time. I heard stories of what Dev Quinn was like before he met the queen. Rhys was never like that. Not even once. I suspect the desire to find his goddess and be true to her was written into his DNA.

Sounds lovely, right? But what happens when you really want to fight and he's a whirling ball of anxiety and confusion because he's being bombarded by energy he doesn't truly understand since he wasn't raised here? His papa was gone before he reached puberty, and while Sasha and Trent did a great job, they couldn't possibly understand a young fertility god. Or what he needs.

Which is to get laid.

The trouble is I'm pissed off with him right now. The other trouble is I'm kind of turned on and it's all about that energy that's pouring off him. I can feel energy from living beings, but normally it's a nice hum from Rhys. Here in this place it's like wave after wave battering me. That sounds violent and it's not. What it's really doing is tempting me, and I have to wonder if this is about what I want or what he needs.

I don't know that it matters anymore. Rhys and I feel inevitable. So much of my fear seems ridiculous. I know why we waited, but there's no reason to wait anymore.

Maybe I'm being affected by this place, too, but I feel freer here. I haven't seen the Drowning Woman at all, and my power has me thinking I can handle him. Even if it's not forever.

I drag his hand up to my chest, placing his palm against my breast. That feels right, too. "You know why."

He pales and pulls away from me. "Shy, don't do that. Not now. I can't control myself."

"That's what I'm telling you, Rhys. I don't want you to control yourself. It's time. You can't think properly, and it's only going to get worse. You need sex. You need a release for all the energy inside you. Tell me you don't feel it. I'm not a fertility god and I feel it. Do you remember what Fenrir was talking about before he and Evan left for the Hell plane?"

Rhys nods. "Yes. His papa's seat of power is a moonlight kingdom. Trent mentioned it would be harder to ignore his wolf instincts there. It's one of the reasons I released him from his promise to wait until Evan is eighteen."

"I'm an adult, Rhys. You're an adult. I no longer house your grandfather's soul. You need this."

His jaw tightens. "And that is precisely why I won't take it from you. This cannot be about my need. I won't use you. I love you, Shahidi. I will wait until you're ready."

So frustrating. "That's what I'm telling you. I'm ready."

He actually takes a step back. "No. You're not. There's something about this place. I suspect there's some kind of energy you're picking up on, and I won't take your virginity because you're under a spell. This is one of the reasons I think we should try to get you back. I don't feel this way in my grandmother's *sithein*."

"How old were you the last time you were in the Seelie *sithein*?"

He seems to think for a moment. "I was eleven. It was a few months before my parents fell through the painting. I almost was taken to the Unseelie *sithein* though. A few Unseelie decided to kidnap me. They intended to use magic to force me to do my duties. I felt the tiniest edge of that magic before I was knocked out. It felt a bit like this."

My heart aches at the thought. He doesn't talk about that time. He's referring to the incident that cost Lee his eye. He's probably afraid, but I worry his fear is going to put us all in a bad situation. "Rhys, are you afraid of sex?"

His eyes roll. "I'm not afraid of sex."

But it kind of makes sense. All of his life he's known this is his power. As a kid it was all latent power, but now it's here and he's ascended to a place no one thought was possible. "You've talked about how hard it was to be in school. How all the teachers wore charms and shields around you and tried to stay away."

Because being around him was enough to cause women to ovulate and several got pregnant, one after she swore she was in menopause. It must have been isolating to a young child. He couldn't control it.

"I'm not a child anymore, Shy. I can control it. I can control myself," he says with grim resolve.

"And if I don't want you to?"

He shakes his head. "You don't know what you want. When the time is right, we'll cement our bond."

He is so annoying. "So I don't know what I want and I'm neither smart enough nor strong enough to fight in a war against the man who murdered my entire family."

"I never said that. I don't think you should have to."

"And you get to make all of the rules when it comes to me."

He stares at me like he knows it's a trap. He falls in anyway. "I am your commanding officer."

I lean in so he can't possibly mistake me. "Then I'll make it easy for you. I quit. Now you don't have to worry about me anymore. I'll fight with Lily and the witches. And you can explain to your sister why her best friend is no longer in her unit. I'm staying with Cassie and you can fuck yourself."

I turn and start for the door.

I hear him growl behind me, and I wish I could say my heart rate didn't triple.

This is it. If he finds his control and lets me go, I will hold the line. I will move forward, and it will be without Rhys Donovan-Quinn. I'll know this is all fear. Know that he picked me because I was out of reach and safe, and now he's trying to buy himself more time by shoving me in a *sithein* and going on about his life.

I reach for the door and begin to open it. A hard hand slams the door closed and I feel him behind me.

My spine straightens as he leans in.

"If you think for one second that I will allow you to leave, you don't know me at all."

So arrogant. "If you think you control me, you don't know me."

I hear him breathing, feel his nose run along the nape of my neck. "I know you. Shy, I am trying to show you that you are not some sort of control mechanism for me. You are precious. You hold my heart."

"But not your body."

He groans and his head leans against mine. "You own all of me. Every cell in my body, every spark of magic I have is yours. And Shy, my cock is absolutely yours. Don't you dare tell me I don't want you."

He rubs against me, and I feel the evidence of his desire.

It takes everything I have not to arch my backside into that hard piece of masculinity. I can feel my own magic pulsing inside me.

I didn't know I had real magic. Not until I stepped onto this plane. It might only ever work here, and I feel drugged by it. I feel powerful and vulnerable all at the same time.

"I want you, too, Rhys."

"Then marry me. I need you to understand that the minute my body penetrates yours I will consider you my wife. I will not touch another woman for all my days."

And this is why I'm scared. "Rhys, we can't know I'm your goddess until we sleep together, and what happens if I'm not?"

"You are. Shahidi, if you say you'll marry me, I'll take you right here. Right now. I'll let my power flow and wake every plant and tree and flower in this *sithein*."

His words wash over me like cold water.

"You can't." Shit. He can't. "I think there would be a few questions as to why Devinshea brought a far more powerful fertility god back to his place. I don't think your father is very open in this timeline. You exploding the gardens will bring too much attention."

I hear him hiss and then his fist pounds on the door.

I didn't think at all. I just wanted, and the tension between us is killing me. I know part of his unmitigated assholery is because he has no place to put his energy. Which is more powerful here. My love is a swirling storm of anger and fear and bad history and magic he doesn't yet understand.

He steps back and I turn. My heart aches at the pain I see on his face, and I will do anything. When my heart seems so full of him, I know my hesitation is going to come for nothing. I know I'll fall into his arms no matter how irritated I am with him.

I love him.

"The temple." He takes a long breath. "We can go to the temple. If it's anything like the one I remember, there's a way to both amplify and nullify fertility power. My great-grandfather was incredibly powerful, and they had to dampen his magic when he really got going. I can take you there."

"Rhys, I haven't said I'll marry you," I say quietly though I know I'm close, but that power of mine still worries me.

"Because you might not be my goddess?"

"Rhys, my power is rooted in death. Yours in life. What if this union takes away from your power?"

"And what if it's all connected?" he offers. "Have you thought about that? You talk about how you stay in shadows, but you literally send souls to the light. The wheel turns. Spring is not possible without the rest of winter. Without death and dying there is no rebirth. You cannot take my pow..." He stops for a moment, his face going blank as though he's trying to figure something out. "Shy, someone is coming. Something is coming. I feel her pull."

There's a knock on the door and I swear I feel a gentle breeze and then the scent of grass and lilacs and apple blossoms. I hear the flutter of birds somewhere in the distance, and warmth creeps along my skin.

The pixies on Rhys's shoulder seem to flex their wings as though puffing up to greet whoever is knocking on our chamber door.

And Rhys himself seems to not be able to take his eyes off the door. Like he knows the power behind it and is intoxicated by it.

Well, it appears he's not going to deal with the situation. He's going to stare like he's waiting for a goddess to walk in. I stride to the door and realize that's exactly what he's waiting for.

An ethereal blonde stands in the hall, her hair covered in pixies, their wings slowly opening and closing. I'm not sure how she does it but there's a gentle glow coming off her. She has the loveliest face

I've ever seen, with vibrant green eyes and lush lips. Those lips turn up in a sweet smile, and the scent of lilies fills the air. She reaches out a hand to me. "You. Please tell me your name."

She's here for me? I was kind of thinking she was here for my boyfriend and we were going to have a smackdown. Which is sad because they always devolve into hair pulling, and mine looks good right now. I reach out and touch her, a flash going through my mind.

Blue skies and green hills. She is the loam of the earth, the light awakening. She is rebirth. The planting season. Flowers growing. Roots spreading until all the earth knows the long slumber of winter is over and it is time to wake. I hear goslings honk and feel the gentle rain that feeds the land.

I have damn tears in my eyes when I finally come out of it. "I'm Shahidi."

Her hands clasp mine. "And I am Ostara. Welcome, Sister Death. It is so good to be in your presence once again. And you have brought a mate. Well-chosen and matched. He is the first elemental we have met in a thousand years. And I want to know who the vampire is."

"Do we speak with Ostara or her host?" Rhys seems to have gotten the power of speech back. "My goddess, this is Ostara of the spring, holder of rains and wind. But she must have a host."

Like Bris lives in Devinshea.

She seems utterly delighted and I swear her smile amps up my own, and then I remember she called me Sister Death and I frown again.

"You are Devinshea's son?" she asks. "I mean obviously you are. You look exactly like him, but I didn't realize he was associated with an elemental. He has returned and brought a new member of our family?"

I look to Rhys because we still have a ruse to run. We don't know this woman. We can't exactly explain. And maybe it's better to keep her in the dark because we gather some intelligence that way.

"Yes, I am the king's son. A by blow from an affair he had with a woman from the Earth plane. He recently met her again and wants to know me. And this is my wife, Shy. So you can release her hand and allow her to come back to me."

I feel my eyes widen at Rhys's cold tone. I would suspect he would be attracted to someone so close to his own power, but he watches her with stony eyes. They've gone to deep jade, the color they get when he's angry. Or possessive.

I look back to Ostara but all I see is a slight tilting of her lips, as though she should have known. She releases my hand and steps back. "Perhaps if you join your husband, sister, he will see I seek no claim on you but friendship and to bask a bit in your energy."

"Her energy is not for you," Rhys insists.

"My energy?" I'm a little confused.

Rhys's hand finds mine and draws me close to his body. "I don't know what she means by it, but it is your energy, not hers. I don't know exactly what her goddess can do since no one has seen Ostara on our plane in millennia."

She glances from me and back to Rhys. "You were not raised in a Fae household? You should know that your powers are always going to be attracted to a Fae with autumnal energy. It is your opposite on the wheel."

"I'm not Fae. I'm human," I explain.

She manages to make her snort sound delicate. "You are far from human, and I feel the Fae energy coming off you in waves. Your power is the power of Faery and specifically autumn. You are part of the wheel. You turn it with your own hands. Your power is ancient, far older even than me. How do you not know this, Spring? You married a death goddess and did not realize how your powers flow from one another?"

Okay. Whoa. "What is that supposed to mean?"

Rhys seems to calm when his hands are on me. "I am not sure, my goddess. I will admit I'm a bit confused. But to answer your question, Ostara, no, I did not grow up in Fae society. My twin is human, and my sister is what we call a companion on my plane."

"The Earth plane." She seems to taste the words. "We are connected to it here. I have been many times, but it's been so long for my goddess. Ostara left with the Tuatha Dé Danann. She's always longed for her home plane. It's why I felt you and your power so keenly. Your spring is rooted in the Earth plane while Ostara's has adapted over the years."

"So you're the host," Rhys surmises. "You go by Ostara as well? I've heard some ascended gods take on the name of their hosts."

"You are not completely uninformed then if you understand what an ascended god is," Ostara says. "As for your question, my name as a mortal was Meadow, though according to Ostara I had many names over my lifetimes. I was born on a far-off Fae plane twenty-five years ago. I am the child of a high priestess and her consort. I struggled with my magic, though I had a happy childhood. I was told my blockages came from a traumatic end to my last life. My people worried I would not find a goddess who would be attracted to me given my bad dreams and flashes of past lives. But when it came time for my attempted ascension, Ostara came to me." A brilliant smile flashes on her face. "She told me I was not damaged, merely waiting to pull the pieces of myself together again."

"You remember your past lives?" I have met several people who claim to. It always makes me wonder where that light takes them and what choices we are given when we pass.

She shakes her head. "Not exactly. I dream some nights. I dream about being murdered, but worse I feel this ache because I know I'm losing more than my life. I'm losing something so important I can't live without it, don't want to. But I can't remember what it is." She waves a hand. "But this matters not. What does is Ostara is with me, and your father can bring her back into her power. It is why we are marrying."

Somehow I don't think the Devinshea who rules this plane is so magnanimous. If he is willing to unleash Ostara's power, I suspect he's going to get something out of it.

"Your goddess was weakened by something?" Rhys asks. "I did spend some time in *sitheins* connected to the Earth plane. My mother found a way to allow us to know the Fae part of our heritage, though only until I reached my eleventh year. This is my first time back in Faery."

Ostara eyes him. Or rather Meadow. I don't think we've met the goddess yet. "And yet I feel your elemental status."

"I ascended on the Earth plane and consider myself the High Priest of all Earthly Fae. May I ask what happened to Ostara that she would be weak? I ask because I once heard a story of an ascended being giving his energy to save a loved one, and he was weak for a long time."

I squeeze his hand because I know this tale. Bris gave his life spark to Daniel to revive him from what Arawn had done. It's one of the many reasons I know the royals don't trust the death god.

"Ostara gave much of her energy in battle many years before," Meadow explains. "There are many who believe she should have waited and watched for a stronger host, but I am glad she picked me." She smiles as though listening to something inside her head and then nods. "She believes meeting you here and now is a sign of good luck. She has been a bit worried about the king, but now you have settled all of her fears."

"How?" I'm pretty sure the answer to this question is going to sting.

She is still, as though having a discussion with the goddess in her body. She finally looks back our way. "It is easy to see the purity of your magic. I can feel it. She worries about what she feels coming off the king. One of the reasons the king left the plane was to cleanse himself. I understand why he had to take control of the kingdom. The things his mother and brother did…" She shudders delicately. "However, no matter his reasoning, murder takes a toll."

"So you believe my father's dark energy was from the acts he was forced to commit to save his kingdom from my uncle and grandmother," Rhys says carefully.

Well, we both know that isn't true, but it's clear to me Ostara doesn't talk to the dead the way I do.

And it's also clear Rhys believes me. Trusts in me.

His energy feeds mine and mine his in ways we do not fully understand.

She nods. "Yes. I know you will hear fearsome stories of your father, but he is not who they portray him to be. I have found him to be a tough but kind man. And a patient one. I do not wish to bind myself to him physically. He is willing to find his affection elsewhere."

Yeah, according to everything I've heard, he does that a lot. I mean a lot. "So it's to be a marriage in name only?"

"For now. I hope when Ostara is strong enough, my feelings might change." She shakes her head. "You don't know that. You can't be certain."

Is that what I look like when I'm talking to the dead? Because apparently I look a little crazy, and I do not take that word for granted.

It strikes me forcibly that I haven't seen a shade in hours. Not since we entered the palace grounds.

I know the Fae are long lived, but this place is ancient. There should be dead around.

"Sorry. She believes we will know when we find our true mate," Meadow explains. "She does not believe it is Devinshea Quinn, but she intends to honor my will. We need her power back on my plane. It has been infected with blight, and our spring will not come. The wheel will not turn. We are left in permanent winter. The king will fix the problem, and we will open our hearts to him."

I kind of think that's a bad plan and Meadow should listen to her inner goddess. "How does he plan to strengthen Ostara?"

"Oh, he is wise and well-traveled. In his many travels across the planes, he met a smart magician who knows much about restoring the spirit and opening doors between the planes."

Both Rhys and I stiffen at the same time. I don't know about him, but I am sure as hell filled with dread.

"And what is the name of this magician?" I force myself to ask the question even as every cell in my body knows the answer.

"Myrddin," she says with a smile. "Myrddin Emrys."

Well, fuck.

Chapter Fourteen

Zoey

I stare at the food set out in front of us and hope that Bibi told the kitchen staff that now's not a good time to kill us all.

I'm hungry. My morning sickness is gone and now baby wants some food, but I worry about that cold iron dust. After all, even when growing a baby abomination, one must consider nutrition.

"It's fine." Dev stares at me across the table. He glances up at the beautifully dressed servants waiting by the entrance. We're dining in the most intimate of the dining rooms. I say intimate, but it still seats twenty, and the open-air walls that look out over the grounds make it seem even larger. "I promise."

I nod and take a bite of the salad, noticing how Rhys keeps staring at our guest. Although I suppose we're in fact her guest.

It's weird since she thinks she's marrying my husband.

"Maybe I should eat in my room," I say tentatively.

The goddess, who told me I should call her either Ostara or Meadow, cocks her head and sends me a quizzical look. "Why would you do that?"

"I suspect my go…Zoey is worried her presence will offend you since we are engaged to be married," Dev says evenly.

Rhys and Shy explained the meeting with Ostara, though we're still trying to feel her out. And to figure out if her Myrddin Emrys is another version of ours. As tales go, this one feels confusing and poorly plotted out. Like the writer was high or something.

Ostara smiles, her teeth a perfect white and eyes sparkling. "Oh, no. I am not offended at all. I'm Fae, Zoey. Even if your husband was the Devinshea I'm going to marry, I would not be offended by his lover. We are not in love. He is simply kind enough to aid me and my plane." She glances around. "I am curious as to why the vampire is not here. The one I saw you with earlier when you entered the palace."

Daniel is busy checking the place out. And by that I mean he's casing Devinshea's rooms, trying to figure out if Evil Dev keeps the important amulets in the same place his mom did. Neil is going with him as backup, and Sasha is doing his Sasha thing. Hanging out in shadows and listening.

"He does not eat," Rhys explains. "Have you never met a vampire before? Is that why you're so curious about him?"

"He feels familiar to me," she says. "Ostara would like to meet him."

See, it's weird when she talks about herself like that. She told us her Fae name is Meadow, but she often goes by Ostara now. Simpler, she said. Nothing about this situation feels simple to me. "I'm sure that can be arranged. So you are from another... Wait. What did you mean by even if my Devinshea was yours?"

Ostara gives us all a beatific smile. "I read energy very well. I thought that was the case, but I have never met Rhys nor his goddess so I could not be sure. Being in the room with this Devinshea makes it all clear. Your energy is off, and not in a way that would let me know you come from another plane. Though I feel that as well."

We all stare at the goddess, wondering exactly how to handle the situation. If she goes to the guards, will they believe her?

"Perhaps we should hold this discussion for a time when we are alone," Dev says, glancing at the servants. Telling me not to give anything away.

Ostara waves a hand. "Oh, the servants in this dining hall are all spelled so they cannot hear unless it is a command for them. Devinshea says it is because of the rebellion, to protect both them and him. The rebels won't hurt the servants if they know they can get no information from them. The king has been hurt many times. I will help him and this land heal."

"I'm not so sure he deserves your help," Dev says with a sigh. "Fine. Since you already seem to understand we don't belong here, Ostara, I am the High Priest of the Fae of a plane connected to the Earth plane. This is my goddess, and the vampire you are so interested in is my partner. Can you get us home to our timeline? We are in danger here. It is clear to me you have faith in this timeline's Devinshea Quinn, but I find myself horrified at the things he's done and worry what he will do if he returns home and finds me and my family in his palace."

"We can explain," Ostara says. "He is a reasonable man."

"I know the spell you are talking about when it comes to the servants," Dev replies, his mouth a flat line. "Did he explain that it is permanent? That those he uses it on can never again hear anything but the commands of the masters of this palace?"

Ostara pales, the pixies in her hair stilling. "We do not have such spells on my plane. You must be mistaken."

"Bibi, could you tell the goddess what you know of the spell and why you were not subject to it?" Dev asks.

Bibi stands, showing herself. She was sitting in shadows by the fireplace, keeping watch. "I am not allowed to speak to the king's fiancée."

"But why?" Ostara rises and gets to one knee, holding out her hand. "I love all of the Fae. Little trolls and brownies are my dearest friends on my home plane. They are beloved. I hate the term lesser. You are not less than a *sidhe*. You are beautiful, little one. Why would I not wish to speak with you? I have been worried that the trolls and dwarves and gnomes are afraid of me for some reason."

Bibi stares at that outstretched hand for a second and then slowly places her own in it. "Mistress, we are not allowed to speak with *sidhe* unless we are serving them. It is the king's command. He hates the lesser Fae. I am only not subject to the spell because I typically work in the gardens, and it is necessary to discuss how and when we will plant. The king gave up his Green Man powers years ago."

"Asshole," Dev says under his breath. "I would like to kick my own ass. Why would I give up my fertility powers?"

"For darker powers that are not compatible," Bibi explains.

Ostara stands, tears in her eyes. "I do not understand. Devinshea told me it was his mother who made these rules, and he is attempting to change them. He told me society changes slowly, but he thought marrying me would help speed things along."

"Devinshea lies," I say and look back at my husband. "The other one, of course. I am curious what happened that changed you here. It sounds like your childhood was relatively the same. At least you had your mother and brother. Bibi, do you know anything about why your king is so angry with the lesser Fae?"

"He is angry with everyone," Bibi explains in her quiet tone, looking at the servants as though they will tell on her. "I know a few things. You should understand that even when his mother was queen, there were tensions, though Miria was fair enough. As a prince he fell in love with a commoner. Have you noticed the courtiers staring at you, Zoey?"

"I have," I acknowledge, though I thought it was simply prurient interest. Now I wonder. "She looked like me, didn't she?"

Bibi nods. "She was a woman who lived in a far-off village. At the time the king was the second son. He was free to pursue his education as he would. They had a son. One who looks very much like your own."

"Lee. In this timeline he doesn't have a twin brother," I surmise.

Rhys snorts. "I'm sure that's made him so much better."

Shy sends him a shut-the-hell-up look and he does. Rhys had not been surprised to hear his brother was causing trouble in another timeline.

"No, there is only the one, and he is not considered proper for the line of succession since his mother was a commoner."

"I can tell you the rest of the story. I know what went wrong. He was not allowed to marry her." Dev sighs. "My brother did not think my goddess was a proper one. He attempted to strong-arm me out of the marriage, but I had been on my own for years. I was strong and held up by my goddess and my partner. So in this timeline, my brother got his way. Likely because I stayed here instead of moving my whole life to the Earth plane. So this me has a bastard son and a version of Zoey who likely loathes me. I would like to avoid an angry alternate of you, my goddess. You can do a lot of damage when you've been wronged. Although…"

I frown my husband's way because I know exactly what he's thinking. "Not happening."

He's got visions of two Zoeys in bed. It would not go well.

"Oh, she is dead," Bibi replies, cutting us off at the pass. "She was killed by a group of ogres, and that is when the prince began spending much time with the royals who prefer the company of only *sidhe*."

Dev looks my way. "So you die and I fall under the influence of the Duke of Ain. That is horrible and makes sense."

The Duke of Ain. In our time, he wanted a *sithein* free of lesser Fae. Devinshea had called the Wild Hunt down on him. But in this timeline, he listened. In this life, he got inside Devinshea's head and corrupted him. I didn't like the idea of the duke hanging around. I might have hated the duke, but he was clever and he didn't mind getting his hands bloody. "Is the duke around? Or is he off plane with the king?"

"The king took most of his retinue," Ostara explains. "It is why the palace guard is so confused. You came back with people they don't know and without any of your normal security. But they also aren't creative thinkers. Eoin asked if I thought something was wrong and I told him you simply found some friends you wanted to impress."

"Everyone is used to the king's mercurial moods," Bibi adds. "And everyone knows he is looking for his lost love. Her name was Zandra. I've heard it said the wizard has promised to find her for him so he can have another chance."

"Well, that makes some sense," Dev admits quietly, his eyes finding mine. "I think we often seek out our soulmates. I have two, and it seems without them I am nothing."

I reach out and hold his hand before turning back to our guest, who brushes away a tear. "Are you all right? I'm sorry to put you in this position. I don't think this Devinshea is capable of truly helping you."

"I fear he is planning something far darker." Dev's accent turns very Irish, and Bris is here. He brings my hand to his lips, kissing it before he stands. "Ostara of the Wind and Rains, I am Bris. I was an agricultural deity on the Earth plane in a place called Ireland."

Ostara smiles, a genuinely delighted expression. "It is lovely to meet you. It's been so long since I met an ancient one." Ostara seems to think, but I believe she's having one of those inner conversations. It's obvious to me these two are not as well integrated as Devinshea and Bris. "My goddess is excited to see you, but she is asking questions. Is the vampire truly your soul's mate?"

Bris frowns but his tone is gentle. "He is Devinshea's. There is no question about it. I worry that is why the Devinshea of this timeline has chosen an evil path. He requires Daniel and Zoey to be complete."

"Daniel." She seems to taste his name on her tongue, and now my worry creeps in. What does a goddess of spring want with my vampire? "Yes, a lovely name for him this time around. He is happy?"

Well, not really right now. He wants off this plane. "He is happy with our marriage. May I ask why you wish to know? Did you know Daniel in some way?"

She takes a breath and shakes her beautiful blonde hair. "It matters not now. Ostara has other questions. I'm afraid she has always been suspicious of our fiancé. What do you think he is doing?"

Bris turns to Shy. "Daughter, what do the spirits say?"

I feel like I'm missing something, but I give my attention to Shy, too. I'll ask Danny later.

A concerned expression sits on Shy's lovely face. "The spirits I met in the forest loathe the king. I believe they would say he is capable of all manner of evil. As for the ones in the palace, there are none. I do not sense or feel them."

"Is that normal?" Bris is unusually anxious, his worry clear. Something is bothering him. Likely the idea of being out of his timeline.

"No." Shy closes her eyes and seeks something the rest of us can't feel or see. When she opens them again, her eyes seem darker, as though she's tapped into power. "I can usually feel death energy. Animals, humans, even plants die all the time. My mother used to describe it as magic. There's a magic to death, an energy that turns the wheel. Even as one thing dies, another is born. Or reborn, as she would say." She shakes her head as though realizing something. "Ostara recently told me. She said the wheel doesn't stop at death. Death turns the wheel. All this time I've been worried my power would harm Rhys's."

"Your power fuels mine as mine fuels yours." Rhys puts a hand on hers, a brilliant smile playing on his face. "Baby, I know you think I should be with some sweet Fae girl, someone whose powers are similar to mine. I know you thought I was attracted to Ostara."

Ostara gasps and puts a hand to her chest. "No. That would be terrible."

Rhys shakes his head. "She smells cloyingly of gardenias and fresh rain."

A brow rises over my soon-to-be daughter-in-law's eyes.

"I am used to it from me," Rhys replies, bringing her hand to his lips. "When we return, ask my brother. I was never attracted to submissive Fae girls. I liked the ones who could kick my ass, and I promise I'm going to be better about trusting you. I'm so in love with you and so afraid I'll lose you that I'm practically making it into truth. If you wish to go to the mountains tomorrow, we shall go." His eyes go to Bris. "My goddess believes there is something wrong with the mountains to the north. She was told there are sluagh there."

Ostara nods. "I have heard rumors about the mountains. That the dead are congregating there."

"Specifically sluagh," Shy explains. "My question is why are there no dead in the palace? I don't sense any wards that would keep them out. Those have to be incredibly strong since it's natural for the dead to be around. Well, as natural as it can be to remain in a state of flux. But there is nothing here. No shades or spirits. It is disconcerting. It's like we crossed a line when we left the forest and now there are no spirits. I'd like to talk to the dead in the mountains and see if they know what's happening. It's obvious that this Devinshea is eliminating what he considers non-helpful Fae. But why would he only do it in the forests? Did he purge his household when he became king? Send them away?"

It is Bibi's voice that answers, tremulous but strong. "He slaughtered many lesser Fae. It is why my master has begun recruiting from the Unseelie *sitheins*."

"So he's the one who sent the chimera," I muse.

"Of course it was Lee who sent a monster to kill us all," Rhys complains, but I also notice he's still holding Shy's hand, still staring at her like she's the sun in the sky.

Like he knows what Ostara explained to her, what she now understands will make a huge difference in her accepting their relationship. Perhaps going on a mission together will seal their bond, though I worry about them making the journey with his face so close to his father's. And apparently the leader of the resistance.

"The question now is why Arawn would send us here. And why would he not be here to greet us or send us further instructions?" Devinshea has taken over the body again, and he stops at the edge of the open-air windows, looking out over the starry night. "It makes no sense."

The door opens and Neil walks in. I stand. Earlier he chose to go with Daniel while Cassie and Brendan stayed with the Cŵn Annwn. They went down to the kitchens to find some food for all of them, and we were going to meet back up in our rooms to decide on which path to take. We're only certain of one thing. We can't stay here.

Perhaps we should all go to the mountains.

"Hey," I begin, looking at my bestie who seems to have found some Fae clothes to change into. "You hungry?"

"Zoey," Devinshea begins. "That's not our…"

That is the moment Neil raises a crossbow and shoots it toward my husband.

Rhys is on his feet in a heartbeat, running toward his father.

Devinshea manages to take the arrow in the arm rather than the chest. He groans as the blood begins to bloom, and Neil is joined by a group of Fae I don't recognize.

I stand and step close to Shy, reaching for her hand.

"Look at his ears," Shy whispers.

I realize what my husband intended to say. Neil's ears are longer, pointed in that delicate way of the Fae.

"Neil," Bibi begins.

But Neil holds out a hand. "In a moment, Bibi. Servants, you can leave or you can die. We don't wish to harm any of you, but we will. The pretender must die for all Fae to be free. Lee, it's time."

Bibi reaches for his coattail, tugging it. "Neil, it is not what you think."

Lee steps inside dressed in all black leathers and looking dangerous. This is my son and not my son. He is older than my Lee, infinitely harder. He has scars my baby boy never took even before his turn made him perfect again. He frowns at Devinshea on the floor, and his eyes flare at the sight of his twin. Well, his alternative's twin. "Another by blow, Father? Damn but your wickedness runs true. He could be my twin. He's evil, you know, brother. Anything he told you to bring you here is a lie."

Rhys stands in front of his father. "He is not your father. He is mine."

"Master, you are mistaken," Bibi says, a bit of desperation in her voice.

"Sir, this is not the king you seek," Ostara tries.

Lee frowns at the goddess of spring. "You are his fiancée. He's going to murder you, too, you know. He wants the energy your goddess can give him. That fucking wizard has done the impossible. He's corrupted Devinshea Quinn further. Well, it stops now. You made a mistake coming back without your witches and your guard."

"Son," Dev begins. "I am not the..."

Lee pulls his bow and arrow.

"No," I yell. "Rhys, do something."

I hear the beginnings of a rumble from outside.

That's not the only sound I hear. Growling.

The servants have made themselves scarce, with the exception of Bibi. There are ten Fae guards backing up the alternate versions of Lee and Neil. As the big white wolf begins to stalk inside the dining hall, some of the arrows shift his way.

Neil. He heard something and he's come. My Neil. We have one shot at surprising them since they are not listening to Bibi or Ostara. "Change, Neil. Show them who you are. Show your Fae version who you are."

Fae Neil turns slightly, and his eyes widen first as he takes in me, and then at the sight of his own naked werewolf self standing in front of him.

"Zandra?" Neil breathes. "Lee, stand down. Something is wrong."

"This is our chance, Uncle," Lee insists and then his bow drops as he sees me for the first time. "Mama?"

Tears pierce my eyes at the emotion behind the word. Like my own baby boy who missed me for twelve years. It's right there in his eyes. The deep longing for the relationship that was stripped from him. A loving mother. A hand in his. Cookies for his belly and stories at night to fill his soul. He is a man. Perhaps older than my Lee. But the child inside still wants his mother. Will always want his mother.

I step away from the women even as I see green vines starting to creep along the open windows.

"Mom," Rhys warns.

I shake my head and move to this version of my son. So alike and yet there's a scar on his chin mine does not have. I stand right in front of him and put my hand to his face, rubbing the deep groove. "Did she soothe you when you got this? I would kiss my Lee's boo-boos and bandage him up even though I would use vampire blood to ensure he healed. He liked the ritual."

Lee's eyes close. "You are not my mother."

"Not in this time," I reply quietly. "But I assure you I love you, and I also promise that man who looks like the monster who sired you is not."

"I am Devinshea Conlan-Quinn," Dev says, his eyes tight. "In my time, I am High Priest of the Unseelie and Seelie Fae."

Lee looks his way but does not move from me. "We have no high priest. Certainly not one we would share with the Unseelie. Why would you name them first?"

"Because the Seelies can be assholes," Dev replies. "I greatly prefer the dark court. It's far more honest, and they don't force my goddess to wear their flowy gowns. She complains. She loves her weapons, and they are far too hard to get to with all that..."

"Fabric," Lee finishes. "My mother hated them, too. She preferred the country because she could wear pants and defend herself. Once she told me she would rather be a goblin."

I've said it before many times. How odd the things that are the same and different. "I have a couple of knives on me and my Ruger."

"What is that?" Lee asks and then shakes his head and steps back. "This is some kind of trick. We have one shot at this. Our witches have taken out the guards. Uncle, we should kill them."

Other Neil is busy staring at himself. He waves Lee off. "You're not going to kill your mother. Even if she's not technically your mother. She's obviously some version of Z. You know I told you about other planes. And we're not killing this magnificent creature. What am I?"

My Neil puts his hands on his hips. "Werewolf. You know I always thought I would make a gorgeous Fae. You are keeping it tight, mister. Proud of you."

Other Neil nods. It's good to know neither of them suffers from self-consciousness. "You, too. Damn. What are you doing to get those abs?"

"Oh, it's werewolf DNA. And this is my body after two kids. I keep telling Z it's not that hard," Neil says with a grin. "Seriously, we're not from this plane or this timeline. We got sent here by a death god who now that I think about it never actually asked us himself. Sent a crone and some dumb hellhounds. That's lazy, right?"

"Or it's a trap," Other Neil acknowledged. "You think they were setting you up to be killed by us?"

"Or you up to be killed by us," my Neil agreed. "And therefore be vulnerable. Isn't it odd it all occurs while King Evil happens to be off plane, and then we find out he's working with our own personal nemesis, Myrddin the Dick Face Wizard?"

"We can't be sure it's our Myrddin." Dev grimaces but he's more relaxed.

"What do you mean?" Lee asks. "Yours? I'm afraid I'm extremely confused."

"That does not surprise me." Rhys helps his father move toward the table. "You were always terrible at school. You would never pay attention."

"What is school?" Lee asks.

Rhys gestures his way. "My point is made. Lee is always Lee. He runs on charm and recklessness and pure emotion. Did you even think about the fact that you are seemingly an army of ten against all of the palace?"

"I feel the weirdest urge to punch you right in the face," Lee says with a sigh and looks at me. "You had two of us?"

"And two girls and one on the way," I admit. "And you were not bad at school. You were a bit distracted. You are very, very smart, son. In our time, you often solve mysteries."

"And catch venereal diseases," Rhys mutters.

"Rhys," Shy groans.

"Well, he is already checking you out, my goddess," Rhys accuses. "I know exactly how he works. He might have a few different scars, but he is Lee. I shared a womb with him. I know what he is thinking. She is mine, Lee. Mine. I do not share."

Lee's lips curl in the most lascivious grin as he takes in Shy. "He's not wrong. I wasn't going to kill you, gorgeous. I was going to offer to take care of you, of course."

Shy's eyes roll. "Yep, there he is."

It seems the real danger passed. For now. "How did you incapacitate the guards? Permanently? Or should we get out of here?"

Maybe we would be safer in a rebel camp. It's not like Rhys and Shy and Neil and his kids don't know how to get along in one.

"We have two witches who are covering this part of the palace and the guard house. It should come as no surprise that the king doesn't inspire loyalty," Lee says. "They won't risk themselves if they think for a bare second that they can get away with it."

"Are they the reason I couldn't bring the vines and trees to my aid?" Rhys asks, looking down at his father's injury. The arrow is sticking out of his upper bicep. "I could pull them from the ground, but they would not come in through the windows."

"You must be strong," Lee says as the Neils start to chat and the others take up positions around the dining hall. "The witches are warding to keep all magic from being performed in the palace. I think you got through those. The windows are warded by the palace witches to keep me out. Fucker didn't think I could find a way around it, but I did. You are truly another Devinshea?"

Dev winces and gives Rhys a nod. He grits his teeth and Rhys pulls the arrow through, blood soaking Dev's shirt. Dev manages to keep his pain to a low groan. His eyes are weary as he looks at the young man who could have been our son. "I am. I am a Devinshea who left the *sithein* for the human plane. My father was human, and I went to live with him as a young man. I took care of him until he died, and then I built his businesses up and one day I met a gorgeous redhead and her vampire boyfriend."

How quickly he forgets. "Not at the time he wasn't."

"A vampire?" Lee asks and his jaw drops. "You are in a ménage relationship with my mother and a vampire?"

"Yes," Devinshea says and flexes his arm. "As you can see, I regularly take his blood so this wound is already healed. Thank you, son."

Rhys pats his father's shoulder and moves back to Shy. "You should expect my dad to rush in the minute he gets close enough to smell Papa. He is protective of his precious blood. You should be happy you have a face he will recognize."

Lee stares at Rhys, an intense look in his eyes. "Were they good to you? Not Mother. She was wonderful. When I close my eyes I hear her singing to me, feel her hand in my hair. See what they did to her."

Rhys is quiet for a moment and his eyes are bright as he takes in this version of his twin. "She was taken from me, too. From us. Me and Lee and Evangeline. Myrddin took our father's crown and sent them through a portal. They did not return for years. We were on the run, and each night I would close my eyes and hear her voice and feel her kiss on my cheek. But I also heard my papa telling me he loves me. I remembered my dad hugging me. They weren't good to me. They were everything to me."

Tears cling to my cheeks and I make eye contact with Devinshea, who watches our sons, absolutely feeling our loss, hearing our son say he missed us, loves us. Wishes we had that time together.

But we must appreciate the time we have now.

"And we are brothers in your time?" Lee sniffles but holds it together.

"You are my deeply obnoxious brother," Rhys returns. "How we are twins, I have no idea. You create chaos wherever you go."

"So pretty much the same," Other Neil snarks. He's beside my Neil, who has no problem standing there with his dingus hanging out. I'm suddenly worried for his husband. They might decide to date.

"I love you, brother. I say that unashamedly and without hesitation. I would give my life for you and I would trust you with everything that matters to me. We are more than brothers. You are part of me," Rhys vows.

"In another time," Lee says softly.

"In all of the times," Rhys replies, his voice strong, unwavering. "Even if you turned out like your father, but you should know I would protect the world from you. I will help you take out this version of the man even though it makes my heart ache to do so because somewhere in there is my papa. He just took a wrong turn."

"A wildly insane turn," Dev complains. "I don't even understand what he's doing. He gives up his Green Man powers? Chooses to not ascend?"

Other Neil moves to Lee's side, seeming to get serious. It's easy to tell that he is Lee's second in command. He likely had a large hand in raising him after his mother was murdered. "He went insane after he learned of Zandra's death. The king was not always as he is now. He was selfish, but I do believe he truly loved Z. He came to our village many times after he pledged he would not marry her. He was even a halfway decent father to Lee for many years. But then the queen declared he must marry."

"My father did not wish to marry," Lee continues. "He was content to be something of a husband and a father two or three times a year. He would come to our village and it would be good for a few weeks and he would be gone again. Mother had a friend who constantly told her she deserved better. But she wouldn't listen to him."

"Let me guess. Sandy hair and dimples? Blue eyes?" our Neil asks.

"Yes, Deiniol did have those attributes," Other Neil agrees.

The thought makes my heart clench. "Is he here with you?"

Lee's head shakes. "No. After Declan Quinn sent his assassins to kill me and my mother, it was Deinny who saved me, who took me to Neil and asked him to hide me. To keep me safe. And then he went to the palace to kill the prince. He showed Devinshea the evidence and that was when my father went mad. In his grief, he killed his mother and brother, took the throne and burned Deinny at the stake because he would not give up my location. I believe by that point, Deinny knew Devinshea couldn't be trusted."

"But you're his son," I say, feeling so much for the tragedies these versions of ourselves had gone through.

"I was his rival at that point," Lee explains. "For all Uncle Neil claims the king was a decent father, I believe he was merely obsessed with my mother and once she was gone, he shut away the tiny part of himself that could love. I'm his bastard, and I'm someone the rebels could rally around. The last with Quinn blood."

"So you're taking his throne?" Dev asks.

"I care not for the throne. Let the damn royals figure it out," Lee explains. "I want peace in my lands. I want all of the Fae to live in harmony again. He has thrown off the balance of the world, and I intend to restore it."

"Is Myrddin from this realm?" I want to know if this is the same Myrddin we're dealing with.

Out of the corner of my eye, I see Sasha walk into the room. "Your Highness, we must move now."

"Oh, why would you leave so soon, my love?"

From the opposite entrance, my husband walks in. My not husband. This version of himself practically glows with dark magic. And his smile is the most predatory thing I've ever seen.

Unfortunately, he's not alone.

"Hello, Zoey. I do believe I told you this wasn't over," Myrddin Emrys says.

And I know we are much too late.

Chapter Fifteen

Shy

My blood threatens to run cold as the wizard looks us over.

This is Myrddin Emrys. The man who killed my family. He's standing right there, and the desperate urge to reach for a blade and tear out his throat is almost overwhelming.

"Don't," Rhys whispers. "He's not alone. Can you feel them?"

His hand slides against mine and he moves slightly in front of me, shielding me with his own body. He's right. I do feel something. There's something here. Something we cannot see.

"My uncle could do it. He kept a hidden guard with him," Rhys whispers. "Be careful. You won't see them until they slit your throat."

One of the rebels hoists his bow up, aiming at the king, but the space around him twists and turns and he's pulled into…nowhere.

"I've never seen my uncle do that before," Rhys whispers.

"Would anyone else like to try me?" the king asks, his lips turned up in a cruel approximation of a smile.

"Z?" Neil stares at his queen, his best friend, but he has to be thinking of Cassie and Brendan. His children. There's a tortured look in his eyes.

Go, Zoey mouths, and in an instant, he's a wolf again, running past the guards at breakneck speed.

"Leave him. He's incidental. We'll take him out later. Everyone important is here with one exception. I told you it would work," the wizard says, putting a hand on the king's shoulder like they're old friends. "I told you I could return her to you. Though you'll have to take care of him first. I suspect he will object to you taking his wife."

Devinshea already moved to stand in front of Zoey, his clothes tattered and bloody. "You will not take my goddess."

"Your goddess?" The king looks her over, his gaze stopping on her neck. "Is that the Goddess Chain? Then you are exactly what Myrddin says."

"Devinshea, they are no threat to us." Ostara stands, her gentle voice tremulous. She puts a hand to her chest as though speaking from the heart or trying to work her will. "They are not here to harm us. They simply want to get back to their own time."

"Oh, they won't allow that, golden one." Sasha stares at her with an intensity I rarely see on his face. "They are the ones who sent us here, and that means they will know who we are and how to kill us."

The Fae guard who had come with Lee all stand at attention, their bodies tense and weapons out. It's obvious they're not sure what to do. It would seem like Myrddin and King Devinshea are outnumbered, but we can all feel the wrongness of this room, the unseen threat.

Lee, however, stands and stares his father's way. "She is not my mother. Not the Zandra you knew."

The king of this land cannot seem to take his eyes off her. "She will do, son. She is the payment I required from the wizard for aiding him with his plans. And for being an excellent teacher. Shall I show you what he taught me?"

The wizard holds out a hand. "Not yet. I told you we must find the vampire king. He is more dangerous than you can imagine. This is why I insisted on the wards and spells we placed on the palace. They will weaken him. He should already be feeling their power. The Deiniol you knew was weak and gentle. This is a version of him unlike any other. Do not underestimate him."

"I can handle any Deinny who comes my way," the Fae king promises. "And any weakling version of myself. I wish to be done with this. I don't like seeing his hands on my concubine. I want to kill him."

"I told you we can't kill him so easily." A tinge of irritation seeps into Myrddin's tone. "Like your fiancée, he is an ascended god. We must separate the god from the vessel and then we can feed from both. Their mortal souls are nothing compared to the gods inside."

And now I know why there are no dead here.

The king of this Seelie *sithein* has turned into a soul eater. It's something I've heard of but never believed in. A soul is sacrosanct. However, if anyone could figure out a way to do it, it is Myrddin.

It makes my stomach roll.

"Rhys, we have to get away. We have to get everyone out of here," I whisper.

I don't know what he's doing with the souls, but we can't risk it. If he's found a way to truly destroy a soul, they won't merely kill us. They will harness our souls to feed their magic. I'm not sure if he wants to destroy the soul or shackle it, tormenting it for power. Either way, I want to avoid it.

Did he do that to my family?

"Fine," the king of the Seelies says, command in his voice. "Guards, take…myself, I guess. Take this thing with my face to the dungeons."

"He will find me hard to separate, my goddess." Bris has taken over the body, his eyes fully emerald. "It will take days. Daniel will find you. We will stay alive. We will survive."

"Well, he's not wrong about the days of torture part," Evil Dev agrees as two guard wind their way out of space and time. One minute there's a whooshing sound and the next there are two large Fae guards, reaching out to bind Bris's hands behind his back. "But I will break him, and I will take his power as my own. It is time I am allowed in my own bloody temple again."

Lee looks my way. Or rather our way. I think his words are truly meant for Rhys. "Yes, my father's temple is alive. It stopped allowing him in when he started eating souls."

"Is that how you got in, you little shit?" Evil Dev's eyes roll. "I should have known. I would burn the place down but it won't let me."

So that's where we run. To the temple.

"It keeps them all out," Lee promises. "The temple is a living being. It knows how evil you are."

"And I will use the power from this entity to take it over again. I will trick it with Ostara's power and then destroy it with the energy I get from myself." The king walks over to Bris. "And you should know that while my guards peel the god from your soul and serve him up to me on a silver platter, that I will be winning back the woman who should have been at my side."

"I think I might enjoy being a queen," Zoey says quietly. "My Devinshea wouldn't take the crown no matter how much I argued. I thought we should. I thought he should be stronger. I knew he was stronger than Miria. Than Declan."

Rhys gasps behind me, his fingers tightening on me, but I know exactly what the queen is doing.

And so does Myrddin. "She is lying, Your Majesty. Do not believe a word she says. She is already plotting."

But it's easy to see the king wants to believe. When Zoey moves to his side, his shoulders come down, he softens. He takes her hand. "I would love to hear about your life, Zandra. I would also love to show you the kind of life I can give you."

"Her name is Zoey," Bris says.

"Her name is whatever I say it is," the king announces and then turns to Ostara. "Take her as well. I never intended to marry you, you worthless fleck of womanhood. I shall eat your weak goddess and then raze your dying plane to serve my friend. Myrddin will use all I give him to free us from this so-called balance."

"I am sorry, my lord." Zoey's tone is soft, though I know the tears on her cheeks are real, I also know she's shifted into a role.

All the books and plays, the stories the rebels told of the history of the royals, served more than to entertain us. While the royals and Kelsey were gone, many works about them were written. Plays and songs as well. To keep them with us. Those tales taught us. Zoey Donovan-Quinn was in this position before. She allowed herself to be taken into custody with the belief that her husband would come for her. She did it to save the people she loved, as she hopes she is doing now. She knows she can manipulate the king. She is buying us all time.

Rhys must know that as well since he stays calm when the evil king takes his mother's hand.

"You would betray me to save yourself?" Bris asks.

I hope he's acting because he sounds so forlorn.

"You know I always take care of myself first," she says quietly.

Oh, she does not. That woman never left a person behind if she wasn't forced to.

Two more guards show up to take Ostara into custody.

She looks pale and fragile as they place her in chains. And then her eyes change and for the first time I truly believe she is ascended. Her goddess takes control of the body.

Searing green eyes find Sasha, and I feel a wind whip against me, the promise of a storm. The whole room smells of rain and electricity.

"I charge you, Oleg Federov," she says in a deeper voice than before. "I look deep in her soul and I see you there. You. Oleg. Save her. You couldn't the first time. You lost her and…" She seems to think, to hunt a mind that is not her own for some knowledge she needs. "You lost her and Natasha. Marta. Her name was Marta. She dreams of you at night but cannot quite remember. She did everything she could for you, for her husband. She gave her life for your daughter. Save her. You might have found other soulmates, but you owe her. I will keep her alive. Come for her."

For the first time since I have known that vampire, tears fill his eyes as they cart out Ostara. He takes a single step toward them but Zoey holds out a hand, and a slight shake of her head makes Sasha stop. His jaw tightens, and I know it's taking everything for him to be still.

But Daniel Donovan is out there, and that means we have to stay alive. It means we have hope.

I feel Rhys's ear against my lips. "If he is the same as my uncle, he can only hold ten. We will only need to deal with six more. I will get you out of here and then we will find my dad and save them."

I nod, praying Rhys remembers his way around this palace.

"I thought she meant Daniel," Zoey says. "When she asked about the vampire, I thought she was talking about Daniel. It's why she thinks you have soul mates. She doesn't understand how long you have been waiting."

"Well, I didn't expect that." Myrddin watches Sasha warily. "Did you find her again? How very sad for you. To look all this time only to find her soul again right before I devour it."

A low growl comes from Sasha's throat, and it's easy to see he's ready to attack. It's also easy to see that would be a mistake.

The room feels tense with anticipation of what awful thing will happen next.

So I pull the focus to me. "Do you destroy the souls or do you keep them somewhere as fuel for your magic?"

Rhys goes stiff, and the whole room turns. Out of the corner of my eye I see Ostara and Bris being taken from the room, magical bindings holding them tight.

Myrddin stares for a moment, pinning me with those pitch black eyes of his. There's a long moment where I swear he's trying to look into my soul. "Fuck me. I missed one. How did you get away?"

"I wasn't home that night." I don't pretend to misunderstand. We're past that, Myrddin Emrys and I. "The night you torched my home, I was at a friend's house."

Myrddin's head shakes. "It was a school night. You should have been... I will kill the dark prophet. I will eat his soul and that of his children. You. He saved you. Guards, take her into custody. I will speak with her in the dungeon. Devinshea, take the rest out and kill them. We need to find the King of All Vampire and his wolves. And then I want to talk to your witches. No one told me there was a seer in the group."

The words threaten to turn my stomach.

He did it. He torched my mom, my sister, my aunts and uncles and cousins, and is mad he didn't get us all.

Something dark opens inside me, and I feel power roll through me for the first time. Not a medium's power. This is ancient. This power inside me is as old as the hills. As long lived as the oceans.

It feels right. Like waking after a long slumber.

The wizard turns, and his eyes widen. "No. No, it can't be. Kill it. Kill it now."

He's pointing at me.

Six guards form, all male and *sidhe*, with long swords or bows.

Sasha takes his shot and jumps the one closest to me.

All of Lee's guards begin to fight, and I hear the clash of swords and whips of crossbows.

The king hauls Zoey out, even as she screams Rhys's and my names. He simply picks her up and walks out, leaving the rest of us behind.

I feel one of the rebels die, his soul lifting up from his body even before it falls to the ground under the guard's sword. I see the spirit, shock on his ghostly face as he is pulled toward the wizard.

He doesn't even have to try. He simply reaches out a hand and drags the soul into his body, light flashing as he is absorbed.

My body aches as I reach out, trying to drag him back, but I don't know how. The impulse is there. It rushes under my skin, but the knowledge is far from me.

I should know. I did know. Once I was this magic and this magic was me.

Swords clang and I'm surrounded by the grunts and groans of battle. Rhys tackles me, taking me to the floor.

I feel his power trying to flare but it's dampened. Myrddin is working some mojo, and I would bet they took out all of the rebel's witches. Myrddin knew about Rhys and his powers, so they are ready for him.

What he isn't ready for is me.

The trouble is I'm only now starting to figure out I have power at all. It's right there. Right in my fingertips, but I can't quite make it work. Terror thrums through me because I can't watch this happen to him. Not to Rhys.

I held back for so long. So long, and now I'm here and I know beyond a shadow of a doubt that if I lose him, I lose the best part of me. I lose the us we can be. I can't.

"We have to go." Lee is suddenly standing over us. "The wizard is held back by the wards, too, but he's taking them down. It won't be long before he's at full power and can kill us all with a glance. I'll take you to the temple. We'll be safe there."

Rhys hauls me up and barely avoids taking a sword to his shoulder. It comes down and hits the ground and Rhys whirls me away. By the time I can look over his shoulder, Lee is gutting the Fae with what I'm sure is cold iron. I see the man's soul begin to leave his body and like the others, it's drawn to the wizard, who doesn't even look up from weaving whatever spell he's working as the male's immortal soul is sucked into his body. And that male was his ally. He doesn't discriminate. He will take them all into his greedy soul.

Sasha makes his way to us, fighting them off with his bare hands. His fangs are out and there's blood coating his tunic as he grabs Rhys's arm. "We're going now."

Lee nods. "We take them to the temple. The king's men can't get in."

I hear a cry and then it feels like the whole world goes still.

Neil. Fae Neil is in one of the last guard's arms, and I watch as he drags a blade over his throat and bright red blood begins to flow.

"Uncle," Lee shouts, but it's far, far too late.

Rhys grabs his brother's hand. "You can't save him."

"I can't..." Lee's face is pale, his eyes tortured. "They'll eat his soul. They'll exterminate everything he is and was and could be again. I can't..."

Neil's soul floats from his body, a confused look on his face, and then he's searching for something. For Lee. He holds a hand out but he's already getting sucked into the vortex that is Myrddin's soul.

I can't. I know him. I know I don't know this Neil, but I *know* him. I know the beautiful, loving, funny variation of him, and I cannot let this pass.

Something opens deep inside of me, something warm and powerful. Like a fire or a boiling pot. Like warmth in winter. That heat flows through me. Strange. I thought any death power would be cold, but there is infinite warmth in this, a calling and longing. There is love in this power.

I hold out my hand, and Neil's soul freezes as though caught between the two of us.

Myrddin interrupts his under-the-breath chanting. Lee said he was pulling down the wards that held magic from this space, but he stops because those wards aren't holding mine at all.

My magic is older than any ward. Wards exists because of my magic. Everything exists because of this sweet heat and light flowing through my veins.

But I am small now. Where once I was infinite, I am now defined and trapped in flesh. I don't completely understand the images flowing through me. They aren't images, exactly. Colors and feelings and impressions of mist and time and a man weeping at what he must do.

Myrddin's eyes glow as he directs his power toward the soul we fight over.

Neil's soul jerks another foot toward him.

His power is greater than mine for the moment. I cannot do it alone.

But just because a soul is dead does not mean his will gone. I can give him a choice.

"Do you see a light?" I ask. "Nothing can stop you if you choose the light. If you choose to move on. He's trying to take you to a place where the light cannot touch."

Neil frowns even as he is moving inexorably toward Myrddin. "I don't see it."

Damn it. For some, it takes a while. His death was so sudden.

"There is nowhere for him to go," Myrddin says with a smile.

But there is.

There's me.

"I offer you my soul space," I say, opening myself to him. I offer that space where Harry Wharton lived for many years.

And Neil takes it. He reaches out, and I realize my power is a golden thread. He holds it and pulls mightily, dragging himself away.

I feel him slam into me and then it's like the world starts again.

Rhys curses and hauls me up and over his shoulder, and then we're running. I barely catch sight of Lee and Sasha covering us as Rhys leaps on the window's edge and over.

We're falling, and I think we're at least three stories up. I brace myself for impact, but vines wrap around us, silky and strong, wresting us from our fall and delivering us gently to the ground.

When I look up, they are doing the same for Sasha and Lee, depositing them on the soft grass next to us.

"Get them!" Myrddin yells.

"The temple is this way." Lee's face is grave in the moonlight. "We have to move quickly. He's almost got the wards down."

We race off into the night.

Chapter Sixteen

Zoey

I *have to stay calm. Calm. Don't let him see you panic.*

It's what I tell myself over and over again as Devilshea hauls me across the palace. That's what I'm calling him now because he's acting like the devil, and I'm going to have to take him down.

What is my Dev going through? Are they already torturing him?

Where is my son? Where is Shy? Are they even alive?

I can't. I can't lose my son. I lost Lee that day in the Council House, felt him die, and even though I knew he would turn, I felt the loss. The loss of his youth and what he could have had as a human. The loss of those years between us, years I should have spent protecting my vulnerable son.

So much fucking loss.

Danny. Where is he? What is Myrddin going to do to my son? To Shy?

I'm a rolling ball of emotion, but I remember this game well. Showing him the truth buys me nothing, and I need something from him. I need him to believe I can be with him. Not today. Not tomorrow, but someday. When the king sets me on my feet, I don't do what I want to do. I don't attack him. I simply stand and let the tears roll down my cheeks.

"Zan...goddess, I never could stand to see you cry. It always killed me. I remember the look on your face when my mother and brother refused to allow us to marry. You looked like this." He appears so much like my husband, the candlelight caressing his golden features, dark hair swaying against his shoulders. In true Fae fashion, the king's hair is long and neatly kept. His hand reaches out and wipes away a tear. "Are you afraid of me?"

I'm fucking terrified of him. "I want to know if my son is alive or if your guards killed him."

His expression softens. "You always were a good mother. I'll give you another child."

He is utterly mad, and I have to find a way around it. "Please, Devinshea. He is my son."

"Lee has proven unworthy to be our heir," he pronounces.

"I am talking about Rhys. My son. The one I gave birth to on the Earth plane." I reach for his hand. "He is here with his goddess, Shahidi. They won't cause any harm. Please. Let them return to the mountain and attempt to go home. He will do it. He will leave me to save Shy, and I want him to."

Anywhere is better than here. Any time is better than this. I know I want them alive far more than I want them with me.

"You would have him leave?" A brow cocks over emerald eyes.

Honesty is the only way to go here. "I would please you and still have my son and daughter-in-law alive. Yes, I would have him leave."

"You do not wish for him to save you?"

Oh, how I hate this role I have to play, but I did it once before. I took Louis Marini down from the inside and I did it by using his ego and his desires against him. I wipe the tears from my eyes. "Do not think because I plead for my children that I will do the same for my husband. The truth is Devinshea is weak and Daniel lost my crown. I told him Myrddin would betray us and he refused to listen to me. Because of my loving husbands I lost twelve years with my children, and I lost my place in the world. So if you intend to give it back to me, I will certainly consider it. But don't mistake my love of power as more than my love as a mother. I do not know how I would survive losing my son. I do not think I can survive it."

He curses under his breath and walks to the massive doors that demark his wing of the palace.

We stood here mere hours before, all of us, and now I feel so damn alone.

So stupid. How could we end up here, tricked by Myrddin again?

I feel the brush of fur against my palm and look down. The Cŵn Annwn are here. All three dogs, looking up at me like they don't understand what's happening.

I wonder where they got the dogs from. Wonder if they're spelled. If they're dogs at all. Myrddin can work some crazy transmutations. The biggest one looks up at me with flaming red eyes that somehow seem to plead with me for affection.

I'm not in the mood.

Devilshea steps back into the outer room. "Well, I think it will please you to know your son got away with his goddess. I believe that asshole I sired is trying to get them to the temple where they'll likely head to wherever the rebels go after they're done fucking up my life."

A bit of relief flows through me. Only a little. "But the guards will be after them? They aren't safe?"

He reaches a hand out, brushing back a strand of my hair, and leans in. "I gave the order to allow them to make it to the temple. I will send word that if they leave quietly, I will not assign guards to follow. Will that do, my love?"

If I can trust him, it will. Not that Rhys will leave his parents behind, but this will buy him time. I sniffle and nod, going into a deep curtsey. "Thank you, Your Majesty."

He takes my hand to lift me back. His lips curl up like he knows he has me now. "You're welcome, Zand..." He sighs. "Zoey. I was arrogant earlier and for that I apologize. You are Zoey but you are her as well. If there is one thing I've learned in my search for you it's that these different versions of ourselves are all the same. Your Devinshea could have been me if not for a few factors. The same way I could be him if not for..."

"My death." I don't say what I really mean. My Dev picked me. My Dev stood strong on his own and told his brother he could bite his ass when he refused to give us permission to marry. He married me anyway. But I have to play to this side of Dev.

And suddenly I know I can. Because he's right. He is the same man. My Devinshea can be selfish. He can be egotistical. He can be brutally stubborn.

Once Marcus and I sat in a park in Fort Worth and he told me I was the only reason Danny and Dev didn't follow their darker impulses. At least with this version, he appears to be right.

Devilshea closes his eyes and takes in a long breath. "I will never forget finding the grave Deinny put you in. Finding the pieces of you they left behind. Monsters. My brother being the worst of them. I knew that day that I could kill or be killed. I could let the monsters take me down or I could become the biggest one of all."

This Dev cares more about his station than mine.

When his eyes open and he offers me a hand, I take it. The Cŵn Annwn follow me to the plush sofa. "I have tea and wine being brought in. Your favorite. From the vineyards of your father. Well, the vineyards of her father. I hope it will please you."

I settle myself in, fighting the deep urge to run as fast as I can. I sit down like it's perfectly normal to relax while my children and friends are on the run. I don't see any sign of Neil or Brendan or Cassie, so I have to believe they got out. Daniel will bide his time.

Devinshea will be tortured.

"How did you steal the Cŵn Annwn?" I ask the question as though it doesn't really make a difference. I idly pet them. "From what I understand they only live in Arawn's domain."

He shrugs. "They are native to here in this time. And the crone as well. She chose to live here when Arawn took on non-corporeal form. Our *sithein* is close to the death god's domain. I suspect that is why. Though he does not visit here often. Myrddin claims it is because he prefers another timeline. I personally am fine with less gods walking my realm."

"So Myrddin came here because he could set us up easily?" I ask, hoping to find some reason for this. I know we are hard to catch, but it seems like a lot of work to go through.

"He wants something else of me," the king replies. "It is none of your concern. He has paid his debt and I will pay mine. I will have all the power I need to protect us. I will ensure you are happy and satisfied, Zoey. We will have the life we should have had. Now, I want to talk about you. Our wine should be here momentarily."

I won't touch it. "I would love to try it. So my father in this timeline was a winemaker? In mine he was a thief."

The king's lips quirk up. "So I have heard."

"Myrddin has told you stories," I say in an unassuming tone. That is completely passive aggressive.

"He has told me you are formidable, and I should not underestimate you. But what I see is the most beautiful woman in the world, a woman my soul meshed with, who completed me in all ways."

But you left her to die. You didn't fight for her. Yeah, I don't say those words out loud either. Instead I lean in. "I felt that way about my Devinshea. Once."

He stares at me for a long moment. "He calls you his goddess. Do you love the god? What was his name?"

"Bris." At least he seems to want to talk. I want to put off the inevitable moment when he decides to take what is his. "Devinshea and I were married in a place called Colorado. Our ceremony attracted an old agricultural deity who matched with my husband."

He winces. "I don't like to hear you call him that."

"But he is. At least until you murder him."

He frowns, and I can see the man thinking. "Yes, well, it did seem like an excellent idea at the time."

"An idea Myrddin planted," I muse. "He's good at that. In my time, my other husband is the King of All Vampire, and Myrddin found a way to strip the crown from him and take over himself."

What I need is some sweet, sweet paranoia. And to find a way to keep Myrddin from killing me just to shut me up.

Somewhere in the background I hear yelling and feel something shake the ground beneath my feet.

And then the doors blow open and my greatest enemy strides through like he owns the place. That's saying something because I once had a real Hell lord as a nemesis.

I killed his ass, and I'm going to take this fucking wizard down, too.

Maybe what he needs is a little poking.

"Well, I hope you're happy, Devinshea," he begins. "They are locked in the temple, and we know the rebels have some way to get in and out of there. I have the wards back up since now there's a damn fertility god in the temple, and we all know how that can go. We need to stay in the palace proper. I got the uncle, but Lee got away with

Sasha and Rhys and whatever the fuck that girl is." He turns on me. "Did you know? Did you know what she is?"

Devilshea stands, and so do I, placing a hand on his arm and glaring at the wizard, who really should know better. "It's Your Majesty."

He frowns my way, shaking his head as though to clear it. "What?"

"You should call him by his title. Your Majesty," I say and know I've gotten a direct hit when Devilshea puffs up a bit. "He is the King of the Seelie Fae and is owed your respect."

"It is rather rude of you to burst in unannounced," the king agrees.

For a moment Myrddin looks like he's going to shred us all, but then his head bows and he proves he's learned a lot over the millennia. "I apologize, Your Majesty. The night has not gone as well as I hoped. I am worried that we did not catch Daniel."

Devilshea simply waves that off and gestures for the servants at the entrance to enter with their trays of offerings. "I was telling my future bride that we're always the same. I assure you I know Deiniol, though he might have a different form. He was a sad sack in this time, and he will prove to be in yours as well. After all, Zoey was explaining how he allowed you to steal his crown." He sits down, tugging me beside him as the servants begin to pour the wine. He offers Myrddin a seat across from us. "It makes one think."

Oh, I really want him to think.

Myrddin looks my way and I can see the hate on his face, but he accepts a glass of wine from the servant and turns his attention back to the king. "My relationship with Daniel is complex. I assure you I didn't intend to steal anything from him. He was my student, and I cared for him. However, when Devinshea and Zoey foolishly allowed themselves to fall into an enchanted painting, he followed. He left his kingdom behind, and someone had to fill in."

"Which is why you had an entire army ready to murder all the vampires in a few hours," I interject.

"How would you know, Zoey? You weren't there," Myrddin says smoothly. "Now, Your Majesty, could we please speak alone?"

Devilshea huffs. "I just got her back. Years and years I've spent without her. You can't imagine I am going to leave her. She is afraid, and I will not have her think me negligent when it comes to my future bride. I have a certain reputation, and she must come to learn that it is not true when she is involved. So if you must speak, you can do so around my future queen."

I can hear Myrddin's inner growl but to his credit he merely sits back. "All I want to say is she is not safe as long as that vampire prowls around. My question is why wasn't Daniel at dinner?"

Dangerous territory. "He doesn't eat. Your Majesty, how much do you know about vampires?"

"Well, I've been to a whole plane of nothing but vampires," he replies, his hand finding my knee as though he can't help but touch me. "I happen to know they only drink blood and tend to eschew things like dinner parties, though their consorts are often Fae or human."

"And the wolves?" Myrddin asks, his tone begging me to come up with an explanation. "I assure you the wolves will eat you out of house and home if you allow them to."

"The wolves are guards. I do not dine with my employees." I'm betting heavily on the fact that this version of Dev doesn't. "And I honestly felt safe here. Sasha is a guard as well. Which is why he was patrolling. I believe the wolves had their dinner in the kitchens. As they would in our own home."

I can feel the approval coming off of Devilshea. He smiles my way. "You know that is the only thing we ever fought about. You...Zandra believed in a world without class or boundaries. It was naïve at best. This proves she would have gotten over it had my brother not killed her. You understand that society needs structure."

Myrddin's expression goes twenty kinds of frustrated. "She is lying. She is playing you. The wolf is her closest friend. He is always at her side. And in our timeline, she is beloved by all manner of lesser creatures. She is constantly feeding the brownies whatever creams her demon butler purchases at Costco."

It's true. They love Yule because the peppermint comes out. And eggnog flavor. "The brownies clean better when they are happy with their cream. It is a minor consideration."

"Demon? You have a demon butler?" the king asks.

I feel the need to tread carefully here. There's an expectation to his tone. A certain prejudice I have to manage. "Your counterpart does. He purchased him at auction. Albert is excellent at cooking and scaring the crap out of anyone his master doesn't want near. He's half demon. You have to be careful but if you get the right one, there's no better servant. Do you have a problem with the Hell plane, Your Majesty? Because you should know Myrddin is in open negotiations with them."

"Yes, I know he's working to cut us off from the celestial planes so we can finally do as we please with no interference," Devilshea murmurs. "But I suppose I didn't think about the implications."

"The implications are power, Your Majesty," Myrddin points out. "The power for the inner planes to be free. The power for your planes to be free of celestial influence. If you had no celestial influence, you would be in your temple right now. You wouldn't have rebels holed up in there."

"The celestial planes don't control the temples. Fae magic does," I say.

Devilshea turns my way and gives me a placating smile. "My love, you don't understand the way things work."

"I understand how he works," I reply.

"And I understand the burden you carry, Zoey," Myrddin says, his eyes narrowing. "Shall we discuss that?"

My baby. He knows I'm pregnant. Goddess, the last time I played this game, Louis Marini tried to beat my babies out of my body.

I'm saved from responding by the door coming open and the head of the guard requesting a talk with his monarch. The king studies me for a long moment and then leans over and kisses my cheek. "I will want to know about all of your burdens. I will take them from you and they will burden you no more. I'll be back."

Yes, that is everything I am afraid of.

When the king is gone, Myrddin leans forward, his eyes black as night. "You understand what will happen when I tell that man you're pregnant."

I'm shocked he hasn't already. "I think it would be an excellent way to murder me. You wouldn't even have to get your hands dirty."

"Oh, if I thought he would kill you, I would tell him in a heartbeat, but he is obsessed with you. He's hunted the planes for you," Myrddin whispers. "And I think he'll do what he did last time if you die. He'll lose his fucking mind. Tell me what you do to him,

Zoey, that he cannot be whole without you."

"I'm his soul mate and his goddess, and don't think Daniel doesn't play his part. This Devinshea was doomed when he wouldn't accept this version of Danny. We all were. What the hell is your endgame here? You could murder the king and take whatever you want from this timeline." It's beyond clear that this is our Myrddin and he can jump timelines. "Or you could find yourself in this timeline and literally fuck yourself. You should do that."

"Such a mouth on you," he sneers back. "And there is no other me. I am unique in the universe. As is that god hiding in your faerie prince and the sad spring goddess. The gods and the most powerful of us are unique in all the planes. The only unique thing about you is that you are always a nexus point. Sometimes that works in your favor. Sometimes it means you die young. But there are many yous. You will find no other version of your daughter Summer, but there are many Evangelines I can get to. She's on the Hell plane, or so I have heard. You sent her with the Hunter. Maybe I'll pay her a visit."

I sent her to Gray's kingdom to keep her away from Myrddin. "If you do, be prepared to deal with Fenrir. And Kelsey. And Gray and Trent and…"

He holds up a hand. "Yes, I will deal with them all at some point. I will certainly deal with the dark prophet. He's the one who foiled my attempts to deal with the seer."

I remember what he said in the dining room earlier. "You killed her family to get to her. You were looking for someone specific. You found some prophecy that talked about Shy."

"I was told the Davis family could be detrimental to my plans," he says. "Any of the major psychics, really, but the Davis family in particular. I thought they were talking about the mother, not the daughter. I didn't realize the daughter possessed any power at all. It should have worked. I planned it carefully. I did it on a night when everyone should have been home."

"But Gray nudged her." I love that prophet. They aren't supposed to fix things but the two I know sometimes take things in hand. If they aren't supposed to do it, then they won't be allowed to.

My children are alive because Grayson Sloane told my butler to get the kids out if anything happened. Just a nudge. Albert listened, and they made it out by the skin of their teeth. It appears Gray's the reason Shy is alive, too.

"And he will pay," Myrddin vows. "Zoey, I need you to understand that I require something specific from the king of this land. You are payment. If you cease to please him, then there's no reason for me to keep you alive. If you turn him against me, then there's no reason for me to not tell him of your pregnancy."

"And if I'm a good girl and simply hate you from afar?"

A shoulder shrugs. "Then I suspect there's little reason for me to kill any of you. You somehow managed to save that idiot son of yours. Now tell me about the seer."

"Shy? I barely know her. She's not powerful. My son kind of has a crush on her, but it's not serious." I will lie and lie and lie to this man.

"Either you are lying or you don't know what she is. Likely a bit of both. I don't think she understands what she is, and I was a bloody fool to use Arawn's name to get you here." He stands and paces. "I should have found another way. If he knows…"

"Knows what?"

He gives me a nasty smirk. "Nothing since she's not powerful and you shouldn't care because the relationship isn't at all serious."

Asshole. I hate this man with every fiber of my being. "Daniel's going to kill you."

"I'm sure he's going to try, but the question is can I get what I need out of your erstwhile suitor before Daniel comes calling. You see even if I don't kill you all, I can leave you stranded here. I got you here with the blue dolerite, but it won't work for the return trip," Myrddin taunts. "You use that door again and you'll simply find yourself on the Earth plane in this timeline. It's interesting. You'll get to see Marini again, dear. Since you were Fae in this time, you weren't around to fuck things up for him. He has more power than you can imagine, and you will be the sweetest treat for him. So you see, I don't have to kill you. I simply have to leave you here."

My rage threatens to boil to the surface. "Then I'll steal whatever key you have."

His smile becomes brilliant, and he holds his arms wide. "I am the key, darling girl. Didn't anyone tell you? I'm part Planeswalker, too. I can walk any plane I like, and I walk through all the times."

"Except the celestial ones." Somehow I don't see him walking those or he would have found Sarah.

The tightening of his jaw lets me know I hit on the truth.

"And if you can't go there no one should. Have you considered the dead in this ridiculous plan of yours? If you cut off the doors to the celestial planes, millions of dead will be trapped. Any who aren't on their way to Hell will be stuck. From what I understand reincarnation happens on the heavenly planes. How do you intend to deal with millions of souls with nowhere to go?" And then the truth hits me with the force of a runaway train. He has considered them. He is counting on them. "You'll force them to Hell."

His eyes practically glow as he contemplates his plans. "Yes, that is the deal I've made with the Hell plane. And there is a unique energy formed when souls cross the barrier. I can use it. I will feast when I close those gates. You think I'm naïve and will allow the demons to overrun the planes, but here's what you don't understand. I don't intend to allow the demons to take the Earth plane. By the time I'm done, I'll take over Hell, too. I'll be more powerful than the Morningstar, and I'll pick my teeth with his bones."

I feel a chill go over my skin. So many souls. Practically endless.

He might be able to do it.

"Now, it appears your vampire husband has fled the grounds so we can have some dinner. I'll have the hounds escorted back to the royal kennels. They've done their jobs," the king says, walking back in. "Teacher, if you don't mind. I would like some time alone with my...with Zoey. We will talk about the mountain in the morning."

The mountain. Shy wanted to go to the mountain. She was drawn to it. I stand and allow Devilshea to lead me away.

The whole time I feel Myrddin's eyes on me and know this is far from over.

Chapter Seventeen

Shy

My slippered feet pound against the soft grass as Lee takes the lead and we race away from the west side of the palace.

Leaving the queen...leaving Zoey behind. And Daniel. And...sweet goddess...we're leaving Devinshea in the hands of the man who killed my family.

It's going to be okay. Lee will make sure of it. You know it's nice in here. I thought it would be a tight fit, but it's roomy.

And I've got someone new in my head now. Or my chest. I don't really know where my soul space lies. I only know that it's full again.

Rhys's hand has a death grip on mine, and the only reason he isn't still carrying me is he's worried about arrows. So he's in front of me and Sasha is protecting my back. The quiet of the night is shattered by gunfire because while Sasha is excellent at all weapons, he really prefers his SIG Sauer. Loaded with cold iron bullets.

Lee races ahead, and I see the temple in the distance.

An arrow thuds into the ground at my feet.

Rhys turns, holds up his hand, and suddenly there's screaming behind us.

Sasha hurries me along. "Don't look."

But I do. I get a glimpse of Rhys's magic. All I've seen my love do is grow things. His magic always seems so protective and soft. But those trees leaning down and skewering soldiers, hauling them back into the sky to hold them there, chests bleeding out…it's not soft nor is this light magic.

Because no magic is inherently evil. Because the darkness is not evil and the light is not necessarily good. Because we are all somewhere in between.

I wish I could say I'm repulsed by his power.

You so are not repulsed. You are totally turned on. Say, I don't know if I can handle that. He looks far too much like my nephew. It would be weird. But you could do the big hot vampire. I would enjoy that.

I have to figure out how to shield.

We make it to the temple without much contest. There's no guard around the temple. No lights or grand gardens. Everything around it feels dead and lifeless.

Until Rhys makes it to the grounds.

Lee tries to shove me through the door, but I get a glimpse of Rhys, his hair mussed and blood on his shirt. As he moves onto the temple grounds, the whole place comes back to life.

Grass that was dull and brown is suddenly a vibrant green. The oaks and willows and rowan trees that appear to be stuck in winter are green and alive again. Flowers blossom in his wake, and the shrubs burst with life.

The door Lee had only managed to partially open swings fully for the god walking toward it. As if the temple knows who and what he is and welcomes him once more.

Lee and Sasha force me inside, and that's when I realize we're not alone. Cassie peels away from the shadows she clings to, and her brother growls her way.

"I'm going," she says with a huff as she walks in beside me. "It's just really cool."

It is really cool. As Rhys jogs up the steps, the torches light themselves and behind us I hear water running where it was not before.

The temple was dead, and it is alive again.

Rhys rushes up the steps, not looking back. His focus is wholly and completely on me.

Well, if you ever worried about whether he cares, the man didn't even notice the world just woke up around him.

It's weird. I had Harry in my head for a long time, but this version of Neil feels different. Like he's slightly too big. My body feels uncomfortable, and I try to remember if I felt this with Harry.

"Everyone inside," Rhys orders. "Cassie, where is your father?"

"He went looking for Uncle Danny," Cassie explains. "He wants Brendan to stay in wolf form and watch over us, but he's going back for our uncles and aunt."

I would expect nothing less. So my other version had kiddos. I didn't find a partner. I was too busy raising Lee. He was seven when she died. He was a handful. I'd like to talk to him before I go.

Go?

"We need to secure the doors," Rhys is saying. "Shy, I want you to go with Cassie and find the safest place you can and secure it however you need to. Brendan, watch them."

"There's no need. They can't get in here." Lee sits on a window seat. The entryway to the temple is made of white marble, green vines with flowering plants climbing around the thick columns. There are four golden bowls that light with fire as Rhys walks by them. Above us the ceiling begins to glow with light as well. "I meant what I said. We're safe. Look. They can't even cross the yard."

They can't. We have spies, and I happen to know that Devinshea has tried everything he can to get back into his temple, and when that failed he attempted to destroy it. Neil's voice is soothing. *And I meant what I said. I'd like to talk to Lee before I go. I thank you so much for saving me. I know the wizard could take me because I was disoriented and confused, and I didn't want to go. But it is my time.*

Rhys looks out the window at the guards gathered round, but true to what Lee said they seem stopped at the edge of the yard surrounding the temple. Even from this distance, I can see they're confused at the change. They look around in seeming wonder.

"They cannot get us in here," Lee reiterates, his expression haggard. "But they certainly took out my men. And my uncle."

His eyes close.

Can you speak for me? One last boon from you and I will go, Shahidi, and leave you the prince. With the god.

"Shy," Cassie begins.

I shake my head. "Rhys, we're fine. We can stay here and figure out our next move, but first my guest would like to talk to his nephew."

Lee's head comes up, eyes flaring. "What do you mean? My uncle? The fucking wizard took him."

Rhys stands in front of the man who looks so much like his twin. "No. My goddess saved him. It is what she was doing when time seemed to slow. She fought with the wizard for his soul and she won." He looks back at me with a wry twist to his lips. "Though this is a new power you didn't tell me about."

His complete faith that I saved Neil fills me with warmth. He couldn't see what was happening. It probably looked to everyone else like Myrddin and I were simply pointing at a space. But Rhys knew what I was doing.

I need to stop thinking he doesn't see me. I need to let him show me what he sees.

I smile back at him, proud that he's calm even though our world upended. Again. "I didn't know about it until tonight. But I will say there's probably more to come. I felt something I never have before. A power. However, right now Neil wants to talk to his nephew before he goes."

Lee stands, tears on his face. "He wasn't destroyed."

It isn't a question. It's an affirmation. It's a settling inside of him. I let Neil's words flow through me.

"I remember the day you were born. I held your mother's hand and Deinny held the other, and then we were a family. Zandra slept, but I stayed up watching you. In awe of how something so perfect could come from your father. He wasn't horrible then, but he was young and arrogant and selfish. You did what he couldn't. You lost everything and stayed true to who you want to be. I adore you, Lee Quinn, and we will meet again. Stay with these people. I don't know why but things are clearer here. They were sent for a reason."

"Yes, so Myrddin can kill them, uncle," Lee argues, but he holds my hands like he's holding Neil's.

My head shakes. "That was the intent, but it will not be the outcome. The wizard falls into traps, too. I love you, Lee, but your mother and true father are calling me. I hear them. He was, you know. Deinny might never have convinced your mother in this last life, but no matter biology, he was your father."

"And you. I didn't fall into selfish pity because I had you." Tears flow freely down Lee's face. "You'll be okay?"

I feel so much love from this Fae. It flows through me, and hopefully Lee can feel it, too. I am merely a watcher in this farewell, but I feel it so keenly. The love, the life that was Neil's. The hope. The odd joy he feels at moving on. "I am more than okay, nephew. I am blessed by the goddess, and you are as well. Stay with them. Take what is yours. Do not be afraid. The time has come. I know you wish for a simple life, but you will be king. Do not shrink away from the power you must take to free them all."

He nods. "I love you. I will be okay. We will be okay."

I feel Neil shift out of me, leaving my body like a whisper, a sweet but cool breeze. He stands in front of me, the proud Fae warrior he was in life. And I swear I can see a glow from a foot behind him. I can see the light.

I have never seen the light before.

There is only peace on Neil's face now. "I know we've only just met, but honestly sharing space like that, you get to know a person. Would you like to know what I see in you, Shahidi? Bravery. Love. So much love. But also fear. You have no need to fear. Death is nothing to fear. You are nothing to fear. When you realize you are the light we are all looking for at the end of our days, you will see things as they truly are. Say his name when you're ready. He will not ignore your call."

He smiles and turns and walks into that light.

"He's gone," I tell Lee and wonder who he was talking about. Who will answer my call?

Lee shudders and nods, obviously trying to control himself. "To be with them again. Thank you." He squeezes my hands. "Thank you. Anything I have is yours."

"And we will aid you in any way we can," Rhys says solemnly. "But first we need to regroup. My goddess needs rest, and we need to figure out how to get my parents back. Bris will keep my father alive for as long as he can. He is very strong. My dad will be working from wherever he is. Uncle Neil will find him. I am worried about Mother."

"And Ostara." For the first time since we came into the temple, Sasha speaks. He looks grim standing in the firelight. Like it cost him to leave the palace. "I must go to the dungeons and free her. I've told you about my wife."

"I might have a way to get you out," Lee explains. "I'll try to make the arrangements."

I remember how the goddess found the strength to point Sasha's way and call him by another name. "Who is Oleg Federov?"

"That was his name when he was alive," Rhys explains. "Before he became Sasha. He had a wife and a child."

"Natasha." I know that part. We keep up with her for him. We follow her socials and have some people in Dallas who watch in case she ever needs her father.

"I suppose I stopped talking so much by the time you came around," Sasha admits. "I was a spy for my government. My government became corrupt, and I objected. I knew they might kill me, but what they did was worse. They sold me to a woman who was experimenting with drugs that took a person's memories. She was trying to create small armies of men who had no loyalty to anyone but her. The drugs took my life but not my skills."

"He could fight, remember how to shoot and do everyday things, but he couldn't remember who he was," Rhys says softly, and I wonder how many times they sat together and talked. Of all the kids, Sasha seems closest to Rhys.

Likely because Rhys was forced to mature so quickly. Because despite the fact that his powers were desired by many, they were also troublesome when he couldn't control them. Sasha wasn't affected by his fertility powers so he could stay close.

"I'm so sorry. How does Ostara know your name?" I realize we misunderstood her. "She asked about the vampire. We thought she was talking about Daniel. She was talking about you. She said she could feel something stirring in her host's soul. Or something like that. Meadow has bad dreams about what happen in her prior life."

Tears pool in the vampire's eyes. I have never once seen this male cry. "Because she was murdered by the same people who sold me. I did not remember her for many years, though she was always in my soul. My wife. My love. I am not proud of who I became when she was no longer a strong voice in my head. When I did not remember her, I was not good. I wasn't as terrible as your father, Lee, but I was selfish and mean at times. And then I remembered.

Sometimes it would happen. A flash like someone briefly turned on a light. I would see a baby in my hands and feel…worthy and good. Like I was where I was supposed to be when I held this girl in my hands. I knew I loved her mother with all my heart. That feeling is why I jumped in front of a bullet to save my brother. It was the first time after I lost my memories that I heard her. I heard something telling me she would find me again."

"Then you were a vampire." Rhys takes over when Sasha seems too overwhelmed. "And you had us. You were patient. You knew she was out there, and these last few years you felt her across time. Across the planes of existence. Across multiple timelines. Sasha, this is why we're here."

Sasha straightens up. "It is one of the reasons. Shy is the main one. This time needs her. Our time needs her." He turns my way. "You must see that you are important and not in a you-will-strengthen-Rhys way. Myrddin is playing with death magic to strengthen himself. You stole from him. One soul. What if you could steal them all? What if you could set them free and he could not use them again?"

"Use them again?" I ask.

"He eats them." Lee settles back on the bench beside Cassie. Brendan is prowling, sniffing and taking stock of the temple. "He uses them for sure, but then they're gone."

"This is not what the world teaches us." Sasha's arms cross over his big chest. "And finding my wife again proves this to me. Nothing is wasted. It is merely transformed. Myrddin is obsessed with Gladys. The Sword of Light. It is the traditional weapon of what we call the *Nex Apparatus*, but it was given many millennia ago to a group of warrior women called the Amazons. I won't launch into a history of how my people ended up subjugating the warrior women…"

"Patriarchy," Cassie says under a cough.

She's not wrong.

"But the sword absorbs the powers of anyone it cuts. What if that is what Myrddin is trying to achieve? Or a variation of it. What if he thinks he can take those souls and use them when the time is right? When he has enough power?" Sasha posits.

"He can't absorb powers. If he could, he would go around murdering any creature with supernatural powers and take them as his own," I reply. "The Sword of Light is unique. It doesn't have to kill to give Kelsey access to power. If Myrddin could do that, he would have shown us before now."

"But he studied the sword for years while Kelsey was trapped." Rhys seems to pick up on Sasha's thoughts. "He wouldn't be able to do exactly what the sword does, but he knows the sword can lock the door between the planes. It stores energy and that energy is what he needs. What if he's storing souls?"

"I'm sorry, what? That wizard who has been fucking with my home wants to close the doors to the planes? That's what my father is helping him with?" Lee is on his feet again. "Just when I'm certain he's at his lowest, he reaches for the stars. Well, I know what Myrddin wants with my father. He's been learning how to gain power through taking in souls. He can't keep them in his body, so he has certain crystals that absorb the soul and lock it into place. From there I have heard he has spells to ingest the soul, to destroy it and use the energy for himself."

"I am almost certain Myrddin is lying to your father. From what I know, no one can trap a soul. You can trick one, but you can't trap it," I explain. "And yet it seems to be what he's doing. It goes against everything I've been taught. I only know that Myrddin needs an enormous amount of energy to close the gates."

"So Myrddin thinks he can close the gate a different way?" Cassie's hands are in her lap, a worried look on her face. "If he thought he could seal the gate with celestial magic, could he think death magic will work just as well?"

I sigh as it hits me. "He figured out something, or at least he's got a theory. A door swings both ways. What if he thinks he can only use the sword to seal the door from the celestial side given where it's magic comes from?"

"I don't think anyone gets to walk those particular planes. Not unless you're invited," Rhys says. "Which is why Mother is looking for the amulet. Shy, please don't tell me you think he's trying to close it from Hell's side because death magic is not evil."

I sigh but don't argue with him because honestly, up until now, it's exactly what I would have been thinking. My witchy sisters always say I need to do some shadow work. Well, I'm doing it in the field and in real time. "No, babe, he wouldn't want that at all. That would close off Hell. The Earth plane is in the middle, and death magic is absolutely Earth magic. It is neither evil nor good. It simply is. It is required."

"Tell me how what you just did wasn't good," Lee says, staring at me with somber eyes. "You saved my uncle."

I'm not certain that was death magic. It felt so lovely, so simple and pure. It felt like home. "All I'm saying is what if death magic or something like it works to close the door from the Earth plane's side. What if he realized closing it from the celestial side means he can't control the lock?"

"He would need so many souls." There's no lack of horror in Cassie's tone.

"He would have to hoard them. I don't know that he can do that on the Earth plane. Too many supernatural creatures, and even the humans would notice if he had millions of souls hanging around waiting to be used," Rhys says with a shake of his head. "It would cause all kinds of trouble. Human souls don't cling together. They prefer to be solitary."

"But the sluagh don't." I know why I am here.

Rhys's eyes close, and he pales. "There would have to be millions."

"He keeps them in the mountains. No one is allowed to go there," Lee explains. "The mountains themselves are considered sacred to the Quinn family. No one can go there, but recently even the villages around them were evacuated. They told us it's because it's dangerous. Right before the last harvest, the king moved them all out. Simply took his soldiers through with the help of the duke and tossed them all into the forest. They weren't even allowed to pack."

"Was that around the time Myrddin began showing up?" Sasha asks.

Lee nods. "That was when the dead began to disappear. I have a friend with a bit of medium in her magic. She was worried when she could no longer hear their whispers, and she definitely believes there are more sluagh in those mountains than our *sithein* has ever held. There was always a small colony of them, but she fears they have grown in a way that is not natural. She has been worried because at some point they will not be contained. Now I know why the king thinks he can handle it."

Because he intends to give them to Myrddin, who will take all that energy and close the Earth plane off.

Rhys nods Lee's way, and suddenly his hand is in mine. "When can we leave? You said there was a way out? How do we know your father doesn't have troops waiting for us?"

"Because they've never found the tunnels we dug to get here," Lee replies with an arrogant grin. "The gnomes who used to serve the temple helped us. When we realized the king isn't allowed in his own temple, we knew we had a way in."

"And how did you get the chimera in?" Sasha asks with a frown. "I do not believe the chimera is native to a Seelie *sithein*."

He frowns. "Damn it. I didn't even think about that. I sicced the chimera on you when I thought you were coming back with my dad. He was brought in by the Unseelie from an outer plane. I have been working with them not only to get certain Fae creatures to safety, but also as a part of the rebellion. They would prefer I was on the throne. I planned on telling them no, but now I have a promise to my uncle. I'm sorry about the chimera."

Cassie waves him off. "The chimera was no big deal. I took him out midair with a machete."

"Really? He was kind of my friend," Lee says.

Cassie winces. "Uh, sorry?"

"How many more assassins do you have hiding? Will they mistake Rhys for your father? He looks much like him. Like you," Sasha points out.

"But our soul scents are different. I had to go with that for our beast friends because they aren't good with faces," Lee admits. "I guess your father and mine share a soul scent."

"I will not even ask how one trains on a soul scent," Cassie says with a grimace.

Lee eyes her. "It's a spell." He turns back to Rhys and me. "We can't leave until morning. The forest the tunnels dump into is full of predators. They're nocturnal, and it's only a half day's hike to my village, and from there we will march to the mountains. At least Shy and I will. I know Rhys must help rescue his parents. I promise, I will take care of her."

I feel my love go stiff and know there's about to be some plants up in here. Probably with vicious thorns he intends to shove up his brother's backside. "Rhys will escort me. I would not go without him. His dad will take care of his mother and Papa, along with Neil and Sasha. I'm afraid our missions have become separate things."

"He won't kill your mother." Lee resettles his pack over his shoulder. "If it helps, I believe he will try to seduce her. Bibi has been watching him. He still talks about her, and when he does it's always about making things right this time."

"You believe that?" Rhys asks.

"I believe eventually he'll do what he does and take what he thinks is his, but he'll want her to want him. He's trying to replay their relationship. She didn't fall into bed with him. He had to work for it," Lee explains. "At least that's what my uncle told me. We also have some pixie spies. I'll let them know to report to the vampires."

I notice a small butterfly peel off the temple wall and fly to Lee's outstretched hand. He whispers to the pixie and she flies off, pausing in front of Sasha. The pixie stops for a moment as though memorizing his face and then it's gone.

"I have faith that my dad will save them," Rhys says and sighs. "And my mother will likely bring down the palace and end up leading a revolution of pixies and trolls and brownies. We must get Shy to the mountain. We can't allow Myrddin to take the sluagh souls."

At least I won't have to fight him. "Cassie, will you come with us? I could use an extra guard."

Lee sends a wink her way. "You are more than welcome, gorgeous."

"Ewww," Cassie says. "You're like a cousin."

Lee shrugs. "Baby, I don't know you here. And you look good." Brendan steps in front of his sister and growls, the hair on his back standing up. "Sir Wolf, I shall keep my hands to myself."

"You do not change. Also, she is fifteen. I will cut off your balls, brother or no." Rhys sniffs and turns back to me. "I can guard you."

I give him a saucy smile. "You wrap me up in itchy vines. She would throw me her second-best machete, and Brendan is good at tracking in case you lose me."

Brendan gives a bark, and his sister throws him a treat before giving me a thumbs-up. "We got you, and also I do look more like I'm a young twenty."

"I mean she kind of does," Lee attempts.

"She does not, and everyone needs to understand that I am in charge. This is Shy's mission, but I am the commanding officer here." Rhys's eyes narrow, and I swear I can see a storm there as he puts his hands on my shoulders. "I will not lose you, and if you run there would be no place I could not find you."

My poor baby god is overstimulated. It's been a rough day for him. For all of us, but this is his worst nightmare. He always has to be in control, and he is simply not now. This is my mission, and losing me is everything he has tried to avoid since the moment we met.

It's funny how I worried about this before and now it seems so simple. We're stuck here for the night, in a version of the temple where he would be married.

Where we will be married.

Maybe I should think more, but I don't want to. I know we're on the run and should focus on what's going to happen tomorrow, but we need something sweet tonight. We're as safe as we can be and have no idea what dawn will bring.

Our fears are often silly in the face of our love. I worried the temple would reject me somehow or that I would feel uncomfortable in it. It all goes back to my greatest fear. That I will not ever belong.

The marble hums beneath my feet. A soft wind caresses my cheek. Like a kiss of welcome. Like a hug from family long unseen.

I do belong here in the temple. This temple is our home. Part of it. We will always go back to the Earth plane. Rhys is the priest of those the Fae left behind. One day—when the war is done and peace lay like a blanket over the plane—we will build our temple there and offer what we are. Life. Death. The beginning of souls turning. Love. We will offer ourselves and our gifts, our magic and our work to our people.

But tonight I have something else to offer him.

"I would never run from you." I go up on my toes and kiss his lush lips. "Show me our temple."

This is my wedding night.

Chapter Eighteen

Sasha

The man formerly known as Oleg Federov followed Lee Quinn through the deepest part of the temple, his mind racing all the while.

Marta.

She had been ten feet from him and he hadn't been able to save her, hadn't been able to put his hands on her, to step in front of her and take whatever pain came her way.

And yet he felt like he was failing as he got further and further from Rhys and Shy and Cassie and Brendan.

Lee stopped in front of a seemingly solid brick wall and tapped on it, three times at the top and then three at the bottom. He turned and looked so much like the child Sasha had raised on the run. The boy had become a man and the man a soldier and the soldier a vampire king. "We have to wait for a few minutes. Someone has to open this door from the other side. From here you can either leave the grounds or get back into the palace, but you'll go in via the servants' entrances. You're on your own from there. Are you sure you don't want to come with us?"

He wasn't sure of anything except the fact that half his soul was here on this plane, and he had to get to her. The kids he raised were old enough to take care of themselves now, but Marta…

He would never forget the way that beautiful goddess had raised her hand and cursed him if he did not come for her host. Oh, she hadn't put it that way, but a Russian knew a curse when it was sent his way.

You owe her.

He owed her everything.

"I have to get to the dungeon," he said slowly, trying to find that calm he'd learned over the many years as an intelligence operative.

"Well, the dungeon is going to be guarded," Lee said, leaning against the wall like he was settling in.

Sasha felt his fangs in his mouth, felt the talons his fingers could spring at a moment's notice. "Then I will make it unguarded."

"I know that sounds like a good time, but it won't simply be Fae guards you're up against," Lee said. "You're up against all the wards and traps the wizard has placed there. Do you think I haven't tried to get in? He takes my soldiers there when he captures them. I've tried to rescue them before and lost more men and in horrific ways."

Sasha's heart felt too tight in his chest. He should have stayed and fought. He shouldn't have allowed them to take her away.

"You would have died." Lee's expression was grim. "And no, I'm not reading your mind. It's a pretty easy bet what you're thinking. So she was your wife and you died, but you didn't die and she actually died. That's a fucked-up story."

"I turned when I died," he explained. "She was murdered because she was trying to find me, but while I thought about going into the light, I talked with some smart vampires and scholars who believe deeply that we find each other again and again. So I became convinced I must wait for her. But it's only been fifteen years."

"From what I understand time runs differently depending on the planes. She could have been born and lived a whole life and you wouldn't have aged more than a few months or years. Though it seems to have worked out for my father since he's now found my mom again and she's pretty much the perfect age for him." Lee's eyes closed. "I see her dying, you know. Over and over again. I was there. I was ripped from her arms, and it was only Deinny who saved me."

"My daughter was only saved because her mother made her hide in a cabinet and she wouldn't give her location up." He thought about it a lot. Prayed Tasha had forgotten. It had been there in her memories the night he went to find her in the orphanage in Siberia. His little girl had been pale and thin and he'd asked a friend to plant certain ideas deep in her psyche. Michael House had left behind the only thing Sasha could give her. The deep belief that her parents loved her. That they would never have left her willingly. That she was beloved and worthy.

While he'd done it, some of her memories had played through the mind connection they had. Michael had dutifully related both the good and the bad.

"So your wife is reborn on a Fae plane and gets selected to be the host to a goddess." Lee chuckled. "You know if you had decided to try to follow her…"

The irony was not lost on him. Fate had a plan. "I would not have been immortal. I could have ended up anywhere, and the timing would have been wrong. If I had not chosen to go on this mission, I would have missed her."

"Yes," Lee said, the warm glow of the torch softening his expression. "Everything fell into place and you ended up in a timeline you shouldn't be in, the only timeline in which you could ever meet her. So it's your turn."

"My turn?"

"The goddess gave you a gift, directing you each time to the right path, to the one that would lead you to her forever. Think of the choices you made along the way. Not the ones you had taken from you. The ones you purposefully selected. You said you saved someone."

Sasha nodded, his emotions so close to the surface. Owen. His brother by bond, not blood. He'd been so lost without his memories. He'd been bitter and mean, but when the moment came, he threw his body in front of his brother's without regret. He'd taken the bullet.

And risen later that night a vampire.

He chose to stay in Venice when he could have gone to the Council House so when the supernatural world exploded, he was there to take the royal children in.

He chose to raise them, training them on the run. He put his heart and soul into them because he could not be there for his own daughter. Because someone else had raised her in love, he did the same for Lee and Rhys and Evan and Fenrir.

For that faithfulness the queen had given him a ring that allowed him to walk in the daylight, to not be constrained by his status. He could walk in the light with his soulmate.

He chose to live and now she was here. Now it was finally right.

How many times had this played out for them? Had he lost her? Would this be their last chance?

Lee sighed. "You made that choice and it brought you here. What I am trying to say is that I've watched a man try to fight fate over and over, try to impose his will on the universe, and I worry she's going to pay again. I don't want what happened to my mother to happen to your Zoey or to Ostara. Everything my father touches dies."

"I will not allow her to die," Sasha vowed.

"But you'll die if you go after her without a plan," Lee replied. "So trust the universe and her. Trust that this time is the right time. Don't panic. I asked about you and Rhys told me you're their general. Be the general. That's who she needs now."

The door began to open, and Lee stepped away from it. A tiny head poked around the corner. A brownie in worn clothes, her head wrapped in a scarf. "Lee?"

The faery smiled and got to one knee. "Hello, Fee. I want to introduce you to Sasha. He's a vampire, and he's our visiting goddess's mate."

"Ostara?" The brownie's eyes lit up. "She is so lovely." And then her face fell. "The king has her in the dungeons. He has found Zandra again and now my sweet friend will be… It's too horrible. We all know what will happen to that poor woman he thinks is his lost love. The rumor is that her husband is in the dungeon as well, though I have not confirmed it with my network."

The word pricked up his ears. "Are you a spy?"

The brownie shook her head. "Oh, no sir. No. I am but a humble servant."

He smiled, a feral feeling in his gut because like recognized like. "Oh, madame, you are a spy, and I am going to beg for your services. On my plane, in my timeline, I was a spy, and I would love to work with you to save Ostara. I will tell you everything I know if you will share your knowledge with me. We can save them."

Lee grins. "With patience, spymaster. That was the other thing he called you. Now you should hurry and get under the wards so you don't turn into a lust-crazed maniac and break those vows right before you're with her again."

Because Rhys and Shy weren't going to sleep alone this evening. They were going to see if they could use the temple to send energy to the dungeons, which were not under the wards. Lee had explained that the wards protecting those in the palace from magic did not extend to the dungeons since the guards there used magic to torture their prisoners. So Rhys and Shy would send their unique magic to Ostara and Devinshea.

Patience.

Fee gestured him into the tunnels. "I think I can take you where you need to go. My network is already protecting the other vampire and the pretty wolf. We have a safe place for you."

All the small faery creatures loved Neil Roberts. Sasha took a long breath, quelling his fear. What place did fear have in the face of hope? "Lead on, madame. I will be forever grateful."

He followed the brownie into the darkness.

Chapter Nineteen

Zoey

"The guard on your door is only there to protect you," Devilshea says as he glances to his left where the bulky *sidhe* soldier stands. One of them. There have been several watching over us. "You are free to go anywhere you like in the palace."

"Anywhere?" I ask in my softest, "oh, hey I'm happy to be here with the dude who kidnapped me" voice. It's sad that I have one of those. Sadder that I've used it way more than once or twice.

He frowns. "Anywhere safe. There are obviously parts of the palace that might disturb your tender sensibilities, but know I will always protect you from our enemies. The rest of the palace is yours, though not tonight, my love. Tonight there is too much going on. There are still rebels on the grounds. I want you to know that my soldiers tracked your son and his mate to the temple where they are currently hiding. I cannot enter. We will find a way to send word that they will be safe if they do not come back. My gift to you."

Ladies, when a man's gift to you is not murdering your son, you need a new man. However, when you're trapped in his palace and he's been known to burn people he doesn't like alive, it's best to give him your most vacant smile and thank his evil ass, which I do now. "Your kindness goes a long way with me, Your Majesty. As did that lovely meal and your company. It's been a long time since I felt so...welcome."

Welcome to steal. Welcome to turn all your servants against you. Welcome to decimate your whole life and not feel a moment's regret.

He reaches for my hand, taking it between both of his. He looks so like my Devinshea, but there's an intensity to his gaze that speaks of some form of madness. I have to be careful with him. "I'm glad. You relaxed once the wizard was gone. I am sorry for your discomfort. He did not explain the animosity between you. He merely told me he knew you."

I consider telling him all about the times Myrddin has tried to murder me and my family. Just weeks before he sent assassins and killed Lee and then locked me in a room with him thinking Lee would turn and drain me dry. Thankfully, Lee was truly his dad's son or he would have. But I think a little lie here might help my cause. There's a reason that might suit me better, even if it's not true. "He does not like me. I sometimes worry I caused all of this trouble."

I still remember how to make my bottom lip tremble. Gotta sell the drama.

"How?" He brings my hand to his lips and kisses my palm with a reverence I know I can use. "How would someone so sweet cause trouble? You were simply caught in a war not of your own making."

Who the hell was I in this time? I surely wasn't myself since no one even once asked me that question. I was probably careful, played my role with as much perfection as I could. I silently thank the Zandra who had lived in this time for setting me up so perfectly. If there is one thing I know a man like this can't stand, it's jealousy. "You don't know everything. When Myrddin and I first met, he offered to take me away with him. I refused. I was married and pregnant at the time. Beyond that, I didn't trust or want him in any way. I loved my Dev. I think my refusal might have hurt my whole plane. He has hated me ever since. I worry this is all some form of revenge for him."

And I see it. The burn of possessiveness. The anger that some other man might touch what he thinks belongs to him. My Devinshea would laugh and tell me to kick his balls in, but this one lost me once and will not have it happen again. "He wanted you?"

I don't wince as his hand tightens around mine. "I did not want him. I only wanted my husbands."

A bit of satisfaction creeps in, and he brings my hand to his chest. "You wanted Devinshea and Deinny. You know he was nothing but a servant here. He worked for your father. He was your friend but you never wanted him. Only me."

"He was my childhood friend, too," I explain. "Life is different where I come from. We went off to college together, and it was easy to be with him. Until I met you. By then it made sense for the three of us to be together. Danny was so powerful."

"I suspect that might have happened here, too, had I not shown up at your father's tavern when I did," he murmurs. "But your love story was always with me. Fiery and passionate. Only with me."

Oh, Danny and I have a shit ton of fire between us, but I'm playing to his narcissistic side. "It's true. My Danny is a vampire, and that was exciting for a while. You know what a companion is? I believe on the Vampire plane they call them consorts."

He nods. "That explains much. He used you for your blood. You loved your Devinshea, but he was weak. And now you do not have to worry. You will be my queen, and once I give the wizard my end of the bargain, we will be done with him. He will not darken our doorstep again. I will make sure of it."

"Does your end of the bargain include closing us off from the celestial planes?"

I realize I made a mistake when his eyes grow sharp and he drops my hand. He turns slightly, and I realize my other mistake.

When his coat rumples a bit with his turn, I see it. The amulet. The one I intended to ask Miria for. The one Danny went searching for tonight. He won't have found it. The king is wearing it as a pin on the tunic he has on under his coat.

It's right there.

The amulet is there and I can take it. I simply have to get close to him.

He steps away. "That is nothing for you to worry about. I know it sounds like a frightening thing, but I suspect you don't understand how much influence the celestial planes have on us." He seems to shake something off. "I don't even understand all of it. I only know I made a deal with the wizard, and I have to see it through. You understand about the Fae and breaking our word?"

Yeah, that can go poorly when it comes to royals. Don't get me wrong. The Fae can lie all day long, but when they swear themselves, they must follow through or face the wrath of certain powerful gods. It makes me wonder if I can figure out a way to call Herne the Hunter down on him. If Herne comes, he will know me. Perhaps he can get us out of here.

Or he will do his job, shoot us all the finger, and head back wherever he wants to be. Honestly, he's kind of a dick.

I nod and think about how to get my hands on the king. It would be easy to offer him intimacy, but it's too early for that. All those words Myrddin put in his head are still floating around in there. I have to prove I'm not exactly what Myrddin claims me to be.

Then there's the risk that if I kiss him, he might not leave.

I know I should be stronger, but I step back. I don't want to go through this again. I survived it once. I don't know how I would do it again even if his face is my husband's. "I do understand, Your Majesty. And you are right. I don't know much about the planes. I have spent my time taking care of my husbands and our children, being the queen. I don't know much more beyond that life."

"And I will give it all back to you. When we are wed, my magic will flow again. You will see. The temple will open, and I will be a proper Green Man once more," he vows. "It all went wrong when I lost you. Now that you are here, things will be right again and you will have your life back as well. I will not fail you the way…well, the way I did in your time."

Oh, he failed on so many levels. There's an odd air of anticipation, and I realize if I don't retire soon, he's going to try to kiss me. I want to put that off as long as I can. "I appreciate it, Your Majesty, and I thank you for your consideration in giving me my own room. It has been a long day."

His expression softens. "I remember. You don't fall easily. I will be patient with you as long as you give me the chance to be. The palace is warded. You will be safe here. Stay in your room tonight. Tomorrow I will show you all I can offer. There's a mirror in the bathing room if you require me."

I raise a brow. "The bathing room?"

He merely smiles and turns and walks away, closing the door behind him. Well, I definitely won't be bathing.

I take my first long breath in hours, shoving my fist in my mouth so I don't scream.

I back up, not caring to look around the room he's caged me in. I'm certain it's beautiful and delicate and potentially deadly. All I can think about is my heart pounding as I let the horror of the night flow over me.

We're here again. Goddess, how are we here again? I fall to my knees, praying there's no surveillance on the room, but I can't...I can't hold it back....

Then arms are around me, and I feel a body moving behind mine.

"It's okay. It's going to be okay, Z."

Before I can start to fight I know it's Danny behind me, and I turn so I can get my arms around him. I love him. I love him so much. So much more than when we were dumb kids and everything was dramatic and overwrought. I joke about wanting adventure again, but I loved our life before we fell into that stupid painting. Quiet days with our children. Dumb arguments with the Council about petty things like who sits where. Dinners when we were all together and we would tell Lee he had to eat broccoli and pretend not to notice when he shoved it in the pocket of his pants.

I thought I loved him when we were young, thought he couldn't possibly have more of a chokehold on my heart, but he does. I clutch him, my arms trying to trap and keep him with me. I lost him once.

Are we going to lose Dev?

"Baby, it's okay. Rhys is okay. Dev is alive. He's alive and he's going to stay that way." His voice is a hoarse whisper against my ear, and I can feel his emotion. "Are you... Baby, did he..."

I shake my head, knowing he feels our position as keenly as I do. And then I realize how dangerous this is. I pull back. He always does this to me. "You have to go. How did you get here in the first place?"

He strokes a big hand over my hair, deep blue eyes taking me in. "Bibi knew where he would put you, and the servants all hate him. They're oathed to him by a spell so they can't harm him or say a word, but they can show a guest how to get through the many hidden hallways and servant entrances and exits. I've been in the closet for the last half hour and don't worry. I have several charms and talismans that Evan gave us. Including the one that will make me invisible to security wards. I can't get through them without help, but they can't see me so they can't sound an alarm."

Evan is excellent with Fae magic, and she made sure we had all her tricks before she took off for the Hell plane. She told us she wanted us to have them even though we thought we were going into friendly territory. She looked at me with grave eyes and reminded me there's no such thing. My sweet girl. "He said he knew she was on the Hell plane."

"Myrddin?" Danny asks.

I nod.

"Well, that was inevitable. It's the first time Lady Sloane has visited her manor. I'm sure all the gossip rags are covering it. Don't worry. She can handle herself, and Kelsey and Fen will watch her like a hawk. Or a couple of really overly protective wolves. Lee won't allow anything to happen to his sister. Did you see him?"

Normally the idea of Hell plane media would amuse me greatly, but I can't stop thinking about what's happening to Dev. "Lee? Yes. There's a version of him here, and he really hates his father. I saw Neil, too, and I'm a little worried he's attracted to himself."

I wish I hadn't been hauled out so quickly. I don't know what happened to them. To any of them.

Danny snorts and hauls me back into his arms. "Our Neil is out there. He sent Brendan and Cassie with Rhys, but he's with us. He found me in the stables where the trolls decided to stash me until they could get me here. Sasha wasn't far behind. They're being led into the palace as we speak. They're going to hide in the servants' quarters. We owe those trolls or I would have to have fought my way out, and Myrddin armed the guards with silver."

I hate that man. "You really don't think you could cut through his guards?"

I'm used to Danny being Superman, completely invincible.

"I don't know if you felt it but Myrddin did something when he walked into the palace. Some kind of ward he activated when he knew we were here. It was always a trap. I can't fly. I feel weak. Even getting my fangs to pop out is a challenge," Danny admits. "It's dampening my senses, too. I need to find that ward or figure out how far from the palace it holds and then I can take them all out, and no amount of silver is going to stop me."

"He either put it in a central location or he's got more than one." Sarah taught me a lot about wards. If it's covering the palace grounds, it's incredibly powerful or he's got more than one. "I'll keep my eyes open, but you need to run if they come after you. He can't cover the whole *sithein*."

"I'll talk to the servants and ask if there's anything new they've seen," Danny offers. "You be careful. I'll try to get Bibi assigned to you."

"Devilshea should have gotten rid of all the non-*sidhe*, apparently." The words hold no small amount of bitterness.

Danny snorts and then sobers. "You can't call him that, baby."

I sniffle, keeping my voice low. "I know. He's wearing the amulet. I have to get close."

"Or once I take down the wards, I can get close, pull off his head, and steal the amulet," Danny offers. "Or we can wait until Myrddin flashes out. I would bet anything the wards require his presence. It's a hefty magic that can keep a vampire king's powers on the fritz. Summer did it but she was with me the whole time. I didn't fight it. I'm fighting the hell out of this. Surely he needs to get back to the Coven House soon."

"I'm not so sure about that. He needs something from the king. It's the only reason he hasn't outed the fact that I'm pregnant." I quickly run down everything Myrddin said to me, including his plans to take over Hell. I don't think he's leaving unless there's an emergency.

"I mean, I could have a conversation with Lucifer, but who knows if he'll believe me," Danny says, shaking his head. "I know he's been using Gray as a focal point, so it's hard for me to believe he hasn't contemplated the possibility."

Lucifer Morningstar is a tricky character, from what I hear. I've only ever dealt with the broody, disgruntled version. The old man who wants everyone off his lawn and can't stand the sound of children's laughter, but I've been told there are other aspects. It makes me wonder which one my Lee and Evan will potentially deal with. Hopefully none of them. "Myrddin said something about Gray. Something about him protecting Shy. He was angry."

A brow rises over my vampire's eyes as he stares at me, his fingers entwining with mine. "I'm unaware of the dark prophet's movements beyond what he did to save our children. If Gray saved Shy from her parents' fate, then I have to believe he did so for a reason. He killed the most powerful psychic families in our world, and many of the individuals. I know he would have taken Shy out even though she was a child at the time. Gray could have easily influenced the situation to get her out of the house for the night. Since she was a kid, Myrddin might have missed her. We're sure this is our Myrddin we're dealing with? I've spent hours talking to the trolls and gnomes and brownies the king didn't spell to silence. There aren't many, but they've figured a couple of ways around the spells. Some of the house servants find they can draw or write things they see in a rudimentary form. The ones who can talk like Bibi have gotten good at translating. They told me Myrddin has been visiting the palace since late summer, so almost half a year."

I have no doubt. "It's absolutely our awful wizard. According to him, he's a unique being. All of the powerful gods are. It makes sense because he's immortal."

"Vampires are immortal, but according to our new friends, I had a doppelganger here. Your closest friend. The king had me burned at the stake for burying you," Daniel points out with a frown.

I thought about this. "You're long lived. You're not immortal. Not really, and definitely not you. You go when I go, buddy. The same with the Fae. Long lived but can be killed. I know Myrddin can be, but I suspect his energy would go into something else. A bit like Bris. Or he's simply a very special boy and I will thank the goddess there's only one of him. But he knows far too much about us to not be our version of the man. I believe him about Bris and Ostara. He said Summer is one of them."

"So she's safe." Danny breathes a sigh of relief for our eldest child. She's in the Summerlands, powering the outer planes with her unique magic. I saw what happened when the outer planes were cut off from the magic as the last queen passed. Before Summer had taken her place, the planes had threatened to mesh together.

Is that what will happen to Earth and Hell without celestial power to keep us separate?

"According to him, but he lies." I feel a dullness pour over me. How long will my children be hunted down? He wants this one gone and she isn't even out of the womb yet. I have to focus. "Do you know how long the king has been in power?"

"Over ten years." Daniel seems to have gotten some history

lessons. "But he goes off plane often, from what I understand. He's spent a lot of his time looking for another version of you. They like it when he's not here. But lately the rebellion has found someone to rally around."

I already know this part. "Lee. He's come of age and he's raising hell. I met him earlier. I hope he's okay."

"According to Sasha and the pixies, he's holed up in the temple with Rhys and the rest of the group." Danny lets a small smile light his face. "It was kind of cool to talk to the pixies. They avoid me at home, but these are spy pixies. No fear. One of them was riding Sasha's shoulder, leading him to where I was. He's with Neil. We decided it was too dangerous to move all of us. I'm worried Sasha's going to try to get into the dungeons before we're ready."

My heart aches for Sasha. I know his story well. Months ago he told us he felt his wife. "I thought Ostara was talking about you when she said vampire. Is Sasha okay? If he moves too quickly…"

"I talked to him. Ostara will keep her host alive, as will Bris," Danny says with certainty. "Sasha is going to try to get to a place where he can watch over them. Bibi says there is a way. But the dungeons are guarded, and I worry if we burst through they'll murder Dev out of spite. I don't know the layout. I need more intel and Sasha and Neil are going to get it for us. Bibi doesn't know a lot about the spell they intend to use to peel Bris off. They've never worked it before, but she thinks they're going to soften him up tonight so it will be easier tomorrow. I suspect they will use Ostara as a guinea pig. I'm not sure what they expect will happen. At least one like Bris cannot be tied to this place. I don't think they can trap him."

"But they can trap Dev?" I know the answer. Dev's soul is mortal. It will linger until it's ready to leave. It can move but not right away. If he dies, he could suffer the fate of the rest of the dead in this palace.

He puts a hand under my chin and forces me to look him in the eyes. "I love Dev, but it's Bris Myrddin wants. It's Ostara. Those ancient souls could serve as real fuel. You know what he's trying to do, right?"

I nod. He told me as much. "He's going to use that power to close the door since the plot with Gladys didn't work." I use Kelsey's name for the Sword of Light. It fits her better anyway. "I can't stand the thought of Devinshea being tortured."

"Well, he's not tonight." Danny sits back against the big bed that dominates the room, drawing me close. "We're causing some trouble. Myrddin really wants to catch me so the servants are helpfully giving reports on where they've seen me and the damage I'm doing. According to the grapevine, there are only three guards on the dungeon, and they are simply there to keep me out."

I raise a brow, silently asking the question.

"And again, I don't know what wards I'll be up against," he says with a sigh. "And you have to get that amulet. I know we wanted to ask the ancestors about how to find Sarah, but now we have another question."

How to return safely to our own time.

"Why don't they fight back?" It's what I don't get. "There are more of them than there are of the king's guard. I understand that he's powerful, but I would fight."

"Would you?" Daniel sighs, and I lay my head back against his chest. His hands go around me, one on the gentle curve of my belly where our tiny abomination sleeps. "From what I understand it wasn't like Miria and Declan were great. They caused their own damage. The lesser Fae thought they could wait it out. If they were quiet and polite. When the king took out the scarier creatures, they thought he wouldn't come for them. Ogres can be violent. Large trolls can be dangerous. Not them. They're helpful. Why would he burn gnomes and brownies?"

"Because he's a fucking monster." Tears are right there again. I know my Dev. It's awful to realize what he could have been. What any of us can be with the right pressure put on us.

"All I'm saying is that fear can lead to dangerous hope. The hope that things will work out even if you don't put yourself on the line and fight. It's all fear in the end, but at least the palace lesser Fae seem ready to do what they can. Sometimes what a rebellion needs is a sign," Danny says. "If we can break Dev and Ostara free, it might be what they need. I promise, I'm not leaving Dev in there one second more than I have to, but he would also want you to be safe. I already tried to get into the king's rooms. Myrddin's been there. He warded the place against pretty much everyone, and they locked up the servants' entrance after a couple of attempts on the king's life, so I can't get to him."

"But I can tomorrow," I say with a sigh.

"I have the utmost faith that you can and will," he replies. "And by then Rhys and Shy will have moved to the rebel village, and we can find a way to join them. I promise you, we will get out of this. We will get home, and we will take Myrddin down."

I sit against him for a moment, simply breathing in his strength. He's the center of my world, he and Devinshea. I don't know…can't begin to comprehend what I would do without either of them.

"Myrddin said if I don't play my part he'll tell the king about our baby."

Daniel whistles softly. "He really needs whatever the king has. Once he has it in hand, he's going to kill the king, and then he'll go after you. He'll try to take you into custody because he knows I'll turn myself in."

I shake my head. "No, he'll kill me because he's afraid of Harriet." I told my husbands what happened at the Council House before I blew it up, but I don't think it sank in yet. "He believes she's an abomination with the potential to kill the world or something."

Daniel is quiet for a moment.

"What do you know that I don't?"

He sighs behind me. "When we got back I talked to the academics about what happened off plane. I explained how you got pregnant."

I'm not sure I want to know what they said. "You talked to Henri?"

"And Hugo. It is not unsurprising that sometimes a latent vampire knows a companion during their human lives. They are often attracted to each other. It's not unheard of for those pairings to produce children."

I like where the words are heading. It's the way he's saying it. There's that hedging tone to his voice. The one that tells me there's a *but* in here somewhere. "And what are the children like?"

"Mostly normal. The few female vampires we have are all from latent-companion pairings."

I try not to wince. Something about vampire genetics makes the overwhelming majority of vampires male. From what I understand there are only two female vampires walking the night today. I've only met one of them and she was…odd, to say the least. But I can handle it. "I survived Lee's childhood." He's silent for a moment and I prompt him. "What else did they tell you?"

I'm proud of myself for not asking the question I want to ask. Why haven't you talked to me about this before now? Why wasn't I in on that conference of yours? That's another fight for another time.

"I'm a vampire king. You're the equivalent when it comes to companions. I believe they are worried that we take more after our ancestors than the others. That our DNA is closer and stronger to what it used to be than a normal latent and companion."

I know this one. "The Amazons? That's who the companions were. Obviously she'll have Amazon DNA."

His head shakes. "No, baby. That's what they called themselves years and years after the fall. I'm talking about who they were before they fell."

"Angels."

"Yes, the Amazons evolved from a group of fallen angels who did not turn demonic. They were warriors who took on the role of protecting humans and eventually became companions. But your ancestry is angelic. And mine is demonic. I'm considered an Earthly demon king who married an angelic queen."

He seems to be trying to lead me somewhere. But I do not understand the road map he's handed me. "And?"

He growls a little, and though I cannot see him I feel his eyeroll. "Harry didn't teach you the crap he taught me. You know you were lucky you got to spend all your time in high school playing around with the yearbook staff."

"Daniel."

"Nephilim, Zoey. Myrddin thinks Harriet is a Nephilim, and if she is, we will have trouble from both Heaven and Hell. If she is, we might wish we let Myrddin close that gate because I fear they will come for her."

Chapter Twenty

Sasha

Sasha entered the servant's quarters deep in the bowels of the palace, feeling the moment the wards came into play. It prickled along his skin, little stings digging in and refusing to let go for a moment. He wanted to turn back into the tunnels, but he had to take a deep breath and banish the feeling. It wasn't more than a moment before he could ignore it.

Naturally the wards were stronger down here in the servant's lodgings. Couldn't let the slaves get comfortable, after all.

He didn't like this version of Devinshea one bit.

"Are you okay?" Fee asked, carefully shutting the door behind them. Like the one in the temple, the seam disappeared and was completely invisible the moment the door was closed. "The wards can make one sick."

He shook his head. "I'm fine." The need to run screaming through the palace, killing everything in sight until he got his hands on his wife, was almost overwhelming. "Tell me about Ostara."

They seemed to be in a shared living space, though they were alone. There was a tiny kitchen, obviously meant to be used by the brownies. Sasha was forced to hunch over until he made it to what seemed to be a living room with ragged couches and chairs. He was pretty sure he would break them if he put his weight on one.

Fee remained in the kitchen area, pulling out a big kettle and filling it with water. "Ostara or her host?"

"You know them both?"

"Not as well as Ione." She settled the kettle over the fire in the grate and moved to knock on a door across the room. "Ione, come out. Stop your crying. It's time to go to work." He heard sniffles from behind the door. "I brought someone you will want to meet."

The door opened and Fee slid inside as though she had to coax whoever was behind there out.

"Sasha," a familiar voice said.

He turned and Neil stood in a pair of pants that didn't quite fit. The werewolf's eyes were wide as he entered the room. "Can we talk now?"

There had been little time in the stables. The network wanted to move them quickly. He only had a few moments to update the king before they moved Daniel to Zoey's room and Neil here. He'd been forced to wait because they couldn't move them all at once.

How terrified must Neil be? "No. I chose to leave. The kids are in the temple. They're safe there, and Lee is going to take them to his village in the morning. Cassie and Brendan are safe and uninjured."

Neil took a deep breath and wiped at his eyes. "Goddess, I never... Being a parent is fucking terrifying. I've been sitting here cursing myself for leaving them."

This was a subject he knew much about. He put a hand on Neil's shoulder. "Sometimes you have to step back. Daniel and Zoey and Devinshea need you. Cassie and Brendan understand. You did your best, and they are safe."

Neil slumped down on the couch. "From what the trolls told me, Daniel is with Zoey."

"He's extracting the queen?" They hadn't been clear on the plan. "If this version of Devinshea..."

Neil held up a hand. "He's going to make sure she's okay and talk to her. If I still know him, he'll be with her most of the night. He's going to ask her to deal with the king while we decide how to get Dev out. If what I've learned from the servants down here is correct, I think there's some more work we're going to have to do. Myrddin is up to something and has been for a while now. There was a reason we had the nice lull in him trying to murder us a couple of months back."

"He was here setting up whatever his plans are, and they have something to do with the mountains to the north. The ones that disturb Shy." Neil hadn't been in the room when the wizard confronted Shy. "He's afraid of her. I can't figure out why."

A brow rose over Neil's icy blue eyes. "Because that girl is hiding a mega shit ton of power. She's far more than a medium, but until now she's refused to even contemplate exploring her powers. I knew her parents, you know. Her mother was a famous medium who worked with the Council all the time. Visola Davis. Such an amazing woman. And she was worried about her daughter."

"I thought they didn't come into Dallas often."

"They didn't. They lived on a hundred acres outside of town. They were kind of a commune for psychics. When they had trouble, one of the wolves would go to their place and check it out. We did regular security sweeps. I didn't interact much with Shy, but I remember her being sweet and quiet."

"What was her mother worried about?"

"They came across a wounded deer. They had a lot of trouble with hunters in that part of the woods. Let me tell you, an encounter with a werewolf will fix that right up," Neil replied with obvious satisfaction. "Anyway, Visola wanted to go and get Shy's dad, but Shy walked up to the deer and leaned down, like she was listening. The deer had a couple of bullets in her hindquarter, and she'd broken her leg trying to get away. Shy talked to it like she talks to the dead now, even though the deer was alive. And after a moment she nodded her head and put a hand on the deer's heart and she took her last breath. Shy told her mother the deer wanted to move on, so she'd turned the wheel."

Sasha felt a cold prickle go up his spine. "Myrddin thinks she's a death goddess? How could a death goddess even be born human? To humans?"

Neil shrugged. "Who knows. All I do know is that I've seen things I can't explain. But isn't that what magic is? Magic is simply something science hasn't explained yet. We exist. We are real. So is she, and that means she has a purpose, and I worry that's why we're here. Why my best friend in the world is going to have to go through this shit again. I would do almost anything to spare her."

Anything but sacrifice his children. Sasha knew the queen's heart. "It is a sacrifice she will make a thousand times, and she is more than capable of handling both the king and Myrddin."

The door came open and Fee walked out, holding the hand of a small troll who had obviously been crying. Bibi walked out behind her, comforting the troll.

Fee presented her friend. "Sasha, this is Ione. She has taken care of Meadow since she was a baby. She is distraught at what has happened to her mistress."

Bibi's eyes lit as she saw Sasha standing there. She leaned in and whispered to the crying troll, who rushed to him, tilting her head up and giving him big, wide, pleading eyes.

"Sir, please save my mistress. You do not know it, but..." the troll began.

Oh, he knew. He knelt down so he was closer to eye level. "She is my wife in her past life. She is my wife in all of our lives."

Neil sat up. "What? You found Marta? And she's an ascended goddess of spring? Dude, there's some freaky sex in your future. I mean if she survives and stuff."

Sometimes Neil was serious and sometimes he was Neil. "I intend to ensure she survives, but I need to get a lay of the land. I have never been to this palace before. I need to know if I can get to the dungeons undetected."

Bibi stepped up. "We have tunnels the king doesn't know exist. I can get you there, but we have to be careful."

"Take me to her."

Bibi nodded.

For the second time that night, he found himself squeezing through tunnels. This one, he hoped, would lead him home.

Chapter Twenty-One

Shy

Rhys takes my hand as we enter the most sacred chamber in the temple. "This is the space where we would perform our rituals. Where we would be together."

I like how he calls them *our* rituals. Something has changed inside me since the moment I realized I could help Fae Neil, that I wasn't merely helpless to do anything but talk to spirits. I feel…settled. Ready.

Our rituals involve sex. Love. Communion of the most intimate kind.

I've literally held other souls in my body and yet I do not know what it feels like to join bodies with the man I love.

"It is also the place with the biggest bed, and we should think about that," a familiar voice says. Lee has followed us around. We managed to shake Cassie and her brother in the small kitchens. Not that there was a ton of food in there. Or at least there hadn't been until Rhys brushed his fingers over the potted fruit trees and shriveled remains of what had once been a garden. The vegetables and fruits had bloomed, growing in seconds as they soaked up Rhys's unique energy. Brendan whined since Rhys can't exactly grow him a pizza, but luckily his sister was prepared. She'd delighted in the peaches she found while tossing her brother some beef jerky.

But we still have Lee with us. He's holding on even after he showed Sasha how to get out with the best chance of getting away from the guards.

Seeing Sasha disappear into the stables without a bunch of arrows going his way was a huge relief.

But now I kind of want to be alone with my...everything.

"It's getting late. We can all bed down in here for a few hours and head out in the morning." Lee eyes the space critically, nose wrinkling at the sight of the stream that flows through the large chamber at the heart of the temple. "Though I'm wary about the water. They could send something through."

"Not unless they want to excavate about sixty feet down." Rhys has a frown on his gorgeous face. "It's actually an underground stream. This is the only place in the *sithein* where the water is on the surface. Also, the temple would keep out anything it considered impure, including anything with malicious intentions. Which is why your father no longer has access to it."

"Yeah, I know about that part, but I don't want to underestimate Myrddin. We should stick together," Lee announces.

"I intend to bed my goddess here and very soon," Rhys replies back, and he looks my way as though waiting for me to protest.

I give him a simple smile.

Lee's lips kick up in a grin. "Yes, I am well aware. It's going to be very helpful to all of our plans. Proceed, brother. I like a good fertility ritual. Do you need any..."

A thick vine wraps around Lee's waist and begins dragging him from the room.

"Have you thought at all about what will happen when we begin?" Rhys asks. "If you're not in the right room, you'll be affected by it, and she really is far too young. I will kill you if you touch Cassie." His eyes narrow. "Or her brother."

"I was joking. Mostly. I am prepared for your magic. There's a room in the temple that is shielded. As I said before the palace is under some heavy wards, though I suspect they'll still feel it." He sighs. "Fine. But you're really no fun. I bet I'm a ton of fun in your timeline."

"You are a pain in my ass," Rhys replies as he gestures toward the door. The minute Lee is out, the door slams closed, and I hear the sound of a lock sliding into place. He turns to me. "Now that the riffraff is taken care of, you can tell me what happened. You were locked into some kind of spell with Myrddin."

I would rather he throw himself on me, but I can understand his worry. I look around the chamber. It's lit with soft lights from above. I can't see them so I have to believe they're magical. They make the room glow. The sacred space comprises three levels. There's the stream below us, with a large bathing pool in the center that the water flows into and out of. It's got stone flooring and steps down to what is a beautifully done cabana. "It wasn't a spell. It was a battle. What did it look like?"

We're standing on the second level. There's an altar with a bowl and candles and various offerings long since turned to dust. I suspect St. John's wort, marigolds, and such were once offered here by those who wanted to benefit from the Green Man and his goddess.

"Like the two of you were frozen in place," Rhys explains, his eyes steady on me. "I tried to get to you but there was some kind of energy that kept me away."

That ancient warmth I felt, the one that I know is mine and yet I cannot give it a name. "We were fighting over Neil's soul. When he died, I realized I could spare his soul by taking him into mine. Myrddin seems to have some kind of spell that drags spirits to him since he didn't actively pull Neil until I stopped the flow."

"You've never done that before and you've seen people die." Rhys is almost too still, like a predator who worries his prey will run if he moves too quickly.

I have no intention of running. Not tonight. We can play that out later.

Why was I ever afraid of this? Am I coming to accept my sexual needs? Needs I refused to think about for so very long. Or perhaps I'm being affected by this sacred place meant for sex. Either way, I don't care. Desire is a drug in my veins and one I fear I can easily get addicted to. I glance up at that third floor. The one with the big bed and what looks like soft, warm quilts. It's dark up there, but we don't need much light. "The souls I've seen either moved on or chose to stay. I've never been in a position where a soul could be destroyed or imprisoned. It was an instinct to save him."

He moves slowly into my space, his big body looming over mine. "That was power, Shy. Raw, unfiltered power. Everyone felt it. I swear it stopped the fighting briefly because it slammed into all of us. I've never felt anything like it."

And he's worried. "I can handle it. I know it seems sudden, but I'm not afraid of it. It's like when I broke free of your vines. I suddenly knew what to do. What questions to ask in that case. I didn't work my will. Simply asked if the vine wouldn't mind helping me out."

"By dying."

"By turning early." For the first time in hours I feel insecurity slip in. "I didn't kill it. It isn't truly gone."

He holds a hand up as though he knows what's going on in my head. "I did not mean dying is bad. It's natural, but up until now all of your powers have been in talking to the dead. What happened today goes far beyond a medium. Shy, can you feel the dead here? From what I understand the king hasn't been allowed inside in a long time."

I close my eyes and send out that part of me that senses the dead things of the world. "There are many creatures buried around the grounds, but they're at peace. This is not a place for the restless dead. This is a place of life. This is where they come when they are ready for the wheel to turn."

His lips kick up in a sweet grin. "You've spent too much time with the witches. You talk like a witch now. The next thing I know you'll be doing shadow work and surrounding us with crystals."

I shake my head. "It feels right. And I know I'm correct about this place. There are no restless dead in the temple or on the grounds right now. But the palace is out of balance. The dead have their place. Even the restless ones. I think I know what Myrddin is doing."

"I don't want to think about him tonight, Shy. I know we should go downstairs and join the others and plan," he begins.

I do not want that. "Or we could bring this temple back to life and show this *sithein* what they are missing. The temple needs you. Can't you feel it?"

His eyes darken, the green of the deepest forest. "In my soul. The temple wants an offering. It's been many years since a high priest brought his magic here. Brought his goddess here and shared their love with it. This temple magnifies our magic."

I don't correct him the way I would have a mere day before. It is *our* magic. Like Ostara said. We are opposites and feed each other, nurture each other in a way we cannot on our own, could not with anyone else in all the planes.

"What exactly does that mean?" My question comes out on a breathy sigh. "Lee said something about wards."

"I suspect the king has warded against all kinds of magic. You saw even the servants wore talisman and charms. If they weren't protected, then a ceremony like what we're about to perform would be felt throughout the *sithein*. However, I'm grateful for the wards since there's an evil version of my father out there who I don't want horny and wild. Lee told me the wards don't extend to the dungeons since they use magic to torture prisoners."

I gasp, understanding what he's trying to tell me. "Your father and Ostara will take in our magic."

"It will strengthen them, and there will be nothing their captors can do about it. This magic slips in and out and finds who needs it the most. It will bring the palace grounds back to their former glory."

More than that. "It will bring hope to the ones who need it."

"Shy, I don't want you to do this to save someone else."

I roll my eyes. "I'm not doing it for the sake of the *sithein*. I'm doing it because I want you. I know I've been reluctant, and it was all about my fear. I'm done with fear. I worried I couldn't stand on my own because Harry was with me all those years, but I was wrong. He was good to me, but he wasn't my power. My power has always been inside me. It isn't a scary thing. It simply is. I am it and it is me, and we have always been."

"When you talk like that, I'm the one who is scared because I realize we haven't begun to find the depths of your power. When you talk like that, I know we're not even sure what you are yet."

He's right, and he should have a choice. "Will you find out with me? Or wait and see?"

His stare goes hard, and his hands tighten on me. "I will allow nothing to separate us, Shahidi. I mean it. I will leave you alone if you do not want me sexually. I will keep my distance if your heart does not want mine, but I will protect you always. You will always be my goddess even if I am not your god."

I was never afraid of him. I was afraid of loving him so much I would be destroyed if I lost him or hurt him.

But he is worth the risk. I go on my toes, my lips so close to his. "Then explore with me. Fight this fight with me. Be the one thing I never have to compromise on. Make me yours in the eyes of your people."

I am already his where it truly counts. In my heart. But he is a leader and there are rituals.

His mouth finds mine, lips soft at first, and then I feel his will. It's there in the way his tongue licks along the seam of my lips, how it invades when I welcome it inside, sliding along mine in a silky glide that somehow has a straight track to my pussy.

Heat pools there, anticipation that suddenly knows it will be fulfilled this time.

He steps back, and for a second I stare at him. Marveling in his beauty. Thick black hair that brushes past his broad shoulders. He pulls his tunic over his head, tossing it away, and there is such lust in his eyes. The god inside is not like his father's. Bris is a separate entity, but Rhys is a fertility deity all on his own, and yet that part of him has been suppressed for so long, there's a sweet madness around him now.

He holds out a hand and starts up the stairs toward the bed. "Come with me."

A command and one I'm more than willing to follow. I let him lead me to what is obviously a space meant for pleasure. As we reach the landing, soft candlelight flares to life, and I see what I did not before. What I thought were curtains are hundreds of pixies. Wings of all colors and sizes flutter against the window, moonlight joining the candles to illuminate this space where we will join our lives and magic together.

Life and death. Spring and autumn.

Rhys and Shy.

The window has no glass in it, but like the palace there's a magical barrier. I can feel a warm breeze, but if Rhys wills it the temple will close itself off. For now it lets in the light from the moon and the stars, the sweet scent of night-blooming flowers caressing my senses.

His face falls suddenly, and a low groan goes through him. "Shy, my pack is back in the palace. Damn it."

His pack. With all the helpful items he brought along. Condoms. There's no pulling out with a fertility god. The pill doesn't work either.

But I asked the vine if it didn't mind moving on early. I have control of my body. I turn the wheel.

Damn. I am not human. Or rather I am human and something more. "It's okay, Rhys. I'm not ready for a child. I won't be for a while."

Our powers are complementary. They only work on each other when we wish them to. I feel it so keenly that I know it's true.

"You can stop me." There's a slight smile on his lips. Admiration.

"I can decide. Our bodies are wheels, too. I decide when I'm ready, and no gorgeous fertility god can get around my will." I move into his space this time. He has never had control over this part of his magic. His father hadn't either. It was only when he took on Bris that Dev Quinn could control some of it. "I am your control, Rhys. I am your goddess."

"My magic flows from you."

"And mine flows from you." We are like the stream that runs through the temple. We meet in the middle, our magic forming a pool we can drink from, luxuriate in, draw from. We do not have to fear our magic. I would not have found this magic without Rhys Donovan-Quinn, and his would be out of control without me.

"You are sure?" Rhys asks, his whole body taut but his eyes hot on me.

As sure as I can be. I know it deep in my soul, the same way I know we were meant to come here. Myrddin might have tricked us, but there is a greater purpose at work.

The wizard really should remember the rule of three. But that is a thought for another night.

I nod.

"Then you should be undressed, my goddess."

I take a deep breath, ready to begin.

Chapter Twenty-Two

Sasha

Sasha breathed deeply, thanking the universe that he wasn't afraid of small spaces. These "tunnels" had obviously been created for brownies and trolls and gnomes. The small Fae creatures. They had not been created for a six-foot, three-inch muscular vampire. And yet he fit. He had to walk sideways, but he fit as long as he didn't breathe too deeply.

"Are we almost there? This is terrible. And the smells…"

Neil had decided to come along. He also decided to complain. A lot. Sasha had shushed him several times, but Bibi had explained the walls were reenforced with magic. Lee had brought in witches to spell the tunnels so they were soundproof. Going out. Not coming in. They would be able to see and hear what was going on in the dungeons once they reached what Bibi called the king's audience room.

It wasn't a part of the tunnel system the rebels had managed to build over the last decade, but they had attached a tunnel to it.

"We are close to the audience room," Bibi promised. "It will not be so crowded."

Neil sighed behind him, but Sasha kept moving. "How will we know the king won't be watching tonight?"

"Because he hasn't used it in years," Bibi replied. "Once he met the wizard he started participating in the torture sessions. I believe it is because the magic works better if he is in the room."

"What do they say about the king's new magic?" Neil asked.

"That it is dark. We all fear it. They say when the king or the wizard has you, there is no coming back. Not even in death," Bibi said quietly, moving with ease. "They say he eats souls."

"I have friends in another timeline who don't believe that it is possible, though there might be a way to trick a soul into trapping itself." When he'd become a vampire he'd stayed with an academic named Marcus Vorenus. Vorenus had been an excellent mentor and they spent many nights sitting around his luxurious Venetian townhouse arguing points of law or history, or in this case, philosophy. "The question is are the rules different here because we're in another timeline. Myrddin can cross them. He might have come here to take advantage of the difference in how things work here."

"I think some rules are immutable." Neil sounded serious again. "It's why Kelsey's in Hell right now. No one believes Myrddin could destroy Liv's soul, but he might be able to hold it somewhere. Or it might hide. What if he's found a way to tempt the soul to go to a particular place?"

"Like the mountains that called to Shy." It wasn't a question. He knew they would have to deal with whatever Shy was here to do.

"The king believes he is eating souls and gaining power from it," Bibi says quietly. "It might be a lie from the wizard, but he truly thinks he is the most powerful king in the history of the Seelie Fae. Why would the wizard lie?"

"Because he needs your king for something," Sasha explained. "In our timeline the wizard has grown desperate. I would bet this is some long-term scheme of his that he's suddenly kicked into high gear. The king wasn't expecting him, was he?"

"The wizard returned to our palace a week ago, and from all reports there was no scheduled meeting. I was not in the room, but we had eyes and ears on them. The king's personal dresser has become adept at a form of language that uses only the hands. He cannot write down the things he hears, but his hand language somehow gets around the spell." She stopped and ran her hand along the wall. In a moment, the bricks receded, a small opening appearing. Sure enough, there was a throne chair and what appeared to be a two-way mirror.

"The room is spelled to be soundproof. The king enjoyed laughing and clapping but sometimes it unnerved the torturers, so he can turn it off or on. He also enjoyed giving orders. What he did not enjoy was getting his clothes bloody."

Though he seemed to have gotten over it now. Sasha stopped at the sight in front of him. There were two Devinsheas in that dark chamber, though it was easy to tell them apart. One was dressed regally and the other one was wrapped in cold iron, his hands over his head, feet barely touching the floor. A high-stress position that would have Dev's whole body screaming in moments and would most likely dislocate his shoulders soon.

"Damn it," Neil breathed as he walked in behind Sasha. "This is why I convinced Danny to check in on Z. If he saw that…"

Devinshea was Daniel's. Vampires were possessive creatures, and Dev and the queen were Daniel's precious blood. He would lose his shit. Like Sasha wanted to lose his because Ostara was in the room, too. Her slender form was tied to a chair. She still wore the gossamer gown she'd selected for dinner but it was wrinkled, the hem covered in the mud they drug her through. Her golden hair hung limply around her torso, and she had been crying.

His heart threatened to break.

She was here.

She didn't look like his Marta, but it was her all the same. If he hadn't been a vampire, he likely wouldn't have known, would have merely believed she was some woman he'd just met who touched him in some odd spiritual way.

How many times? How many times had he looked at her face and known they were meant to be?

This time…this fucking time would be forever. This he vowed.

"It's honestly unnerving being in the same room with him," the king said as he looked Devinshea up and down. "I think he's thinner than me."

"Well, I'm not feasting on the souls of my enemies, you whacked-out bastard," Dev spat back.

"Please," Ostara began.

Dev managed to turn his body slightly her way. "Shut up. Let me do the talking."

It was said in a harsh grind, but Sasha knew the words beneath it. Right now Ostara was a side project. There seemed to be three guards in charge of the dungeons. One was stationed by the door, but the other two were behind Devinshea. It was obvious they were already at work since Sasha's friend had several round burn marks on his torso. His previously white shirt was in tatters and now a muddy red brown, but he was healing right in front of them.

The king nodded, and one of the guards hauled a long poker out of the raging fire blazing in the furnace. He didn't hesitate to shove it into Dev's shoulder, steam rising where it sank in. Dev's jaw went tight, teeth gritting, but only a low moan came from him.

The guard pulled the poker out and stepped back. In mere seconds it began to heal.

"What is this magic?" the king complained, looking utterly disgusted with the fact that his wounds wouldn't stay.

A long sigh came from the doorway. Myrddin stood there. "I told you he's on vampire blood."

"The vampires here don't heal others."

"Because the vampires on this plane are *baobhan sith*. It's not the same. They don't share blood the way the vampires on the inner planes do," Myrddin said. "Devinshea has been on it a long time, so it will take a lot of damage to get it out of his system. He's Daniel's lover, and that means Daniel shares blood with him. Daniel's blood is powerful. I believe I told you this won't work right away. Between the god inside him and that damn vamp blood, this could take a while."

"Or I could drain all the vampire blood out of his body and then the problem is solved." The king snapped his fingers. "Get me a blade. I'll slit his throat and this can be over."

Sasha felt Neil tense beside him and knew they were about to have to make a choice.

Even as the guards handed him a long cold iron blade, Myrddin was shaking his head. "I told you, Your Majesty, if you kill him immediately, the god will flee. You have to separate the god from the man in a very specific way. It's the only way to take the god's energy yourself and regain the power of your temple."

"Bullshit." Neil's arms crossed over his chest. "Nothing can hold Bris. I don't know what the hell he thinks he's doing, but he's absolutely conning that king."

The king sneered and moved in, dagger still in his hand. "Maybe I don't care about the temple."

Sasha would give it to the wizard. He was a cool customer.

"All right, but I'm not sure why you need a goddess if you won't have a temple," Myrddin said.

"The temple will open to me when I have a proper goddess." He held the dagger under Devinshea's chin. "Tell me something. Do you have a temple in your timeline? I suspect you do."

"I have two," Dev replied. "In my time, I am the bridge between our tribes. Seelie and Unseelie claim me. My goddess can power any number of temples but only if the temple finds the god worthy."

"The Unseelie are impure. They are the assassins of our world. Did you know my brother used Unseelie infestations to kill my beloved? And all because I would not take a bride. Do you have any idea what they did to her?" The king sneered, showing his distaste.

"Probably a lot of what they tried to do to me. Did Mother send Declan to the Unseelie *sithein*? Did you follow?" Dev asked.

"Of course not. We have no relations with the dark court," the king replied. "None except planning our wars."

"Well, she did send my brother, and I went with him. It's odd how time refines and shapes memory. For so long all I thought about was how they forced me. We were caught by a rogue group. My brother got away. I did not. I remember how awful it was, and that was all I thought about at the time. But now I remember how a group of trolls found me, lying there. Spent and aching, and they took care of me," Dev said. "The Unseelie has its monsters. And its kindness and beauty and love. The same way we do. The temple rejects you because you are the Seelie monster. Just because someone calls you light, doesn't mean you are good. Because someone calls themselves clean does not mean they are worthy. It simply means they understand neither word."

The king chuckles, a wholly unhumorous sound. "You are weak. When you're dead and that god has fled in terror, I will show your goddess what we can truly be."

Dev's head shook. "You will be left with a dead *sithein*. It's already in the process, isn't it? Your kingdom is dying because there's no such thing as an evil Green Man. Your magic was a gift and it's gone now. You were unworthy."

The knife moved to Devinshea's throat, and a fine trickle of blood began. "You are the unworthy one. You allowed the wizard to take your kingdom. You were foolish enough to fall into our trap again. You don't deserve her."

"I defied my brother and Mother for her," Dev declared. "I didn't treat her like a dirty secret. When she had our babies, I was there. She didn't labor alone and suffer without my aid. I held them in my hands. Two. I was gifted two children, and then another beautiful girl. Your son hates you. You are the king of a dead *sithein*, barely holding on to a populace that hates you, too. They loathe you, Devinshea. They see down to your cowardly soul. The only reason they haven't risen up is you found borrowed magic, and when Myrddin gets what he wants from you, that will be gone and your head will be on a rebel pike. You killed it all. All of this death and horror because you were a coward."

"Is he trying to get murdered?" Bibi asked with a shudder.

"He knows exactly what the man is afraid of, who he is because deep down Devinshea is honest with himself. Even when he's wrong," Neil said with a sniffle. "Goddess, how will I tell Zoey if he dies?"

"He won't." Sasha saw Myrddin's hand come up, his fingers twisting slightly. "You see that? He's having to be subtle about it, but I would bet he's working some kind of calming spell. You said the wards weren't up here, right?"

Bibi nodded. "The king likes to use magic against his enemies, and it's hard with the wards because he's never been good with it. He thinks he's some kind of magic wielder now that the wizard has taught him some things, but he is still a bit inept. The guards had to take down the wards because the king's own magic couldn't overcome them even after they were trained to. That's not what they told him, of course, but they had to do something. Myrddin himself has had to come in to strengthen the spells holding us from time to time."

Sure enough the king took a step back, sneering at the version of himself currently in chains. "I will have my temple back. When I take the god, the temple won't be able to keep me out. And I will take my bride in our sacred space, and all will be right with the world again."

He turned and stormed out.

One of the guards started sneering Ostara's way, an unholy light in his eyes. "I don't think he cares about you, pretty girl. Didn't look at you even once. I don't think he'll care what I do to you."

Dev found the strength to kick out and send the fucker stumbling and falling forward.

So all the guards were on him again.

Sasha breathed a sigh of relief. He owed Devinshea.

Myrddin *tsked* as the guards punched and kicked Dev. "Prince, you never learn. She's of absolutely no value. She's weak. Her goddess was trapped for too long without form, and it will take years and years for her to recover. I brought her over because I needed to show the king how to separate a god from a host. Well, I need to make sure I do it properly. Practice does make perfect and all. Poor thing really thought she was saving her plane. Women are easily led. Promise them a few baubles, a tiny bit of power. Saving their people from hunger and they just go right along with it. Gentlemen, give me a moment."

The guards stepped back, retreating to a part of the dungeon where Sasha's gaze couldn't track them.

"Yes, I'm sure my wife is going along with all of this because that asshole version of me offered her a new shoe collection." Dev spat some blood from his mouth, barely missing the wizard.

Myrddin frowned at Dev. "She's being perfectly obnoxious. I would have given him anything else, but he would take no other prize. I know it's a mistake, but if I don't sit down here and talk with you, I'll have to deal with…well, the other you, and strangely I like you more. Or perhaps not strangely. You're a likable chap, Devinshea. I found you quite a nice lad to talk to when you weren't fighting me."

"I didn't fight you because you put a thrall stone in my head," Dev bit off. "But please continue. I would love to know why we're in this specific position."

"Like Lucifer, I often attempt divination. I use a demon or witch as a focus so I can calculate which paths to take. Imagine my surprise when that idiot Olivia had so much power, she could show me not only different outcomes on our plane but how the timelines would fracture in any given scenario. By the way, you not returning at all actually went quite poorly for me. At some point your human security team would have went looking for you when their contracts were up, and that shockingly led to my untimely death at a rather large blond man's hands. Working with Olivia's power taught me how to jump into a different timeline. Such an odd place. People were happy and thriving and working together to heal the world. It was unnerving. I didn't like it so I tried again. Eventually, I found this place that has, shall we say, some unique properties. I don't know if your mother's *sithein* would work the same way since it's technically on the Earth plane. These Fae lands form one of a thousand different Fae planes. I suppose this timeline broke off when your grandfather chose to leave the Earth plane entirely and found a home. Either way, I doubt your mother would have given me what I need."

"And what is that?" Dev asked

"Energy, of course. I've always known my plans to use the Sword of Light to close the door to the Heaven plane might not work out, so I've looked for other sources of energy," the wizard admitted. "This particular plane has mountains that amplify a specific resonance. But the land is attached to the king. I need his help, so that meant I needed to find a way to give him something he wants."

"Zoey."

The wizard's eyes rolled. "She must have a magical pussy. Too bad it's attached to her personality. I truly hate that woman. However, you're correct. He would only take his lost love. He intends to spend his immortal life with her. I'm supposed to be working on how to make her immortal, by the way. I'll be long gone before then, and she can deal with him."

"Oh, none of us are truly immortal." Dev rolled his head as though trying to work the kinks out. His body was already healed, but he had to be in pain. "You should know I intend to bury that fucker, and then I'll deal with you."

"I'm sure you'll try, and I don't know about that. Immortality, that is. I recently ran up against some magic I haven't felt in millennia. Magic I was certain had been destroyed," Myrddin said with a low growl.

"Good for you. I hope it swallows you whole," Dev replied with a shit-eating grin.

At least one of them knew what to do. Ostara sat quietly. She was being sweet and patient and allowing Dev to take the risks.

And then he noticed her shoulder move slightly.

Damn it. She had a knife, and she was trying to cut her way out. They would hurt her. He felt a growl start deep in his chest.

And a thrill of pride run through him. His Marta hadn't been some simpering thing. She'd been fierce. When he went missing she went up against a corrupt system to find him, and when that system came for her she ensured their daughter survived.

She was always a warrior.

"She's trying to escape." Though he knew Myrddin couldn't hear him, his voice went to a whisper.

"But where would she go?" Bibi asked, her eyes wide with worry.

Myrddin only had eyes for Devinshea. "I was talking about my plans and how you fit into them. My point is I will keep you and that bitch wife of yours alive as long as I need to in order to get the king to do my bidding. Or I can kill you all now and try to find some backwoods version of her who will likely last all of two days before he realizes no goddess can power a god who gave up his magic. It's your choice. As long as he's torturing you, he's likely not raping her."

"Told you it's all a con," Neil whispered.

"You can't pull Bris off me," Dev said boldly.

"I can," the wizard assured him, "but unfortunately I can't make him do the new and insane Devinshea's bidding. Even if you tell him, he won't believe you. So if you want to survive, you won't try that psychological shit when I'm not around to calm him."

"Why don't you kill him and take whatever the fuck you want?" Dev's eyes narrowed. "It's attached to him. You need him. Is it DNA? Because if it is, you could use me. Get my wife and partner out of here, give my people safe passage back to our timeline, and I'll do it."

"I almost believe you." Myrddin looked him over as if trying to decide what to do. "I might be willing except Daniel is out there. I really hoped he would die or get caught. I have certain spells going that will weaken him, but he is still the king. It would have made things so much easier if he simply died. Now I didn't tell you all of this simply to entertain you. I am well aware how resilient Daniel can be. But your group is split now, and the kiddos are locked in the temple. I've already got soldiers looking for those tunnels. I'm not a complete fool. They're also looking for Daniel. I could flee and give up my plans and leave you here. It might be the easiest thing to do."

Dev let a moment go by. "Or?"

"I could get what I need. I can only do that if you allow your wife to pull the king under her spell. I will tell you that woman is already working her magic on him. I need a day or two."

Dev's head shook. "So I get tortured and you leave us here to deal with the fallout."

"Or I get what I need, take care of the king, and you and yours have a new kingdom to rule over," Myrddin offered. "Think about it. It's not bad. I can find a way to ship the rest of your clan over and then we all get what we want."

"Like I would trust you," Dev replied.

"If you distract him, I will keep my word." Myrddin's gaze was securely on Devinshea. "If you don't escape and allow the queen to play her part, I will destroy the king and leave you be. I will send my witches to tell your children and your people how to join you here. If you are still here in the morning and do not attempt escape, we will make this bargain. If you are still here in the morning, we will make it official. It will be a promise to a Fae king on Fae land."

"Fuck." Neil let out a long huff. "He's serious. Dev has to take him seriously because if he doesn't follow through, Dev can call Herne down on him."

"Only if he stands in the same space and calls him out." Bibi obviously knew the rules. "He's betting Devinshea won't be able to find his way back."

"Any Quinn would be able to call the Wild Hunt." Sasha had heard the stories. The Wild Hunt was a way to enforce promises both to and from royal Fae. Led by Herne the Hunter, the Wild Hunt could be called down on anyone who lied to a royal or a royal who lied to them. They were something of a check and balance in a world that had few of them. "All we would need to do is find a way to get word to Lee or Evan. Even to Devinshea's brother. If Myrddin can find the right magic, so can we. But he's trying to buy time."

"And we have to as well," Neil replied. "We have to buy time for Rhys to get Shy out of here. To get my kids out of here. Then we can figure out how to force Myrddin to take us home. If nothing else we take the stones and go back to the mountain and find another door. At least one of us does. But it would be better if we simply forced Myrddin to take us."

Myrddin stopped, his head tilting up as though he was scenting the air. A long frown came over his face and then Devinshea sighed and smiled.

"I think that temple is going to come to life tonight, and it won't be for your boy, asshole," Dev said with a grin.

Myrddin cursed and was turning to the door when the guards prowled back in the room.

"Do you feel that?" Neil asked. "It's faint because I've got a charm."

Sasha watched the guards because he definitely felt it. Faintly. He had a tat on his body that protected him from Rhys's unique magic. As one of Rhys's foster fathers, he'd been forced to find a way to counteract the fact that sometimes a young fertility god's power went a little weird. He'd been the lucky one. He could get a tat. Trent Wilcox was a werewolf and had to depend on charms and wards like Neil.

"I think I need to..." Bibi put a hand on her chest. "I cannot be here... I must get back behind the wards before I lose control."

The troll ran back to the tunnels.

Because Rhys's magic was thrumming through the air.

"If you let them hurt her, I'll give you nothing," Dev was saying.

That was the moment Sasha realized the guards were circling Ostara. They were under the influence of all that magic, and she was the only woman close to them.

"I have to find a way in." He couldn't leave her there. Couldn't watch what they would put her through.

Myrddin's gaze went greedy. "They're so full of lust they can't help themselves. They'll fuck her over and over again."

"It's rape," Dev pointed out.

"It doesn't have to be," Myrddin replied and held a hand up. The guards stopped, seemingly frozen in place. Myrddin turned to Dev. "I'll make it easy. All you have to do is be here in the morning and we'll negotiate the rest then. Let's make this promise a simple one. I will not go and kill your wife if you promise to stay until morning when we negotiate further."

He was putting Dev in a position where he could wiggle his way out of staying.

"I told you I would think about it and give you my answer in the morning."

"Yes, that was before your son decided to screw everything up. I'm not a fool. Daniel will use this time to free you," Myrddin countered.

Dev's jaw went tight. "He won't. He won't save me because he knows it puts our wife in more danger. He won't come for me until he's freed her."

One of the guards put a hand on Ostara's shoulder.

Sasha felt a low growl start in the back of his throat.

"Myrddin will kill us all," Neil said, holding him back. "I've watched him kill twenty wolves with a twist of his hand. Please wait. Dev is trying, and they are both feeding off this energy. She might surprise you."

"Give me until tomorrow," Myrddin offered. "I cannot simply leave you without guards, but no one I send here will be prepared for that magic your son is putting out. Even I feel the effects. A deal from a royal Fae. You will stay here until tomorrow and I will send them away."

Devinshea nodded. "Until tomorrow, and then all bets are off."

Myrddin turned toward the guards and twisted his hand, the guards stopping in an instant. "Find your satisfaction elsewhere."

The guards ran out.

"I suppose you'll feed on this magic," Myrddin said, his gaze tight. "I have to get back to the palace and pray the wards hold. You should hope so, too, or it's your wife who will bear the brunt of it. Think about what I said, Devinshea. We will make our true deal tomorrow. I want it properly witnessed."

Sasha took a long breath and put a hand to the mirror. She was so small, seemingly frail. That body housed his soul's mate.

"Are you okay?" Dev asked. "Take a deep breath and let the magic in. My son's energy can help heal you."

Ostara's shoulders moved again and then her hands were free. She stood and her eyes were wholly emerald, with no hint of white. "Thank you, Green Man. And I will thank your son as well because he is giving me energy I haven't felt in hundreds of years." She turned toward the mirror. "Well, are you coming to save us or not, Oleg Federov?"

Chapter Twenty-Three

Shy

I start to bring my hands up but something catches my wrists. Flowering vines. Purple buds seem to wink at me as they caress my skin. Those vines of night-blooming flowers hold my hands slightly out while another, thicker vine snakes it's way to the top of my bodice. I see a wicked-looking thorn there.

"Rhys Donovan-Quinn, what am I supposed to wear tomorrow?" I ask even as I feel the delicate material begin to tear.

His lips curl up. "Cassie has clothes with her. You're not hiking in that dress."

Cassie does not have my breasts, but he's right about one thing. The ethereal gown I'm wearing isn't going to hold up against the tunnels and then the forest. I'll find something that fits me properly when I get to Lee's village.

"Now hush and let me see you." He stands back and looks so much like the prince he is. Slightly arrogant. Wholly in control.

The thorn tears through the fabric like a knife through butter, leaving my gown gaping open and my breasts on display. Cool air tickles my flesh and my nipples peak immediately. While the air is slightly chilly against my skin, there's another place that's warming up.

My arms drop and the vines allow the dress to pool on the floor before catching me again in their embrace.

The vines wind around my arms, and they're so soft I know he's manipulating them. Flowers bloom along my skin, wrapping me in his power. This is Spring worshipping me in his way, and I am surrounded by him. They wind up my arms and over my torso, curling around my breasts, and I wonder what I look like to him.

"Fuck, you are so gorgeous, baby." Rhys's eyes take me in, roaming my body like I'm a work of art he needs to study. "I knew you were beautiful, but you are so much more."

"How do I get you out of those clothes? I can't exactly have spirits rip them off you."

A brow rises over his eyes as he approaches, careful to step around the glossy green vines covering the floor. "Rip? I assure you it's far more delicate than that. See."

He twists his hands and two thin strands of the greenest ivy climb my legs and wind under the undies I'm wearing. It's the only thing I have on that's not Fae approved, but I do like my cotton bikinis. They're dragged down my legs, and I step out of them. "You are still fully dressed."

"I'm not as pretty as you."

A lie. He's a Greek god. Or rather a Fae one. He could be a marble statue in any number of art museums. I've watched women fall over themselves to get a look at him.

And he never noticed. Not once. Oh, I'm certain he thought women were attractive, but this man has never given me the slightest indication he wants anyone but me.

My fears are my own, and I let them go in the face of his love and devotion.

His expression falls and his hand comes up, fingers brushing away a tear. "Shy, if you're..."

"I was thinking about how much I love you."

He takes a shaky breath. "And I love you. I've loved you from almost the moment I met you. I knew very quickly I was made for you."

I have to smile. "Someone taught you right."

"Well, my mother would have put it that way."

"And I was meant for you," I reply. It was odd. I meant to say made, but it didn't feel right on my tongue. Like I was made for something else, that part of me that sees the dead. But the part of me that loves and lives is meant for him. Since walking into Faery, I can feel parts of myself coming to life. Or rather coming online after a long, dormant sleep. "Rhys, something is happening to me."

He nods. "You are coming into your power and that power is Fae." He kisses my forehead and both cheeks. "I do not know what would have happened if that bastard hadn't thrown my parents to the winds and murdered your own. I have to believe that at some point you would have shown your powers and they would have brought you to the Council and we still would have met but without all of the trauma between us."

He's right. My family was well known to the Council. When my power started showing any signs beyond what they understood, they would have brought me in to help understand them. When they realized the powers were Fae, I would have been brought to Devinshea Quinn, who would have taught me and introduced me to his son.

We were always meant to be, and there is nothing Myrddin Emrys can do about it.

"And if my powers are dangerous?" It is the only thing I fear now.

"Listen to me, love. There is nothing dangerous about you. The power would only be dangerous if you were. I spent my life being told it was dangerous to be around me."

"Only if you didn't want a bunch more kids," I reply.

He hushes me with a kiss. "I was a child and I couldn't control it, and no one wanted to be around me. Adults would see me coming and walk the other way. You did not have to endure that, and I am grateful. Your power is coming to you at a time when you can handle it. When we can handle it. If we find out that you can blow out the world with a thought, I'll sleep easy knowing it won't ever happen."

He's wrong. There are reasons I might. If I lost him. This. This is what I feared because I'm already so deeply in love with him I can't imagine a world without him. What would I do if he was the one down in the dungeons?

"You would find a safe way to save me. You would trust that I could handle it until you could come and get me," he says, his mouth hovering above mine.

I didn't realize I spoke the question aloud. And I wasn't sure he was right. I can be reasonable about many things. He is not one of them.

But the thoughts fly out of my head as he kisses me, his tongue sliding against mine. The vines that hold me tighten deliciously, and one of them runs down to my thigh, coming dangerously close to the apex of my being right now.

"We have a war to fight, Shy, and I promise I am going to stop being an overprotective ass. I'm going to trust you and be calm and have faith in your abilities," he vows. "I will trust my wife, my love, my goddess."

He steps back, and I'm suddenly raised in the air, my feet leaving the ground as those seductive vines carry me toward the bed. It's the oddest feeling. I'm floating like I weigh nothing at all, and I know damn well I do. I feel delicate and airy and precious, and when I'm laid out on that soft quilt and Rhys stands between my outstretched legs, I feel something I so rarely do.

Powerful.

Rhys stares at me for a moment and then drops to his knees. He's positioned me perfectly. I know this is technically both of our first sexual experiences, but he doesn't need a lot of tutoring. His brother might have had to practice to become good at pleasing a lover, but it's in Rhys Donovan-Quinn's freaking DNA. His jaw tightens and the vines ease my legs apart again, giving him more space. He reaches up, hand trailing from my throat over my breastbone and down. He runs his palm over my belly, an act of pure possession, and moves again to right above my pussy. "Do you know how long I've waited for this?"

I do. As long as I have. "Forever."

"Forever," he agrees and then he lowers his mouth to my pussy and I can't think anymore.

Pure sensation flows through me, lighting up every nerve in my body. Even as I feel the warm caress of his tongue on my most sensitive flesh, I sense something happening in the temple. The lights around us seem to pulse, and the wave of Rhys's unique magic breaks against me, body and soul.

I am not ready to be pregnant. I have to tell my body because that magic of Rhys's is very seductive.

But I can handle it. So much of his overwhelming power flows from me and I give him control and take it for myself. We can enjoy this magic, share it with the people and beings who need it, and only use it for ourselves when we choose. We are in control together in a way we never were alone.

His tongue runs over my pussy again and again, each stroke sending waves of pure pleasure through my body, and I can practically feel myself glowing with it.

When I look down my body, I see that he is the glowing one. His eyes are pure emerald orbs, his skin sun-kissed, forming the most beautiful contrast to mine. The sun and moon. Starlight and sunbeams.

The world as it should be.

I let my head fall back and give over to the pleasure. The first orgasm hits me when he sucks my clit between his lips as his fingers slide deep inside my body, caressing some spot I never knew existed. I fall over the edge, breath stopping for a moment as the whole room is bathed in a golden glow that seems to come from the walls themselves. Like the temple is connected and the heart has found the rhythm of our own.

Rhys gets to his knees, chucking his clothes in an eagerness that brings a smile to my lips. The vines have slid away, caressing me one last time as though they love me, too.

But now is Rhys's time.

For a moment he's the teen boy I met, the one who had been slightly shy. Already a soldier and confident in battle, but he hesitated when it came to me. The boy who followed me in those first days, standing far away as though he knew I was nervous but he would not allow me to be unprotected.

He knew before I did.

We are in a foreign land. An alien time. Surrounded by enemies, his parents in danger. And I will not allow this to be anything but joyful.

I hold out my hand, my naked body on display. A comfortable display because this is easy and magical between us. "Tell me the words to give you."

His head shakes slightly, and he looks so gorgeous in that golden glow that bathes the temple. "Someone in my grandmother's court would have to do it for it to be legal."

"Rhys, you are not of your grandmother's court. You are the High Priest of the Earthly Fae and will never live and serve in a *sithein*. You are the authority of your court. I don't need my marriage to be acknowledged in any Faery court but our own. I assure you the brownies and trolls and huldrefólk who worship you as much for your kindness and love as your power will accept it."

His shoulders come back, and there's that bit of sexy arrogance I love so much. "Then in this temple, I affirm that I want to marry you, to bind my life to yours through this world and time and all the others. What say you, goddess?"

He climbs on the bed and offers me a hand. It takes a lot to get my focus off his... Gods that is a beautiful cock. It's thick and long and seems to be pointing my direction. I should probably be nervous but there's this silky magic flowing off my soon-to-be husband that curls around me like a warm blanket of lust. I get to my knees, not caring for a second that my pussy is so wet I can feel it on my thighs. His hands are still soft with my orgasm, but I slide my fingers around his as we kneel, staring at each other. Out of the corner of my eye, I see more pixies have joined us, covering the walls with their winged beauty.

"In this temple, I affirm that I want to marry you, to bind my life to yours through this world and time and all the others."

He brings my hand to his. "I don't have..." He smiles suddenly. "I was going to say I don't have a proper binding ribbon."

I know exactly where he's going. "But you do."

A vine of deepest green suddenly flows from the open window, winding around our arms that lay together forming the handfasting part of our wedding.

Rhys's eyes sparkle as moonlight joins the golden glow, coating him briefly in silvery light. "Do you wish to be my goddess? You will be the maker of my magic, the keeper of my spirit, the protector of my heart. You will hold nothing back from me and give me every piece of you, the good and the bad, the light and the darkness. You will be mother to my children. You will be my partner, my love, my goddess in all things. Are these vows you enter willingly and with an open heart?"

"I do," I say, the words forming a promise, a warmth in my soul.

I feel him squeeze my hand before he continues. "You are my true goddess. I will be your protector, your defender, your lover. I will pour my magic into you and be grateful, for that magic flows only from you. I will hold nothing back from you but give you every piece of me, the good and the bad, the light and the darkness. I will be father to your children. I will be your partner, your lover, your god in all things. These are vows I make with a willing and open heart. I love you, Shy."

The vows are said by the soldier, the leader of the Earthly Fae. The last by my best friend. Tears spring to my eyes. "I love you, Rhys."

He leans over and brushes his lips against mine. "Wife. I have known I would use that word for you since the day we met. I am so sorry I don't have a Goddess Chain for you. We will make our own traditions."

"Because your mother is still the Goddess of the High Priest of the Seelie and Unseelie." I am unbothered, but I know he feels like it's not complete. "I assure you we can find…"

A gray dove flies in from the window and drops a delicate gold necklace over our bound hands.

I stare at it for a moment and know that necklace belongs to me. The vines that bind us flow away and Rhys holds up the same chain I have seen around his mother's throat. A large pixie flies to his shoulder, bending in and covering his ear. His eyes widen and then he nods and bows his head as the pixie takes to the air once more before settling in with the large kaleidoscope.

"She says it should have been Zandra's, and since her own son didn't inherit the Green Man powers, she wants you to have it. The king has tarnished their magic, and this is their thanks for giving it back to them," he explains. "The temple is pure once more, awake to them and all who worship with an open mind and heart. The temple, she says, will call to those who wish to fight, will be a beacon of freedom and love once more."

The last words are whispered as he drapes the Goddess Chain around my neck. It's gold, and the amulet hangs just over my breasts.

Then he is kissing me, taking me back to the softness of the bed. It's easy to open my arms to him, spread my legs for him to make a place there.

"Shy, are you sure?" he asks as I feel his cock slide against my labia.

I don't think he's sure I have the power to cancel out that fertility magic of his. I give him a smile. I am coming into my own powers. I am death and rebirth, and both happen at my will. "Make love to me."

He stares into my eyes as he gently enters my body.

I wasn't expecting pain. One doesn't receive pain sexually from a Green Man. Even this first time is pure pleasure, but the care he takes warms me. He works his way inside, kissing me the whole time. His body against mine, skin to skin. Like we are one flesh.

And we are.

He groans as he fully breaches me, his cock as far inside as it can go. "It feels so good. So fucking good. So fucking right. This…this is right."

It is. This is sheer perfection, and there is nothing between us. No worry or fear. No self-consciousness. No one else in the world can come between us here in our place of love and power. I can feel the very walls breathe with us, like the whole temple is coming back to life as my husband works over me. I let my nails dig into the strong muscles of his back while I lock my ankles around his waist, not wanting to give up an inch of him.

He finds a rhythm that matches our beating hearts, our breath, the pulse of our souls against each other. It isn't long before I scream out his name, the orgasm so much stronger this time because he's with me. I can feel his pleasure. It joins my own and sends me to a place I never expected to see. A place where I am not alone.

Rhys falls on top of my body, and I wrap my arms around him.

The sky seems so much closer now, the moon and stars shining through the window at the top of the temple, and then I realize. The shine isn't simply coming from the night around us.

It's from us. Our bodies glow, gold and silver weaving together.

"Love you, Shy," he whispers as he starts it all over again.

All in all, a hell of a wedding night.

Chapter Twenty-Four

Sasha

S*he can feel me. The way I can feel her.*

"Sasha's here?" Dev asked, his neck craning around to see.

Ostara stared at the mirror. "He is. I felt him moving through the palace. He's behind this wall. It's so odd. I felt the moment he entered the plane, like a piece of Meadow fell into place and she had the chance to be whole again. Even if he is your soul's mate, he might have information that will settle my host's issues. She still dreams of her traumatic past life. She left something behind."

"Sasha is not my...," Dev began. "We heard you say vampire and thought only about Daniel. Ostara, we came here with two vampires. One is my partner, Daniel Donovan, and the other is our general. Sasha, once known as Oleg Federov. Since I've known him, he had one goal in his whole vampiric life. To live long enough he could find her again."

Ostara's green eyes turned to Sasha even as he was frantically trying to find the seam in the wall that would allow him entrance. It had to be there. The king would want to enter from time to time and play with his prey.

"She would not take a husband," Ostara said to Devinshea even as her eyes seemed to find Sasha. "She would not take a lover. She felt so deeply inside that she was missing something. Someone. She can't remember, but the knowledge is in her soul. It is how I know. I can read her history, see her past lives. It is always you."

"There's a slight breeze here, and I can smell the other room." Neil was calm and collected. He ran his hand over the wall and Sasha heard a click.

The door opened slightly and Neil pushed through, rushing to Dev while Sasha followed.

He stood in front of Ostara, the moment so surreal it almost felt impossible. She was beautiful, but then she always was. She was the most beautiful woman in the world to him.

"I selected her because her soul meshed with mine," Ostara explained. "I did not know it at the time, but the universe brought us together for a reason. Because I long for the kind of love you have between the two of you, but I have never found it. I love her. Through her I know I can love you, and I can give her what no one else can."

"Forever," Sasha whispered. "You can give us forever."

Ostara looked to him. "You already have forever. It's just interrupted over and over. What I can offer is a long time together in these forms. Time to rest and love and learn each other so well you can never truly be separated again. But I understand the jealous nature of the vampire."

Sasha felt a wave of wonder suffuse him. He couldn't help but chuckle. "Perhaps if you were another male I would struggle a bit, but I assure you my jealous nature will be tossed aside if I have to choose between it and her safety and happiness. As it happens, I don't feel anything but the deepest gratitude for the goddess who is willing to bless us with her strength and wisdom. Ostara, I honor you, and I would bet a lot that I will come to love you since I happen to know how this works. You chose her because your soul recognized hers. You are close in values and how you love and live."

Ostara nodded, a lovely smile coming to her face. "We are. I think she is a part of me I've been seeking."

"Sasha, you have to convince this idiot to let me get him out of here," Neil was saying. He stood by Devinshea, frowning at the high priest. "He does not need to stay in chains all night. We can get him, get Z and the kids, and get out of here. Danny's with Z right now. I'm not sure what rooms they're in, but we can take the servant halls and I can track them."

There was only one problem with the scenario. Myrddin had trapped them all since no one was going to leave without Devinshea. "He promised."

Ostara turned to the werewolf as well. "The priest made a bargain in the old ways. He cannot leave or he risks bringing the Wild Hunt down on his head and that of his family. In the past, the hunt has sometimes taken all the family line. Perhaps Herne will be kinder to a fellow ascended one, but perhaps not. He cannot take the chance. The wizard knew this could happen."

Devinshea looked to Sasha. "He did, but he didn't make her promise the same. Get her out of here, Sasha. Take her back to her own plane and live the life you were meant to."

"I can't..." The idea of leaving the royals...of leaving Rhys and Shy and Cassie and Brendan floored him. He raised Rhys.

"Of course you cannot." Ostara stood at his side, her color so much better than before. She seemed stronger, a faint glow starting to come from her skin. "You must help your friends, but we should get Meadow out of this dungeon. The king has a reason to be patient with Devinshea and Bris. He will spend his anger on Meadow and me. Though this energy is doing me a world of good, I have been weak for a long time."

"Get her out of here. I can handle it," Dev said.

"Or we could get you both out of here," Neil argued.

"And then we all get ripped apart by the Wild Hunt." Dev shuddered. "Neil, I understand and appreciate you wanting to save me, but there's more going on here, and we have a better shot at getting home to our timeline if we figure out exactly what Myrddin is planning. Whatever it is, it will affect us and the people we love. He has no care for this timeline. He is only in this version of my home because it gives him some kind of edge."

Though it knotted his gut, Sasha had to agree. "This has to do with Shahidi. You did not see the way he reacted to her. He was frightened that she was here."

Dev's eyes were bright green, his gaze steady. "Myrddin believes he tricked us into coming here, but I know better. The universe placed us here. The goddess wanted us here so we can do what we do best."

Neil's lips curled up in a begrudging smile. "Fuck up all the bad guy plans and save the world?"

Dev winked. "Exactly. Sasha, you are our planner. If this were your chess game, what pieces would you move right now?"

It was hard to take his eyes off Ostara, who now stood beside him, hard not to take her hand and pull her against his body, but he was dealing with the goddess and not the woman right now. The goddess who knew him, who understood who he was. Meadow was a different story. Would she remember? Would this magic that Rhys and Shy were making change things for her? Open her mind to their shared history?

He had to focus on the now. They had chaos because of that magic, and chaos was cover, but it would only last so long. "If I am the cold, hard general or the soulless spymaster, I would ask for you and Zoey to sacrifice for the greater good of the mission. We need to figure out what Myrddin wants from the king and how to shut it down. We cannot do that if we are on the run. Queen Zoey is smart and resourceful. She will figure out how to handle this worse version of you. Daniel can listen from the shadows. You...well, sadly there are things to be learned in your position, Your Grace, though it will not be pleasant. Neil and Daniel can work with the serving class to fuck everything up and cause chaos while Rhys and Shy figure out why the mountains call to her. And I can get Ostara to a safe place and return to lend my aid in any way I can."

"The safest place for me is with the servants," Ostara said. "This palace is massive, and there are rooms no one but the house servants know exist. This magic I feel is going to destroy the spells the magician and king put on the serving class no matter the wards, and if they're smart, they won't allow them to know. I get the feeling they have waited a long while to be able to rise against their tyrant king. I thought I could help to sway Devinshea away from his brutality, but I was also prepared to fight him once I regained my strength."

"He was never going to give it to you," Dev said.

Ostara's head bent slightly, a show of respect from a goddess. "I know that now. But you would. There once was goodness in the man, and there could be again. Remember that. I will go with Meadow's mate. I will heal and be ready to aid you in any way possible. If there is no ready way to get back to your timeline, I will consult with the scholars on my plane. They know much of the mystic ways. You came in with some interesting crystals. Dolerite. We have long believed it aids travel in ways that do not involve distance."

So they might not be stuck. There was so damn much to do and so little time to do it. He held out a hand to her.

She smiled and took it.

He turned to Neil. "If I know Rhys, he's waited a long time for this. He'll be at it for a while, and anyone not directly in the palace will feel the effects strongly. You should be able to move fairly freely outside the wards. Consider Bibi's quarters our home base. I'm taking Ostara there to her personal maid. You make sure Dev is fed. I get the feeling they won't care about him starving tomorrow. Take him off that damn hook and make him comfortable for the rest of the night. Dev…"

"Don't die." Dev seemed to understand the assignment. "You'll get me out when the time is right."

Neil was already helping Dev down, and he would put him back up when the time came.

There was no more reason to wait. He held Ostara's hand and led her out of the dungeon.

After another long walk through too small hallways, Sasha breathed a deep sigh of relief as they made it to the door leading back to Bibi's shared quarters.

The troll sat on the couch, holding the hand of Ione, who was still weeping. She looked up as the door opened and was on her feet in an instant.

"My baby," she sobbed as she launched herself at Ostara, who smiled and lifted the much smaller troll into her arms.

"Oh, sweet Ione, she missed you as well. When she thought she would die, she wept at the thought of never seeing you again, good mother," the goddess whispered.

Sasha took it in. The sight was odd. Ione, small and weathered, and so unlike the gorgeous Meadow. Ostara was merely a light inside her body. The beauty was all Meadow. She'd been raised in these strange, wonderous lands. She was Fae. She was love and light and had an embodiment of spring in her soul.

What if she didn't want a vampire?

He stayed back as they spoke in hushed tones. Bibi walked over to join him.

"I'm sorry. The magic the Green Man weaves is potent. I was worried I would shame myself," she admitted. "I can still feel it here, but it is like a distant song. However, I noticed Hubbie. He is one of the lowest servants. He cleans floors and washrooms. He spoke to me for the first time in years."

Then the magic was doing what Ostara thought it would. Or rather undoing. She'd told him the wards couldn't keep out some parts of the magic. "You need to get word to everyone to pretend. Pretend they are still under the spell. Otherwise, the king will likely put a stronger one on them. Tell them to bide their time. The Green Man and his goddess are here now. All will be well. They need only wait for the right opportunity."

Bibi's dark eyes shone in the candlelight, and he could see hope there. "I will begin spreading the word. I know who to talk to and who to...well, who to deal with so we don't have problems."

"If you can, access weapons. Hide them. Do you have any witches close by?"

Bibi's head shook. "Not in here. He killed all the ones who worked in the palace, but there are some who would not leave the forests. I can send word."

"Have them make charms to protect every servant from the king and the wizard. Sew them into your clothes. Hide them in your personal spaces. How many will fight?"

"All but a few, and honestly, after so much time under these spells, I would be surprised if they weren't willing to simply stay out of it," she explained.

There came a time in every authoritarian regime when the populace had enough. He had fought his own and lost because they were not ready. It appeared these Fae were.

"I will go with you." Ione wiped her eyes and smiled. "I know I am new here, but I can help spread the word. I would like to offer my room to my darling girl." She tilted her head up to look at Sasha. "Ostara tells me you are the one in Meadow's heart. The one she can't forget and can't quite remember. Take care. She needs you."

Bibi and Ione left, going to do their spy work, and he was alone with the only woman who had ever had his heart.

And the goddess she shared a body with. Alone in a too-cramped room where his head nearly touched the ceiling and he worried he would break the furniture.

Ostara stared at him. He knew it was her by the fully emerald eyes. A bit like Rhys's since he ascended. Vibrant green, without a hint of white. She faintly glowed, and he realized that glow wasn't merely hers. It was Meadow's. He'd mistaken it for the glow of the goddess.

"You're...she's a companion," he said, his fangs growing long.

"Companion?" Ostara asked.

"In my home, a companion is part angel. She glows to my kind. As supernatural creatures we are...how do you say...compatible on every level. Companion blood makes a vampire stronger, faster. Vampire blood heals and keeps the companion young and vital."

Ostara nodded as though she understood. "Ah, a consort. That is what we call such men and women."

So there were differences. "It's almost always women where I come from."

"A strange place then," she said and seemed to come to some decision. "She is afraid. It's why she wants me in charge of our body. She didn't know how important this moment would be. She doesn't remember her past lives except through what I have told her I see."

"Is she afraid of me?"

Ostara's lips tilted up, an amused expression. "She has not had a man. You are large and intimidating."

He smiled at the memory. "She said that to me the first time I asked her out. She told me I might be what we call a bad bet if I turned out to be the violent type." He sobered. "I am the violent type, Ostara. I tried to use my mind to help my people, but when I could not remember her, I fell into violence. It is my nature."

"But when you did remember her?" Ostara prompted.

"I tried to be the best husband, friend, human I could be. It's why it fell apart. She brought out the best in me, and I had to stand up for what was right. And Tash...oh, our daughter made me want to be everything. To be beyond what any man could be."

Tears pierced those green eyes. "Natasha is what was left undone. Her baby. She tried to protect her."

He took her hands in his and looked into those eyes as if he could stare down into her soul and see his wife nestled there. "Natasha is beautiful. She is strong. She survived because of her mother's love, and now she thrives with the family I found for her. They love her, Marta. She has sisters and brothers and cousins. She lives in America with a family who gives her everything she could possibly need. When I became a vampire and remembered my life, that man who saved you in the dungeon, he and his family and friends helped me find her. I got to see her one last time. I was weak because I had so recently turned, but I had a friend see into her soul and plant a truth there. She knows we loved her. Deep in her soul, we are still with her. Still giving her strength. Put that fear and guilt aside. If you can never love me, I will be satisfied knowing I gave you this comfort. Our daughter lives and loves and is happy, and somewhere in her soul, she remembers us. We live on in her."

If he could only give her this, he would find a way to be content.

Ostara's eyes changed, the jewel tones pulling back to still glorious green eyes, but they were normal. Meadow's eyes. Marta's eyes. Her name could change. Hell, the eyes themselves could change, but the spirit behind them was always the same. Loving. Strong. Resilient.

"Tasha?" The name came from her mouth like a prayer.

"Natasha. In our lives she was Natasha Federova. She is now Natasha Taggart. She is happy. She is loved. You did so good, baby." Tears fell from his eyes now. He was here. How many times had he wished he could be here, telling her all the things he needed to say? All the things he hadn't because they had been so abruptly pulled out of their lives. "You did everything right. I was so…I am so sorry to leave you."

"You didn't." She stepped back, and he felt the distance as she seemed to go deep inside herself. "You were taken. You didn't mean to go. Goddess, this magic… I can see more clearly."

"You can still feel it?"

Her eyes flashed, and he knew she was talking to the goddess inside. "He can't keep this magic from us. This is a gift. This magic is our magic, too. They can keep the lust away but not the energy of spring, not the awakening. There are no wards strong enough to keep it out. It will be the same for your Devinshea. This magic will fuel him for days. For us, it is allowing me to see where I could not. Oleg. Sasha. You have had many names, and I loved them all. You did not mean to leave me. You never mean to leave me. Every life we cling and try to remember, promising ourselves we will not forget."

Something settled deep inside Sasha's soul. She knew him. He was not alone. Even if she never wished to touch him, he was not alone. "I will never forget you again."

She moved in front of him, her head tilting up, eyes shining with tears. "You will never be lost again…Sasha. I like this name. I like this man you have become."

"Not a man at all," he replied. Her light was brighter now, like she'd instinctively dimmed it knowing how attracted he would be to it. "I am a vampire."

Her lips curled up. "And I am host to a goddess."

"You are a goddess. You are my goddess," he whispered reverently. "I have always worshipped you."

"Then show me. Show me how you worship me." She let her head tilt back, giving him her throat.

It was an offer he would never refuse.

Chapter Twenty-Five

Zoey

I stare at myself in the mirror and realize I'm this man's Barbie doll.

I mean there have been times in our lives where that was certainly true of my Fae husband. For Danny, clothes are just an obstacle to his final destination, which is me naked, but Dev likes to dress me up and show me off.

It rankles with this man.

The *sidhe* maid finishes tying the bow around the waist of my dress and steps back. She's been silent most of the time, only answering my questions, and it takes me a moment to remember that she's under a powerful spell. She cannot talk unless I speak to her directly.

She's thin, far more than is natural, and she doesn't glow the way I've found most Fae do. Not like *Twilight* or anything, but most *sidhe* I've met have this brightness to their features no matter their skin tone.

A bit like Shy. Huh. I never considered it before but my son's goddess—and after the magic I felt last night she's absolutely his goddess—has that bit of glow around her. Though she was born on the Earth plane, I now think she has Fae in her background.

"Are you all right?" I ask quietly.

The woman's eyes widen as if shocked I would ask. "I am fine, my lady. Thank you. Is there anything else you require?"

"Some information, if you can," I say, glancing at the door. Daniel promised there's nothing there that would give anyone special access to my conversations. That was oddly all in the bathing room. I'd been careful when I used it earlier. Careful in the way I let him get brief glimpses, little looks, and then I would hurry away because I'm such a delicate princess and no one ever saw me naked before. Only him.

He doesn't need to know how many people have seen my hoohaw in the name of fertility rituals.

When I awakened, Danny was gone. He held me until I managed to fall asleep, but it took a while since we both sat up, feeling those waves of magic pulse against us. Familiar and yet uniquely theirs.

There were definitely wards to keep out magic, but Rhys's had slipped under them, weaker than they would be without the wards since they didn't send the palace into a frenzied orgy, for which I will forever be grateful, but they were there. I heard the king screaming at his guard to do something about it, but he didn't come into my room.

Danny and I had been on the outside again. Our son bound himself the night before—a ceremony that should have been joyous for us all. And Dev was held in shackles as his son took his rightful place.

Another sin I place at Myrddin Emrys's feet.

"Of course," the woman says, her head bowing.

How much has this woman gone through? "What's your name? I'm Zoey."

Her head comes up. "My name is of no consequence."

"It is to me. It's so much nicer than hey, you." I give her a smile and step back from the mirror. "You did a wonderful job, by the way."

She glances to the mirror, wariness clear in her eyes.

I wave off the fear. "It's not spelled. It's only a mirror. I checked it with a charm my baby girl made. She's excellent with Fae magic, but she comes by it honestly. Her father is a high priest in our timeline. Did you know that?"

Her face flushes, and her voice goes low. "I heard this. That he serves both courts."

I nod. "He does, but he prefers the Unseelie. Don't get me wrong. He wouldn't deny his Seelie brethren, but if he had to choose it would be the Unseelie. They're less pretentious."

She bites her bottom lip, and her eyes go wide again.

Damn it. Communication is going to be so much fun here. "What's your name?"

"I am Grenelda."

"Are you Seelie?"

"Of course." She winces as though something hurt her. "I do have some Unseelie blood, but please do not tell the king. My father was part troll. I can pass."

I feel for her. And I'm glad apparently no one ever asked the question directly to her because it appears she cannot lie. Not even to protect herself. "There is nothing wrong with being part anything. Except asshole. Your king's got a lot of asshole in his background."

That earns me a slight smile.

Though if she can't lie, I need to give her truth to tell. "Although he is handsome and seems kind." I wink at her. "I could definitely come to love him, if you know what I mean."

Her smile widens. "Yes, Zoey. That is good. If I am asked, that is what I will report to him."

I doubt the king will ask her, but I've given myself cover. I can get to the question I really want the answer to. "Do you know what happened at the temple last night?"

She nods. "Oh, yes. Or rather I have seen what happened to the temple itself. It's so beautiful again."

I didn't see it when we came in. "What was it like before?"

"Before last night or before the king took over?"

"Both," I say.

"It was beautiful. Peaceful. It was open to all when his grandfather was king," she begins quietly. She frowns. "I am not usually able to speak so much. Usually the spell only allows a few words."

"My son's magic is the language of Faery. His magic got through the wards last night. I felt it." Danny and I talked about how Rhys and Shy finally giving in to longing would affect the *sithein*. Years and years of pent-up need had flowed out the night before and despite the wards, it would affect everything here. "I'm sure the king will tighten it up again when he realizes, so perhaps you should all remain cautious."

"You are not here to take her place." Grenelda slaps a hand over her mouth as though she can't believe the words came out.

I am so pleased I can't begin to express it. If Rhys's magic can break the king's stranglehold, I can work with that. "I am not. I came here to see my mother-in-law and ask for her aid. You see, in my timeline, Myrddin Emrys stole my husband's crown and twelve years of our lives with our kids. I need to find a friend of mine who might have the only magic that can counter him and free us, but I need the ancient amulet. The one the royals use to talk to their ancestors. I certainly didn't come here in hopes of dumping the husbands I love in favor of a bad version of one of them. What do you think?"

I give her the question because I'm sure it's easier for her to reply that way. Even without the spell, they've had years to learn when not to talk, when their voices could cost them much pain and suffering.

"I think he wears it most days," she replies quickly. "I do not know how often he uses it, though. He doesn't believe in listening to his ancestors. Especially when they give him bad news."

"Do you remember the last time he did use it?" I'm surprised since at least in our time, it is only to be used as a last resort. Dev is worried they'll be angry with us, but I don't know where else to turn. Finding Sarah and Felix and Mia is the most important thing I can do.

She nods. "He asked how he could get back into his temple. He was so angry the day he realized he couldn't even walk onto the grounds, and neither could anyone who follows him."

"Follows him or is forced to work for him?"

"I cannot walk on the grounds, either," Grenelda admits. "At least I couldn't before. I am afraid to try."

The spell would have the king's signature on it. The temple's magic would recognize it. "Do you know if Myrddin can go into the temple?"

"I don't think so. The temple doesn't seem to like what he does."

"He destroys souls."

She nods. "No one can know exactly, but there are dark rumors that the wizard has taught our king new ways to find magical energy in hopes of getting back inside his temple. I believe some of the lesser Fae still find ways. They enter to help the rebels. The king guards the lands around the palace vigorously, but it is said there are tunnels he has not found, and that is how they get in. Please do not tell him."

"I would never tell him," I vow. "I need you to understand that the lesser Fae are important to me. In my time I am their high priestess, and I love them. I honor them. What your king has done to you and them is evil. I will do anything to help you, but from what I understand there is no rebellion among the palace staff. Not among the *sidhe*. Could anything cause them to risk rebellion?"

She nods slowly. "Yes. I think what happened last night might sway us. Especially since that magic seems to have dimmed the king's spells that keep us quiet and submissive."

"What happened?"

A smile crosses her face. "The temple is alive again. We felt that sweet magic flow, and it filled my soul. I woke in the middle of the night and I felt...love and hope. I cried. I have not been able to cry since the king forced this curse upon me."

I didn't realize it went beyond ensuring obedience. He shut down their emotions? They haven't had emotions in years until the night before when they felt the marriage of a god to his goddess.

"One more thing, Your Grace," she says as I hear shouting out in the hallways. She leans forward. "I have heard rumor that there was a theft last night."

Shit. All eyes will be on me then. "Of what?"

"The Goddess Chain," she whispers as the floors shake lightly, a sign that someone is coming. "The one he should have offered Zandra."

We don't have much time left. "Do you know anything about my husband?"

Her lips curl up. "I know the guards are surprised at how little damage their torture did to him. They are not warded in the dungeons. They felt the full magic. The guards ran fleeing because they were in a full lust. Still, the injuries they gave to the Green Man should not have healed the way they did. And I heard Ostara was not there this morning at all. They fear the king's anger at losing her."

The door begins to open, and I whisper to her. "Pretend you are normal. Don't let him know you can talk freely."

Devilshea strides in, his face an arrogant mask.

I turn, offering him a deep curtsey which also gives him a good view of my breasts. "Your Majesty."

He stops, and I can sense his irritation. "You…you look lovely this morning."

"I want to know where she was last night," a distinctly unwelcome voice says. Myrddin steps into the room, and he looks to Grenelda. "You, girl. Where was she last night? She is your charge, correct? You stayed in the outer rooms in case she needed something."

The king sighs. "I didn't want her to think I didn't trust her. The guard on her door told me she did not leave."

Grenelda stares at the wizard, a blank look on her face. "Yes. No. I was in the servant's quarters."

The words came out like she had to push them.

She's good at this. Thank the goddess.

"I was in this room all night, Your Majesty. I did not leave," I say, telling him no lies.

The king sighs. "It appears there was a theft last night, and the wizard believes it was you."

"I know it was her." Myrddin looks a bit ruffled this morning. Like something's thrown him off his game. Whatever it is, I'm here for it. "She is a known thief in her timeline. She stole the Goddess Chain, and she's going to use it to some nefarious purpose."

Now I'm a little confused, and it's time for some honesty since the sucker is still around my neck. I pull it from my bodice. "I have worn this for years. You accuse me of stealing something that belongs to me."

The king stills, his eyes on the chain. "It is similar but not exact. The one that belongs to me is slightly larger, and the crescent moon is done in silver, not gold."

"Of course not. You took the other one," Myrddin accuses. "I believe you stole it from its place in the library and you found a way to smuggle it to your son. He is using it to transform the temple."

Myrddin doesn't know everything. He is of the inner planes, a child of a human and a demon. He has been the mentor to the King of the Sword since there was first a king. He doesn't understand Fae magic. He probably thinks it's too soft to harm him. I pull the chain over my head. "I did not leave this room, and this is my Goddess Chain. I was given it by Declan Quinn in the name of his mother,

Miria, the Queen of the Seelie Fae. I have worn it since our wedding night. Your Majesty, do you want me to give it to you? I am certain the wizard will tell you I am wearing the proof of my crime. I'm sure I changed it just enough to fool you. I can't defend myself in any other way."

"My mother gave it to you?" He takes it and holds it up to the light, inspecting it.

"It was actually your brother. He was her emissary that night. He did not want to give it to me, but Dev forced his hand," I reply honestly, not bothering to clarify that it was another Declan Quinn entirely. I'm starting to worry there is something wrong with the king's brain and he can't think completely straight. "He thought we should not marry. He thought I should be kept as a mistress and Devinshea should screw as many pretty Fae girls as he could."

A bitter expression crosses his face as he brings the chain back down. "Yes, that was his argument. My mother's as well. Zandra was low born, and it wouldn't do even when it was obvious she was my goddess and my magic was so much stronger when she was with me. I spoke with your Devinshea last night before the temple went insane. It unsettled me." He holds the chain and looks to Grenelda. "What did she say to you this morning? Anything about me? Did she ask you to help her get away?"

Grenelda's mouth opens, and her head shakes as though she's not sure which question to answer first.

Myrddin sighs. "I told you. You have to be specific. Girl, did this one say anything concerning?"

Grenelda nods as though the confusion is gone now. "No, sir."

"Did she say anything about me?" the king pushes.

"Yes," Grenelda says.

"Well, what was it?" the king asks with utter impatience.

"She could…she could fall in love…with you." The words come out haltingly, stumbling over each one.

A perfect performance. I lower my lashes as though the revelation is too emotional for me.

He comes to stand before me. "You could?"

Myrddin actually groans.

I let my eyes meet the king's. All I can think about in this moment is somewhere beneath me my real husband is held in chains.

"It's what I said, but I understand if you cannot say the same of me because you think I'm a thief."

"Think? You are a thief. You pretty much introduce yourself as a damn thief," Myrddin complains. "You are proud of it."

I shake my head. "I was once, but I have children now. You can't think I go around stealing things. I left that life behind long ago. I never thought I would have to be anything again but a wife and a mother. Now I have to face a life where we are perpetually at war, with my children in constant danger because my husbands won't do what they need to do to protect them."

"Which is why you want a man who would burn the world for you," the king says, and he holds out the Goddess Chain.

I bend my neck and allow him to return it to me. It settles between my breasts. "I simply want to be safe. I want to know my children are safe."

"Well, he can't keep your children safe," Myrddin replies. "No one can."

"You doubt me?" The king turns on the wizard, moving to my side. He holds his hand out, a silent request.

One I dare not refuse. I let my hand lay on his, the gesture regal in nature, a king about to lead his queen.

I am not his queen, and I will lead this game.

"I do not, Your Majesty," I say and look to Myrddin.

The hate on his face is blatant and pure before the courtier is back. He bows toward the king. "Of course you are more than capable of protecting anyone you wish to. But none of this solves the problem we're facing. Someone has the Goddess Chain, and they are using it to power the temple."

"Then destroy the temple. I'll build another one," the king says. "I'll build one for me and my goddess."

"I have explained to you that the temple is necessary to the *sithein*. To the whole plane," Myrddin explains. "Even if I could destroy it, it would likely take everything close with it. And by close I mean within sight, and that includes the mountains."

A long look passes between them, and I know they're talking about the mountains that called to Shy. My daughter-in-law is on to something, and I have to pray Rhys will allow her to investigate.

Or that she'll insist.

"Then find a way to cut it off from the rest of the palace," the king says with obvious frustration. "Look. I appreciate what you've done for me thus far. Your teachings have been invaluable, and you will get what you came for. But she is not fully mine yet and cannot be until I have the god's power for my own. Until then, I cannot go to the mountains with you and unlock what you need. So work on cutting the temple off. Find a way in and desecrate it so its power is dimmed."

"I don't know that..." Myrddin's head bows. "Of course, Your Majesty. I will work on the temple and my own projects and report back to you. As to our future queen, be careful with her. She will lie and cheat and do whatever it takes to save her family."

The king's eyes narrow. "If you feel she cannot love me then your portion of our bargain is unfulfilled, and we should do something about it."

Myrddin holds a hand up, and I finally truly understand the quandary he's in. He can't tell this man I'm pregnant because I'm the prize and the prize has to be perfect. The king has to desire the prize or he won't give the wizard what he wants. What he needs so desperately. "Of course she can, Your Majesty. This one is the right one. It didn't work before, but it shall this time. You will see. I'm only asking you to take things slowly and be cautious or you might...lose her again."

Oh, I don't like how that sounds. I don't think he's talking about taking me to the mall and oops, I thought she was at Ulta but now she's gone. This feels like losing me in the most malicious way possible.

"Come, Zandra." He fumbles over my name, and I see the recognition of wrongness, but a stubborn will hits his features and he does not correct himself. "I have a lovely breakfast set out for you and then I thought we would tour the palace. I want a nice day with you."

I just want to get through it. Danny's going to try to break Dev out this evening, and Rhys and Shy should be going on the run this morning.

I smile. "That sounds wonderful."

I follow him out and pray Myrddin can't get to the temple.

Chapter Twenty-Six

Shy

"I hate him." Rhys kisses my cheek and rolls onto his back. "I don't even know this version of my brother and I want to punch him in the face." He sits up in the bed where he became my husband and stares at the door. "Go away."

I blink in the morning light and feel the most delicious ache in my muscles as I stretch. I can't even remember the number of times this man made love to me the night before. He was insatiable and seemed to find a way to make me hungry every single time. "He's not going to go away. We're supposed to flee this morning and go hang out in a village that will absolutely not be as comfortable as this bed."

It's perfect. Like it is made for me.

"Do we have to flee before we've even had proper morning sex?" Rhys complains.

I'm pretty sure we had that right before dawn, but I don't correct him. I sit up and look around for my clothes. I find a robe laid out and wonder if a bird brought that in, too. The thought makes me touch the only thing I'm wearing. The Goddess Chain.

Rhys smiles and his fingers come up to touch it. "It's beautiful on you. One good thing about coming here. I never thought to see you wear this." He turns it over and traces the details. "It's different. I like the silver here. Shy, I think we were meant to be here, and this is yours."

I can't argue with him. The chain hums against my skin like it's so happy to be mine. "I think we're meant to be here for many reasons, and the main one is in the mountains. I have questions for Lee. For Fae Lee."

Rhys sighs and leans in for a kiss before rolling out of bed. "Fine. I'm hungry." He pulls on the robe at the end of the bed, the larger one obviously meant for him. Immediately he's got ten pixies on him, the gorgeous creatures landing on his shoulders and in his hair. He barely notices as he jogs down the stairs and I hear him whispering to Lee in a low growl.

He slams the door and turns my way. "Come, my goddess. Let's take a bath and Lee will return with breakfast and news of last night. Will it bother you if he's in the room while we're in the bathing pool? I get the feeling he wants to move quickly."

Ah, such an odd question if I didn't live in the equivalent of a *sithein* for the last several years of my life. Technically Frelsi and its New Zealand equivalent are pocket worlds created by our witches, but they're filled with Fae and supernaturals, and I'm pretty sure when Lily and the witches were decorating they were all into hobbits.

When I first got to Frelsi, I was surprised by the lack of modesty. What I realize now is it isn't modesty my friends lack. It's shame. Wolves and other weres don't freak out when they change back to human form and find themselves naked. Witches do not mind dancing in the moonlight with no clothes on to strengthen a spell. Or to just be comfortable in their skin.

I won't even go into the Fae. It took a lot of care for me to wait to see Rhys's full beauty on our wedding night. I've seen his brother, and everyone knows what Fenrir looks like.

I have a decision to make. I've always known if I became his goddess, there would be some public nudity.

I slide out of bed and stretch and decide to forgo the robe. The water should cover me. Mostly.

As I walk past the robe, the pixies land on me. My little ones. I love the pixies in Frelsi, but this feels right. Like something changed inside me last night and I can accept the affection they have always wanted to honor me with.

Rhys gives me a once over, his lips curling in a decadent smile. "We're going that way, are we?"

I give him a prim curtsey. "I am the wife of a High Priest of Faery. Should I cower and hope no one ever sees my body?"

Rhys chucks his robe, too. "Your body is a freaking gift to this world and all the rest, my goddess. Lead the way." He gestures for me to take the stairs to the bathing room. "Is it me or is this place nicer than it was last night?"

"Much nicer," a deep voice says, and I find a gnome staring up from the bottom of the steps. "I don't think I've ever seen anything so nice in all me days."

Well, that changed. I stop two steps above him and frown down. "What happened? There were no spirits here last night."

Rhys stops behind me. His hands go to my shoulders. "Friend or foe?"

"I am a friend of the true king of the Fae, Lee Quinn. His father is the betrayer," the gnome announces. "And dat is why I was killed in me own garden this morning by that wizard arsehole. I think the fucker was tryna steal me soul for some reason, but I came here instead. Always loved the temple. Thought I wouldna see it again."

"Friend," I say, and my brand spanking new husband moves around me, hurrying to the steamy pool.

"Thank the goddess." He walks right in, leaving me behind. He sighs as he sinks into the water. "It's freezing. We need some fireplaces."

It's good to know now that he's had some sex, he's relaxed. I move around the wee one and join my husband because he's right. It's chilly. "They killed you for speaking out?"

I'm curious about what happened in the hours since we separated from the royals. I need to stop calling them that. They're my in-laws now. I think Zoey will appreciate it immensely if I stop calling her Your Highness or Your Grace.

The gnome follows me. "Aye, they did, though I think he was looking fer a reason. He was in a right rage this morning. I'm sure it's about how the temple has come to life."

The door opens just after I descend into the bathing pool, and Lee strides in carrying a tray and followed by Cassie and Brendan, who has found his human form once more.

He's got two mugs in his hand. "Guys, these women showed up sometime after the big sex bomb went off, and they made all kinds of food. Thank the goddess because I went through all the jerky in Cass's bag."

Cassie's eyes roll. "The two pound bag."

He stares her way. "Yes, you only had two pounds. Did you intend to starve me so you get all the inheritance?"

She snorts. "Yeah, we don't have that, brother, and one of our dad's is immortal, so we won't be collecting that anytime soon. Now that I think about it, it was Vamp Dad who packed my go bag. I know because he included a couple of face masks. We needed them last night. It was a lot."

"I liked it," Lee admits as he moves down the stairs with the tray. "It was cucumber and melon. Smelled nice, and my skin is smoother." He stops and gives me a come-hither smile. "Hey, there, Shy. You are looking lovely this morning."

I turn to Rhys, half expecting him to come out of the water and attack this version of his twin. He merely smiles and winks my way. "You are beyond lovely, my goddess."

"Eww, they did it," Brendan says as he passes me one of the mugs and then Rhys the other. "I can tell because Rhys doesn't look like he has a stick up his ass."

"Duh," Cassie replies. "That's why we were stuck in the safe room for five hundred hours." She turns to me. "When you are redecorating, you need to take into account that the people seeking refuge from your spicy times might need like a TV or a couple of extra beds. Maybe a full-service kitchen. I had to listen to Lee tell me battle stories and then a bunch of crap about how closely bonded he was to the chimera thing. I told you. Not sorry I killed its ass."

"That wee thing killed a chimera?" the gnome asks.

I nod his way. He's sitting on the edge of the water, his feet dangling, and I can see a thin line where they slit his throat. I feel for him, though he seems perfectly happy to be here. His head tilts back as he looks up at the sun through the skylights as though he hasn't seen it in forever. "She did. She's fierce. So my question is how did you escape getting sucked into wherever Myrddin keeps the souls of those he kills?"

"My question is how did the priestesses get in, and where have they been hiding?" Rhys says, picking up a muffin. "This looks delicious."

"They took to the woods years back when my father desecrated the temple. I think they were called by the magic you and Shy created. We could feel the vibrations from it, and it would have been so much fun if I could have participated, but no, you shove me into a safe room with a way too young for fertility rites girl." Lee's gaze goes between Rhys and myself, but I don't think he's at all disturbed that the two of us are naked. "Do you know how long it's been since we were blessed with fertility rites? Not that I need a baby, but I've been told it's the best sex ever. That's how long it's been. The last time it happened I was a babe."

I suspect it would have been an orgy. Now I'm worried about my mother-in-law. There is a man who is obsessed with her. "Would it have hit the palace?"

Rhys moves to my side, sipping on the tea he's been given. "You mean would it have hit my mother."

Lee's head shakes. "The palace is far too warded for them to have gotten anything but the edge of it. From what I heard this morning, it did hit the dungeons."

"Oh, aye," the gnome says. "I heard them guards talking about how none of their torture came to aught last night and that the spring goddess got away while they were in the woods wanking off. I laughed, and that was when the wizard took me out. I also might have called him a charlatan and thrown some very rich fertilizer at him."

I wince. "He says your papa is better this morning, and so is Ostara. Sasha got her out. I suppose they left Devinshea because of what could happen to Zoey if they didn't have him. I suspect Dev wouldn't leave." I hate the thought of him being there, but he has given us some cover. "The magic did what we hoped it would, and the wards held. And my new friend threw shit at Myrddin."

"Who is Shy talking to?" Lee counters.

"A newly dead creature," Rhys replies. "Do you know of any who would be bold enough to hurl crap at the wizard?"

Lee grins. "That sounds like any number of creatures I know."

"Dead... Baby, does the dead person have a name?" Rhys asks.

"Hasn't introduced himself yet. He's a gnome. Died this morning in the gardens," I reply.

"Not Benfal," Lee says with a frown. "I love Benny. Tell me it wasn't him."

The gnome grins. "Tell him I love him, too. A good lad. Far better than his father."

Before I can pass on that message, Lee continues. "But you weren't there when he died, so you couldn't have saved him. How did he get away?"

"Oh, I felt the pull, but the temple was far stronger," the gnome says.

"He felt the temple's magic and was drawn to it," I explain to Lee, but I have more important questions. "Someone else mentioned they felt pulled toward the wizard. So you can feel him forcing you?"

"And it weren't like that. It wasn't force. It was a song calling to me, telling me I can move on. But the temple meant a lot to me and I heard its song, too. I chose."

Now that revelation changes things. I thought I was fighting Myrddin himself. It sparks a memory in me. One I didn't realize I had, but I suddenly know it's true. I turn to Rhys. "He's got some kind of spell that's tricking the dead into a trap. I was worried he had the same kind of soul space I have and he was pulling them in, but I just remembered the dark prophet told me I was unique. I'm the only one with a space like this, that can hold a whole soul and not have it affect me long term. How did I remember that? The day I met your grandfather, Gray Sloane was there. He taught me how to let Harry in. He explained that it wouldn't change me the way it would other people. You can house a piece of soul or a ripped up soul for a brief time, but they can stay in me and I'll still be in control."

"I'm confused. I thought the wizard was eating souls," Lee points out. "That's what he told the king. He convinced my father he could take back his power by eating souls."

"Most of my research says the soul is sacrosanct." Cassie spends a lot of time with the academics. And Evan and me.

"The theory is the soul can't be destroyed," I explain. "But naturally Hell tries, and so does Myrddin Emrys. At least that's the working knowledge we have. However, it goes against the reports we have about Myrddin taking pieces of his witches' souls when he needs to keep them in line. That's one of the reasons Rhys's twin and their sister are on the Hell plane right now. Looking for Liv Carey's."

"Well, the tales here are that the king eats the souls of those he kills," Benny says gravely. "It's why so many fall in line. It's one thing to die. Quite another to be utterly destroyed. But it weren't the king calling to me. It was something beyond the wizard, too. I wanted to go somewhere, to join them."

A chill prickles along my spine. "Did you want to go to the north?"

He nods. "To the mountains. They sing to me even now, but I like it here. It's quieter here. Much."

I turn to Rhys. "He says when he died, he was called to the mountains."

Lee nods. "So this is about the sluagh. What if he's been sending the dead to the mountain and trapping them, forcing them to become sluagh? To what end?"

"I'm not sure, but we need to figure it out," Rhys says, starting in on another muffin. "Or we could stay here for a couple of days."

I turn to stare at my husband.

His eyes go straight to my breasts, and I realize I need to sink down a little more. "Well, it is our bonding time, my goddess. And you don't have to do that on their account. You're a fertility goddess now. You're supposed to walk around in your gorgeous skin knowing no one will touch you or they risk the wrath of the god."

Lee actually bows his head and looks serious for a moment. "He is not wrong about that, Your Grace. I am irreverent at times, but you bless our *sithein* with your presence, and you should understand that every Fae here will consider you holy."

"Except your father and Myrddin Emrys," Cassie points out. "And anyone who happens to be under their spell."

"Don't know about dat," Benny says. "I think the rites disrupted the spells. It's why I flung that shit the wizard's way. For the first time in years I could feel again. I never had the whole can't talk spell, but everyone in the palace and on the grounds were under the pall of the king. It made things dull and kept us submissive. You will scare the crap out of them all, Your Grace."

"Because we brought the temple back to its beauty?" I ask.

"Because you bring hope," Benny corrects.

"You bring hope," Lee replies at the same time. "You are a rallying cry. You are a pause in the misery that allows my people to remember who we are, what we can do when we are together. This temple is the heart of the Seelie Fae. Not simply of our *sithein*. The Green Man is a reflection of who we are as a people, and when he becomes corrupt it is up to us to fix the problem. You are revolution, Your Graces, and that is why I know you will cut this short and come with me to the village."

Rhys growls and frowns my way. "I don't like him."

But he knows he's right. I know how to calm my irritated sex god. I look to Lee. "Go and get everything ready. We will join you in half an hour."

Rhys growls.

"An hour," I say with a sigh.

In moments we're alone with the exception of Benny, who is still staring at the sun.

"Do you see a light?" I ask.

His head tilts down, long white beard against his chest. "Of course. I see several. You are the strongest."

I give him a smile because I'm absolutely certain he's flirting with me. As I'm a naked, newly married woman, I can't blame him. "That's sweet. I'm talking about a light you can move through."

"Yes," he says with a nod of his head. "You're talking about a door. You're talking about the first door, the oldest one."

A pretty way to put it. "If you go through, you begin again in some way."

"Is it hard, goddess?" he asks, and he's staring at me with wonder.

I feel Rhys's hands on my shoulders, but he doesn't do anything. Merely lets me know he's with me. "Hard?"

"To be the door and never know what's behind it? You do, you know. You know. It's in your heart. You're confused because it's been so long."

The way he's looking at me... "Since what?"

"Since you were born the first time. Since he had to hide you," Benny whispers. "I was there. I served him, *un sanctaidd*. She belongs to the world. *Mae hi y llwybr i dragwyddoldeb.*"

"She said that to me. What does it mean? It's Welsh, right? I thought you spoke Gaelic." The words unnerve me, cause those tears to pulse behind my eyes because I know I'm close to understanding.

But I'm also close to knowing something hidden. Something lost. Something that might need to stay lost.

He stands and his expression gentles. "All of his followers speak his language, sacred one. You are the path to eternity. She's coming. She's fought so hard to get here. Do not be afraid. Call his name when you need him. He will always come for you."

And then he dives toward me. I put up a hand, though I know he can't hurt me. He's non-corporeal. But instinct has me backing up against Rhys and holding a hand out.

He falls against it, and a gold light shines and he is gone.

What the hell just happened?

"Are you okay?" Rhys asks.

I hear the sound of rushing water that is not from this stream. That sound is soothing and this one…so familiar and yet so deeply frightening.

The Drowning Woman is here. She floats ten feet away.

I turn to my husband, wrapping myself around him and trying not to cry.

Chapter Twenty-Seven

Zoey

I sit in the middle of a lush park and thank the goddess for all of Dev's lessons on protocol when it comes to dealing with the high Fae, and in particular the Seelies. It makes it less awkward for me to know how to sit on this grand quilt beneath me and still look very much the lady. I circled my skirts around my bent knees and made sure my ankles are covered. My boobs are on serious display. Such a weird culture, but I know how to move through it. I keep my eyes downcast for the most part. As they would say in my time, I am all kinds of demure and mindful.

I wonder what my younger self would have done in this situation. Probably taken the knife in Devilshea's hand and attempted to murder him with it.

"It's odd." The king took off his formal coat when he declared this the perfect picnic spot. He's in a snowy white tunic that's been unbuttoned to show off his golden, muscular chest. "According to the head of my guard, some of the servants were affected by whatever happened in the temple last night. I use certain spells to make it easier for them to work, and the magic seems to have lessened the hold."

Though he calls this a picnic, and we're sitting on the grass that is absolutely greener than it was the day before, there are ten guards with us and three servants who drug out china for us to dine on, including the delicate cup I hold in my hand and pretend to sip from.

There are some mistakes you never make twice. I have a charm Evan gave me that would detect any kind of spell or poison, but I can't use it in front of him so I pretend to sip. Bibi brought me a canteen of water early this morning. I hid it in the closet along with the bread and cheese she gave me. More importantly, she gave me news. Danny is hidden for the day. We decided the night before that we must figure out what Myrddin wants before unleashing hell on everyone. The last thing we want is Myrddin running away and leaving us stranded. Daniel is going to send news that he is willing to talk to Myrddin. He's not, but it will buy us some time.

And I pretend to not be horrified by his behavior. "Affected? How?"

I hope they were smart enough to pretend, but I'm sure it's hard for them. Thankfully my own maid had done a spectacular job of fooling him.

"I think the ones who wandered out of the wards had the bonds we forged broken. The gnomes especially were...feisty today. I've found bonding to the palace and their king makes them more satisfied."

It made them into wordless zombies who couldn't feel or use their own voices. It made them slaves. I stare at him for a moment, trying to see anything of my Devinshea inside this monster. "Tell me why you didn't marry Zandra."

He waves me off. "It simply wasn't done."

"But you wanted to."

"I did. I wanted to badly." He leans back, giving me a lovely view of his profile. His hair is slightly longer than Devinshea's. "But my brother convinced me such a marriage would bring shame to my family."

"You were embarrassed by her."

"Never. No. It was always my brother."

It's clear to see he had been, but I have to frame everything as Declan did it or I will lose him. "Declan didn't like her because she wasn't royal? She seems to have not been impoverished. You told me her family owned a vineyard."

"She was somewhat wealthy, but she was only a quarter *sidhe*. Her grandmother was a troll. The kind that can pass as human but still a troll."

"Well, you're only half Fae," I point out.

His brows rise. "Where did you hear that? Are vile rumors going around? I assure you I am fully Fae. Why would you...he isn't." The king seems to think about it for a moment. "Your Devinshea took after our father? Was your Declan also a halfling?"

This is news I was not expecting and yet it somehow makes perfect sense to me. Of course he's an arrogant prick. He's literally never had to face what my Dev did. He never had to face discrimination. He was a pampered royal, and the first time he didn't get what... I have to slow down. There has to be more to this. I know this man. He can't simply be evil. "Not at all. In my timeline you're twins, but Declan takes after his Fae side while Dev got his grandfather's Green Man powers and his father's mortality."

He shudders like he can't think of anything worse. "It must have been hell for him. Growing up, I mean. They would have seen him as bad luck. I'm honestly shocked that my mother allowed him to stay in the palace. I don't think she would have killed him, but she should have sent him to the Earth plane with the humans."

"She didn't realize he was mortal until he was three, I believe. By then she simply loved her child. She couldn't send him away." I can't help but remember this man didn't want his child. At least he didn't seem to. "A mother's love is powerful."

"I suppose so," he agrees. "I wouldn't have thought it of Mother. She was a bit cold and distant. She thought only of the throne."

"Perhaps because she wasn't forced to face that choice. I obviously didn't know Miria before, but I know she loves her son. She made some mistakes with him, but they all came from the fear that she could lose him."

"She welcomes you?"

"She gave us permission to marry because she was so desperate for her son to come home," I explain. "He left the *sithein* shortly after she tried to force him to procreate with a woman he didn't care for. She was worried they would lose his Green Man powers, and quite frankly, she was scared she would lose him altogether. Following our fears often means walking into self-fulfilling prophecies, but she learned from it. When Dev requested the Goddess Chain, she sent two envoys. Declan and Padric."

"Who is that?"

Another piece of the puzzle. "He was the head of your mother's guard and all of her armies. She was also his long-time lover."

A look of recognition crosses his face. "Her childhood sweetheart. Yes. I heard some speak of him. He died before my brother and I were born. Long before. I don't think she ever got over him. So he is alive in your time. I suppose he loathes me."

He knows nothing. "He treats you like a son."

My answer seems to throw the king off. "Why would he do that?"

"Because he helped raise you. Devinshea, did you feel nothing for the child Zandra gave you?"

He seems to think for a moment. "He was an amusing child, though I never spent much time with him. I only saw him when I managed to get to Zandra's village and honestly, I was far more interested in her. I did love the way she lit up when she saw him. She was a good mother. She could have had servants, but she preferred to take care of him on her own. It's how Deinny got in."

I would bet Deinny was in her life far longer than merely after her son was born. I would bet he loved her always. "He was a father figure to Lee?"

"He and that friend of hers. Neil, I think."

"He's my best friend in our time," I tell him with a wistful smile. "Of course he's also a werewolf."

Devilshea sits up a bit straighter. "Yes, there's word of a wolf prowling around last night. I hope for your sake he leaves with your son and that vampire version of Deinny. I don't like the idea of that man with power. Why in all the planes would I make the decision to share you with him?"

"Because you love him, too," I reply quietly, hoping for the same thing but knowing neither Neil nor Danny would ever leave Dev and I in this position. They might wait and watch, but they would never, ever leave us alone. "You don't share me. It might have started that way, but we're a happy threesome." I mentally wince because I'm giving too much away, but I can't help but poke him to see if there's some good there. "Well, we were until Myrddin came along."

"I sleep with him?" He sounds shocked.

I can't help the salacious grin that covers my face. "Sometimes there's not a lot of sleeping going on."

He stands suddenly, pacing the length of the blanket. "I am...unnatural?"

It takes everything I have to not roll my eyes. "That's your brother talking. You are a Green Man. You are sex on two legs. You are love and commitment and joy, and why would that have boundaries beyond the ones of your own heart? I can blame my Devinshea for many things, but knowing and honoring his heart is not one of them."

"Because he defied the crown for you? Because he gave into unnatural desires?" The question comes with a sneer that absolutely makes this man less attractive.

I lower my eyes because I've seen what I needed to see. He wanted Deinny but feared reprisal from his family. He wanted them all together but when he couldn't have her, he allowed his guilt and grief to lead him to do monstrous things. "Forget I said anything, Your Majesty. Why are we speaking of this when we could speak of more pleasant things?"

He is quiet for a moment. "You are so like her. I suppose we're speaking of it because I didn't get to tell her. I didn't get to say how much I wished I had scooped her up and left the plane. We could have gone anywhere. Deinny had a plan at one point. We were friends back then."

I would bet they had danced around being more. "He had a plan?"

"He thought the three of us should take Lee and leave. He wanted to go to the Earth plane to find my human father. The one my mother tossed aside when she was done with him. Apparently he had some friends from the Earth plane, and they looked him up. He was wealthy, and Deinny believed he would have welcomed me. He thought we could be happy there. As friends, of course."

Bullshit. If they hadn't had some kind of physical interaction, I would be surprised. In this timeline's Daniel, the connection between them made him want to risk everything for a chance at real happiness. However, this Devinshea was too mired in his own miserable devotion to royalty that he couldn't. Or could he? "Is that why? Did your brother find out you were going to leave and he killed Zandra?"

"He couldn't stand the shame I would bring on our name."

"This is a very different *sithein*. Miria's court in my world lived for gossip, but there wasn't shame involved in having relationships. Your brother has slept with every pretty girl in the *sithein*, and he doesn't care what their class is," I point out.

"Declan might sleep with them, but he would never have thought to marry one. He might have fathered a bastard, but he wouldn't have dared to publicly claim him. He would have given the mother money and went on his way. I wanted to claim Lee. For her sake. I suppose I didn't want her child to be ashamed of me, but I didn't get the chance." He sits back down, and there's an air of shame around him.

I can use that. I don't mention that he had years to claim Lee but he hadn't. I can point out how different he and his counterpart's lives are. "Well, my Declan did have a child with a woman he considered unsuitable, and they are married to this day."

Not happily, from what I can tell, but Declan does love his son, Sean.

"He married a commoner?" The question isn't whispered with disdain. The king sounds shocked but almost envious. "And Mother didn't disown him?"

I am going to be way nicer to Padric the next time I see him because he seems to have done Miria a world of good. It's interesting to know how deeply the love and affection of the right person can change who we are and the choices we make. Terrifying but interesting. "No, she encouraged the marriage, though it wasn't to a commoner. He married the Unseelie princess."

"He married Chima? They hated each other here." The king shakes his head. "I heard she died in childbirth. It was six months after our last meeting with the Unseelie. My brother and I both went as envoys. It was one of the worst times of my life."

"Because you were caught by a group of Unseelie who raped you while your brother ran away?"

Dev's eyes close. "I rather hoped that hadn't happened to him. I'm surprised he would so readily accept a male in his bed."

"Danny isn't some random male. He's Dev's best friend, his partner. Yes, they sleep together and there's a lot of passion between them, but there's also the shared experience of loving me. It's not always easy. I don't know what I was like here, but I'm trouble where I come from. A whole lot of it."

"And they share the job of loving and protecting you." He stares off in the distance for a moment. "I suppose Deinny and I did that as well, in our way. Or rather Deinny took care of her while I took care of myself. When I look back on it, I wonder if she really loved me in the end or if she was afraid of me."

Yes, he should ask those questions. Asking those questions will never fix the past, but they might save his soul. "She could do both. I assure you. I can love and be disappointed at the same time. We're imperfect creatures. We're always going to fight, to be upset, to wish things were different. In a marriage, getting through it all with honesty and love is the measure of how successful it can be."

"And when did you realize you couldn't trust them?"

Danger. I need to not overplay my hand. He still has to believe he's got a shot with me. "When they didn't listen to me about Myrddin." Damn, but there was some truth there. I understand now they were under a thrall stone, but there's a tiny piece of me that knows it would have been hard for me to get them to listen even without it. I still remember how Daniel had looked at the wizard when we first met him, how sad he'd been at the thought that Myrddin chose to walk the Earth with Nimue instead of mentoring him. "Daniel is what's known as the King of the Sword. He carries an ancient sword meant for kings who rule during particularly important times. It was a system set up millennia ago by the Heaven and Hell planes. To keep Earth in balance. Myrddin is the king's mentor. But he decided to take the power for himself this time. I always knew something was wrong with him. I knew it from when we met, and they wouldn't listen."

"Your anger is more about the lost time with your children than it is the throne," the king surmises. "Losing the throne and the crown are just things you threw in for me."

Yes, this is a delicate line. "I have to think of my children, Devinshea. Yes, they are my primary concern. I don't really care about the crown. I loved the man, not the king. Not the high priest."

He nods as though he expected the answer. "You are so much like her it worries me. It makes me think I'll disappoint you like I disappointed her."

"Did she tell you that?" I ask.

"Not in so many words, but how could she not be? I left her

alone."

"You left her with her best friend," I point out.

"And made it plain that if she were ever to be with him physically, our relationship would be over. I knew she loved him but by the time she was willing to open herself to his love, she was pregnant. I could have stepped back and let them raise the child. If I had done what I needed to do, she would be alive and Deinny would be alive. They would be a family," he admits.

"You didn't mean to hurt me. I might have been lonely without you, but if I stayed true to you it was because I loved you. If she was anything like me, she didn't let fear rule her. She made conscious decisions." I give him the words because I think he needs to hear them. But there are things he must atone for. "But why kill Deinny?"

"I couldn't stand the way he looked at me after. After I took my revenge." His head drops. "We had a fight. I was drunk. I used some potent drugs to try to forget how my brother looked when I ran a sword through his gut before taking off his head. Deinny said some things to me I didn't want to hear, and I gave the order. I regretted it when I was sober again, but it was done. They all think I feel nothing. They do not know the weight of guilt that presses on me."

"Devinshea, I am not her. You are trying to recreate a relationship that can't exist."

I think I have him for a moment and then his expression clears, and I watch him make the choice to stay mired in this course he chose so long ago. "It can. You will see. I will be better this time. This time I will make things right. I already started by allowing your son to take over my temple. We will have to fix that, but I think it proves I can be a better husband for you. And you will come to enjoy the crown and throne. I think your husbands didn't do it right. Servant, bring my fiancée another pillow."

I sigh inwardly because we'd gotten so close.

And then I feel something whiz past me and hear a terrible thud as an arrow launches itself right into the king's shoulder.

I take a deep breath and pray I survive this battle.

Chapter Twenty-Eight

Sasha

Sasha woke to Meadow staring down at him. She studied him with those glorious green eyes, her blonde hair curling around her shoulders. If she was worried about wearing very little clothing, she didn't show it.

"I thought Earth plane vampires could not be awake during the daylight hours. I have read some books on the subject. Mostly by Vampire plane scholars. They enjoy studying what they like to call their less evolved cousins."

He frowned and then smiled again because she was here and she was beautiful and he was now utterly, hopelessly addicted to her blood. Companion. She was his companion by all legal rights since he'd convinced her to drink from him as well. Ostara had explained to her host that his blood would strengthen their body. And the bond between them. "They are not wrong. While King Daniel and a class of vampires we call academics have the power to daywalk, I must use magic." He held up his right hand, showing off the ring. "This allows me to be in the sun, to be awake when I need to be."

"Or I could do this." She placed her hand on his chest, and her eyes changed as energy pulsed through him.

Through his chest, his heart. That warm wave seemed to go straight to his cock. It filled with blood and strained against his underwear. He couldn't help but gasp.

He'd allowed Rhys to share some energy with him when he'd known he couldn't feed from sex energy. He'd known his wife was somewhere out there and he couldn't force himself to betray her. Even if she hadn't known who he was. Vampires fed from blood and sex, and he cut himself off from half his energy, so Rhys had given him just enough to survive.

This was more than survival. This was power. A tidal wave of sex energy flowing through him. Like Devinshea gave Daniel.

He wouldn't need the ring anymore. Not as long as he had her. He could give it back to the royals and they could give it to one of their warriors. Someone who could work in the shadows and strike when no one would expect.

He groaned and tried so hard to fight back the orgasm that threatened. He had fed from Meadow the night before and given her his blood as well. She'd groaned and moaned in a way that had him panting for her. He'd felt her orgasm, but she'd been weak. She fell asleep in his arms and he carried her to bed, gently undressing her down to her light chemise. He gathered her into his arms and laid in the darkness for the longest time, simply breathing her in.

So he was horny. Super fucking horny, as his American friends would say.

And she was by all accounts a virgin.

She was smiling as she broke contact with him, her eyes back to normal. "Ossie says that should take care of you for a while. I'm afraid she might have had a relationship with a vampire in the past. She enjoyed it. She's worried, though, because vampires can be possessive of their companions. Is that why you didn't make love to me last night?"

He turned her way. "My darling, I didn't make love to you because you were exhausted and running on emotion. I have to give you the choice to be with me, and that means allowing you time to make the decision."

"So you're not opposed to caring for both of us?" Meadow asked the question with an air of expectancy.

Oh, he was over that. He didn't have to think about it. Ostara had already proven herself to him. "Do you love her, Meadow?"

"Very much," she replied with a smile. "She came to me when I was low. I didn't know why, couldn't remember my dreams with the exception of how terrible they were. She saved me. There was something inside that told me I wasn't in the right place."

He sat up, not an easy task in the small bed. They were forced to cuddle all night and his feet hung off, and it was the best sleep he ever had. "But you were."

"I know that now, but at the time I felt," she seemed to think about what word to use, "so far away. I didn't understand it, but I was too far from you. Now I know. If I had been born near you, I would have been human."

"If you had been born on my plane, in my timeline, you would be roughly fourteen years old," he pointed out, trying to ignore his insistent cock. "I would have to protect you and stay away from you for years."

"I don't like the sound of that," she replied with a frown, and her eyes were on his chest.

"You are not afraid of me?"

She shook her head. "Another good reason to have been born Fae this time around. I was raised around all manner of creature. They do not frighten me. Though now that I think about it, perhaps I need better senses when it comes to danger since I thought marrying the evil king would be a good way to save my plane."

He had almost forgotten. "You need the marriage for your kingdom. You said something about a blight."

"We have not had a fertility god or goddess for many, many years," she explained. "My people were struggling, and then Ostara was discovered. She had been trapped by men who thought to use her power. They died, but she remained in the prison. One day some curious children found the cage they held her in buried in the sand of a cave. They freed her but she was weak. She found me and I ascended. However, she was still weak. We heard word of a wizard who could funnel energy to non-corporeal beings."

"If it's Myrddin, he cannot. Or rather wouldn't. He's not known for his good deeds." This was what he needed so he didn't fall on her and scare the hell out of her before she was ready. He needed to think the problems through. "You said Devinshea sought you out as his bride."

"I believe he heard about my ascension," she explained. "There are several Fae planes in this timeline. I come from one that accepts both Seelie and Unseelie Fae. My plane is not directly attached to the Earth plane, as this one is. From what I understand there is one Seelie plane and one Unseelie plane both attached."

That was how it was in his time. From what he could tell, the land remained the same. It was the people who changed given what forces sculpted them. "I know the royals traveled to several different Fae planes other than the attached ones."

"I lived on one founded by a group of Fae who hated the wars between us and wanted to live in peace. Which we do for the most part. My mother is Unseelie and my father Seelie. So both tribes are represented by our crown. But when we lost our Green Man no one would help us. After so many years, not even the gnomes could make it work. We thought we would have to find new lands or be taken back into the *sitheins* here. And then Ostara brought us hope but even inside me, she was a shadow of her former self. So we met with witches who put us together with Myrddin. He brokered the marriage between us and Devinshea, and it seemed perfect because Devinshea did not want physical relations with us. He was honest about finding his love. He wanted only her but would accept a political marriage."

"My darling, then what did he get from the marriage?" Marta had been somewhat naïve. She believed the best in all people.

"Apparently he got to try to peel Ostara off me and eat her soul." She laughed. "Sorry. Ostara is calling me a silly girl for believing that. She says you cannot eat a soul, as your friend Shy could attest. Though she does appreciate that is a question we should have asked. We were naïve."

"Shy? What does she have to do with it?"

"Nothing to do with it, but your friend should be able to put the pieces together. Ostara believes she now knows what the wizard is trying to do," Meadow explains. "She didn't understand why he has spells and charms to draw in deceased souls. She felt them, knew what they were, but it didn't really register. She's so much stronger now, and that means her memories are stronger as well. The magic from last night truly revitalized both of us."

"He's trying to draw in souls? To what purpose?" His body was humming with energy.

"I don't know, but perhaps Shy would since she is made of the energy that turns the wheel."

He'd heard the phrase before but he didn't understand. "I'm confused by that. I've known Shahidi for several years. She's never shown powers beyond being able to talk to the dead. It's been very useful. She's trained hard, and she's good at hand-to-hand combat and several weapons, but I don't understand what you mean by turning the wheel."

"The wheel is life," she explained. "Think of it like a year. You are born in the spring. You live in the summer. You die at the end of the fall and rest during winter. You make your choices during that sleeping time. It's different for all people. Sometimes that winter is the blink of an eye because the soul knows what it wants. Sometimes the soul lingers. It watches and learns. The soul makes a choice to move forward, to stay somewhat where they are, to change forms entirely. I made that choice, Sasha. It's why I trust what is between us. Whatever I saw when I passed into this turning, I knew being born Fae would lead me here."

He reached for her hand, bringing it to his lips. "And I am so grateful for your choice, my love. But how would Shy turn the wheel?"

She stopped for a moment, obviously listening to the voice inside her head. "Ossie says she's made of an ancient magic. She looks human but she is not. She says it's been at least two thousand years since she felt the presence of that magic on any plane. You see while there are many different versions of human and Fae and other creatures, there are those whose souls are completely unique."

This he had figured out. "Gods like Bris. Goddesses like Ostara."

She nodded. "Yes. And, if I'm correct, beings like the wizard Myrddin. The simple fact that he can cross timelines without using the stones proves this. Shy did not need the stones. When you are ready to go home, she can get you there."

If she was right, then he could get them all out now. But he had to be certain. "Because of this magic she has?"

"She doesn't *have* the magic. She *is* the magic." Meadow frowned, an expression that did not mar her beauty in the least. "She does not know, does she? She believes she is human, which is why I sensed the small distance between her and the Green Man. She worried she would not be enough for him, but the real question is the opposite."

"Shy has always worried her magic is too dark for Rhys, though for a long time she had a passenger. A bit like Ostara, though Harry didn't have the same power. He lived in her soul space and he was Rhys's grandfather."

Meadow smiled. "Soul space. A pretty name for it and a bit true. Ossie is wondering how the magic found its way to become somewhat human. Arawn destroyed it when it became clear he would have to retreat with the Fae. It was too dangerous to keep in Annwn. He had certain symbols—you might call them objects of power. The Golden Torc, the Cloak of Invisibility, and the Cauldron of Rebirth. The cloak was given to a group of powerful beings who were creating a race of kings."

Huh. Now he knew where Daniel had gotten it. Or rather Myrddin, since he'd been the one to give it to the king. When Daniel had gone missing, Albert had brought the cloak with the kids, and it had proven invaluable over the years. "I don't see what this has to do with Shy."

"You will. Patience, my love. He still has the torc. He wears it while in Annwn. But the cauldron was the most important object in all of the Fae world at the time. Though you should understand he ruled over humans, too. It was only when they pushed aside the old ways that the gods left the plane."

"I don't know much about Welsh folklore. What did the cauldron do?" Sasha asked.

"What didn't it do? It could feed armies. It could bring the dead back to life. What it mostly did was keep the wheel turning. It was life and death and regeneration. The cauldron could kill or give life or stop life altogether."

"Yes, I can see where that would be very dangerous."

"So dangerous if it found its way into the wrong hands," Meadow agreed. "So Arawn was forced to hide it. He couldn't destroy it entirely, but he could use his magic to get it down to the tiniest piece of the original cauldron. A bit of light and magic and he stood on Snowdonia and flung it out across land and sea and air. He made sure it was so far away no one in its new land would recognize it."

A chill prickled along his spine. "Magic like that, it grows. It changes if allowed to."

She nodded solemnly. "Yes, and in this case, it likely morphed into something like the building blocks of a human, waiting for the right ingredients to become magical again."

His stomach threatened to turn. "You are telling me Shy has the power of the Cauldron of Regeneration in her genes?"

"No. I am telling you that Shy is the cauldron reborn, and I worry Myrddin will use her if he can. Ossie believes the wizard is planning to use the souls he's trapped in the mountain to some terrible purpose. If he filters them through the right spell, he could gain incredible energy."

"Enough to, say, close the gates between planes?"

She nodded.

Sasha stood. The reunion would have to wait. "We need to stop them from leaving. They could be walking into a trap."

He raced to get dressed and hoped they would make it in time.

Chapter Twenty-Nine

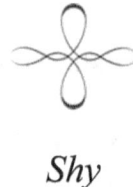

Shy

I don't like tunnels. I'm really more of a walk out in the sunshine or the moonlight girl. Either is acceptable. But the tunnels Lee is leading us through makes me think of being buried alive, and I have to force myself to breathe.

It doesn't help that I can hear her behind me. I hear the water rushing, a river of misery I can't run from.

How did she find me here? I've never known a spirit to be able to move the way she does. She follows me from place to place when every other damn spirit I've seen is tied to where they died.

I have to accept the fact that this spirit isn't haunting a place or a time. She is haunting me.

"You okay, baby?" Rhys is right behind me, his hand on the small of my back most of the time, reminding me I'm not alone. Reminding me that by all Fae rights, I have a husband.

I turn slightly so he can see my face in the torchlight and give him a tight nod. At the end of our line, behind Cassie I can see the Drowning Woman. She stays back but she is here, still following me everywhere I go. "I'm fine."

His brow rises and his arm curls around my waist as he pulls me back against him and whispers in my ear. "Liar. But understand, I will take care of you. I will find a way to break this curse."

I'm not sure I would call it a curse. The Drowning Woman is attracted to my power. I need to stop thinking of her as a burden and start thinking of her as a…client. I need to start viewing her through an adult lens and put aside the fear from my childhood. Everyone in my life right now has told me I need to view myself and my power differently, and I saw it last night. My power doesn't hold Rhys back. My power attracts him as his does mine. Life and death. Spring and autumn. We need each other, and it's a beautiful thing. "I need to find a way to help her move on."

"There's my wife," he says, and I hear the pride in his voice. "She cannot hurt you. I would never allow it. I know I don't have your power, but I would find a way."

I believe him. I tilt my head up and he kisses me. My body immediately responds, the bonds of the night before hugging me close.

"Do you have to be so, like, emotional and stuff?" Lee says with a shudder. "It's bringing the mood down, brother."

"See, I know he means that *brother* as a friendly term, but I know what my brother would say," Rhys grouses.

It makes me smile. He and Fae Lee have bickered like he and Vampire Lee do all the time. Since they were children. "The very same thing. Lee struggles to understand complex emotions."

"I do not," Lee argues. "I understand all the emotions. I just think they're unseemly. Anger and humor are really all I need to get by. And horniness."

"You definitely understand that," Cassie replies. She moves behind Rhys, with Brendan prowling after them. He's back in wolf form. "I would bet you've never had a serious girlfriend. Or boyfriend."

Lee shrugs negligently as we reach one of what he calls the resting points. They're slightly larger spaces in the tunnels where the rebels store food and water and weapons. "I try to keep things light."

"I saw you hitting on the priestesses last night," Cassie accused. "Like five of them."

Lee's lips kick up in a salacious grin. "I didn't merely hit on them, sweetheart. I had some fun with three of them after the kiddos were all put to bed. That lust magic might not make the priestesses insane, but it does something for them."

"Eww," Cassie replies with a shake of her head.

Rhys reaches for his canteen and refills it. He huddles to one side, keeping me close. "Do you need anything, my goddess?"

"Just to be out of here. How much longer?" I ask. When we're out in the sunshine, I'll be able to breathe again.

"About an hour more. Sorry. We're taking the longest route because that's the one that dumps out close to our village," Lee explains, tearing off a piece of what looks like jerky and tossing it Brendan's way.

The werewolf bounces up and catches it, swallowing it in one big gulp, and then he stops and turns, beginning to growl.

Rhys immediately steps in front of me, a long blade in his hand.

I have to admit, my husband looks superhot when he's defending me.

But then I hear a familiar bark and the Cŵn Annwn are running in. I note they avoid the Drowning Woman as though they know she's there. They seemed to have been running toward us at breakneck pace, but they slow and carefully avoid her.

They don't bark or growl. They don't seem to see her as a threat.

Brendan growls again as the biggest hound tries to sniff his butt. He definitely sees that as an affront to his dignity.

Cassie giggles as they edge past her. "I think they're just being friendly. I wondered where they went."

The big hounds make their way to their target. Me. All three crowd in, trying to get near me. There's nothing unfriendly about them. They're big dogs looking for cuddles and treats. It's hard to remember they're supposed to be hellhounds.

"The king had them held in the royal kennels," Lee replies, looking down at them with a vague smile on his face. "I'm pretty sure he was going to…" He draws a hand across his throat in the universal sign for get rid of in the meanest way. "My father's not a pet person. Hey, guys. Did you seriously think these were real Cŵn Annwn?"

"How were we supposed to know?" Rhys asks with a huff.

"Well, you're Fae for one thing. I suspect you have some in your home *sithein*. These are kind of runts."

Then I would fear seeing the real thing.

"I didn't spend a lot of time there except when I was a child,"

Rhys admits. "There weren't a lot of hellhounds on the planes where we hid out. But there were dinosaurs."

"What is a dinosaur?" Lee asks, absently petting one of the hounds.

I shake my head because we are not going there. "They're extinct in every plane that counts now. So these aren't Arawn's hounds? Your father said something about them being from this plane. Would the crone have been, too?"

"If it's the same crone I'm thinking of, she used to be one of the King of the Dead's councils. At least on this plane," Lee replies. "From all accounts she's the real thing. I know many Fae visit her for her wisdom."

"So she would have been working for Myrddin, but she could also have told the truth about some things." Rhys seems to know where my head is at. He's asking the same questions I have.

"Very likely, though I'm not sure when she was last in Annwn. No one has been in a long time."

"How would you know?" I ask.

He seems to think about the question. "I guess I wouldn't. No one's come back. Which since it's a land of the dead makes sense. What I do know is every soul that has died on this plane in the last year hasn't gone. Our witches tracked the energy."

I can guess. "They're going to the mountains in the north. But there has to be a cutoff point because I met some spirits in the forests where we came out."

"But that forest is connected to the tunnels we found on Snowdonia." Rhys has put on his thinking cap, and his big brain is working. He might have been forced to flee traditional education at the age of eleven, but Sasha taught all the kids how to think critically. Well, he taught Rhys and Evan at least. Fenrir is more of an emotional thinker, and Lee thinks with his dick. "The legends place Snowdonia atop Annwn, the Welsh version of Hell."

I shake my head. "Annwn was never Hell. It was the afterlife. The idea of Hell is a Christian belief. Viewed in that way, Annwn would be more like Heaven, but I get your point. It would also likely have some effects on the land around it. Perhaps there's a reason those spirits wouldn't go further into the forest."

"The proximity to Annwn protects them," Rhys agrees. "There

might be other distances that would be safe, but we can't count on that. Whatever spell Myrddin's put in to attract the souls of the dead is definitely working in other parts of this *sithein*."

Lee nods. "From what they can tell. We're not allowed close to the mountain. My father has guards on all the trails. It's been going on since shortly after he first met with Myrddin. We had a couple of spies make it to the mountains, but they didn't come back." Lee gets to one knee as the hounds roll around and offer their bellies up. "We've had some disturbances as well that led our witches to believe something is wrong."

"So he did something to the mountain." I think carefully about what the gnome told me. "Something that attracts the recently dead. They're drawn in through Myrddin or the king. Likely via some spelled object they're wearing. If one could see it, it might appear as though the soul was being consumed."

"Are you telling me my father isn't a soul eater?" Lee asks.

"I don't think so, but it might be possible to use those souls as fuel for something. I don't know if it would destroy the soul however. I think that might be impossible. But it could damage it." I consider the problem as my hand strokes down Fluffy's back. I like the fact that they're here. They weren't responsible for tricking us. They only wanted some affection and treats. "A spell like that could disrupt the balance."

"Balance?" Cassie asks as her brother hides behind her because Caddoc is still trying to get a whiff of him. "What balance is there to death?"

"A soul needs to move on, and most do. It's why the sluagh colonies aren't filled to the brims," I explain. "The truth of the matter is most people move on quickly because they're ready. Otherwise, the world would be filled with spirits, and they would be restless. So restless they would disturb the waking world around them. I suspect that's why no one is allowed near the mountains and why your people never came back."

"They're dead, too, aren't they?" Lee asks, his expression grim.

"I think we can count on it," I reply. "That many restless dead forget they're trying to move on. They become angry even if they were not in life. They know they're not in the right place, and after a while they seek revenge for it on anyone they can."

"Myrddin needs my father because of his access to the mountain," Lee says with a huff. "Why didn't I think of it? We know he's holding them there, but they had magical properties, too. Those mountains have long been ruled by my family. It's where we hide our treasures. The sluagh actually guard some of them. I think he needs my father to access the mountain and get what he needs. He has to have my father alive to perform his ritual, and the only way to get him to agree was to give him what he wants."

"My mother." Rhys leans in, his arm going around my waist.

"He's also convinced my father that he can take his temple back if he integrates with Bris," Lee explains.

"Why bring Ostara into it?" Cassie asks.

I think I've figured that out. "She's the experiment. They found a fairly weakened ascended goddess. If they can find the right spell to peel her off her host, then they can do the same with Bris. Bris is a non-corporeal spirit. They might think he could get sucked into the trap, and let me tell you, his soul moving on would be the big bang of that kind of magic."

I shudder at the thought of it. Bris leaving could be everything Myrddin needs to do his will. To close us off. When that is done, he will open the gates to Hell and Earth will become a warzone like nothing we've ever seen.

It must be stopped at all costs.

"That might be enough to close the celestial planes off." Rhys takes a long breath. "And he thinks you can stop him."

He's talking to me. Of course he is. I don't understand it. "Me?"

"Yes, my love. You. He's afraid of you," Rhys says. "I want nothing more than to take you to Lee's village and hide you away, but you are the key to all of this."

"He's terrified of you, Shy," Lee agrees. "I saw it in his eyes when you were fighting him in the dining hall. You are what he didn't count on. He thought he would get Rhys's parents."

"But the trap was about me," I point out. "The crone came for me. Not the king and queen. Not the high priest. Me."

"Which is why we have to consider the fact that the gods we call are not always the ones who answer," Lee says solemnly. "What if my father and the wizard sought to trick your parents by hiring the hag, but the hag tricked them? What if, after all these years, she still loves the god she worked for? She is a divination witch. What if she saw what must happen and gave it the push it needed?"

"Like the dark prophet did." Rhys nods. "This is all dependent on you, my goddess. I can stand by your side and accept whatever fate brings us, but you will lead us down the path. You will win or lose this battle."

Tears spring to my eyes, and I am so afraid of his words. Because they ring true. "I have no idea what I'm supposed to do."

I feel my power, but I don't know how to use it. I don't know what I'm supposed to be. I only know I'm more than I thought I was.

Water caresses my toes and I glance their way, thinking someone must have spilled. When I look down I see my bare feet in the mud of the pond that father used to fish in, and for a blink I am there. I feel the sun on my face, the warm winds of a Texas spring on my skin. It's almost dark and Mama will call me in soon, but for now I stand beside my father as he whips the fishing pole into the pond and waits.

"Such a feral child," he says with a grin. "You know we buy you shoes, Shy."

I smile his way. "But I like the feel of the earth between my toes. And the sky above me."

My father grows serious and he stares my way, his eyes going dark. "Because you are earth and sky. You are the bubbling cauldron we were all born of. When you need him, call his name. He always meant to find you again."

I blink and I'm back in my adult body and the floor is dry again, but I look to the Drowning Woman.

She sent me that message. Why? She never has before.

Or has she and I was too afraid to see it?

I am earth and sky. I stand in the mud and feel the tug of a thread that runs to the core of the planet. I tilt my head up and that thread runs from me to the heavens above. Earth and sky. Moon and sun and all the planes.

Power bubbles up. I can feel it.

And it frightens me.

"Shy?" My husband stands in front of me, gently tilting my head up. "Are you all right?"

"She sent me a vision," I say quietly.

"She?" Lee asks.

Cassie gasped. "The she? The creepy water spirit? Is she here?" Cassie turns, machete in hand like she can fight a non-corporeal spirit. I know she would try for me. "How is she here?"

"She found a way to follow me." I look past Cassie but the Drowning Woman is further back now, or perhaps she used up energy sending me that vision. She's not as solid as she was before and sounds more distant. "What are you trying to tell me?"

The hounds have taken space around me, like they're letting me know they are there for me.

Why would the hounds specifically want to be with me?

Why would Matilda, the crone, call me *yr un sanctaidd*? The sacred one. I thought she was trying to pull me, to get me to do what she wants, but now I wonder. Had she been the trap for me? Or for Myrddin Emrys and the king of this plane?

I see a hand come out of the water as though she's trying to touch me, and then she's gone.

"Well, that's frustrating." I look to Rhys. "She's gone. She somehow sent me a vision of my father."

"Why would she do that?" my husband asks.

I'm not sure. "It started out as something I remembered. My father would go fishing in this pond on our land and I would sit with him. I would sometimes play in the mud, and he would tease me for being feral. But then one day I cried because that seemed like a bad thing to be and he told me to never think that. He told me I was made of earth and sky and I had found my way to him." Tears pierce my eyes as the memory flows over me. The sweetness of my father laying down his pole and getting into the mud with me. "He told me I was a gift to my family, a gift from the old ones, and that one day I would understand." I shake my head. "How did I forget that? He told me I was made of earth and sky, that I should never apologize for liking to play in the mud. But he wasn't talking about mud. He knew. He knew I would have these powers."

"Your father was a telekinetic," Rhys points out.

I love that he listens to me. My family might no longer be on the Earth plane, but Rhys knows them through my stories. He encourages me to keep them alive even when it would seem easier to forget. It was one of the first ways I knew he cared about me. He was a teenaged boy and he would sit up late with me and ask about my family and tell me about his. We bonded through loss, but it became something beautiful. "He was, but every now and then he would have the sight, as my grams would call it. Not divination. He would see something as it was rather than as it wished to be seen. He could see trolls through their glamours. I think he saw me that day."

And loved me. Wanted the best for me. Wished for me to step into my power and use it for good.

"So there's a weird ghostie in here with us?" Lee shudders a little. "I'm not sure I wanted to know that. Can't you send it along, Shy? Like you did with my uncle?"

He really understands nothing, and he doesn't listen. He was probably either thinking about his next meal or who he could hit on when I explained the first time. "Your uncle was ready to move on. The Drowning Woman is not. So she follows me. When she does what she needs to do, she will find her path."

And it's up to me to figure out what she needs to move on. We're connected somehow, but that is a problem for another day.

Today I have to deal with Myrddin.

"Are we rested up?" I ask.

And Brendan starts to growl.

I look down and the hounds move in front of me, hair coming up on their backs.

"Shy, when I tell you to run, you do it," Rhys commands.

"I'll get her out of here," Cassie promises.

"Follow the signs back to the temple." Lee stands beside his brother and then moves so they are back to back. Like they've done this before. The trouble is we're at a crossroads where three different tunnels meet.

It would be super nice to have some big-ass power right now. I want to throw up a shield around us but I'm still just me, and the power bubbling inside me doesn't cover the living world. My hands are useless as my adrenaline rushes to the surface.

"Who's there?" Lee takes a couple of steps forward, into the tunnel to our left. He tilts his head to speak to Rhys. "This tunnel leads back to the palace. It's how we get into the servant quarters."

"Is it a friendly?" Rhys asks, not taking his eyes off the tunnel in front of him.

"I don't know," Lee admits. "Who is there? Identify yourself or we're going to have a problem."

A light appears in the darkness, small at first but getting bigger.

"Shy, run," Rhys says.

I can't leave him. "What if it's coming for you?"

"Run, baby," he pleads.

But the light is already there, and it has one target. Me.

The ball of light hits my chest and, in a blink, I'm transported.

Cold winds whip around me, and I am alone at the bottom of the mountain that hums for me. Hums? More like screams. What was a mere whisper in those woods is now a roar.

The dead are here, and they are restless. They want. They need. They will do anything to get out of here.

I put my hands to my ears in a useless attempt to stop the screaming.

"Well, I rather thought this place might bring you low."

I look up and my horror is complete.

Myrddin Emrys stands in front of me and he has Devinshea Quinn wrapped in bindings. He's covered in blood, and I feel horror splash across me as I realize why.

His hands are gone.

Myrddin cut off his hands.

The screaming pulses through me, and I faint dead away.

Chapter Thirty

Sasha

Sasha held Ostara's hand as he rushed through the too-tight tunnels and into the king's viewing room. He expected to see Devinshea there, tied back up after a long night of healing.

Instead he saw Neil where Dev had been. He wasn't tied to the post, however. He was upright, his head slumped forward, his body covered in blood and a long silver spear sticking out of his torso. The spear held him to the post. The shackles where Dev had been hung were empty, dangling over Neil's still form.

There was blood everywhere.

Ostara gasped and started to rush for the door they found yesterday.

He held her back, fear flooding his system with adrenaline. "We don't know who else is in there."

"He needs help," she insisted.

"And we will give it to him, but we can't help him if we're immediately attacked." Neil's body was moving slightly, breath entering and exiting his body. He was a tough kill, and whoever had tried hadn't finished the job.

Sasha noticed the altar someone had placed in the middle of the dungeon. Myrddin had been hard at work, and he hadn't waited until dark. What made him lose his patience?

"What happened?" a deep voice asked.

He turned and Daniel was there, his face ashen. His shoulders were slumped like he was tired beyond measure. "My king, where have you been? You didn't come to Bibi's last night."

Bibi had promised she took the king to the queen's chamber and that he would be safe there until morning.

"It was a bit crowded. I stayed in another room until I took a meeting this morning. Where is Dev and what the fuck happened to Neil?" The king stood in front of the mirror. "How do we get in? He's alive but he won't be for long. That's silver, and we don't know what kind of spells Myrddin worked. Something big from the looks of it."

"I suspect Myrddin took Devinshea, and it looks like Neil tried to defend him. He was probably angry that Ostara got away," Sasha explained. He hadn't seen anyone moving. He would be able to tell better if they were alone once he was in the room. The wall cut off his senses. It was time to get in, get that spear out of Neil, and figure out what the hell had happened. He pressed the door open. "Stay behind me."

Ostara rushed past him. It was fitting. Marta never listened to him, either. If she thought she could help, she would risk everything.

She moved before the werewolf, looking at the place where the spear entered his body. "He could bleed if we take it out. He's already lost a lot of blood."

"Oh, he'll bleed." Sasha looked back to Daniel, who was trying to get his sleeve rolled up. What had happened to the king? "But I'll handle it. Vampire blood can heal a lot of damage, and he's a werewolf. It's only the silver that's holding him back. Once we take it out, he'll begin to heal." Unlike a custom bullet, which would leak silver into Neil's bloodstream, the spear simply held him there, kept him in a state where he couldn't heal. Myrddin hadn't pierced the heart, so Neil was alive. Sasha would bet Myrddin thought he had. "Why don't you see if you can help my king? Do you have any energy left?"

She stood and nodded. "Yes, after last night I have a bounty. It will not harm me or make me weak to share some with your king. The energy is still pulsing through, and I feel it out here even more."

"We're going to fix you, my friend." Daniel studied Neil as he spoke. "I got hit with something a few hours ago. Something new. I've felt weak the entire time I've been on this plane, but this… It had to be a spell of some kind, probably something to do with that wicked altar. I don't think it was particularly meant for me, but it took all my energy. I wasn't behind the wards. I was meeting with some of the guards. The ones who want to join the rebels now that they're out from under the spells used on them. In the middle of the meeting, I felt this wave, and then I could barely move. I forced myself to go to the tunnels, to get back to base, but I saw you come in here."

Neil's eyes opened, weariness and pain plain in his expression. "It was Myrddin. He's moving into end game. He said he can't wait any longer because he thinks Zoey is going to screw everything up, and now he believes he can use her to get to Bris and avoid the whole soul-peeling thing. I don't know how, but he believes it. He's going after Shy, too. He thinks he can use her to put Arawn in a bad position and keep him and the other ascended gods out of the war. Daniel, I think he went to Hell last night and something happened."

Daniel nodded. "Well, we knew he was meeting Lucifer. I would bet he went to get some advice. Lucifer might be interested in Shy as well if she's as powerful as we think she is. Do we know where he took Dev?"

Tears slipped from Neil's eyes. "I don't know. Daniel…he took Dev but only after he… Goddess, I can't even say it."

There was so much blood. Could it all be Neil's?

Daniel managed to lose more color. "What? What, Neil? What happened to Devinshea? We were supposed to have more time. After last night, Dev should be strong. He should have been able to fight Myrddin off after soaking in Rhys's magic."

Sasha braced himself. If Devinshea was dead, the king would never forgive himself. Sasha would never forgive himself. He'd left Dev here.

"He couldn't do magic. Myrddin blindsided him with a spell. I didn't see all of it. I just know by the time I was aware, Dev was immobile and… I can't. I'll never get the sight out of my head. He worked a dark spell. He wanted to locate where Shy was. He pulled death magic. It's what you felt, but he needed dead magical flesh to do it. Daniel, he cut off Dev's hands," Neil managed, though he was having trouble breathing.

Sasha felt his gut turn. He'd done this. He'd left the high priest, and he was in bed with his wife while Dev had been…

"So he can't do magic." Daniel looked like he was going to be sick. "Dev isn't fully Fae. He's half human. He can't control magic with his mind. Not even with Bris. He doesn't need much more than a few finger movements, but he has to use them. Myrddin took his magic. He might have cut him off from Bris. Goddess, he's alone and completely at Myrddin's mercy."

"He saved me, King Daniel. Please allow me to give something back to you." Ostara was in control of the body, and she was obviously going to stay calm. "I suspect the spell the wizard used to find Shy sucked up all the death magic in the area."

Daniel put a hand on his heart. "I think you're right. I've felt this way once before when Arawn fed off me. He did it in small doses, and then all at once when he was in danger."

Ostara nodded. "I can feel the remanent. The wizard figured out a way to take your magic, too, though I think he was probably trying for someone else. He was likely trying to drain Shahidi. It won't work. Shahidi isn't death magic, per se, though he might be able to find her by using it."

"She's in the temple," Daniel said with a sigh. "She's safe. Let's get Neil healed up first, and then we'll make our way there. Or rather you will. I'm going to extract my wife. If Dev isn't down here, there's zero reason to keep her in play."

"It's not going to work." Sasha stood beside Neil and put a hand on the spear. He couldn't heal with that silver splitting his body. "Shy and Rhys were going to allow this plane's version of Lee to take them up to the mountains. She should be either in the tunnels or at Lee's village by now. I'm sorry, Neil. This is going to hurt."

Neil's head shook. "Nothing can hurt more than watching Dev… Nothing. I tried to stop it."

Of course he did. "It's not your fault. This is Myrddin's."

And so was what he did next. He pulled the silver spear from Neil's body, watching blood spurt from the wound as he caught the werewolf with his free hand. He tossed the spear away and bit into his own wrist and put it to Neil's mouth, cradling him. It had been a long time since the wolf had any blood. His husband's and Daniel's would have been best, but the king was in a bad way. The only reason Sasha wasn't was because he'd been inside the wards when the wizard unleashed his powerful magic.

Neil drank for a full minute, and Sasha heard the sizzle of Ostara's magic as she gave Daniel some of her unique energy. It was very close to Rhys's, which came straight from his father. Daniel had fed on Devinshea's magic for years. This was what he needed. This would give him a major boost, though he would need to feed from his companion to be back at any kind of power.

"The fucker used Dev to create the spell. I wasn't expecting it. I was asleep in the watch room." Guilt coated Neil's confession. "I was planning to wake up and get Dev back in his torture gear before they showed up, but they returned long before dawn."

How long had Neil been hanging there?

Daniel took a long breath and his fangs were out, eyes glowing blue as he inclined his head to Ostara. "I thank you, goddess."

"He stayed so he could spare me." Meadow's eyes stared up at him, shining with tears. "He could have run but he made a deal with that wizard so I didn't…"

He knew exactly what Devinshea saved her from and what he owed the male. "We will find him. We will figure out how to help him. We need to find his hands if we're to have any chance at giving him back his magic."

King's blood could work miracles. They would find a way to get Dev's hands back. They had to. Devinshea couldn't lose his magic. His family depended on him.

"He destroyed them," Neil said dully. His side was already healing, and he looked so much better color wise, but there was a hollow look to his eyes. "Myrddin burned them for the spell. He wanted to make sure Devinshea can't work any kind of magic ever again. He's going to pull Bris off his soul and send him into the mountain. He thinks he can do it. All he needs is the king and Zoey. I think he realized how much power he held when Dev made that deal with him last night. He thinks Dev will make another deal to spare Zoey's life, and because we're in Faery it can be enforced through Dev's line."

"Yes, that will work on Dev and Bris alike," Daniel agreed. "They'll do whatever he wants to save our wife, and they won't play around if they think for a second the Wild Hunt could tear apart our children. But he didn't work a spell to make a deal. He did that to find Shy. Why the fuck would he need Shy? Does he want her to talk to his victims?"

"She's more than a medium," Sasha said, looking around. The dungeon was quiet, but he could smell blood. He caught a glimpse of bodies in the background. Neil had defended the high priest well, but Myrddin's magic likely swayed the outcome.

"She is so much more than a medium." Meadow stood beside him, her small hand finding his and giving him a squeeze. "Ostara knows her. Well, she knows what she is, what she was. She contains the best parts of Arawn's magic. She is both death and life magic. At one point in time, she was the Cauldron of Rebirth. She could feed armies, revive the dead, turn the wheel of time. She was…is the power of life reborn."

"But she doesn't understand her own power." It was the reason he'd jumped out of bed, though he wanted to stay with his wife. Shy was in danger, and Shy was a danger. If what Ostara said was true, she had immense power and no ability to use it. "If Myrddin knows what she is, he could potentially use her to send Bris where he wants him to go. I don't know how it works, but I have to think Bris might not have a choice if Myrddin can tap into Shy's power. Or he's going to do exactly what Neil said and use her against Arawn."

"I have to find Zoey." While Daniel looked better, there was still a slump to his shoulders.

"Myrddin will need the king," Meadow pointed out. "From what I understand, the mountains where he's holding the souls is keyed to the king's family. They keep certain treasures there and have for centuries. It's a sacred mountain, and the entrance is guarded by wards that can only be opened with the king's blood."

"Would Dev's work?" Daniel asked.

She shook her head. "I don't think so. While they might look exactly alike, the king is fully Fae and your Devinshea is not. I think one of the reasons the mountain worked for the wizard as a holding place is the fact that those wards are keyed to only one man. The only other with a possible chance of opening it is his son. Lee might be able to because he is a son of the royal family, but I cannot be sure."

"So he will have to get the king to open the mountains to him," Sasha mused. "I doubt this version of Devinshea does anything he doesn't want to." He winced as he realized what was going to happen, might be happening right now. "Zoey will work as leverage to make the king do his will. She works for both Devinsheas. Damn it. Do we know where she is? Is she still in the palace?"

Neil stretched, his eyes dark as he looked around the room and then took a deep breath through his nose. "She hasn't been down here. I need to change and then I'll be able to track her."

"She was in her room when I left her." Daniel looked sick again. "I shouldn't have left her. I shouldn't have fucking allowed Myrddin to have Dev. I shouldn't…"

The king was normally a calm presence, but Sasha understood. His partner was injured—possibly irrevocably—and in the hands of their greatest enemy, and his wife could be next. He couldn't think like a king at this point. He was a terrified husband, and he wasn't anywhere close to full power. He hadn't been since they walked through the doors to this plane. There was something about the sun on this plane that took more out of Daniel. Sasha felt it, too. But he spent less time outside, and he had a full dose of companion blood and Ostara's magic. "Neil, change and help us find the queen. Can you track the other Devinshea?"

Neil nodded, getting to his feet. "I can track anyone, and if you get me close to the wizard, I promise I'll kill him this time."

Daniel's head shook. "No, you won't. You'll get Z and Shy out of there, and I'll save Devinshea. You know the prophecy. I want to kill him, too, but the dark prophet is never wrong. Our only goal at this point has to be to get our people out of here and stop whatever Myrddin plans. You taking a shot at him likely means we lose you."

Neil nodded tightly. "I'll get her out. I'll get Shy out. We'll run for the door. It doesn't matter where we go. We'll find a way."

"You leave us if you have to," Daniel insisted.

"Or I can lead you to my home plane," Meadow offered. "The safest way off this plane is a door not far from the mountains. You cannot use the door you took without access to the blue dolerite, but my plane is accessible through a stable door. We have to pass through the Earth plane, but the door to mine is in a city called Los Angeles. My timeline's Earth plane is a place of peace and harmony. It is not dangerous to travel through."

"Well, that's a change from ours," Daniel said with a touch of bitterness. "We will need to hide our powers."

Ostara's head shook. "Not at all. The Earth plane residents know about the other planes and are very accepting. Like President Taggart says, horns and tails don't make you an asshole. Your attitude does. He encourages tourism, too."

Daniel ran a hand over his hair, pushing it back. His claws were out. "We start in the palace. Sasha, kill anyone who tries to stop us."

Sasha nodded as Neil changed and a large snowy white wolf was suddenly in the room.

Neil took off.

Sasha took his wife's hand.

The chase was on.

Chapter Thirty-One

Zoey

Fear floods my system as I roll toward Devilshea.

I know I should run, but in this moment it's like my Dev is hurt. It's pure instinct, and I can't think straight. All I see is my husband with an arrow in his shoulder and a rasping sound coming from his chest.

"Dev." I kneel over him.

"Zandra," he says between gritted teeth. "Run. You must run."

Now he sounds like my Dev. I glance around and the servants are fleeing, but I don't see where the archer is.

I reach for a knife. It's small, but I need some kind of weapon. "We need to get that arrow out of you. If they're smart, it's cold iron, and the longer it's in, the more likelihood it kills you. It's going to have to go out the back, I think."

"You have to run." His hands grip my arms, and I see a bit of desperation there. "Go. Can't live through your death again."

"I'm going to kill her," a deep voice says.

Eoin is walking toward us, and he is not alone. He has several of the king's guard with him, and he's dressed for battle.

Confusion sets on the king's face. "What is going on? Eoin? Why aren't you chasing whoever shot me?"

I know the reason. "Because he's the one who shot you."

"I will admit you are far smarter than the you who lived on this plane," he says with a smirk my way. "Zandra was an idiot. She truly believed he would come around and marry her one day. He never would have."

The king tries to push himself up.

Two other guards draw down on him.

"Don't fight, Dev," Eoin says with a *tsk*. "They're out of your spell now so they're a little angry about spending the last couple of years as your mindless zombies. Thanks for not doing that to me, by the way. I know. We were childhood friends. The best of friends. But I'm weary of you always chasing after this one woman when you could have had them all. And the wizard pays more."

"Bastard," the king hisses.

Eoin shrugs. "Certainly, but at least I'm not so bespelled by a woman I would chase her across planes of existence and ruin my soul for love."

"No, you did it for money," I point out. My fear has ramped up, and I have to force myself not to put a hand over my belly where my daughter lies. Them not knowing about Harriet might be the only thing keeping her alive.

Though the wizard knows, and apparently that's who this asshole is working for.

He nods, no shame at all in his expression. "Yes, a much better reason to sell one's soul, if you ask me. Now because you have no one to defend you, let's get you ready to pay your bill to the wizard."

I stand, putting myself between the king and his guard. I'm pretty damn good at defending myself. Though it's been a while.

"What are you doing?" The king struggles to get the question out.

I pick up the decorative sword he placed on the blanket when he sat down. "Giving this asshole a hard time."

"I will go with you if you allow her safe passage." The king struggles to his feet. "I will do what the wizard wants if you only spare her."

I'm shocked because I've seen nothing but selfishness from this version of Dev. It's like someone took all the empathy out of him and this is the shell we are left with. But now, facing pain and death, he finds something of the soul I've known for years.

He takes the sword from my hand even though he winces at the weight. His left arm is useless and he tosses the sword away with his right. He stands in front of me. "Go. Find your real husband. I'm not a fool. You love him. You were placating me. Find him and be happy."

Tears pierce my eyes because there is still some measure of good in this man.

"I think she's about to find him." Eoin gestures to something behind me, and I realize we're circled by guards who have no intention of letting me go. "Both of you are needed for this ritual of the wizard's."

I have to try logic. "You know what he's trying to do, right? He's trying to close the door between the celestial planes and the Earth plane, leaving Hell and Earth alone."

"Don't know. Don't care. It won't affect us here, so that sounds like an Earth plane problem," Eoin says with a smirk. "We'll be fine on this plane. I'll take over as king, put down that son of yours and his rebels, and we'll live like kings. Because we'll be kings. At least I will."

"It won't work that way," I argue. "If he closes the door, it won't simply be for one timeline. That door to Heaven is not ruled by time. It will affect everyone."

Eoin shrugs. "Not how he explained it to me, and honestly, I don't care. I'm tired of watching a man I once admired humble himself for a woman. He could have been great, was great. When he slaughtered the creatures he thought murdered his beloved, he had a backbone. He took out his competition, and it was a magnificent thing to see. I had some small hope when he announced his betrothal to Ostara that he might let go of this ridiculous dream that he could get you back. But it was all another plot. You are the only thing he thinks of, and if the wizard didn't point out that we need you, I would kill you here."

Well, of course he needs me. I'm sure he wants to kill me himself, but I'm stuck on a couple of words. "Thought killed me? What does that mean?"

Devilshea holds my hand, trying to get me behind him, but it doesn't matter since we're surrounded. He's not thinking straight, likely because of the arrow in his chest. "He is talking about the creatures my brother sent to assassinate Zandra when I refused to marry. He thought to make it look like a random assault by goblins and trolls, but I knew he sent those monsters after her. I knew they had to be taken out. Animals. They aren't like us. Some can be managed, are necessary, but the wicked had to be removed from our society."

Ah, but that wasn't what Eoin said. I've found the villain always wants credit in the end. Sometimes it's their downfall. "It was you."

Eoin's smirk widens. "It was me. But I made sure to make it look like goblins tore her apart. It was fun. Such a dumb bitch. All I had to do was pretend I was taking her to you and she followed me. She cried, you know. She called out your name, Devinshea. She truly believed you would come and save her. She believed right up until the moment I slit her throat."

The king practically vibrates with rage and starts toward Eoin, but he doesn't get far. He groans as another arrow hits his back, the thud a sickening sound to hear.

"Don't fucking kill him," Eoin complains. "We get nothing if we don't deliver him." He stalks up to us, completely unafraid. "You're going to do everything the wizard tells you to or we'll kill her. Am I understood? If you do what he asks, you'll be allowed to take your bitch to the Earth plane and eek out whatever existence you can find there."

He's lying. There's zero chance Myrddin lets any of us live. Oh, he might have as long as he was certain none of us could get back to the right timeline, but it's clear to me he wants more than to leave us in prison. He'll kill me simply to take out the threat Harriet poses, but I'm not about to point that out. I need to stay alive as long as I can because my Devinshea is going to be in trouble, too. Daniel will find a way to come for us. He always does.

I put up a hand to stop Eoin from coming too close. If they kill this Dev, they might not need me. "He's going to do everything you ask."

"Is he now?" Eoin asks, a challenge in his tone.

The king nods. "As long as you don't harm her. But Eoin, you should know I will be a good boy until I get off this plane and ensure her safety. And then I will find a way to make you pay."

If that dire threat concerns the guard, he doesn't show it. "I'm sure you will try. I think I'll close the doors to this plane for a while.

Until I've taken power and turned this place around."

"You won't be able to do it without a Green Man," the king says with a bitter bite. "I should know. I lost this place the day my temple decided I was unworthy. The temple will not open again."

"It already has." Eoin looks like this is a problem he has already solved. "Your bitch here brought along a fully Fae Green Man. A fucking elemental. All we have to do is capture him. We'll cage him in the temple and his magic will feed our lands. The wizard is going to help us. He says he has a spell that will keep the Green Man in stasis, and he won't give us any trouble."

"The temple doesn't work that way," the king argues. "It's not merely looking for power. It wants a partner. It wants... companionship."

Oh, I was going to be way nicer to our temple when we finally return to it. I'm going to say hi and everything. And talk to it because it's a very good temple. Eoin is also being extremely optimistic. "Myrddin is out of here the minute he has what he wants. He won't bother to track down my son. By the way, he's going to be harder to deal with than you think. He's not merely a Green Man or an elemental. He's a warrior, and he will fight."

"Then he will lose," Eoin concludes. He points his sword. "Get in close. We're going to meet the wizard and finish this. Tonight we dine in the palace, and it will all belong to us."

A grand cheer goes up, and I know there will be no talking this man out of his foolish plan. I will have to figure it out once we get to the wizard, though I can try to delay as long as possible. When Danny realizes he can't find me, he'll send Neil, and we're not so far he can't find us. Neil can track me almost anywhere.

I need time. I need to buy my son time to get Shy somewhere safe, time for Danny to save Dev and then me.

I always need time, and it's almost always the one thing I don't get.

"He can't travel like this." I gesture to the king and his wounded torso. "I assume that's cold iron. If it stays too long in his body, it will kill him, and then Myrddin won't get what he needs."

Eoin sighs as though all of this drama is extremely boring. "I suppose you're right, though I can't have him healing too soon." He nods to one of his guards. "Secure the king."

One of his men rushes forward with shackles I'm sure are made of cold iron as well. They will make his wrists ache and send pain through his body, but they won't kill him. Those arrows will. I start forward to try to find the gentlest way to remove them, but his men are at work on that as well.

The king shouts out as one of the men pushes at the arrow. He falls to his knees, the arrow still lodged in his shoulder, but now it's sticking out the back. The man takes a knife and slices through until he can pull it out the other side.

The king is in a heap on the ground, the contents of his stomach on the grass next to him after they're done and both arrows are removed in the most savage way imaginable.

I drop to my knees beside him, trying to help him up. He's covered in blood and pale. I hope my Devinshea is only half as bad.

I hate. I hate that I hate. I hate what Myrddin has done to me because I hate that man. If I were a witch, I would forsake myself to ensure his demise. I would hex and hex and hex him. I would pour my soul into each spell, giving away pieces so the world is safe from him.

I am the worse version of myself because that male exists and thrives.

I try to help the king stand, offering him my shoulder to balance against. He's pale and unsteady as he gets to his feet, but he forces himself to face Eoin.

"Do not harm her. Let her go, Eoin. We were friends once. She is the only person I have ever loved. Honor our friendship. Let her go," he says, his voice shaking.

I can tell him it won't work. I can certainly tell him that I am not the woman he loved, that he didn't love her enough. Instead I stand there and wait for the inevitable because there's nothing else to do. There's nowhere to run, and I can't get into a fight because they've already shown they don't mind lodging an arrow in a person. The problem is if they lodge one in me, they might hit my daughter, and I cannot risk that.

Eoin's head shakes, and he pulls out a sphere. It's a familiar one. This has to be a gift from Myrddin. Sarah played around with them as transportation spells. A *sphaera motus*.

"I don't trust you, and the wizard was specific about who I was supposed to bring." He stands close to us and drops the orb.

It hits the ground, and there's a whirring sound and the world goes fuzzy. I hold on to the king, and in a flash we're in a completely different place. The bubble around us dissipates and I'm suddenly cold, harsh winds blowing my hair back.

I look up and recognize the mountain. Not this one, but the same in our timeline. This was where we'd once looked for the Blood Stone all those years ago, where Danny had taken on a frost giant and at the end of our successful smash and grab I was sold into sexual slavery to a goddess named Nimue.

Good times. But I doubted this trip to the mountain would end the way that one did.

"You need to run if you get the chance," the king whispers. "He won't need me for long, and I don't believe he has any intention to honor his word. I was a fool."

"Yes, you were," a familiar voice says. "You were a complete idiot, and it was my pleasure to work with you."

I turn and Myrddin has a tent set up. He stands in the doorway, completely at ease as though it's not frigid here.

As though death doesn't hang over the mountain. Even I can feel the weight of it.

The king groans as the guards haul him toward the tent.

I think seriously about running, but there are two guards at my sides, each taking an elbow.

"Queen Zoey," the wizard chides, his dark eyes on me. "You want to leave so soon? I'm afraid I have to insist on you joining our group. I have so much to show and tell you. I recently left a meeting with your brats."

"You saw my children?" Fear is so much colder than the wind because there's a smirk on his face that tells me he knows something I don't know.

"Yes. Just last night. It's why I had to leave for a while. They've gotten awfully cozy with Lucifer Morningstar and that whore Lilith. I was rather surprised when she showed up." Myrddin stands in front of the entryway, blocking us and leaving me to feel the bite of the wind. "Naturally she fucked me over, but what else should I expect from the woman who spat Nimue from her womb."

Nim's mom? She never mentioned to me she had a mother. I kind of thought she sprang fully formed from the lake she guarded. I had a hundred questions, but only one mattered, and I couldn't ask it because he lies.

Are my children alive?

I force down bile because I'm about to be at his mercy and he will have none.

Myrddin studies me for a moment. If he feels the cold, he doesn't show it. He folds his arms over his chest. "That son of yours outmaneuvered me. Lucifer owed me a boon and I meant to collect Dean since they so thoughtfully brought him to the Hell plane. Unfortunately, Lee is fucking things up in all timelines, and I had to make do with tossing your little girl off a balcony and into the pits of Hell. Demons are probably polishing off her bones right now. Or they're having a good time with her. I don't really care as long as she's dead at the end of it. You take my child, I'll kill yours, Your Highness."

He lies. He lies. He fucking lies.

I force the words through my head over and over because if I don't believe them, I will break utterly. I cannot... Evangeline is not dead. She was there with Kelsey and her brother and Fenrir and Trent and Gray. They would not allow it. Fenrir would give his life for her.

Is he dead, too?

Is Kelsey in mourning?

It's too much. Far too much. I can't begin to process.

He lies and lies and lies.

"Nothing to say, my queen?"

He lies. Give him nothing. He's doing it to get a rise out of me, to put me off. My daughter is not dead. Not dead.

How far could the fall be? She's on her father's blood. She can take a lot of damage. Fenrir would follow her. He would defend her. She is alive.

"I think you broke her," Eoin says. "Pretty funny."

Myrddin turns the guard's way. "Watch what you say. I might hate the bitch but she's so far above you it's ridiculous. She's a damn nexus point. She literally makes fate. Her choices change the world. Which is why I have to get rid of her at some point. Unfortunately, it won't be today. Come in, Your Highness. See what your choices have cost you this time."

He steps back, and I suddenly don't want to know. It's an

instinct. Something terrible has happened. I don't purport to be psychic. Not even close. I'm also crap when it comes to magic. I am what Myrddin called me. A nexus point. It means I have no particular fate and affect the world around me with my choices. I know we all do, but for me it's on a world-ending fate level. I've had angels betting on whether or not I could change the fate of the world, and here we are again and I don't want to know. I don't want to see what he's brought back.

Is it evidence of my daughter's fate?

My stomach is in knots as they pull me in. I shrink back, not wanting to allow Myrddin to touch me, but he stops and his hand grips my chin, forcing me to look at him.

"Do not think Daniel is coming for you," he says with gravity. "I used a death magic spell earlier today in order to locate someone important. It is much like the one that nearly killed him all those years ago, though I wasn't close enough to really do the deed. He would need Devinshea and the god attached to Devinshea's magic in order to get any kind of strength back. I like to think he's lying on the ground somewhere, half dead and thinking about all of his choices. He'll know that's where he was when his precious blood died. You'll note that I made it impossible for Devinshea to ever do magic again. He'll be grateful when I put him down."

He turns my head and I take in what he wants me to witness. The king is in his shackles, his hands over his head, feet barely on the floor. But he's not alone. At first my eyes... They don't work because I can't be seeing what I'm seeing. Devinshea. My faery prince. He's bound to a pole, chains wrapped around his body, and he's covered in blood. So much blood. His shirt is off but I can't see a patch of clean skin.

And that's when I realize something is wrong with his arms.

They stop in bloody stumps. His hands. Those hands that caressed me, that stroked over my skin and gave me comfort... His hands are gone.

"Do not look, Zoey," the king says in an oddly tortured tone. Like he feels my husband's torment. "He would not wish you to see him this way."

It's his words that spark me to movement. Because Devinshea would not want me here in danger, but he will not care if I see him.

He did nothing wrong. The wrong was done to him and I promised. I fucking promised nothing would keep me from him. No sickness. No fucking wizard.

I shove at the guards and rush to my husband, tears making the world a watery mess.

"Devinshea?" Goddess, is he already dead? I don't know what I'll do if he's already gone. And Evan is gone and Fen is…

His eyes open, and I can see the weariness there. "My goddess. How I wish you were not here." But he manages a smile. "Have I told…how much I love you? How good it's been to be your husband?"

Tears stream from my eyes because this sounds like good-bye. "Don't you dare."

"My love, I don't have a choice. He brought you here to force Bris to leave me," he whispers. "He knows Bris would stay until the end and give him nothing without some threat."

In that moment, I don't care. For all I know Danny's dead and Neil's gone. For all I know I'm the last one left and I don't… I want to be with them. I want to go wherever they go. *Please don't leave me here alone.* "Tell Bris to stay. No matter what he does to me. Stay and we can go together. All of us."

It's what we planned. To live together. To go into the next turn hand in hand. To spend as little time apart as possible.

Dev's eyes are a dull green, and I realize how close he is to that next turn, to rounding the corner and fading into something new. "No, my love. You have to stay. On this Bris and I are in full accord. When the time comes, we will sacrifice for our goddess. And our daughter." His eyes fill with tears. "You have to stay alive for Harriet."

I shake my head. "He won't let me live."

"I will." Myrddin stands mere feet away, and it's all I can do to not attack him. I only don't because it won't do any good. "I made a deal with a Fae royal. Two, really, and Devinshea kept up his end of the first one. It was why he was sitting there waiting for me when I returned to this timeline this morning. After dealing with the situation on the Hell plane, I realized I'm hesitating because I want to meet my son. It's selfish and all too human of me. No more. I have what I need and I'm going to do what I promised I would. Free us from the celestial planes."

"What deal?" I demand, wondering exactly what Devinshea and Bris have offered in exchange for my life.

"If I don't harm you, Bris will leave the body when I command," Myrddin explains. "Once Devinshea is dead, you will be allowed to leave."

"No." Devilshea twists his body on the rack, turning to his counterpart. "You cannot trust him. When you are dead and she is dead, who will call the hunt on him?"

"It's recorded in Hell," Dev replies. "I am not a fool. I would not agree to the deal without a satan present. Myrddin is only half demon, but the rules apply. The satan will check on Zoey and if he cannot find her, he is empowered to call the hunt."

"Were your hands part of the fucking deal?" Devilshea asks, his voice tortured.

"He took them before he brought us here," my husband replies simply. "But I would have given them up. I would do anything, give anything to ensure my family survives. Zoey, no matter what he says Daniel is out there. Daniel and our children. You must get to them and be with them. They need you."

"They need you, too," I say, all of my emotion rising up like a damn wave. "Harriet needs to meet her father."

"If only Devinshea was Harriet's father," Myrddin mutters.

"You would give everything for her?" King Dev asks, staring at my husband. "You gave your magic. You are not full Fae. You must use your hands. Why would you give up your magic?"

"It comes from her." Dev speaks to his timeline twin, but his eyes are on me. "That's what I found out. My magic always came from her. From loving her. From building a family with her and my Daniel. There is no magic without her, so it was an easy choice to make. My goddess, you are the center of my world. Never forget it. Know that if there is any way, we will find it. Bris will try to find a way to come back. I will try to wait. Know that I am somewhere in all the planes and all the timelines loving you, missing you, looking for you."

I can't. I put my hands on his cheeks. "Please don't go." I wrap my arms around him. "Please."

"You have to save Shy," he whispers. "She's in the back. He's going to either kill her or figure out how to use her. I would have added her in to my deal, but I thought she was with Rhys. Save our daughter-in-law, my goddess. I will do the rest."

The rest being dying for Myrddin's plot.

Myrddin's hand grasps my arm, hauling me away from him. "I think that's enough. It's time for the king to make good on his deal. You see I had to find a way to keep the souls in the mountain. It's sacred in this timeline. The Quinns have preserved it as a holding space for their great treasures and a way to honor their dead. The only way for me to work spells on this land is for the king to open the doors. I already tried using your husband's blood but apparently the spells know he's not the real king."

"So sorry we couldn't help you," I say, turning to look around and trying to figure out where Shy is. Devinshea gave me a gift when he whispered in my ear. He gave me a mission.

Save Shy.

I see a figure on the floor. She's slumped over. I want to scream at Myrddin, but I pretend I don't notice.

The guards pull the king off the rack and start to lead him outside.

"Stay with them. Don't take your eyes off her," Myrddin orders as Eoin pushes his king out into the cold again. "I'll be back for you, Devinshea. Do not forget our bargain."

The minute the flap closes I run to Shy. Despite what Myrddin said, the guards don't seem too interested in me.

I drop to my knees and pray my daughter-in-law is alive.

Chapter Thirty-Two

Shy

I come awake to the sound of a familiar voice pleading with me.

It's hard. Myrddin hit me with some kind of spell. Something to make me sleep, and I can feel that I am bound, my arms and legs tied by his magic.

I am trussed up and ready for slaughter.

"Shy? Shy, please wake up."

The queen? I open my eyes and realize it wasn't merely horror that caused me to faint dead away. Nope it's magic. I didn't realize it at the time. I saw my father-in-law and nothing else mattered, but now I feel the remains of whatever spell he sent my way.

It makes things foggy, but I can clear it out.

"Are you okay, baby?" The queen puts a hand on my forehead like I'm a child and she's checking for fever.

It's been a long time since I had a mother to fuss over me. It feels nice.

That's when I realize the queen is not alone.

The Drowning Woman stands over her, her hands moving in and out of the water with what feels like desperation.

She can follow me anywhere. I can change timelines. I can move off plane. I can get hit with a transportation spell and she can find me.

I stare at her. Why? Why would she follow me through time? Across the universe? To torment me? Or is it for another reason? Something the terrified child in me cannot see. What if I am exactly what Matilda said I am? *Yr un sanctaidd.*

Because you do not know death, either. You can see yourself as a cold, pointless thing, or as necessary and warm and loving as birth itself. Like all things, you decide how to see the world around you, and by choosing your vision, you form reality.

I choose the form of my reality.

What if the thing itself doesn't change—always was, always will be the same—but how I see it makes the difference?

"Talk to me, Shy," the queen begs, and I see the tears in her eyes. "Can you move? I don't see rope but you're not moving."

Because I'm bound in magic. I find it hard to speak as well. I think he plans to take me somewhere, and this is how he will transport me. He put me to sleep, took my voice, paralyzed me and bound me in chains no one can see.

Poor guy. He underestimates me. There are some magics that might work, but I shrug this off.

"I'm fine," I promise as I stretch my arms and move for the first time in what feels like hours.

I catch on the spirit that's followed me and wonder how I never noticed her hands. I always notice the blood, the scars, but not the actual color of her skin. Where the hands are not torn, her skin is a deep brown. Like mine.

I allow the queen to help me sit up.

"The wizard said you would be asleep for hours," a tall Fae with a crossbow in his hands says. He has the look of one of the palace guards. "He said you would not be able to speak even when you woke."

"She's not dangerous," the queen begins. "She's a medium. Do you know what that is? She can talk to those who've past on. She's not a danger in any way."

I wouldn't go that far. Now that I'm awake I can feel my blood humming. I'm close. Close to all those restless souls. Close to… Devinshea.

Oh, my heart aches because I feel him.

He's dying. The only thing keeping him alive is the god inside him.

"Don't try anything. I'm not allowed to kill you, but he didn't say the same thing about her," the guard explains and moves back as though we're not a real threat at all.

Which at this point we aren't.

The mountain calls. It's hard to think when those souls are so damn near. They're screaming in my head.

And I can't seem to come to terms with the fact that Devinshea is going to die. How do I even comprehend the outcome? But I don't see a way out. I feel power, but I don't know what it means. I can break Myrddin's bonds, but I don't know how to stop him. If my power is death, to turn the wheel, then how do I do it? I'd asked that vine Rhys tied me up with. I don't think Myrddin will agree to begin again. He likes where he is. He has all the power. He won't allow me to send him through.

That's what I did. I sent the vine through. Not a light. The vine doesn't have a spirit the same way a conscious creature does, but it has energy, and I transformed that energy into something else. Something new. The energy wasn't gone, merely changed form. But I forced the change.

Can I force Myrddin to change? Do I have to get my hands on him? How do I fight him?

"We need to find a way to get you out of here," the queen whispers in my ear.

I can feel water on my skin. The Drowning Woman is so close. So close. Closer than ever before. She's right beside the queen, almost standing in her space.

"There is no way out," I reply. I know it deep in my bones. I was always going to be here. The trick Myrddin played was to get Devinshea here. That's obvious to me. But why, then, had Mallt-y-nos talked almost exclusively to me? Why had she insisted I come? "Arawn didn't call me. Myrddin did this to bring the royals here."

"To bring me here." Dev looks so pale.

I allow the queen to help me stand, and I am face to face with the Drowning Woman. I want to look away but I don't give in. I stare at her. "I don't know why you're here, but I promise if I survive this, I will find a way to help you."

The water seems to almost calm for a moment, and I can see a glimpse of a face.

It is almost familiar to me.

And then I hear the screeching of all those souls in the mountain. I put my hands to my ears as though I can cut them off.

I can't. It turns my stomach, but I have to fight through this. I force myself to walk to my father-in-law. "Yes, Myrddin did all of this to put you and the queen into the position where he can force Bris into whatever trap he's laid. Rhys and Lee and I discussed the fact that the crone he sent actually lives on this plane. She left Arawn's service long ago, and it seems she was likely bribed to do Myrddin's bidding."

Dev's green eyes show a spark of life. "But she convinced us to bring you here."

"What if instead of doing Myrddin's bidding, she's still working for the god she loved?" Zoey muses. "She knows more about Shy than we do. If she sent her here instead of merely doing the job she was paid to do, then she must think you can change the outcome."

"But I don't know how." I put a hand to my forehead. It's so loud.

And then it's not. Then what I hear is the soothing sound of a river rushing by. Of a pond in a rainstorm. Of waves gently crashing.

The Drowning Woman has one of those mangled hands on me. I feel the chill where she touches my skin, but I don't pull away.

I make my reality, and I have let fear rule for so long.

I reach out and touch her. Which is really simply touching my own skin, but it is a gesture. "Thank you. I can think now." I turn back to my in-laws, my head in a better place now. How had I ever thought that sound menacing? It's a sound from my childhood. I focus in on one. The sound of the creek behind our house. It would ease me to sleep on long nights. I would put my feet in the mud and know I was connected to the earth. Lift my hands to the sky and feel the way my soul stretched to the heavens. Earth and air were mine. Are mine.

"I think you might be here so I have one last chance to say good-bye," Dev admits quietly. "I don't want to give up, but I cannot allow Myrddin to harm my wife and our child. Shy, is the space Harry stayed in still open? Or have you found a way to close it?"

This cannot be why I am here, but I still reply. "It is open. I would never close my soul space. I wouldn't want to even if I knew how."

"I won't stay long, sweet girl. Only long enough to say good-bye." His head turns and he stares at his wife. "I will find out if that bastard killed our daughter. If he did, she will be waiting for me, and I will make things right between us. Wherever we go, we will go together."

"Or you could not go at all." It's easy to hear the panic in the queen's voice.

"Do not touch those chains or I'll have you in them, too." The guards are still watching us. We are not alone.

Zoey bites back a cry and steps away, her eyes on the stumps where Dev's hands used to be. "We can find a way out. You don't have to die. Shy is right. She's here to stop this."

I feel something shift. The cries briefly become louder, but then the spirit beside me seems to amp up her power. "I think the king did his job and opened the door."

I feel a rush of agreement. The Drowning Woman thinks so, too.

Why do I get the feeling she is proud of me? It's the oddest thing. It's almost like she's sending me a message.

I am so proud. You can do this. You were born for this moment.

It's almost like she has a voice. A familiar one.

I have an inkling, but I can't give in to it now. Time is running short.

"Then it's my time," Dev says, and it's easy to see he's trying to put on a brave face. "My darling goddess, I love you. Be brave. Be Zoey. Take care of all of them for me."

Tears pour from the queen's eyes. "I can't do this without you."

"You can," he promises. "You can and you will, and I will be waiting to be reunited with you and Daniel again."

The door to the tent opens, and he is there. Myrddin's presence soaks the space in dark, selfish magic. His eyes narrow when he sees me. "Guards, get the seer. I don't know how she managed to get out of my spell. It should have kept her asleep and incapacitated for days. I want her in chains, and then we'll add her soul to my pyre. When we slit her throat, her magic won't matter. Devinshea, it's time. I have the mountain open, and I have a door to the Hell plane open. The souls have one place to go."

I feel the panic of the Drowning Woman as two guards wrest me away. "Dev, when the time comes, choose me."

It's as much instruction as I can give him. I know the Fae version of Neil made the choice. He wasn't swayed by the call of the mountain. He chose.

Myrddin can't force the souls to do his bidding. But he can trick them. They will think they are walking into the light, but the light Myrddin offers will send them to Hell no matter their religious beliefs. I have to think it's a portal of some kind that will gather energy and allow Myrddin to work his will.

"He will choose his wife every time," Myrddin says as he stands there, energy flowing off him. His eyes are obsidian orbs, and black veins cover his body. This is the wizard in his purest form. In his magical power. "Choose her now, Devinshea, or I will kill her where she stands."

The guards haul me back, their rough hands gripping me, and I hear a crack of thunder and rain start to pelt the tent above us.

Myrddin's eyes narrow but he ignores it. He has an ornate knife in his hand and points it Zoey's way. "I'll carve the child out of her and force you to watch. I won't wait for the Wild Hunt to do her in."

The guards hold Zoey in place, too.

The only comfort I have is the Drowning Woman who stands near Myrddin now, and I feel her menace.

It is for him. It is not for me. What if there was never menace in this spirit for me? What if I created that because I was not ready to face her? Not ready to lose her again. What if I always knew when I truly saw her face, I would have to let her go?

"I'm going," Devinshea says. "Or rather Bris is. I love you. Zoey, say my name. One last time."

I'm sure she says it, but I don't hear because my mind is stuck on that request.

Say my name.

His name.

Call his name when you need him. He will always come for you.

When you need him, call his name. He always meant to find you again.

I wondered whose name, but I know it deep inside now.

I feel the moment Devinshea Quinn dies. I can see Bris's soul, see how anguished he is as the priest's body fails him. His head slumps over and his spirit walks my way, his hand to his heart.

"Goddess, you are beautiful, Shahidi. This…you glow like the warmest hearth, like the promise of comfort in winter." He stands in front of me even as his wife goes to her knees.

"Do you feel the pull?" I have to know if it's more pronounced here.

"Who are you talking to?" Myrddin asks. "He should be in the mountain by now."

"Tell him I'm gone. Tell him I couldn't resist. But there is no pull. Not for me. Oh, it hums and beckons, but I know where the light is. It is inside you," Dev says, the saddest look in his eyes. He's whole now. The most beautiful spirit I have seen. As though death cannot change the attraction of a Green Man. He glances up at the canvas roof. "My son is here. He's come for you, but you know what to do next. May I accompany you on this journey?"

"Shy, tell him I love him." The queen barely manages to talk through her tears.

I have to be cruel to be kind. I cannot let Myrddin know they are both still here, Devinshea and Bris. "He's gone, Your Grace. He's with the sluagh now." I nod briefly Dev's way to let him know he is welcome before turning to Myrddin. "Bris is merely waiting. He has to make the choice, right?"

"I cannot trick a god, but I can force him," Myrddin admits. "It's time, Bris. Do my will or I will kill your goddess."

Zoey screams, and I see Bris as he was in life. A giant of a man, muscular and broad. He wears a wreath of vines around his red hair. He has a straight jaw and lips meant for smiling and kissing. He reaches out to Zoey but cannot touch her.

I wish she could see him in all his glory.

"I'm sorry," Bris tells me with a sorrow that is palpable. "I made a deal to spare her, but I fear nothing will if the wizard gets his way. My energy will allow him to close the door, and I can only stay for so long before he will know I am not complying. Call his name, Shy. It's the only hope we have. I must fulfill my end of the bargain or the Wild Hunt will come for my family. I have to do this, but I believe you can offer us another way. If you break Myrddin's spell before the last soul enters, we might be saved. If you break it before the door is closed, I might be able to lead them out again. Do you understand?"

I nod because I know what I have to do now. I know how to find my power.

"Whoa," Dev says, staring at Bris with a smile of approval. "Dude, you are very attractive. And very Irish."

Bris bows. "Devinshea, it was my honor."

Dev's spirit bows as well. "And mine, brother. Thank you for everything. See you on the other side."

"We will abide in the Summerlands," Bris promises. "And make a home there for our family. When you get the chance, tell the queen her daughter lives. I can feel it now that I am in this form fully again. Her daughter lives, and so do they all. Evangeline is safe."

And then Bris is gone, and I hear a booming from the mountain as Bris joins the others, feel Myrddin's satisfaction.

"It begins," he says with a nasty smile.

He says *begins*, but what he's really talking about is the end. The end to hope. The end to real life. Definitely the end to death because how will anyone move on if they are cut off from the light?

I know why Hell is backing Myrddin Emrys. They will be the only choice for in between spirits. Hell will fill with souls. Damned. Not damned. It won't matter when they're the only game in town.

"Guards, kill the seer," Myrddin orders. "She better be a corpse when I return. I must do what I need to fully open the mountain and send all those souls to their new home."

He rushes out of the tent like he has a job to do.

"Dev, if you're coming, the time is now," I whisper.

He slips into my soul space.

And I am ready.

"Arawn," I say. "Come for me."

In a heartbeat, I am in another place. I am in Annwn.

Chapter Thirty-Three

Sasha

Sasha stood at the north end of the palace and looked up at the sky in the distance. The mountains were likely a day's hike away, but he feared Myrddin hadn't needed to jog.

"We didn't find anything in Aunt Zoey's rooms." Cassie had both Neil and Brendan in wolf form on either side of her. Sasha could see her claws were out, too, though the smart, brave girl had never managed a complete change. Not even on full moons. "Dad seems to think she's not in the palace at all. He found a trail leading out to one of the gardens. Her maid says she went to have a picnic with the king."

"I know the spot." Lee joined them, Rhys following.

Ostara sat near Daniel on a bench. Despite the energy she'd given him, it was clear the king was still in a bad way.

That must have been one hell of a spell. He didn't want to think about what Myrddin could do if he was standing in the same space as Daniel. If they survived this encounter, he was going to have to rethink his battle plans. Sometimes he thought Daniel Donovan was invincible, but he wasn't, and the wizard knew exactly how to hurt him.

"We should follow Neil and Brendan," Sasha ordered.

Rhys stepped forward. "No. My mother isn't at some picnic. He's already taken her. I noticed the guard isn't here, and Bibi told me the king took only a nominal party with him. They should be here. They are not on assignment. At least not one from the king. I believe they are working for Myrddin and they have my mother. He wouldn't have taken Shy if it wasn't time for him to do whatever he is going to do at that mountain."

"You don't want to check the site to see if your mother is still there?" Sasha posed the question, though he knew the answer.

"I don't have to." Rhys's eyes were on that mountain. "I know."

"I agree with the Green Man." Lee looked so much like his counterpart it was hard to remember this wasn't the young man he'd raised. He stood beside Rhys, looking every bit like his twin. "We should go to the mountain. I'll find us some horses."

Sasha shook his head. "It would still take half a day. Can we find a witch who knows transportation spells?"

It was the only way he could think that they might have a shot. If Myrddin was implementing his plan, he would do it quickly and without hesitation. Every second they weren't there brought them closer to losing Dev, the queen, and Shy.

He couldn't stand the thought of losing any of them.

"Or I can take us there." Meadow stood, smoothing out her skirts. "I can catch an eddy wind and have us there quickly."

"We don't have those kinds of winds this far south," Lee explained. "Or else I would have offered as well. The winds to the north are the only place to find an eddy."

Meadow looked slightly arrogant for the first time. It was a look that threatened to send Sasha's libido into overdrive. If they weren't about to go into battle. "We do not need some north wind. While I cannot both make and catch a wind at the same time, lucky for me, Walking Spring is here. Rhys, would you do the honors? Make it a fast one and large enough to carry us all."

Rhys stepped forward, his eyes glowing green. He turned slightly toward Daniel. "I don't suppose I can talk you into sitting this one out, Dad?"

Daniel growled and stood, forcing his shoulders back. His fangs were out now, and his eyes a deep sapphire. "They are mine."

"Well, at least I know where I get it from. All right, then." Rhys tilted his head back and closed his eyes, and the world seemed to shake with thunder and lightning.

Sasha looked to Meadow, who helped Daniel stand. "When we get there…"

Her chin turned up, eyes flashing, and he was damn near transported back to another life. Shortly after their wedding he thought he heard something moving in the night and told her to hide in the closet and she'd given him that look. Right before grabbing his backup pistol and following him.

I watch your back always, husband.

The rain was starting to fall, but that wasn't why the world was watery. Tears. Sweet and cleansing tears fell from his eyes as he remembered.

If she died in this battle, he would go with her. No matter what. He would not allow them to be separated again.

"When we get there, what?" She asked the question with no small amount of challenge.

He moved into her space, towering over her, but with the firm knowledge that his physical strength was no match for her. She was the strongest woman he ever met in all of his lives. She was the best part of him. He leaned over and kissed her forehead. "When we get there, watch my back, love."

Her eyes closed, and she leaned into him. "Always."

There was the sound of wind whooshing overhead, violent and threatening. Like he suspected a hurricane would sound, but he held his ground. The group moved in, surrounding Rhys and Meadow.

She reached out a hand, the other lifting toward that wind above them. She yelled over the cacophony of storm Rhys was creating. "Hold on."

In an instant, he was in the storm.

He forgot what it was like to want to empty the contents of his stomach on the ground and hold his head after a long night of drinking. That's what it felt like being tossed and turned inside the eddy wind. The ground below flashed by, and he caught glimpses of lightning and felt his body shake with the cracking of thunder.

And then he was falling. Right on his ass.

Daniel managed to catch Neil first, and Lee landed on his feet, turning so he could catch Brendan's wolf, who seemed to be trying desperately to find the ground, all four legs spinning.

Cassie dropped down in a perfect imitation of Black Widow, one knee on the ground, fist balancing her, head down. She grinned as she looked up. "That was so fucking cool."

Rhys managed to stay on his feet, brushing his clothes off like nothing happened.

Meadow was last, but she eased down out of the cloud like she could ride the very air around her. She sighed as she hit the ground, straightening her skirts. "You did not enjoy the journey, husband?"

Oh, he had not, but he loved the sound of her voice calling him that name. He hopped up, each movement easy and graceful. Even his eyesight seemed better since he fed from her the night before. His companion. His love. His wife. "Any journey with you is a wonderful one."

She grinned his way even as the rain began to fall again. "I promise next time will be easier. It's obvious the king has done this before."

Daniel nodded. "I have, and I can safely say you are a much better driver than my partner. Who is here." He closed his eyes and took a long breath. "I can smell him and my wife."

Rhys's irises filled his eyes. He was more god than man now and seemed larger than he was before. As though his magic broadened his physical form. Sasha noted that the grass around him had grown and the tall aspens seemed to bend, trying to get close to the Green Man. "My mate is here. She is frightened."

Neil and Brendan moved toward a path that seemed to lead out of the woods. Neil barked and his head came up, letting Sasha know he had the scent.

"Son, be careful." Daniel stood in front of Rhys. "Myrddin is dangerous. We need to rescue them before we take out our rage on him. Do you understand?"

Rhys nodded and began to follow his uncle.

"I'm letting Ossie take over for now. Know that we are so eager to continue whatever path this leads us to as long as we share it with you," Meadow said, looking up at Sasha. "Whatever happens. I think we were meant to find each other in this fashion. I think she was meant to complete us, to be with us forever."

He reached for her hand, bringing it to his lips and letting the feeling of peace wash over him. "We will be together. You and I and Ostara. Come what may."

It was in their wedding vows. They said the normal things. Sickness and health—though apparently they should have added in something about a crazy woman taking his memory and experimenting on him for years—but they added the words *come what may*.

She went on her toes and kissed him, and when she lowered herself down again, Ostara's eyes were staring at him. "You mean this? You can love me?"

He followed his instincts and pulled her close. This was what Zoey had always known. Bris was a part of Devinshea. Ostara was a part of his wife. They had not always been together, but they found each other in this life. This time it was right.

Even if it might not be for long.

He hugged her tight. "I already love you, *dushka*."

She shuddered as though a sense of deep relief passed through her. When she tilted her head up, there was alarm there. "I can feel something. We have to move. There is dark magic at work here."

What began as rain rapidly became snow given the high altitude they found themselves in. All around them was winter, with patches of green where Rhys and Ostara walked. Sasha followed them up the trail. Now he could smell the high priest and the queen. He could smell blood and fear and desperation.

"Is that who I think it is?" Daniel asked, standing beside Lee. If he felt the cold, he didn't show it. He stood tall, his claws out. Whatever the king was feeling from the spell Myrddin had sent out, he wasn't going to allow it to stop him.

Up ahead, Sasha could see a dark-haired man, his hands in shackles. He wore nothing that would tell Sasha he meant to come into the mountains this day. His tall body shivered in the wind.

"Is that Dev or the other one?" Cassie asked.

"It's the other one," Sasha replied.

"How can you tell?" Cassie held her machete like it was a lifeline.

"Because he still has his hands," Lee said with a long sigh. "That is my father, and he's about to open the mountain. Do you see the stone?"

There was a large white stone sitting at the base of the mountain which soared up into the clouds above them. The stone looked almost like an altar, and even from this distance Sasha could see there was some kind of writing on it. "Is it ceremonial?"

They began walking again, trying to stay out of sight of the wizard, who could use the distance between them to his advantage. He didn't need to be close to kill them all.

"It is basically a key," Lee explained as they started down the path. Meadow had deposited them on another mountain, the one closest to where the wizard stood. She'd found a space a thousand or so feet up, Sasha estimated. Now they had to carefully make their way to the valley. "The royal family keeps both treasures and their darker secrets in that mountain. It is considered sacred and cursed."

"Making it the perfect place to lure in several million sluagh from across the planes," Daniel continued. "He found a way to bring them in but not let them leave. It's a trap for souls, and now he's going to have the king open the door so he can send them through whatever spell he's planning."

"Something to drain their energy," Sasha surmised. "We need to stop him. We have no idea how it will affect other timelines."

"No, we do," Daniel argued. "If Myrddin is doing this, then he's figured out how to send it across space and time. He wouldn't bother if he only thought it affected one timeline, and not even the one he's invested in. We should have brought a bow."

Lee moved down the trail, stopping briefly to point toward the wizard. "Wouldn't work. Do you see the faint sheen around him?"

Ostara nodded. "Yes, he's in a protective bubble. He has a shield. Such a coward. I don't like the king, but I feel sorry for him in this moment. We should hurry."

"Where is Shy?" Rhys asked. "He has to be holding Shy and Mom and Papa somewhere close."

Neil raised his snout as though answering the question. He pointed a paw to his left, signaling he meant to go that way.

They were almost to the ground when Sasha saw two guards were moving the King of the Seelie Fae into position, near the sacred rock. One of them had a long blade.

Ostara raised a hand, and Sasha felt the earth beneath his feet tremble slightly.

Daniel moved in beside her. "I'm going to ask you for patience. I know you want to save whoever you can, but if Myrddin knows we're here he might kill his hostages. We need to get to wherever he's holding our people."

Ostara nodded. "All right. I will wait." She gasped as the king was stabbed through the gut and placed on the altar. His blood soaked the stone, and it felt like the heavens above them quaked.

"We have to move." Sasha nodded the wolves' way. "Get us there and fast. Find the queen."

He glanced behind him and noted that Myrddin wasn't walking. He smashed a sphere and was gone in a puff of dark smoke, leaving the guards behind.

The king lay on the altar, but Sasha could see him still breathing. His blood had opened the door, and now he was a useless husk.

He had to make sure Devinshea didn't suffer a similar fate.

"I can't fly here," Daniel said, running to keep up with the wolves. "The winds are even worse than the ones in our timeline."

And he was still weak.

"I see a tent up ahead," Lee shouted. The winds were picking up, and now that they were lower, it was raining again. It started to come down in hard pelts, a sure sign Rhys was panicking.

But in this case, if a storm held up the wizard, Sasha would live with it.

A hard wind whipped past him and then a softer one that warmed him. Ostara caught up, running beside him. Warmth spread over his skin as her gentle winds surrounded him.

There was a cracking sound as they made it to the tent, Neil leading the charge. A guard stepped out but Neil ran past him, leaving the man to his son, who immediately went for his throat. The guard went down in a gurgle of blood while Cassie took out the one beside him, gutting him with an ease he wasn't sure he should be comfortable with. And yet Sasha felt a paternal pride in the young woman as she handled the guard and moved to her brother's side, talking to him and seeming to ease his natural blood lust.

"Come on, buddy," she was saying. "Time for snacks later. Save our auntie now."

"Where is she?" Rhys asked the question as the winds picked up.

Sasha made it to the tent with Ostara and saw Daniel already had

Zoey in his arms.

Neil growled at the wizard but every time he got close, some invisible barrier pushed him back.

The queen was sobbing in her husband's arms, and that was the moment Sasha saw the body on the floor.

Devinshea's body. Unlike his timeline twin, he was not breathing.

From the queen's reaction, there was no life left in the priest.

"You are too late, Daniel." Myrddin practically glowed. "You cannot take me down. You know it. Everyone knows it. That version of Lee is useless here. Shall I kill him? Or let him witness the new world rising?"

Myrddin snapped his fingers, and suddenly they were all back at the altar.

"I can't reach him," Ostara said, desperation in her eyes. "I cannot pierce the armor he wears. I don't understand it. It feels...wrong."

Likely because whatever spell he wore was from the Hell plane, and Ostara's magic would be useless there. Myrddin had brought a piece of Hell to protect him.

"Rhys." Zoey was on her feet, shoving aside her grief to get to her son. "Shy disappeared, but I don't think Myrddin did it. I think she did. I didn't hear what she said. I was..."

Rhys's eyes were the deepest green as he turned to Myrddin. "Where is my mate?"

"What do you mean she's gone?" Myrddin suddenly didn't look so sure of himself. "Guards, find the seer."

"Where would she go?" Ostara asked.

"To find help," the queen insisted.

"There is no help to be found," Myrddin countered. "I made a deal for safe passage for you and your family, but I can defend myself, and I never said I wouldn't pull more energy off the vampires. I don't think this one was outside the wards."

He reached into his pocket and brought out an obsidian sphere.

Sasha immediately felt the effects. His heart rate slowed, and he could feel his strength waning.

Daniel hit his knees, Zoey falling with him.

"You cannot touch me, Green Man," Myrddin said from behind

his protection. "I am filled with demonic energy. I am whole with it. I renounce my angelic side. I am a true demon lord, and I will use your power to aid me. The king has given his blood to open the mountain. Now witness as I close the door on our oppressors."

The mountain screamed and shook as a good chunk was blasted through and the door to Hell opened.

Sasha felt his vision begin to go and prayed he could survive the wizard's assault.

Chapter Thirty-Four

Shy

I turn and despite the fact that I know I'm on a timer, I can't help but wonder at the beauty I see around me.

Annwn. They call it the Welsh version of Hell.

The Welsh did not get the same memo the Christians did.

Life abounds here. Green forest and waterfalls. Mighty trees and soft ground at my feet. It's stunningly beautiful. I find myself on the banks of a serene lake, the waterfall in the distance. All around me there's some kind of festival going on. I smell pies baking and meat frying. Families sit on big blankets and enjoy the day.

Well, that's not what I expected.

Devinshea. I feel him in my soul. I feel his sorrow, but he is calm. He refuses to give in to confusion and rage like so many others. What I really feel is his will to do the right thing.

He would have been the most magnificent father-in-law.

"Me, either." I say the words out loud because we're not in synch the way I was with Harry. Harry and I could talk in my head, but it took a while for me to figure out how to do it. Devinshea is different. His mind works in a way Harry's did not. Or I suppose I should call it his soul. "Matilda told us, though."

Yes, I would like to have a word with the crone.

A big white rocket runs my way, and I'm suddenly assaulted by a happy hellhound. Fluffy.

"How did you get here?" I pet the big beast, and we're joined by the other two. Caddoc and Emyr bounce around me.

"These little ones belong to us. I allowed Mallt-y-nos to take them for a while. I did not understand why she felt she needed a break at the time. There are things not even a god knows. I allowed Mallt-y-nos her sabbatical, and she brought you here. Now it's time to call them home," a deep voice says. "It's time to call all my people home. I'm afraid I've been hiding."

Oh, I have a few things to say to... Dev begins. And then he's suddenly standing beside me. "...Arawn. Shy, I need you to translate for me. You are a massive ass."

The King of the Dead manages a smile while crossing his arms over his chest. "Dev, it's good to see you. I am ready to hear whatever you have to say. Also, you don't have to hide inside *yr un sanctaidd* when you're in Annwn. You are welcome here. I know we've had our issues, and you can't know how I regret the last few decades I spent in the Unseelie *sithein*. I allowed myself to become something less. Can you tell me how she is?"

I do not have time for this. "Your Majesty..."

He shakes his head. "You do not call me that. You are... *yr un sanctaidd*. I bow to you."

I'm not sure what he means, but somewhere out there my husband needs me. "I need to know how to defeat Myrddin, and I need to know now."

"You're worried time is moving," Arawn says, nodding as though satisfied he can fix the problem. "I assure you we can spend days here in Annwn and I will have you back to your husband within moments of when you left. You will miss nothing. But you should also understand that you cannot defeat Myrddin alone. You don't have what you need yet."

My heart threatens to stop in my chest. "I can't save Rhys and the rest of them?"

"Arawn, there has to be a way." Dev stands next to me, lending me his strength.

"Yes, there is a way, and the dark prophet laid it out." He chuckles, and it's an affectionate sound. "Although he didn't reveal the whole plan, did he? He knew exactly who you were, Shahidi. He could have told me."

"And you would have...?" Dev asked.

Arawn sighs. "I probably would have screwed everything up since I would have wanted to see her. I'm certain the only reason Myrddin is surprised by her existence is the fact that he didn't know what she was until now."

I have to hope this male is telling me the truth and I'm not missing my chance to save my family. For some reason, I believe him. For some reason, he feels familiar. "Yeah, I'm still a bit confused. So I'm this sacred one and I'm somehow connected to you. I don't know that you've noticed, sir, but I don't have a lot of Welsh in my background."

The softest look comes over the death god's face. "It's in your soul, Shy. I have never understood humanity's need to classify and separate by traits that are meaningless in the end. The essence you were first formed with was made of Welsh land and magic and pieces of my soul. The way you appear now is mere coincidence. The power was granted to me by whatever being controls the universe."

"You're a god," I point out.

"Little *g*," Arawn corrects. "Not big, though you should know those who claim the one god only for themselves do not know the heart of the universe. Think of the gods as pieces of the creator, emissaries, so to speak, because humans are tied to their bodies and common physical features as something to create community around."

"I think what you're saying is we are often intolerant to those who look different than us so the creator has to come to humanity in forms we can understand." Dev sounds very academic all of the sudden.

"So while I rule this way station some call an underworld, I don't control the universe, and I am just as ignorant as humans about some things. The dark prophet is playing a dangerous but necessary game because all the gods fear Myrddin. Long ago Heaven and Hell worked out a deal to keep balance on the Earth plane and Myrddin was created. Through the millennia he has gained power, and now he has done what we all feared he would do."

"Chosen a side," Dev says grimly.

Arawn nods. "Grayson Sloane is obviously playing a game of

chess, putting all the pieces in place. It is not time to kill the wizard. He is too powerful for even you. For you alone, but you will not be for long. Even today Myrddin set another on her path, and long ago he did the same for the third. The men are necessary as both power and obfuscation, if Grayson is doing what I think he is. This will always be a war won by women, *un sanctaidd*."

"Why do you call me that and why am I here if I cannot save them today? I don't…I don't know what I'll do without him." It is so odd since I started this whole thing certain I would walk away from him, and now I can't imagine it. Can't imagine my life, my heart, going on without him.

Panic threatens to overwhelm me.

"Calm," Arawn says in a gentle but firm tone. "Find your calm. All will be well if you will it. You cannot kill him but you can defeat him, and you won't do it with violence. You will do it the way you were created to do it. You will offer those he would harm choice and light and a chance to start again. Like you offered Devinshea, though it is not yet his time."

"How?" I ask because I still don't understand why I'm sacred.

"What do you mean by it's not my time?" Dev asks.

The King of the Dead gives him a mysterious smile. "My cauldron gives opportunities. She allows for change, for rebirth, and she can allow those who have made mistakes to make retribution if they choose. I see the way every creature could die. See the most likely way each will die. I do not see this death for you, Devinshea. I see a long life with your family, and oddly a gentle fading, your children by your side, when they are gone."

"I won't outlive them," Dev says. "We all know that despite taking Daniel's blood I am mortal and will die."

"And yet that is not what I see for you, High Priest," Arawn says gently. "There is a way, but I cannot influence it. It is up to him. If he truly sees what Shahidi can do, what she is made of, it could sway him."

"Who?" Dev asks.

"Have faith and all will be well," Arawn promises before turning to me. "You wish to know what you are? Like I said I was granted permission to create you, but you stand before me magnificent on your own. Shy, I created you and I was forced to destroy you when I knew I could no longer keep my corporeal form. It was that or hide you in Annwn forever, and you were meant to be in the world. You were a gift for the living creatures of all the planes."

The truth hits me. I suppose somewhere I have always known. I knew it when I felt the deep connection to earth and sky. When I first felt a creature pass and wished it well on its journey. I thought those moments the fanciful ideas of a creative child, but I was closer to the truth then. When I was a child, my mind wasn't muddled with the problems of living. I simply was and knew the dying rabbit or butterfly could use my kindness.

And so I turned the wheel and released them.

My mind flies back. Through the ages, because I was not human until I took this form.

I bubble and boil. I feed the armies of the Earth plane. I offer rebirth to those who choose me, passage to those ready to be something else.

I am life and death and eternity in the form of a cauldron. While I appear to be cast of iron, the truth is something more. I am energy. I am rest. I am the end and beginning of the experience of life.

And then I am small. I am dismantled because I am dangerous. I am flung to a new land where Arawn believes I will be safely hidden for all of time.

I want more.

I want to know why they wish for the wheel to turn. Why they make the choices they make.

I want to know what I am truly made of, to understand the world in a way I cannot in this form.

So I turn my wheel. I become a mote of dust, a blade of grass on the savannah, a drop of needed rain. I become the smallest of creatures, bacteria replicating, and then an ant with mighty strength. A bird on the wind and mouse skittering around. A beloved cat and fierce lion, and then I find my way into my mother's womb and after centuries and centuries, I am Shahidi.

And I know what I was born to do. It's the same thing I am made of.

Love.

Tears kiss my cheeks, sweet knowledge and peace flowing through my veins.

I see this place with different eyes. It is even more beautiful than before because I realize Arawn created it as a replacement for me. Annwn is an underworld in name only. It is what he called it. A way station. These beautiful souls are resting and readying for their next journey. They are making decisions about where to go next, what they need to work on. How they can help more, love better.

This is what Myrddin seeks to stop. Our choices. He wants to send everyone to the Hell plane, to one existence for his own selfish purposes.

I can stop him.

"I have always asked the spirits I talk to if they see a light." Emotion wells inside me. "Did I keep them from it?"

Arawn takes my hands in his, and warmth fills me because death does not have to be cold. It can be a warm blanket at the end of a long day, the sunshine on my face just before twilight. It can be hope for more, for another chance. "Never, my child. You never once kept anyone from the light. They simply found another one. You aren't responsible for all the dead of the world. But you are the hope for the lost ones."

"Because you are the light, Shahidi." Dev gives me a gentle smile. "When I died, I heard the call of Myrddin's spell, but it was nothing compared to your light. It is…the promise of peace. You are nothing to fear and everything to be grateful for. Like the lives we live. The time we have. You make us appreciate what we were given and anticipate what is to come."

I sent them searching for the light.

I am the light.

"You are ready." Arawn's jaw tightens as he holds my hands and turns to Devinshea. "Is this what it feels like to have a child? I created her but this…this is her own growth. I am proud of her in a way I did not anticipate."

"Yes, that is what it means," Dev replies. "Being a father means you have to love no matter what happens. It means you have to accept your circumstances and forget your regrets because your children mean more."

"I was always afraid of grief. Afraid I would one day mourn them," Arawn admits. "It's why I denied Nimue."

This is something I have learned. I wonder if I would have had

Arawn not been forced to change me. If I was never out in the world, would I have learned this important lesson? "Grief is temporary. Mourning is different. It's a gift in a way because it reminds us how deeply we loved and were loved. We have to find a way through grief, but mourning is something we can hold close because missing those we lost can be sweet, too. Mallt-y-nos told me I need to view death differently. Perhaps it's time you viewed life through a different lens, Arawn."

He squeezes my hand and nods. "Yes, it is. Tell Daniel I am going to the Earth plane. I will wait for Nimue to forgive me. I know a couple of great assisted living homes in Iceland. Tuesday night bingo is off the hook, as the young people say."

"They do not say that anymore," I reply with a genuine smile. My fear is gone. There is nothing left but the deep belief that I will win.

He responds with a smile that lights his usually grim features. "I was never good with slang. But I will be there. And if the King of All Vampire needs me, I will be there, too. I think it's time I got the old gang together. Hades is pretty fun, though he has some beef with Hel. And Kali is a genuine treat. I mean as long as you don't piss her off. Yeah, we could cause Myrddin Emrys some trouble."

"I will let him know," Dev responds.

Arawn leans over and lays a gentle kiss on my forehead. "Fly free, my cauldron. You deserve all the love in the world. See things the way they are now, free of fear, your ancient eyes lit with new fire."

I feel Dev slip back into my soul and then we're in the midst of battle.

Chapter Thirty-Five

Shy

The cold bites into me and I feel the door to the Hell plane is open. It is a gaping maw in the center of the valley, red flames spewing forth, and the stink of brimstone fills the air.

He's already opened it, Shy. Devinshea's voice is steady in my head. *You can do this. You can save the rest.*

I can save them all.

It's not too late. I see the souls pulled into the Hellmouth, watch as they try so hard to avoid it but cannot. They have no other option.

I will give them one.

"Shy." Rhys rushes to my side. "You have to get out of here."

I lean over and brush my lips across my husband's. "This is my time, Rhys. You have to let me do what I was born to. Give me some of your strength, love. Ostara told us. My autumn. Your spring. We are what turns the wheel. Summer is work and winter is rest, but real change comes from us. I intend to offer them change."

He is the most beautiful thing, this man I found at the end of my long journey. He is a gift to me and I to him. How had I ever thought I wasn't enough for him? I am what he needs. He is youth and fire, and I am wisdom and comfort. We belong together.

He steps back as Myrddin turns my way. I can see the protective magic around him now where I could not before, but then I can also see the glow coming off my skin.

I realize that it's more than protective magic. The wizard is lying, but then that's what he does.

My mother-in-law rushes out of Daniel's arms and stands in front of me and Rhys, staring down Myrddin though she doesn't have an ounce of battle magic. She puts her arms out and gestures as though I should hide behind her.

"You will not hurt my son or my daughter."

That's who Zoey Donovan-Quinn is.

And suddenly the Drowning Woman is beside her. Both women—one alive and one who even in death would not let me be alone—stand in front of us. Protecting us.

"I don't have to hurt her," Myrddin announces. "She can do nothing. I thought she was more than she is, but it's apparent now she is useless. Those souls I collected are all going to Hell, and I have the power. The spell collects the energy that is created when a soul passes to Hell. I will have all the power I need."

"Or I can show them another way. Mama, could you call to them for me? You've never once felt the pull. You can show the ones who are already inside the way back," I say to the Drowning Woman.

She didn't drown, but it's odd how spirits present themselves. I don't know why she became this water spirit beyond the fact that her name is Visola. My grandmother was looking for an African name and found Visola. She said it was a gift she could give her daughter from her ancestors.

I blink back tears. It means longings are waterfalls.

My mother came to me the only way she knew how.

"Who's here, Seer? Who did you bring with you?" Myrddin looks around like he can find the threat.

My mother emerges from the water for the first time.

"The Drowning Woman is your mother?" Rhys asks.

I nod.

She is beautiful, too, Shy. She can do the job, Dev says deep inside me. *She can lead them back.*

I know it in my soul.

Visola Davis, my mother, reaches her hand to me, and it is not frightening. It is not desiccated. It is the gentle hand of the woman who loved me so much she found a way to stay close even after death.

She gives me a smile from behind the water which now I can see truly is longing. Longing for me. Longing to make sure I am safe.

"Find the Irish god," I whisper so the wizard cannot hear. "He will help you. Tell him he honored his promise by going in. There was nothing in his pledge that said he couldn't come back out."

She then turns and I watch as she flies to the Hellmouth and disappears inside.

"I told you there is nothing you can do."

There's something wrong with the wizard. I tilt my head and open my senses. I confirm the lie I detected earlier. "Myrddin is not really here. He might have been at one point, but he's not now. The protective circle around him is hiding the fact that he's sending a shadow of himself. I suspect he needs to gather the energy somewhere else. Likely from his base on the Hell plane. Zoey, he can't harm any of us, and if those souls he sent through leave Hell while the door is open, it will reverse the energy and he will be left with nothing useful. Rhys, Neil, if you wouldn't mind taking care of the guards, it might take my mother a moment to pull her Pied Piper routine."

My husband gets a feral grin on his face. "With pleasure, my goddess."

Neil growls and takes the one closest to Sasha and Ostara. He plants his teeth in the man's neck and the blood flows. Rhys is much more efficient, though not much neater. The trees around us lean over and the guards scream as they are impaled and hauled high into the air, gravity pulling their bodies down and down, impaling them on the branches.

"Hey, you didn't leave anyone for me," Lee complains.

Cassie has a grin on her face as she stands over the guard she did in. She nods to her brother. "I think this one's safe to snack on."

"He's not really here?" Daniel asks as he stares at the altar where the King of the Seelie Fae has managed to sit up. There's a deep longing in his eyes.

That makes me ache, Dev says. *He knows it's not me, but he can't…*

"All will be well, father-in-law," I promise him. "Let me deal with this first."

"I suspect he has not been here since he transported us from the tent," Ostara explains, and if she's bothered by the amount of blood spilled around her, she does not show it. She simply gets into Sasha space after he drops the corpse of the guard he took out and huddles close to him.

Sasha found his wife and she's a freaking goddess.

A weird joy suffuses me, and I know it's going to be all right.

"I have to go back and see if there's anything I can do," Daniel begins. "He's tough. He might be alive."

Zoey puts a hand on his arm. "He's gone, Danny. I don't want to believe it either, but you can't bring him back. He's... We have to concentrate on getting our kids out of here now. If Myrddin closes the door there will be all kinds of trouble. Maybe we should go to the mountain and try to figure out how he's doing it."

She cannot see what I can and can't feel the shift in magic the way her son and Ostara do. My poor mother-in-law is trying so hard to save us.

"Mother, there is no need for worry. My goddess is going to handle it," Rhys says with great confidence. It fills my soul.

"It doesn't matter if I'm there or somewhere else," Myrddin announces. "You will still bear witness... What?"

The wizard turns, and I swear I can see a shadow like someone is trying to bring him news. His face goes tight, and I see his mouth moving but he's being quiet about it. Not so quiet I don't hear him curse.

He calls himself a wizard. Well, he's a little like the Wizard of Oz in this moment. Hidden behind a curtain, all his magic falling to something real. My magic.

His is selfish and temporary. My magic moves the world.

Rhys ignores Myrddin entirely. "Would you like sunshine or a lighter rain, my goddess?"

Ostara joins us. "Sunshine would be nice."

"There is no winter allowed here today. Today, for an afternoon, I declare it to be spring." Not that winter was too rough in the *sithein*, but here in the mountains it definitely feels like it, and I want joy and warmth for what is about to happen.

And it will happen. I already feel them. And I see the first spirit out of the Hellmouth. My mother bursts free of the spell and flies up.

The sun comes out, gentle breezes bathing the mountain valley, and I can feel the grass grow beneath my feet.

Something happened in those moments she spent inside the Hellmouth. Gone is all vestige of her previous state. She is who she was in life. Petite and vibrant, with curls for days when she doesn't keep her hair in braids, and a smile that warms the darkest night.

Bris is behind her, flying up to float beside her as they guide souls out.

"Guide them to me. To my light," I say, the words sounding right on my tongue. Like I knew them before, though the language was different. "I am Death. I am a door to whatever happens next. Come into me and begin again."

"Shy," my mother-in-law gasps. "You're…"

Glowing. I glow with invitation, and they take it. I feel the first of the sluagh fly through me.

Feel his cool presence. In life he was a farmer. A half-troll who was killed because the king feared his size and ordered his family slaughtered. He holds on to his two sons, also killed and then trapped by the wizard. He holds them close so they won't lose each other. So they can be together wherever fate leads them.

I feel his love and gratitude as he flies into eternity. Into whatever way station waits for him and those he loves.

I hear shouting but I pay no mind to it. I don't need to. My husband and our family and friends will take care of me. He won't allow anything to happen when I'm in this vulnerable time. Or am I? I don't feel vulnerable. I feel my gift.

Each soul who passes through has a story to tell, a life to share, and in those seconds it takes to cross over, I take them in. I open myself and let them fill me.

I feel when all who were trapped have passed, and yet they do not stop. Some of these souls were stuck in Hell for centuries, but when they saw my mother and Bris, they took the chance that their long suffering could be over. They realized Hell is a choice they made, and they can make a new one.

When the last moves through, my mother stands before me.

Myrddin is screaming about some contract, but Daniel is arguing with him. Something about the deal being fulfilled.

I'm sure I'm right. The deal Dev made was completed with his death and Bris willingly entering Hell. No one said I couldn't bring them back.

But I ignore the argument because I see her again.

She holds out a hand. "Hello, baby."

Tears stream down my face as I hold her hands in mine. "Hello, Mama."

"Your mother?" Rhys straightens his shirt. "Your mother is here?"

"Her mom? She was in the mountain?" Zoey asks, her face still red from crying. "I thought Myrddin killed her."

"He did. She's been following me ever since," I say, never taking my eyes off my mom. "I was afraid of her. She was the first spirit I ever saw. Connecting with her brought me into my power."

"I'm sorry I scared you, baby. I thought I was taking on a peaceful form. Things get confused on this side, and then I couldn't change. I was as stuck in my fear for you as you were in your fear of me," my mom explains, her voice sounding ethereal. She's wearing white, and it contrasts with the beauty of her skin. "But I'm not afraid anymore. I can move on now because you have a family again. I suppose I needed to know you had a mother who would take care of you."

I look to Zoey. "She says she can go now because I have a mother again."

Zoey bites back a cry, and Rhys puts an arm around his mom's shoulders. "I am, Shy. I will be your mom for as long as I live. I won't... I will survive for my children's sake. I will honor my husband by taking care of us all."

I feel Dev's deep sorrow.

And I see the King of the Seelie staring at Zoey.

Oh, is that what Arawn meant?

Shy, Dev begins. *I should talk to them and then I will go.*

"Trust me," I whisper. "There is still a chance."

"I love you so much, my baby girl," my mother says. "But I would love to see your father and sister again. To be with my family. You have found your soul's mate, and I am so happy for you. He's stubborn, but I can feel his love for you. Be happy, my love. I know now what a gift you were to us all. Thank you for picking me to be your mom."

Tears stream as I offer my mom the door. "Thank you for teaching me how to love."

"You always knew," she says and then she hugs me, arms

reaching around, and she is gone. "It's who you are."

A deep sense of peace grounds me in the moment, and I reach for my husband, hopeful I have one last job to do.

* * * *

Zoey

"He didn't get what he needed." Daniel stands beside me, reaching for my hand. There's a smile on his face. "Shy did it. Not only did he not get what he needed, there were a bunch of souls in Hell who followed her mom and left with the sluagh. From what I can tell Lucifer showed up at the end of his transmission, and he was pissed."

Danny seems elated with the outcome, but then he sees the king and it's like all the air is let out of him.

Because he remembers. He remembers Dev is dead and for once he can't open a vein and bring him back. He can't make a deal and have our family whole again. He is powerless in this moment, and my heart breaks for him.

For all of us.

How do I tell my children I lost their papa? They just got him back and now he's gone.

How can I be standing in this beautiful place, evidence of spring and life all around me, when his corpse is down in the valley? The world should stop like mine has.

And yet I have to move on. Isn't that what I've learned? I can stop, mire myself in misery, but we're still in this place and my children—our children—are still not safe.

"We have to get to the mountain. We go back to the palace, get the blue dolerite, and try our chances," I say, tears blurring the world, but I am firm in my conviction that we will survive this. We will take my husband home. "We have to…"

I can't make the words come out of my mouth.

"We have to get Dev's body." Daniel can, though they come out the slightest bit shaky. He pulls me close, wrapping his arms around me. "I can't…"

"Zandra." The king has managed to stand, the stone behind him coated in his blood. He pulled the cold iron knife out of his gut at some point and the guards forgot to finish him off.

I hate that he looks like my husband. I hate that he's alive and Dev is not.

Goddess, I need to purge this hate from my soul. It's going to kill me.

"Her name is Zoey." My daughter-in-law steps in and I watch Rhys tense, but he restrains his need to cage her. He's getting better. The bond they formed is doing exactly what Devinshea thought it would. "Your Highness, she is not the woman you loved, but she is connected to her."

Devilshea puts a hand to his gut as though he needs the pressure to stay upright. "She is every bit as lovely and fierce and good as the Zandra I loved. And Deinny…your Daniel is more fierce than he was, but every bit the friend. I was not as brave as your Devinshea. I was not as good."

Shy moves closer, and though she no longer has that vibrant glow she had while working her magic, there is still almost a halo around her. "You can be. Devinshea understands because he felt all the impulses you did. He is inside my soul space, so I will let him speak now."

Though her voice doesn't change, I can hear my husband as she allows him to take control.

Dev is here.

"He's where Harry was," Daniel says, every word tight and emotional.

Neil takes up space on my other side, his wolf rubbing against my leg. It's comfort. He's giving comfort and letting me know he's here.

I hold Daniel's hand and stroke Neil with my other as my husband speaks from beyond death.

"The difference between the two of us is one little trick of DNA," Dev says from Shy's mouth. "You were born fully Fae and I was not. It led me to leave the *sithein* while you stayed. I wasn't welcome. You were. So I had nothing to lose when I left and found my real life. Though you should know, I thought about not leaving the *sithein*. I thought about simply doing what my mother asked. By the time Declan attempted to break my relationship with Zoey and Daniel, I had been on the Earth plane too long and was unmovable. You did not get the same experience. You are who I could have been had things slightly changed. You learned to be a royal, and there are hardships there, too. You are taught loyalty to the crown above your own heart. You were scared and decided you could have both, but our world does not work that way. Now you have a choice to make. You do not have to stay selfish. You watched a thousand souls choose to begin again. You can, too. You can start by helping my family get home."

"Devinshea?" Daniel asks.

Shy turns my way, and somehow her smile holds my husband. It's there in the lopsided grin and the way her eyes soften. "I'm here. You should know Myrddin either lied about Evangeline or she survived on her own. She is alive."

A shudder of pure relief flows through me.

Dev is not finished. "Our daughter-in-law is a remarkable woman. Make her tell you the tale. And you should warn Nim that Arawn is waiting for her. He's going to join us and maybe bring along a couple of friends. Us." She sighs. "You and Daniel. He's going to join you and Daniel."

"Dev, is there any way," Daniel begins.

Her head shakes. "No. I'm not going to take up space in my daughter's soul. I won't disrupt our kids' lives like that."

"We can find a balance, Papa." Rhys's eyes shine with tears. "Maybe stay and we can consult with the witches. Maybe we can find a way for you to exist on our plane."

"You need to understand that your wife is arguing with me," Dev says through Shy. "She is offering to host me for as long as possible, but I figured something out during these days. When Myrddin took my hands my first thought was I would be useless without them. I mourned my magic, and there was a part of me that wanted the death I knew was coming because I didn't want to live without my magic. But son, it was always you. My magic was always you and Lee and your sister and your mama and Dad. If there was a way I would take it, but I can't. I love you. I will always love you, and I need you to take that message back to your siblings and Albert and Zack and all of those who made my life so special."

I'm crying again. I will be for a long while, so I don't bother to wipe my eyes. "I love you forever, Devinshea. I will take care of them."

"I will take care of them," Danny promises and wraps me so hard in his arms I can't breathe. I feel the shudder of emotion go through him and his tears on my skin. I hold on to him.

"Vampire, can you fix this body?" The king's soft question breaks through my misery.

Daniel doesn't let me go, but I feel the growl go through his body. "Leave us be. The more I remember you are here, the less chance you have of surviving the experience."

"He was different, too," the king says ignoring the warning. "My Deinny wasn't fierce. He was gentle and kind, and I loved him, too. When Zandra died, I wanted to be with him. I wanted to drown myself in his comfort, but I was taught that was wrong. In my head he tempted me. I didn't kill him in a rage. I lied about that. I had him executed because I was awash in guilt and grief, and I couldn't handle how I felt about him."

"Precisely why he should be here and you should not," Daniel shoots back.

"Danny," Dev admonishes. And then I feel a change and Shy is back in charge. She looks to the king. "He can, Your Highness. Daniel can fix the damage to your body."

"Could he fix it even if it was worse?" the king asks, and his eyes take a far-off look. "What if the damage was enough to release my soul? Could he fix it even then?"

"I am not going to fix you. You just admitted to killing my counterpart here, and you had a hand in Zandra's death, too," Daniel announces.

But he isn't thinking. "He might be able to help us get home."

The king shakes his head and moves closer to us. He has Dev's bravado. "I know nothing of timeline jumping. That was all the wizard. I can walk the planes, but I cannot fix the time you would be in. And Dein...Daniel is right. I did have a hand in my love's death. Because I did not honor the love I had for her. Or him." He turns to Shy. "Is it possible, Lady Death?"

"Don't call her that," I say.

Shy holds a hand out. "It's okay, Mother. I've learned that word is not so frightening. And yes, Your Highness, it is possible. But you are not dead."

"The vampire can fix the damage and I can begin again?" There's a hitch to the king's breath that makes everyone in our party stop.

As we realize what he is offering.

I move out of Danny's arms, my heart hesitating, scared to believe. "You would give your body to him? Shy, how is it possible?"

"The body is nothing more than a vessel for our souls. The body will recognize our Devinshea," Shy explains. "I don't even think I'll have to guide him. Once the king is dead and he exits this plane, Dev should be able to sneak in and be alive again. Arawn promised us this is not the way Devinshea dies."

Hope bursts through my system, and I bite back a cry.

"You want this?" the king asks me, stroking a hand on my cheek. He doesn't flinch when Danny growls.

"Do I want my husband back?" I ask, searching his eyes. "Yes, but I can't ask you to do this."

"I can," Danny counters.

The king smiles. "I think my life would have been different if my Deinny had your Danny's fierceness. I think it might have brought out my own before it was too late and it was twisted. I don't know if we can start again, my loves, and I only know I do not wish to hurt you more than I have. In this moment you are my Zandra, and I will do anything to make you smile one last time."

He steps back, and I notice he has the cold iron dagger in his hands.

The world seems to stop as he holds it to his chest.

And plunges it into his own heart.

He falls to the ground. I rush to get to him, dropping to my knees as he holds the dagger in.

Blood slips from the corner of his mouth but there's a smile there. It is nothing like the smirk I'd seen before. This was a bit of real joy.

"I hear them." Tears slip from his eyes. "They are quite cross with me. But they waited. I think Deinny is going to have words." The smile goes brilliant. "Even if you haul me to Hell, at least I'll have your hands on me again. Yes. I will tell him. Lee." He turns his head and looks for the son he never acknowledged. Lee gets to one knee but says nothing. "I leave you the kingdom. You'll find everything you need in the mountain. It's open now. Share what I've horded with the people and bring the Seelie back to the glory I took from them."

Lee nods solemnly. "I will, Your Highness."

"Just once, Lee?" he asks.

"I will, Father," Lee offers.

"Then I can go." His eyes glaze over, and I swear I feel the moment his soul leaves his body.

"Danny?" I pull the cold iron from his chest.

Danny and Sasha are there. Danny bites into his wrist. "Sasha, pour some over the wound. We're fighting the cold iron."

Ostara drops to her knees. "I can take that burden from him, but it will be quicker if you do as your king asks, love."

Ostara places her hands on the dead king's chest, and I can see a glow where she touches him.

Sasha pours blood from his wrist over the wound to the king's heart.

Lee stands on one side watching. Rhys comes to my other side and takes my hand, holding it tightly while we wait.

"It will be all right, Mom." For the first time in a while Rhys sounds like my son and not a soldier or a Green Man. "It's going to be okay."

"Where does this optimism come from, my son?" I ask.

His smile turns sheepish. "My goddess, of course."

"Fuck, that hurt," a familiar voice says and the king's eyes open. Devinshea's eyes open. "Cold iron sucks. It is a freaking crime. You need to make it illegal, Daniel."

Danny leans over, putting his hands on Dev's cheeks. "Dev?"

"In the flesh. Well, in the new flesh. Hey." He reaches up and cups the back of Danny's neck. "Are you all right, my king?"

Danny hauls him to sitting position and wraps his arms around him and does what he almost never does. He cries. He puts his face in the crook of Dev's neck and cries. I drop to my knees and join them, arms around my husbands.

I look up and Shy is with Rhys, a smile on her gorgeous face.

"Thank you," I whisper.

She bows her head.

Dev's body stiffens for a moment and then relaxes. He squeezes us tight. I can feel Bris's magic. It flows over us. "Easiest integration ever. Bris is happy to be back."

And I am blessed beyond compare because I have my family.

Chapter Thirty-Six

Shy

"I don't know. I think I should feel more evil than I do." My father-in-law stretches for what I'm sure is the one thousandth time since we got back to the temple the night before. "Instead I feel amazing. This is what it feels like to be fully Fae? No wonder my brother is as arrogant as he is. Hey, I think I can easily kick his ass now. Not only am I fully Fae, but I got the whole ascended god thing going."

Lee asked us to stay the night and for Rhys and I to power up the temple one more time before we go to the mountains and try to find our way home.

Rhys was happy to give in to that request.

I'm still a little sore because my husband got incredibly creative.

The temple is humming with power, and not merely from ours.

Ostara was beaming this morning, and I already saw how all the plants in the palace exploded, and it looks like ground zero was the room the royals used the night before.

Three fertility gods getting their freaks on really made the fields grow.

They gave off so much energy the Fae here were able to store the majority of it for rituals their new king would perform later on to keep the temple charged.

"I will be happy to watch that," Daniel says, a smile on his lips.

He's right back to his normal fully charged self. I even saw him taking a flight to check out the mountain we're going to visit later today. He wanted to make sure there were no more weird lion/goat/snake things hanging out, even though Lee promised there weren't.

"I will, too. I love it when someone punches my uncle." Rhys winks my way as he joins us in the parlor where we've gathered to make our plans.

I know Sasha has a big decision to make.

The general paces in the corner, walking by the window that looks out over the temple and then turning and making his way back to the big bookshelves. I saw Ostara at breakfast but I haven't since, and I wonder if they had a fight about their next move. Or if Sasha is trying to find a way to say good-bye to us so he can return to Ostara's home plane.

"You know we're still going to have to make nice with them," I point out. "We didn't get what we came for. We're no closer to finding the Days, and now that we know the amulet here is a bust, we're definitely still going to have to see your Fae family. Besides, I think your papa wants to show off his fancy new body."

The amulet is out of magic. It appears the king used it all.

Rhys sighs and sinks down to the sofa beside me. "Yes, he is insufferable right now. I guess I never thought about how different it would feel to be half human. I always thought it was about how long he would live. It's so much more."

Devinshea Quinn is stronger than ever. He will be tougher to kill, his magic mightier than before.

And he is immortal if he chooses to be, but I doubt he will.

The biggest change, he told me, is he can work magic with his mind. Those hands he lost are back, but he no longer needs them. Not for magic.

He does seem to get them on the queen a lot, though.

"I'm going to miss Sasha." Rhys settles in beside me, leaning his head against mine. "He was like a father to me." His hand slides against my hand, fingers tangling together. "Are you all right?"

In between all the wild sex the night before, my husband held me and listened to stories about my mother. He let me cry and laugh and took my tales into his own heart so I am not the only one who remembers them. He was tender and sweet and everything I needed. "I'm good, babe. It's like I can truly mourn them for the first time."

He brings my hand to his lips. "I'm glad, my goddess. Have I told you today how fucking magnificent you are?"

I smile. "Three times already."

Something has opened between us, some deep and peaceful connection I can feel even when he isn't in a room with me.

"Then I owe you at least three more," he vows.

"Rhys, I need to talk to you about not killing the death god," his papa says, looking cool and crisp in his Fae clothes.

I turn to my husband. "You can't kill Arawn."

Rhys shrugs. "I can try."

I sigh. "He is going to be our ally, and he's going to bring in more allies. We need all the allies we can get, and when you think about it, he's kind of like my dad in a way."

Rhys's head shakes. "He is not. You are a goddess of your own making. You managed to transform from a magical tool to a magnificent woman with power we couldn't have imagined. You did that all on your own."

My father-in-law smiles at me. "He isn't wrong and Shy isn't wrong. If we find our way back, we will still have to go and visit my mother. The amulet in my *sithein* works. We know it does since it was recently used to blow up my club."

"Sorry," Zoey says with a wince.

This sends Neil and his kids into a fit of laughter. They spent the night behind a wall of wards since the lust magic was heavy. A good time was had by all, Bibi reported. And Neil did a great job making sure his kids had none of it.

"We tried several times to use the amulet last night, and it's out of magic," Dev admits. "I suppose this Devinshea used all the magic from it."

"My father kind of sucked the kingdom dry," Lee says as he strides in. There is a thin crown of gold around his dark hair. He accepted the crown late the night before, and the nobles fell in line when they realized the temple was working again.

All Fae creatures are once more welcome in the Seelie *sithein*. He has a long way to go, but he will get there.

The *sithein* is coming to life again, and I've already seen a spirit on the edge of the river.

She told me to mind my own damn business when I asked if she wanted to move on. Cranky spirit.

Daniel sits on the sofa opposite me, an arm draped around my mother-in-law and an indulgent look on his face as he watches Devinshea. "I think we can handle your grandmother, son. And you are going to be quite a revelation. You and your goddess are powerful enough no one is ever going to fuck with you again. You two decide when and if you perform rites for them."

"Rhys and Shy are Earth plane gods," Devinshea says. "I will inform my family and the Unseelie of this. They serve the Fae who did not leave. It won't sit well, but they will accept it. I am still the high priest. Unless you've changed your mind, Rhys."

My husband's head shakes. "Nope. You can be the High Priest of the Seelie and Unseelie Fae. I'll take the misfits. Oh, look, the pixies woke up. They had a long night."

I giggle as they land on my skin, tickling me a bit. There is nothing so magical as being covered in pixies.

They do not fear me, and I no longer fear myself.

"Hello, little ones," the queen is saying as they land on her as well. She winks my way. "And the Goddess Chain looks good on you."

I reach for it. I already feel connected to it so it's sad I have to say good-bye. "I love it, but I think Lee must give it to his goddess."

"I'm not going to have a goddess," Lee says, gesturing for me to keep it. "I am not a Green Man, and I think we should have our high priest be separate from the king. The Unseelie claim they have a powerful Green Man. I'm going to meet him and see if there's any way he'll help us out. I think it could check my power...provide a balance. We need that."

"Yes, I believe I've heard the theory," I reply as I ease the necklace back into my bodice. "I'm happy to hear they're willing to open negotiations."

"Me as well." Lee looks slightly uncomfortable in his formal wear. I heard Bibi had put her foot down when he wanted to receive the crown in his undershirt and slacks. She was going to make an excellent aide to the king. She was already treating him like her wayward son and bringing him in line. He looks to Sasha. "I suppose you're heading out with the rest of them. I wanted to thank you for everything. I had a chance to talk to the others, but I need you to know you're always welcome in my kingdom."

The vampire steps forward. He takes a long breath and looks to Rhys first. "You know what I have to do."

Rhys stands and nods. "Of course. Sasha, you have to follow her."

Daniel's head drops back and he groans. "Damn it. Are you sure, man? I don't know how to run that spy network of yours."

Sasha looks so torn, his jaw tight, a sad light in his eyes. "My wife has a plane she must save. She was willing to marry this Devinshea to save it. I cannot ask her to go with me and I cannot leave her. I will never leave her again. Not willingly."

Ostara glides in, a wide smile on her face. No. It's Meadow, but they work so seamlessly together it's hard to tell them apart. She's carrying a beautiful moonstone shaped into a sphere. She needs both hands because the crystal is so large. "Hello, I'm looking for…there he is. King Lee, you will understand when I tell you my engagement to your father is done and I must leave with my husband."

She's perky and smiling today, and I'm here for it. She brings the scent of fresh flowers with her, and I breathe it in. I'm ready for spring.

"Yes." Sasha puts on a good face and stands beside her. He leans over and kisses the top of her head. "I was resigning my position as the leader of the king's army. I am eager to see your home, my love."

Meadow frowns up at her husband. "You're resigning in the middle of a war that is going to potentially affect every person on every plane and in every timeline?"

Sasha looks a bit taken aback. "You have to help your people."

She nods. "Yes, and this is for them. I set the moonstone out and it stored a lot of fertility magic. There was so much last night. An abundance. This will restore our temple until we can find a Green Man."

"You will come with me?" Sasha puts his hands on her shoulders as though he needs to see her eyes, to know her truth.

"I will go where we are needed." Meadow straightens her shoulders. "Our daughter is on your plane. I understand that she can never know me, but I can watch over her. She is the only child we will ever have, and I am content with that, but I will not leave her."

Rhys's hand squeezes mine, remembering my mother had done the same until I was safe.

Well, as safe as I can be in the middle of a war where I am apparently going to be a big part of the fight.

This will always be a war won by women, un sanctaidd.

The question is who will be in my sisterhood?

"As for my plane," Meadow says, turning to Lee. She hands him the large moonstone. "I need you to go there and give this to my sister. She will know how to use it. I think you two might get along."

"Actually, it turns out I have a lot to do here," Lee hedges as he holds the stone. "But I can find someone to act as my emissary."

Meadow's brow rises. "My sister is known as the most beautiful woman in all of the *sithein*. Men fall at her feet. I suppose it's best you don't go because I doubt she would give you the time of day."

Lee straightens up and puts on what I like to think of as his player face. "Oh, well, we'll see about that."

Meadow seems thoroughly pleased with her plotting. "Her name is Mia, and send her my love."

That name. It makes Rhys stand and his mother frown.

We have to find our Mia, and we still have no idea how to do it.

"I will find Arawn when we get home," I promise. "I didn't have time to ask him. Perhaps we can use Annwn. It isn't a Hell plane."

Devinshea claps his hands like he's thrilled with the idea. Or he's just happy to have hands. "Yes. It was definitely a celestial plane. We can use it as a starting point. I think if Nim asks, he can't say no. He's back on the I love Nimue train, and I haven't even told him Myrddin cut her head off yet. He's going to do anything he can to fuck the asshole over."

I foresee visiting a lot of assisted living homes. And I forgot to tell him we're moving to New Zealand. Hopefully he'll get the message.

Hopefully we'll get home.

We have to get home.

"Knock, knock," a feminine voice says. "I hope I'm not being a bother."

I feel my jaw drop. "Nim?"

Everyone is on their feet now as the gorgeous woman with long dark hair and a whole body dressed in a flowy gown walks in.

"Nimue, what happened?" Zoey rushes to her and throws her arms around her friend. "You have no idea how happy I am to see you. How did you find us?"

"I want to know how she grew her body back so fast," Danny admitted.

"Zoey," Neil's voice is low, and his eyes have the light of his wolf in them. "That's not Nimue. She's smells like brimstone."

Daniel reaches for his wife and the fake Nim frowns.

"What happened to my daughter? Why would she need to regrow her body?" the woman asks.

"Nim has a mom?" Neil asks.

"My name is Lilith. Layla is my daughter, though I suppose I shall have to learn to call her Nimue," the woman admits "Her father is made of lies. He gave her up to become some balance to the wizard. I hate him as well. You should know he attempted to murder a girl who claims you are her parents."

"Evan?" All of the royals are around Lilith now, but Zoey asks the question. "You know my daughter."

"Yes, and apparently you know mine," Lilith returns.

"Nimue is my friend," Zoey explains. "I met her years ago when she gave Danny Excalibur and named him the King of the Sword. But then she woke up Myrddin, who was supposed to mentor Danny, but he put a thrall stone in her head and in Danny's and Devinshea's and he basically roofied the fuck out of her for like eight years, but then she woke up and she freaked out because Myrddin had taken over the Earth plane supes and she did not sign up for that gig and he cut her head off and stuffed her in a magical box and kept her in my closet with my shoes, but then I sent some Hidden Folk to find my lost bag of holding and they brought her head back instead, so she's regrowing her body and I think she might need some therapy because of all the rapey shit Myrddin did to her."

Lilith's eyes go wide. "I will kill him."

Zoey shakes her head. "There's like a prophecy and stuff. We got it handled, but we could use some help getting out of here. We're in the wrong timeline. I heard my daughter is alive, but is she all right?"

Lilith seems to soften. "Evangeline is physically fine.

Emotionally is another thing entirely. She has gone through a change. When that massive asshole tossed her off Lucifer's balcony, she was forced to accept the physical changes she was trying to avert. It's not bad. She has wings and some other powers she needs to learn to use. She has asked me for sanctuary for the time being."

Zoey stifles a cry.

Devinshea moves in behind her. "Why would she need sanctuary?"

"She's scared," Rhys says. "She's been afraid of this change since she had to take primal blood to survive. Has she become bat-like?"

Lilith nods. "Somewhat, but not in a way that would keep her from passing for human. It's too much for her, and she needs a break. I have offered for her to stay in my kingdom. It's a refuge of sorts. I take in a lot of strays. Not that she is one, but I believe surrounding herself with them, with caring for creatures who need her love and kindness, will heal her. However, I explained I would speak to her parents, to let you know she is safe. I will send you updates."

"Is Fenrir okay?" I ask, knowing the answer.

Lilith sighs. "He is sad, but she needs this space. She still loves him. Still loves you all, but I ask you to honor her wish."

"I don't even know you, lady," Daniel begins.

But Dev steps up and offers her a hand. "I do, Lilith. First woman, I ask that you help my daughter as we have aided yours. We love Nimue and count her as part of our family, and you are welcome in our kingdom. As for Evan, please tell her we love her and accept her and what she needs. Tell her we will take care of Fenrir. We will make sure he is safe and cared for and has everything that is necessary. Apart from her."

She squeezes his hand. "I will take you up on that, High Priest. You have that look about you. Now you are definitely in the wrong timeline. Does this have anything to do with the rumor that the Hell plane recently lost several thousand guests and Lucifer is cross with Myrddin?"

I hold up my hand. "I did that."

She nods my way. "Excellent. Good job, though don't think Luc will kill him. He's all for the insane close-off-Heaven thing. He has daddy issues. Now, let's get you back where you belong."

"You can do that?" Zoey asks.

Lilith stops for a moment before answering. "I got here, didn't I. Are you ready?"

Dev steps back. "So ready."

Lilith snaps her fingers.

And we're in Frelsi again.

"Hey, you're back. Girl, you look good." Josie sits on a rock to my left. "Do you really have to go to New Zealand? It's boring when y'all are gone."

"It's our timeline," I say with a smile. "Josie's here."

"We're home," Rhys says with a sigh of relief. He takes a deep breath as though something about being on his home plane settles him.

"Yeah, about that," I begin because I see a problem now. "I am not living with your brother and Fenrir."

The biggest smile crosses his face. "I think we'll find our own place. Until then we can probably get Fen and Lee out of the house by having sex as much as possible."

There's a problem with that. Lee would want to watch.

"Where's Zoey?" Neil asks.

We look around. We're all here. Cassie and Brendan and Lee. Meadow and Sasha are here. Danny and Dev.

But no Zoey.

We've lost her.

Chapter Thirty-Seven

Zoey

I turn on the infamous first woman when I realize I'm the only one in my party still here. It's me and Lee—still holding his moonstone—left in the parlor, and I wonder if I'm being tricked once more.

"Is there a reason you separated me from my husbands?" I ask in my iciest tone. A thought occurred to me, one that threatened to make me sick. "Or did you send them somewhere else? Who are you working for?"

"Lady who looks like my mom, do you need me to kill her or something?" Lee asks in an oddly polite tone, like he's really not sure the etiquette for dealing with a girl throwdown over one of them sort of kidnapping the other.

Lilith frowns. "Of course I sent them somewhere else. I sent them to the place I saw in the Fae's mind. Someplace called Frelsi. The wolves were thinking about it, too, as was the vampire. As to the timeline, your bodies naturally want to be in the proper timeline. How did you get here? Was it a spell? Or did you use the blue stones?"

Well, no one could say she didn't know her way around the universe. "We were given stones and told to go through a doorway that led us here. We thought we were going to the Seelie *sithein* in our timeline."

She nods as though listening. "Yes. You needed to go there because there's a… I believe you're describing an amulet, child. Yes, I can see it. It does not work here?"

"I'm sorry, who are you talking to?" I ask.

"Look, lady. I don't know how you got here but this is my kingdom and she's sort of my mom in some weird timeline where I get to be this supercool vampire and sleep with everyone, and I don't end up with a crown I don't want and a weird sphere that's apparently full of energy, so I'm going to have to ask you to leave," Lee announces.

I feel for the kid. "You need to go and meet Mia. I think it will change your life."

His eyes widen. "Because I like her in your world."

"You are obsessed with her in my world, and you're lost without her," I explain. "Now I think there's something wrong with this woman, and I need to have a chat with her."

After all, according to her, she has my daughter.

"I think she would talk more if we put her in the dungeon," Lee offers.

Lilith waves a hand, and Lee is suddenly gone.

"You have to stop that." I round on her. "You can't disappear people."

"He didn't disappear." Lilith takes a seat on the sofa like this is a friendly girl's chat. "I sent him to the place where they need the moonstone. I pulled that out of the ascended goddess's head. She was thinking about her sister, Mia, and I saw her bedroom and then you mentioned Lee should meet Mia, but you were thinking of the other Mia. I quite like this plane. I'm super powerful here. Usually I can only read soul's." She gasps as though having a revelation. "Oh, of course. It's not the plane. It's Harriet."

I put a hand to my belly. "I never said I was pregnant, and don't you tell me I'm showing. Because I'm not."

"I would never. You look beautiful, Your Highness. Or I suppose since we're in Faery I should call you Your Grace." Lilith pats the seat next to her. "Seriously, you have my daughter. I would not betray you because it's not my nature, but I certainly wouldn't fuck you over before I've even seen her. It's been so long. So many lifetimes between us." Her eyes close and when they open there are tears shining. "I am known as the mother of demons. That was the price I paid for defying my creator and denying Adam. A harsh lesson to learn, and yet I would do it again. Sometimes I wonder if my punishment was to try and try and try to give birth to a child who could truly love me. Like I hurt my creator so he would let me feel what he had. And then I gave birth to her. Don't get me wrong. I have a couple of sons who I get along with. My sweet Tix is a joy to me, and I take such pride in him, but Layla... I knew she held a real piece of me, something the others did not."

"Nim is a good friend." Okay, she's getting to me, and the truth is Evan is an excellent judge of character. "I don't think she knows she had a mother who was looking for her. I definitely don't think she knew her name was Layla. May I ask what happened to her father?"

Lilith's eyes narrow. "Well, I was having a bit of a bad-boy moment."

"That era lasted a while if you're called the mother of demons," I point out. I mean we all had one, right?

"Yeah, well, I married the asshole, or at least one aspect of him. You know he can be really charming when he wants to be, but then he sends in the misogynist prick and steals your only daughter and sends her to be the Lady of the damn Lake, apparently, and thinks I won't notice because I just love being the Queen of Hell."

My jaw drops. "Dude, you married Lucifer Morningstar?"

"And divorced him, and let me tell you that was no easy feat. I tell you this because I need you to understand how far I've come. I have some amount of peace on my little slice of Hell. I spend my time showing the broken creatures of our plane that there is more to life than torture and neglect. Whatever has happened to my daughter, I will help her. And that means I will help you because according to Evan, she likes you and your family. You saved her."

I shake my head. "She's saved us, too, and I feel bad for leaving her to Myrddin, but I didn't know about the thrall stone. I thought... Well, I hate what I thought, but she forgave me."

"Which is why I wouldn't harm you," Lilith points out.

"But you know more than you should. Evan might have told you I'm pregnant."

She shakes her head. "She didn't. Harriet did. I know it sounds odd, but I speak angel. Such a weird language. You're carrying a Nephilim child. I want that story at some point because we haven't seen one in thousands of years. You are trying to get to a celestial plane."

"Yes." I don't know that I like how much she knows or how she knows it. "She talks to you?"

"Like I said, I can read souls, and hers is quite vibrant," Lilith admits. "It's only the fact that she's Nephilim that I can hear her. I was made part angel. I think that's where the creator went wrong because angels can be a bit stubborn. Then he went and made Adam from clay and Eve from Adam. You know they were a bit boring, right? Most exciting thing that woman did was eat that apple."

I would normally love to listen in on her very interesting family drama, but I'm kind of stuck in my own. "I do need to get to the celestial planes, but I can't figure out how to open that door without dying. Trust me. I've called on a couple of angels I know about a million times. They aren't answering."

"Because we're in a crisis, and the creator prefers to let us solve some problems on our own," she says with a huff. "No. We have to assume Heaven knows what's happening, and they are going to let things play out. But you have a secret weapon. I wouldn't be surprised if that bit of angelic light isn't your guardian angel's way of sending you a weapon no one will see coming."

"She's not a weapon." But isn't that how we're viewing Mia? Do I have any right to take her out of her safety and plunge her into war? Yet, I know what her mother would want. She wanted us to find them. She wanted me to bring them home.

"Think of her as an advantage," Lilith says. "She's the one who will take you where you want to go. Her soul holds angelic magic, and that means she can navigate the celestial planes. Because she's in utero, she can take you with her."

"Harriet can get me to Sarah?"

Lilith nods. "Yes. All you have to do is ask her. Picture who you're looking for in your mind, and if she's on a celestial plane, Harriet can take you there. Then because you're on a celestial plane, she can take you all back to your home. She cannot transport you across the Earth plane. She would have to access Heaven, and that will get increasingly dangerous because if you do this, she will be on their radar, so to speak."

I don't like the sound of that. "I thought you said she was a gift from them."

"From the angel who watches you," Lilith corrects. "But not all will agree with that angel, and there are those in Heaven who think

Nephilim are abominations. You'll find the same in Hell."

"Yes, that's what Myrddin called her." I can't help the bitterness to my tone.

"If you think finding your friend could turn the tide of this war, then you should do it because your daughter will still be in danger." Lilith stands. "Now, it's time to make your choice. I can send you to your timeline or you can ask Harriet to take you where you need to go. Either way, if you need me, all you have to do is call. It's been a while since I spent time on the Earth plane. And I promise, I will take care of Evan. She simply needs time."

I wish my daughter would come home and heal with her family, but I suspect her family is part of the problem. We have to be patient. "Thank you. I think I'll find my friend. I'll talk to Nimue about you and send word."

Lilith's head bows and then she is gone.

I hope she's right.

I put my hand on my belly and think about Sarah Day.

When I open my eyes, I'm in a completely different world.

Heaven. Though not the place with the pearly gates.

I breathe in, and the air seems warm and gentle in my lungs. There is a gauziness to this pastoral place. I stand in front of a rustic cabin. In the distance I see a flock of lambs and... Is that Felix?"

"Hello?" a familiar voice says.

Sarah. Relief floods my system. Sarah is standing there, though she looks way different than the last time I saw her. Her hair is a natural brown and is in a braid that reaches her waist. She looks like she's been shopping in medieval Walmart in her long skirt and peasant blouse.

I don't care. I'm too happy to see her. I wrap my arms around her. "Sarah, I'm sorry it took so long."

It takes me a moment to realize that she's not hugging me back.

I step away and there's a confused look on my friend's face.

"I'm sorry. Who are you?" she asks.

Not the way I meant for this to go.

Damn it.

Evangeline, Fenrir, and the whole Thieves gang will return in *The Rebel Princess*.

Author's Note

I'm often asked by generous readers how they can help get the word out about a book they enjoyed. There are so many ways to help an author you like. Leave a review. If your e-reader allows you to lend a book to a friend, please share it. Go to Goodreads and connect with others. Recommend the books you love because stories are meant to be shared. Thank you so much for reading this book and for supporting all the authors you love!

Sign up for Lexi Blake's newsletter
and be entered to win a $25 gift certificate
to the bookseller of your choice.

Join us for news, fun, and exclusive content
including free short stories.

There's a new contest every month!

Go to www.LexiBlake.net to subscribe.

Discover the Faery Story Trilogy
By Lexi Blake
Now available

Bound
Book 1

A stranger in a strange land

Megan Starke has given up believing in knights in shining armor. With an unrewarding job and a failed marriage, no one would confuse her life with a fairy tale. No one is coming to save the day or carry her off to a romantic fantasy. So when she wakes up in a magical world and discovers she is to be the grand prize in a fierce and bloody tournament, she isn't sure if she's having a sexy dream or a horrible nightmare.

Two kings without a kingdom

Beckett and Cian were raised to be the saviors of their people. Prepared all their lives to lead the Seelie Fae, prophecy proclaimed they would find a bondmate whose love would complete them and unleash their magical powers. But the thrust of a traitor's blade stole that future and now it threatens to take their lives. Struggling in exile, their glorious destiny has become a curse. Unless they can find the perfect woman to save them, they will descend into madness and ruin. When all hope seems lost, Beck sees Meg and knows she's the key to their salvation.

An epic battle begins

In a world filled with dethroned kings, upwardly mobile vampires, and dangerous, feline-loving hags, Meg will need all her strength to survive. Finding herself caught between Beck and Cian, she's willing to do whatever it takes to claim her happily ever after.

* * * *

Beast
Book 2

A playboy who needs to grow up

Fresh from his latest tabloid scandal, vampire playboy Dante Dellacourt has been given an ultimatum. Either he takes a consort and settles down, or his family will disown him. Unwilling to lose everything he has, he reluctantly agrees to find a wife. Marriage is just another kind of contract, after all. No one said anything about love being a part of the bargain.

An outcast who has only known hardship

Exiled by her pack, Kaja is a werewolf without a home. Her life was never easy in the frozen tundra she grew up in, but it was familiar. Waking up in a foreign landscape, surrounded by bright lights, loud noises, and far too many people has left her overwhelmed. Frightened and with no one to trust, she savagely fights to get free of this strange new world.

A passion strong enough to change them both

Called to defend the gnomes of the marketplace, Dante is almost blinded by the radiant light coming off the fierce werewolf. Kaja glows like no consort he has ever seen. Gorgeous and wild, she calls to him in ways he had not dreamed possible. For Kaja, she finds in Dante a man unlike any she has ever known. They could not be more different, but she finds him irresistible.

In order to claim his werewolf bride, Dante must first discover how to overcome their differences. Will he tame his ferocious beauty, or will she unleash his inner beast?

* * * *

Beauty
Book 3

The princess in the tower

In one horrifying night, Bronwyn Finn lost her family, her kingdom, and the princes who had haunted her dreams for years. Left alone, years pass as she fights for survival and craves revenge against the uncle who took everything from her. But she's never forgotten her Dark Ones. Now she hides along with her guardian, but the war rages ever closer.

Two dark princes

A tragedy marred Lach and Shim's lives. The future kings of the Unseelie Fae are obsessed with finding their promised wife—Bronwyn. Lach and Shim have never stopped believing that Bronwyn is their mate. She is the bond that connects the halves of their shared soul.

A destiny that will change a kingdom

With the blessing of the renegade kings, Beck and Cian Finn, Lach and Shim begin a dangerous quest to find their bride before Torin and his hags take her life.

Across two planes, a war will rage. Lives will be lost. Love will be found. And the Seelie Fae will welcome their true kings home.

Love the Way You Spy

Masters and Mercenaries: New Recruits
By Lexi Blake
Now available!

Tasha Taggart isn't a spy. That's her sisters' job. Tasha's support role is all about keeping them alive, playing referee when they fight amongst themselves, and soothing the toughest boss in the world. Working for the CIA isn't as glamorous as she imagined, and she's more than a little lonely. So when she meets a charming man in a bar the night before they start their latest op, she decides to give in to temptation. The night was perfect until she discovers she's just slept with the target of their new investigation. Her sisters will never let her hear the end of this. Even worse, she has to explain the situation to her overprotective father, who also happens to be their boss.

Dare Nash knew exactly how his week in Sydney was going to go—attending boring conferences to represent his family's business interests and eating hotel food alone. Until he falls under the spell of a stunning and mysterious American woman. Something in Tasha's eyes raises his body temperature every time she looks at him. She's captivating, and he's committed to spending every minute he can with her on this trip, even if her two friends seem awfully intense. He doesn't trust easily, but it's not long before he can imagine spending the rest of his life with her.

When Dare discovers Tash isn't who she seems, the dream turns into a nightmare. She isn't the only one who deceived him, and now he's in the crosshairs of adversaries way out of his league. He can't trust her, but it might take Tasha and her family to save his life and uncover the truth.

About Lexi Blake

New York Times bestselling author Lexi Blake lives in North Texas with her husband and three kids. Since starting her publishing journey in 2010, she's sold over three million copies of her books. She began writing at a young age, concentrating on plays and journalism. It wasn't until she started writing romance that she found success. She likes to find humor in the strangest places and believes in happy endings.

Connect with Lexi online:

Facebook: Lexi Blake
Website: www.LexiBlake.net
Instagram: www.instagram.com
Twitter: authorlexiblake

www.ingramcontent.com/pod-product-compliance
Lightning Source LLC
Chambersburg PA
CBHW051523250626
47156CB00001B/211